P9-DNX-402

Keeping *the* Republic

Keeping *the* Republic

Ideology and Early American Diplomacy

Robert W. Smith

NORTHERN

ILLINOIS

UNIVERSITY

PRESS

DeKalb

© 2004 by Northern Illinois University Press

Published by the Northern Illinois University Press, DeKalb, Illinois   60115

Manufactured in the United States using acid-free paper

All Rights Reserved

Design by Julia Fauci

Library of Congress Cataloging-in-Publication Data

Smith, Robert W., 1967–

Keeping the republic: ideology and early American diplomacy / Robert W. Smith.

   p.   cm.

Includes bibliographical references and index.

ISBN 0-87580-326-1 (alk. paper)

1. United States—Politics and government—1775–1783. 2. United States—Politics and government—1783–1809. 3. Republicanism—United States—History. 4. United States—Foreign relations—1775–1783. 5. United States—Foreign relations—1783–1815. I. Title.

JK116.S65 2004

327.73′009′033—dc22

2003027083

To my mother, **Claire W. Smith,**

and to the memory of my father,

Robert W. Smith Sr.

Contents

Acknowledgments

My first acknowledgment is to someone who is not here to read this book. My father died in 1993, when I was just beginning the dissertation this book is based upon. Like John Adams, I first became interested in politics listening to my father, and this book is a product of the bond between us. I cannot begin to calculate my father's influence on me, or my debt to him, or how much I wish he could be here to read this. For the last ten years, my mother has listened with a sympathetic ear to the idiosyncracies of someone writing a book, and my brother, Matt, knew what topic to avoid when we saw each other.

Part of this book began as my honors thesis at Syracuse University; I would like to thank Robert McClure, James Roger Sharp, William Stinchcombe, and Stephen Saunders Webb for helping this young scholar along. Next, I would like to thank my dissertation committee at the College of William and Mary: Edward Crapol, Charles F. Hobson, Michael McGiffert, and the late John Selby. Their suggestions and attention to detail saved me from various errors. My outside reader, Joseph A. Fry of the University of Nevada–Las Vegas, graciously stepped in on very short notice. For help turning the dissertation into a book, I would like to thank Katharine Graydon, James Read, Martin Johnson, my editor at Northern Illinois University Press, and the anonymous reviewers for NIUP.

The College of William and Mary and the Virginia Society of the Cincinnati provided financial support for the dissertation. I would like to thank the following for help with my research: Daniel Preston of the Papers of James Monroe at Mary Washington College; Special Collections and Interlibrary Loan of Swem Library, and the Omohundro Institute of Early American History and Culture at the College of William and

Mary; Alderman Library and the James Madison Papers at the University of Virginia; the Massachusetts Historical Society; the Library of Congress; the National Archives; the American Antiquarian Society; and Princeton University.

Finally, I would like to thank my friends from graduate school, particularly (but certainly not exclusively) Richard and Ginny Chew, Mary Carroll Johansen, Chris and Chris Joyce, Lynn Nelson, David Rawson, and Antoinette van Zelm.

Keeping *the* Republic

The Republican World

When asked at the conclusion of the Constitutional Convention what the delegates had created, Benjamin Franklin answered that they had given the American people a republic, "if you can keep it." Keeping the republic placed a double burden on the founding generation: preserving liberty and free institutions at home and defending national interests abroad. John Quincy Adams captured this duality in 1837 when he observed that "the Declaration of Independence recognized the European law of nations, as practiced among Christian nations, to be that by which they considered themselves bound, and of which they claimed their rights." In American thought, the liberties of individuals and nations proceeded from the same source. American foreign policy would therefore be conducted on the same principles as shaped American government.[1]

Under a commitment to republican government, Americans in the founding generation saw no division between foreign and domestic spheres. The story of early American diplomacy is therefore the search for a republican realpolitik, a diplomacy compatible with republican institutions at home that recognized the realities of world politics. John Adams, Thomas Jefferson, James Madison, and Alexander Hamilton shaped foreign policy using the same thought that formed the republic itself. Each made foreign policy decisions based on the need to preserve republican government, and the need to do so in a hostile world. Either in concert or in opposition, they provided the intellectual underpinnings of the republic and its diplomacy. Republican ideology is the key to understanding both why Adams and Hamilton reconsidered the nature of the republic after the American Revolution and hence altered their diplomacy and why Jefferson and Madison retained essentially the same ideological framework for their entire careers.

The papers of Adams, Jefferson, Madison, and Hamilton reveal the depth and breadth of their reading as well as their sources for foreign and domestic policy. Adams's diary and autobiography show a mind steeped in the classics of English Opposition thought. At various times he listed James Harrington, Algernon Sidney, Lord Bolingbroke, "Cato" (Trenchard and Gordon), and Baron de Montesquieu as his influences.[2] In 1771 Jefferson recommended the works of Montesquieu, Bolingbroke, Sidney, and John Locke.[3] Thirty-six years later, Jefferson had cooled on Montesquieu, had added the *Federalist,* James Burgh, and Adam Smith, and again listed Locke and Sidney.[4] On January 23, 1783, Madison submitted a list of books for a proposed library for Congress. Aristotle, Harrington, Locke, Sidney, Burgh, and Charles Davenant numbered among three hundred recommendations.[5] "Apply yourself, without delay, to the study of the law of nature," Hamilton wrote in 1775. "I would recommend to your perusal, [Hugo] Grotius [Samuel] Puffendorf, Locke, Montesquieu, and [Jean Jacques] Burlamaqui."[6] As Forrest McDonald has observed, the theoretical materials for republican government did not all fit together.[7] The founding generation saw no one author or thinker as the only source for republican truth and had no philosophical difficulty accepting and rejecting the same author on different points. For example, the founders embraced Montesquieu on the need for balanced government but rejected him on the proper size of a republic. Adams, Jefferson, Madison, and Hamilton repeated this process with other thinkers, dissecting the thought of Harrington, Bolingbroke, Sidney, and others and often reaching opposite conclusions using different aspects from the same thinkers.

The four figures in this study agreed on two broad principles of republican foreign policy. The first was that preservation of republican government demanded political separation from Europe and neutrality in Europe's endemic wars. Not even Jefferson's enthusiasm for the French Revolution trumped the principle of neutrality. Europe was, in Thomas Paine's words, "too thickly planted with kingdoms to be long at peace." The second principle, to which Paine referred, was that a republic would conduct its affairs in a different fashion than a monarchy. Paine's argument combined the republican assumptions that monarchies were prone to war and that wars, which tended to augment executive power to the point of tyranny, were fatal to republics. Neutrality would prevent encroachments of monarchy from without.[8]

Republicanism therefore limited the tools available to enforce neutrality and separation from Europe. Even Hamilton, who did not have the same qualms about power as Adams, Jefferson, and Madison, drew a sharp distinction between power exercised by a republic and an absolute monarchy. A republic was a government of limited powers and could not, for example, establish standing armies, raise taxes at will, or conduct wars by executive fiat. Such policies were hallmarks of royal despotism. "The spirit of monarchy is war and enlargement of dominion,"

Montesquieu wrote, "peace and moderation are the spirit of a republic." Thomas Paine agreed, writing that "in England a k—— hath little more to do than to make war and give away places."[9]

The United States had to find measures of defense that did not endanger republican government. With a permanent standing army (as understood in Europe) ruled out, the choice generally fell between a navy or some sort of economic coercion. A navy paid for itself by protecting commerce and avoided the dangers posed by a standing army. Economic coercion—denying American agricultural exports to Europe and its colonies and closing the American market for manufactured goods—promised to substitute for any military system.

The United States existed in a world full of governments that did not have the same self-imposed limits as a republic. Consequently, American leaders did not always have complete freedom to base diplomacy on purely republican principles. The alliance with France during the American Revolution, to cite an obvious example, was a deviation from the idea that the survival of the American republic depended on separation from European politics. American statesmen had to strike a balance between diplomatic necessity and ideological commitment, to find policies that would secure diplomatic goals abroad without endangering liberty at home.

The four figures in this study agreed that a republic was based on the virtue of its people. Yet virtue had different meanings at different times. Three versions of virtue can be discerned in the thinking of the early republic: classical virtue, whig virtue, and yeoman virtue. Adams and Hamilton went from classical to whig; Jefferson and Madison based their diplomacy on yeoman virtue. All three forms of virtue had theoretical roots in the republican canon; and all four statesmen sought to harmonize republican theory with diplomatic reality.

Classical virtue was drawn primarily from Greek and Roman models, extending to the seventeenth-century English revolutionaries. Classical virtue meant a devotion to the public good, republican government, liberty, and the subordination of private interest. The role of government was to produce this virtue. The highest form of public service (and the best way to demonstrate virtue) was to take up arms. In 1769 Alexander Hamilton wished for a war to lift him from obscurity to fame. In 1775 John Adams lamented he was not a soldier. As a classical republican following seventeenth-century English writers, Adams saw the possibility of universal liberty and of reshaping world politics to American wishes: "I always consider the settlement of America with Reverence and Wonder—as the opening of a grand scene and Design in Providence, for the Illumination of Ignorant and the Emancipation of the slavish Part of Mankind all over the Earth," Adams wrote in 1765.[10]

In foreign policy, classical virtue saw republican government as an advantage. A people animated by classical virtue would be able to defeat a larger, stronger, and better-equipped enemy. Self-denying Americans could endure greater hardships than self-indulgent Europeans, making American trade a powerful weapon. Foreign involvement represented a sort of moral contagion, which would be contained by limiting contact with Europe to trade. Adams and Hamilton did not necessarily believe that the United States could spread republican government, but they did believe that other nations could be forced to adopt American principles regarding trade and freedom of the seas. The diplomacy of classical virtue expected the most out of the citizenry, and it was the most fragile form of virtue. The nagging question was whether the American people were up to the level of self-sacrifice demanded of them. The parallel question was whether Europe was as morally weak as presumed. Classical virtue entailed various inconsistencies, such as encouraging free trade as a weapon while denouncing the desire for gain and desiring to reform European commercial practice while taking advantage of Europe's vices.

Whig virtue, drawn primarily from the English Opposition thought of the eighteenth century, came from a reexamination of the moral fiber of the American people. Adams and Hamilton had personally experienced what they considered the moral failure of their fellow citizens. Whig virtue sought to mitigate rather than suppress private interest and therefore reduced personal virtue to respect for the constitution and adherence to the law. Adams redefined the public spirit to mean support for a balanced government with fully independent branches. "If it were to be asked, What is the most sacred duty and the greatest security in a Republic?" Hamilton asked in 1794, "the answer would be, An inviolable respect for the Constitution and Laws—the first growing out of the last." While still recognizing the natural rights source of liberty, whig virtue emphasized that the possibility of preserving liberty was limited by historical circumstance. If Americans, who had more liberty than anyone else, had difficulty establishing a republic, there seemed little hope for other peoples. "Strait is the gate and narrow is the way that leads to liberty," Adams wrote in 1821, "and few nations, if any, have found it." Adams and Hamilton believed, with Montesquieu, that the laws must match the spirit of the people. Hamilton wrote that "what may be good at Philadelphia may be bad at Paris and ridiculous at Petersburgh."[11]

In foreign policy, whig virtue did not expect the world to adopt American principles. Geography—rather than an elevated public spirit—was the key to a republican diplomacy. Defending the republic meant keeping it out of the quarrels of other nations. No cause, be it freedom of the seas or the spread of liberty, was more important than the preservation of the republic at home. Adams and Hamilton were completely agreed on this. They disagreed on exactly why separation preserved the republic. Hamilton feared that involvement in Europe's wars would destroy the union by disrupting the nation's commerce and inviting foreign influence. Adams believed the best way to enforce separation was through a navy, which in turn would protect commerce and avoid the dangers of debts, taxes, and armies. Hamilton did not share Adams's fear of power. This difference explains why Adams and Hamilton seemed very similar during the Washington years but very different during the Adams administration.

Yeoman virtue was the mirror image of classical virtue, replacing the sword with the plowshare as the primary weapon. In 1816 Jefferson described a republic as "the equal right of every citizen, in his person and property, and in their management." The farmer at his plow was independent and resistant to corruption. "Corruption of morals in the mass of cultivators is a phaenomenon of which no age nor nation has furnished an example," Jefferson wrote in his *Notes on the State of Virginia*. "Dependence begets subserviance and venality," he continued; it "suffocates the germ of virtue, and prepares fit tools for the designs of ambition." The private interest of the farmer to maintain his independence was at the same time a public interest and a natural bulwark against corruption. Jefferson and Madison never doubted the yeoman virtue of the American people, and they never underwent the reconsideration of republicanism and diplomacy experienced by Adams and Hamilton. Yeoman virtue drew on a combination of the agrarianism of seventeenth-century republicanism, the fear of power in eighteenth-century Opposition thought, and a political economy that emphasized free trade. Agricultural production gave the United States the upper hand in its relations with the world. Like his classical counterpart, the yeoman republican saw the possibility of universal liberty and a common interest with other republics. In 1795 Jefferson cheered what he believed to be the triumph of republicanism in the Netherlands and France and argued that the "ball of liberty" set in motion by the United States "will roll round the globe."[12]

The foreign policy of yeoman virtue made the preservation of an agrarian political economy a main goal of diplomacy. Specifically, this meant gaining the free use of the Mississippi River and a free trade with Europe and with Europe's colonies in the West Indies. The ideal government would use the power of the American farmer to secure these ends. Like Adams and Hamilton early in their careers, Jefferson and Madison assumed that the moral weakness of Europe (here manifested as a dependence on American trade) gave the United States the upper hand. Yeoman virtue sought to avoid war, as war would bring debts and standing armies, both fatal to republican government. Jefferson and Madison went further, hoping to avoid a navy as well as an army. In their formulation of yeoman virtue, Jefferson and Madison backed themselves into a theoretical corner. If economic coercion did not work, the republic was doomed. When economic coercion failed (as it usually did), Jefferson and Madison ascribed the failure to external factors rather than to any flaws in yeoman theory itself.

The preservation of the republic, as both an independent state and a specific form of government, was the central goal of American diplomacy in the early national period, yet it is something of an understudied topic. The study of republican thought and its impact on the revolutionary era has generally focused on domestic issues such as constitution-making and political economy. The vital question of the connection between republicanism and diplomacy has received comparatively little attention. The last study to take ideology and early American diplomacy as its exclusive focus was Felix Gilbert's 1961 book, *To the Farewell Address*. As the book appeared before the explosion of ideological studies in the late 1960s, it suffers from two major defects. First, Gilbert gave the more theoretical French enlightenment primacy over the English political thought, which spoke more directly to the American experience. Second, Gilbert posited a static ideological model that did not consider how actual diplomatic practice changed the nature of a republican foreign policy. Gilbert moved from the Model Treaty to the Farewell Address without showing how the republic and its founding ideology changed in the interim. Bernard Bailyn and Gordon Wood put the Commonwealthmen and the English Opposition at the center of American republicanism. Yet despite the fact that Harrington, Sidney, "Cato," Bolingbroke, and Burgh all wrote extensively on foreign policy, there has been no revision of Gilbert's work, viewing diplomacy through the lens of republican ideology.[13]

In fact, the study of the ideological origins of American foreign policy has usually been the province of twentieth-century specialists. In *Ideology and U.S. Foreign Policy,* Michael Hunt saw three themes from the founding era that shaped American diplomacy: the idea of national greatness, classification by race, and a generalized fear of revolution. These concerns do appear in the founding era, but as Hunt formulates them they belong to the twentieth century. Other students of foreign relations have either denied or lamented that a connection existed between domestic principles and diplomacy. Hans Morgenthau argued that in the history of American diplomacy "political thought has been divorced from political action." He divided early American foreign policy into a "realist" period (dominated by Alexander Hamilton), in which diplomacy was conducted in terms of pure power politics, and an "ideological" period (dominated by Thomas Jefferson), in which diplomacy was formulated in moral terms but executed in terms of power. George Kennan perceived a "legalist-moralist approach" to American diplomacy, which he blamed on "the memory of the origin of our political system." He argued that American diplomatic difficulties came from a misguided effort to "transpose the Anglo-Saxon concept of individual law into the international field and make it applicable to governments as it is applicable here at home to individuals."[14]

Foreign relations provided the severest tests for republican government and deserve equal treatment with constitutional issues. If the proper distribution of power within the branches of government was the central question of republicanism domestically, the distribution of power among nations was the ultimate diplomatic question.[15] Furthermore, a focus on republican ideology gives a truer picture of early American diplomacy than the realist-idealist dichotomy, which presumes that one set of statesmen could divorce political thought from diplomatic action while another could not. Republican ideology influenced Adams and Hamilton as well as Jefferson and Madison.

FOR IDEAS CONCERNING THE RELATIONS between men and between nations, Americans turned to two categories of thinkers. The first category consists of "republican" writers, stretching from the ancient Greeks and Romans to English Opposition writers. Opposition writers included the seventeenth-century republicans James Harrington and Algernon Sidney and the eighteenth-century Real Whigs John Trenchard and Thomas Gordon (who wrote jointly as "Cato"), Lord Bolingbroke, and James Burgh. The second category consists of writers more concerned with natural law and natural rights and may be broken down into three subcategories: those writers who were primarily concerned with the emerging law of nations, such as Hugo Grotius and Emmerich de Vattel; those who wrote on constitutional issues, such as John Locke and Charles Secondat, Baron de Montesquieu; and political economists such as the French Physiocrats and the Scottish Common Sense school. All of these theorists sought to discover and codify the natural laws governing human conduct. Authors such as Vattel represented a foreign policy analog to the constitutional writers who influenced the revolutionary generation.[16]

The classical authors of Greece and Rome were the foundation of colonial secondary and college-preparatory education, supplying many of the key concepts of American republicanism: the idea of balanced government, for example, derived from Aristotle and Polybius. Polybius credited Rome's expansion to its balanced constitution. Americans read classical history not to understand the classical world on its own terms but to extract moral examples. Americans often saw ancient Greece and Rome as models of public spiritedness, and they could adopt classical models such as Cato or Cicero and condemn as enemies of republicanism others such as Caesar or Catiline, without sharing all of the assumptions of classical society. For diplomacy, the most important difference between classical and modern republicanism was that the classical state was designed to wage war, and Americans generally sought to avoid war as subversive of republican government. Furthermore, American republicanism generally, though not unreservedly, accepted commerce as a public good, whereas the classical world feared commerce.[17]

Montesquieu praised Sparta as a model of the classical spirit. "The sole aim of Sparta was liberty; and the sole advantage of her liberty, glory," he wrote. Samuel Adams embraced the classical spirit and linked it to a holy cause, hoping that Boston would become a "Christian Sparta." The American republic was founded in war and as such used the martial aspect of the classical tradition when needed. In general, in a republic, war was to be avoided, but when war was inevitable the classics served as a cultural reservoir to provide a republican justification for war. John Adams, for example, spent his executive career trying to avoid war, yet he believed that, had the United States remained at peace in 1812, "the American Nation would have been, as timorous as a Warren of Hares."[18]

James Harrington's 1656 work *The Commonwealth of Oceana* serves as a bridge between the ideas of the classical world and those of the English commonwealth thought of the seventeenth and eighteenth centuries. Harrington followed Aristotle and Livy in proclaiming a free commonwealth "the empire of laws and not of men" and, like Aristotle, believed "that a commonwealth of husbandmen (and such is ours) must be the best of all others." Harrington believed that power followed property (meaning land), and that widespread private holding of property guaranteed freedom. A balanced government, with an agrarian law and rotation in office, could produce public spirit by giving more people a role in public affairs. The proper government would create the men who would defend it. Harrington denounced the idea that "'good men . . . will make us good laws'" and argued instead "'give us good orders, and they will make us good men' is the maxim of a legislator and the most infallible in the politics."[19]

Harrington intended to cultivate the public spirit, manifested in martial virtue. This spirit depended on the character of the people rather than the size of the public treasury. "I do not offer you a nerve of war that is made of purse-strings, such an one as hath drawn the face of the earth into convulsions," he wrote, "but such an one as is natural to the health and beauty." Harrington believed that England's "middle people" made better soldiers than French peasants. An army consisting of the landed citizenry would not threaten liberty, as would a professional army under royal control and beyond the reach of the people's representatives. Harrington did not fear power in the hands of elected rulers, and he accepted the Roman idea of a temporary dictatorship as compatible with a free commonwealth. Only a free people had the warrior spirit necessary to preserve a republic born in war. "If you lay your commonwealth upon any other foundation than the people," he wrote, "you frustrate yourself of proper arms and so lose the empire of the world."[20]

Harrington's republic, with a citizenry perpetually in arms, was like Rome naturally expansionist. Oceana was "a commonwealth for increase." Rome lost its liberty because of its unequal distribution of property, not its expansion. A properly balanced commonwealth could command the sea as well as the land. "The sea giveth law unto Venice, but the growth of Oceana giveth law unto the sea."[21]

Liberty not only permitted but demanded expansion. Harrington's republic was a crusader state destined to bring liberty to the oppressed nations of the world. "This is a commonwealth of the fabric that hath an open ear and a public concernment," Harrington wrote; "she is not made for herself only, but given as a magistrate of God unto mankind, for the vindication of common right and the law of nature." He called for England to "spread the arms of your commonwealth like a holy asylum unto the distressed world, and give the earth her sabbath of years or rest from her labours, under the shadow of your wings."[22]

While the idea of the crusader state would not become part of American thinking until the twentieth century, the revolutionary generation shared the dream of the spread of liberty. Seventeenth-century thought deemphasized the historical roots of the rights of Englishmen in favor of a theory of natural right. "The sacred rights of mankind are not to be rummaged for, among old parchments, or musty records," Hamilton wrote in 1775. "They are written, as with a sun beam, in the whole *volume* of human nature, by the hand of divinity itself; and can never be erased or obscured by mortal power." Natural right included a right of rebellion and implied that any society could move from tyranny to liberty, regardless of historical circumstances. Jefferson's assertion of the right to "alter or abolish" a tyrannical government was not limited to America. The possibility of universal liberty hinted at in the Declaration of Independence reflects the thought of the seventeenth century rather than the more pessimistic Opposition thought of the eighteenth century.[23]

Harrington may be seen as an example of one thinker used for various purposes. Jefferson and Madison adopted the agrarian basis of Harrington's republic as a model for an American republic. Adams, at least early in his career, endorsed the idea that good laws could make good men. Throughout his career, Hamilton retained the idea that a properly balanced government could safely exercise great power.

Like Harrington, Algernon Sidney saw that the purpose of the state was "to make men better, wiser and happier" and that a well-balanced constitution, containing monarchy, aristocracy, and democracy, "makes good men."[24] Sidney's republican virtue also had a martial component, and he believed that a people fighting for liberty could not be tyrannical. A professional army could easily turn on the government it was meant to defend. Sidney looked to the Roman republic as a model, noting that Rome's conquests came as a republic. Sidney showed a "preference to those constitutions that principally intend war, and make use of trade to that end." Furthermore, he thought it "better to aim at conquest" than merely to defend one's territory. Like Harrington, Sidney's republicanism demanded expansion, but, unlike Harrington, Sidney cast expansion in terms of national interest rather than a crusade for liberty.[25]

Both Harrington and Sidney were concerned more with giving a government balance and the proper spirit than with limiting its power. A properly balanced commonwealth could exercise great power without danger to liberty. Harrington and Sidney advocated aggressive foreign policies because they did not fear the tools of diplomacy when placed in the right hands, and Hamilton agreed, as is shown particularly in his aggressive policy toward Spain in the 1790s. But Jefferson, Madison, and to a certain extent Adams took the eighteenth-century Opposition Whig view that power was always something to be feared, particularly in the tools of foreign policy.

The Glorious Revolution, seemingly a moment of triumph for the Commonwealthmen, changed the nature of Commonwealth thought. The Whigs believed William III delivered England from Stuart absolutism. William's constant wars on the continent forced him to give Parliament a permanent share in the nation's government. When William asked for a permanent standing army from 1697 to 1699, the Whig pamphleteer Daniel Defoe defended the measure out of necessity and argued that an army paid for and regulated by Parliament was perfectly safe. John Trenchard countered that a standing army was dangerous under any circumstances and that only a navy and a militia were compatible with England's constitution and physical situation. Trenchard shifted the argument from the danger of power in an unrestrained monarch's hands to the danger of power in anyone's hands. The debate between Defoe and Trenchard in the 1690s in many ways foreshadowed the debate between Hamilton and Adams in the 1790s.[26]

William's wars altered the fiscal as well as the political establishment of England. The political economist Charles Davenant was not only, as Rodger Parker observed, the first to apply the commonwealth tradition to the settlement of the Glorious Revolution, but he was also the first to introduce the issues of trade and political economy to that tradition. Davenant moved away from Harrington's focus on martial virtue and argued that trade was "the strength of the kingdom, by the supply it breeds of seamen." Davenant advocated an economic model similar to that in the Netherlands, which embraced productive activity of all sorts. "It is not the extent of territory that makes a country powerful," he wrote, "but numbers of men well employed, a good navy, and a soil producing all sort of commodities." Trade was not an unalloyed good, as it might bring luxury and corruption. It was, however, necessary for power and a condition and consequence of liberty. Davenant abandoned Harrington's imperial republic, believing that expansion would end only in tyranny. "Commonwealths, well founded, would be eternal, if they could contain themselves within a reasonable territory."[27]

Finally, William's reign also reoriented English foreign policy by making England the primary opponent of French hegemony. The accession of the Hanoverian King George I in 1714 made continental entanglements unavoidable. Robert Walpole spent most of his first decade as prime minister constructing alliances with France and Prussia in order to protect Hanover. Fear of war with Spain and Austria in 1729 prompted Walpole to raise taxes to build an army and pay for German mercenaries, leaving the government open to the charge that it put Hanover above Great Britain. In the 1730s Walpole realized that his political system depended on peace, and he sought to limit European commitments. Opposition figures, however, attacked his passive policy as vigorously as his active policy. French commerce in America boomed in the 1730s, especially with the Newfoundland fisheries, allowing France to challenge Great Britain as a naval power. Worse still, Walpole acquiesced in the Spanish crackdown on British smuggling in the West Indies. Parliamentary outrage allowed Walpole's opponents to force him into war against Spain, and eventually out of office.[28]

The satirist and Tory pamphleteer Jonathan Swift sketched out the beginnings of the Opposition critique of Ruling Whig foreign policy in his 1711 pamphlet *The Conduct of the Allies*. Swift attacked the Marlborough ministry for pursuing a backward strategy. The ministry, Swift argued, sacrificed men and money on a continental war when the correct strategy was to focus on the navy. Great Britain had conquered German provinces on behalf of Austria, Swift continued, while Austria was slow to move against France. Swift concluded that Great Britain could not depend on continental allies for its safety.[29]

The outbreak of war with Spain in 1739 revealed what the Opposition considered the proper strategy: emphasis on the navy and on the colonies, with no continental engagements. Naval power avoided the need for a standing army and paid for itself by protecting commerce, thus providing revenue, and was therefore the means of defense most compatible with free government. Opposition thought accepted the idea of a balance of power among nations but interpreted it to mean among continental nations while Great Britain stood apart. In this position, the Opposition recognized its debt to Queen Elizabeth, who had strengthened the navy and sent the "sea dogs" to raid Spanish commerce. In focusing on a war in the colonies, the Opposition owed another, unacknowledged debt to Oliver Cromwell's Western Design. Cromwell assumed that an attack on the Spanish colonies and plate fleet in 1655 would pay for itself.[30]

Lord Bolingbroke was the Opposition figure most connected with foreign policy. He began his political career in 1700 as a member of Parliament. Tory leader and secretary of state Robert Harley chose Bolingbroke as secretary of war in 1702, but both were replaced when Marlborough and the Whigs came to power. Harley and Bolingbroke returned to office in 1710 with the purpose of ending British involvement in the War of the Spanish Succession. The Tories were satisfied with French defeats in Italy and the Spanish Netherlands and feared the war would produce a fiscal burden that would increase the influence of the Bank of England. Bolingbroke completed this task as the principal British negotiator of the Treaty of Utrecht in 1713. Bolingbroke's career in public office ended with the death of Queen Anne in 1714. He opposed the Hanoverian succession and joined the Pretender's forces in 1715.[31]

Bolingbroke spent the last thirty-six years of his life as a critic of the course taken by British politics. He produced a body of work that John Adams began reading in the 1750s and had read through five times by 1813. Bolingbroke saw the Glorious Revolution as the founding moment in modern English history, "a new Magna Charta," a triumph over parties. Parties soon reemerged in English politics and according to Bolingbroke fell into three groups: opponents of the government, opponents of the constitution, and opponents of the constitution who supported the government. In this formulation, public virtue meant support for the constitution. The third group was the most dangerous, Bolingbroke believed, and was responsible for public debts and taxes that degraded the nation's spirit and morals and threatened the independence of Parliament, which Bolingbroke considered the "keystone of liberty."[32]

Bolingbroke saw the unity of domestic and foreign policy, and he believed the same spirit that unbalanced the constitution was undermining British foreign policy as well. He equated a belief in a balanced constitution with advocacy of a balance of power among nations. He sought to avoid European politics and rejected the Harringtonian approach to diplomacy. Isaac Kramnick considers Bolingbroke's view a realpolitik, devoid of any other considerations. Contrary to Kramnick's argument, however, Bolingbroke always based his view of the balance of power on its relationship to balanced government at home. In his opinion, the safest position for Great Britain—politically, economically, and diplomatically—was to remain apart from the alignments that formed the European balance. The great irony of the Glorious Revolution was that the king who saved Great Britain from tyranny was the same king who drew England too deeply into continental affairs. Unlike Walpole, Bolingbroke believed that the balance of power within Europe would take care of itself. "Great Britain," Bolingbroke wrote in *A Dissertation on Parties*, "should maintain such a dignity and prudent reserve in the broils of Europe, as become her situation, suit her interest, and alone can enable her to cast the balance." In *Letters on the Study and Use of History*, he criticized the "rage of warring," which created an oppressive system of taxation, and the "rage of negotiating," which preserved it. Bolingbroke argued that Great Britain "inhabits an island" and was a neighbor to the continent rather than a part of it. Such an isolation from European involvement, he declared, would allow Parliament to "take all Opportunities, by saving *unnecessary Expenses,* to pay off *our Debts,* and ease the People of their *taxes,*" cutting out the roots of the Walpolean system. Bolingbroke placed British interest above reforming the world and cited Queen Elizabeth as the model monarch: "She considered the interest of no kingdom, no state nor people, no not even the general interest of the reformation, as zealous a protestant as she was, nor the preservation of the balance of power in Europe as great a heroine as she was, in any other light than relating to the interest of England."[33]

Bolingbroke counted on trade to give Great Britain the power to act as arbiter of the European balance of power. Like later Scottish political economists such as Adam Smith and David Hume, Bolingbroke linked trade with freedom and wrote that British wealth depended on trade, particularly the American colonial trade. Trade had its political uses. Bolingbroke inserted an Anglo-French commercial agreement into the Treaty of Utrecht, hoping that the promise of reciprocal trade would gain a French alliance against Austria. Parliament feared French competition and rejected Bolingbroke's articles. The navy was the foreign-policy tool best suited to protecting trade without risking British liberties. The army, Bolingbroke and other Opposition writers believed, was a vehicle for tyranny and, if foreign policy was conducted correctly, an unneeded expense. "The sea is our barrier, ships are our fortresses," Bolingbroke wrote, "and the navies that trade and commerce alone furnish, are the garrisons to defend them."[34]

Bolingbroke tied together his ideas on foreign and domestic policy in *The Idea of a Patriot King*, published in 1749. Bolingbroke had largely given up the hope that Parliament would reform itself. Virtue was not impossible to achieve, he believed, but the way of corruption was much easier. He struck a modern note regarding the presence of political parties and factions in societies: "Thus factions are in them, what nations are in the world; they invade and rob one another: and, while each pursues a separate interest, the common interest is sacrificed by all: that of mankind in one case, that of some particular community in the other," he wrote. "This has been, and must always be, in some measure, the course of human affairs, especially in free countries, where the passions of men are less restrained by authority."[35]

The solution to factionalism and corruption was the rise of a charismatic leader whom Bolingbroke called the Patriot King, and without whom the "way of salvation will not be open to us." The Patriot King would defeat factions by transcending them and by drawing the nation to the example of virtue, that is, a renewed reverence for the constitution. "As soon as corruption ceases to be an expedient of government, and it will cease to be such as soon as a Patriot King is raised to the throne, the panacea is applied," Bolingbroke wrote. "A Patriot King is the most powerful of all reformers; for he is himself a sort of standing miracle," he continued, "so rarely seen and so little understood, that the sure effects of his appearance will be admiration and love in every honest breast, confusion and terror to every guilty conscience, but submission and resignation in all." The Patriot King may favor one faction or another, as the situation dictated, "but he will espouse none, much less will he proscribe any." Regarding specific policies, the Patriot King "will not multiply taxes wantonly, nor keep up those unnecessarily which necessity has laid, that he may keep up legions of tax gatherers."[36]

John Adams can be most closely connected to Bolingbroke, but others shared the vision of the virtuous leader. John Taylor recalled that "Mr. J[efferson] contemplated in raptures the idea of a patriot king!" Bolingbroke's model for the Patriot King was Queen Elizabeth, who "united the great body of the people in her and their common interest, she inflamed them with one national spirit: and, thus armed, she maintained tranquility at home, and carried succor to her friends and terror to her enemies abroad." Bolingbroke credited Elizabeth with encouraging English trade and giving "rapid motion to our whole mercantile system." He attacked James I for squandering England's advantages. Elizabeth's reign offered further proof that England was easily defended under the right monarch. As an island, England had no powerful neighbors and did not have to undertake continental engagements. Elizabeth recognized that England was first and foremost a maritime power, and she cultivated naval power. She knew that England had an amphibious character. "Like other amphibious animals, we must come occasionally on shore; but the water is more properly our element, and in it, like them, as we find our greatest security, so we exact our greatest force," Bolingbroke wrote.[37]

John Trenchard, the senior author of *Cato's Letters,* agreed with Bolingbroke that Elizabeth's reign was a golden age. In his 1698 work *A Short History of Standing Armies in England,* Trenchard contrasted the glory of Elizabeth with the folly of James I. In *Cato's Letters,* which ran from 1720 to 1723, Trenchard and Gordon shared much with Bolingbroke. Like the younger Bolingbroke, "Cato" saw a reformed Parliament as the foundation of British liberty. In Letter 70, "Cato" recommended the election of legislators "who are not already pre-engaged, nor, from their circumstances, education, profession, or manner of life are likely to be engaged, in a contrary interest." "Cato" did not last long enough to become as disillusioned as Bolingbroke. *Cato's Letters* ended with Trenchard's death in 1723, and Gordon later became one of Walpole's propagandists.[38]

"Cato," fully agreeing with Bolingbroke's view of foreign policy, was fearful of continental alliances and standing armies and favored trade and the navy. "What did England gain formerly by their conquests upon the continent, but constant wars, slaughter and poverty to themselves, and to their Princes precarious foreign provinces at English expense," Trenchard and Gordon wrote in Letter 93, reflecting on recent British experience in continental politics. Conquests bred armies, they wrote in Letter 95, and "all the parts of Europe which are enslaved, have been enslaved by armies."[39]

The navy was the proper weapon of a free people. In Letter 64 "Cato" argued that "despotick monarchs, though infinitely powerful at land yet could never rival Neptune, and extend their empire over the liquid world." "Cato" drew a direct equation between freedom, trade, and naval power. Merchants naturally sought out free countries, as trade "cannot long subsist, much less flourish, in arbitrary governments." Trade was the foundation of naval power, both as a training ground for seamen and as a source of customs revenue. Commerce had the added virtue of giving employment to those who might become troublesome at home. Like Bolingbroke, "Cato" gave the colonial trade a high priority, arguing in Letter 106 that, "our northern colonies do, or may if encouraged, supply us most or all of the materials of navigation . . . which management would soon make us masters of most of the trade of the world."[40]

The implication of Opposition thought on military and diplomatic affairs was that Great Britain, separated from the continent, had the best chance at freedom. The Netherlands had escaped the fate of the rest of Europe but were constantly at risk. "Almost all Europe are witnesses of the brutish havock which the conquerors make, and of the dismal Scenes of Ruin that they leave behind them," wrote "Cato" in Letter 93. The equation between isolation and liberty passed whole into American thought. Thomas Paine, in *Common Sense,* recognized Britain's unique place when he wrote that "Freedom hath been hunted round the globe. Asia, and Africa, have long expelled her. — Europe regards her like a stranger, and England hath given her warning to depart." Even though England had turned against liberty, liberty had survived there longer than anywhere else.[41]

Opposition foreign policy, emphasizing colonies and commerce over continental objects, enjoyed a brief and partial ascendancy during the Seven Years' War under William Pitt. Pitt entered Parliament in 1734 and soon joined the Patriot group, which was influenced by Bolingbroke and which formed the parliamentary opposition to Walpole, and particularly opposition to Walpole's Spanish policy. Pitt's appointment as secretary of state for the southern department (covering France, Spain, and the colonies) made him responsible for the main theaters of the Seven Years' War. Although obliged to protect Hanover, Pitt reversed the British strategy of the War of the Austrian Succession by putting continental strategy in the service of his American strategy, rather than using the colonies as bargaining chips over European objectives. Pitt sent troops to Hanover and subsidized Prussia to tie France down and prevent it from mounting an effective counteroffensive in America.[42]

James Burgh (1714–1775) represents the culmination of eighteenth-century Opposition Whig thought. Burgh echoed many Opposition themes in his book *Political Disquisitions: An Enquiry into Public Errors, Defects and Abuses* (1774–1775). Burgh also served as a direct link between Opposition thought and its American adherents, personally sending a copy of *Political Disquisitions* to Adams, who called the book "the best Service, that a Citizen, could render to his Country." Burgh believed that the promise of the Glorious Revolution had been betrayed from the beginning. After William arrived, "one of his first works was to plunge us into the very vice [a standing army] which has enslaved all the nations of the world, that have ever lost their liberties." William dragged England into his wars in Europe and started a trend that worsened under Queen Anne and the Hanoverians. To Burgh the standing army was the ultimate tool of oppression. "No nation ever kept up an army in times of peace, which did not lose its liberties," he wrote. Englishmen need look no further than Cromwell for proof "that a man of courage backed by an army, is capable of any thing." Burgh summed up Opposition military thought in book 3: "A Militia with the Navy, [is] the only proper Security of a free people in an insular Situation, both against foreign invasion and domestic Tyranny." Like Bolingbroke and "Cato," Burgh emphasized the colonial contribution to British power, arguing that the colonies consumed the most British-made goods and were a general national benefit.[43]

The Opposition Whigs contributed two important ideas to the connection between republicanism and foreign policy. The first was the need to take advantage of physical separation from Europe; Adams, Jefferson, Madison, and Hamilton all accepted this premise. The second idea was that the tools and conduct of foreign policy constituted a potential danger to republican government. Adams's views of the 1790s were closest to the Opposition Whigs and shaped his conduct of the Quasi-War with France. Jefferson and Madison accepted these two main ideas but went so far as to see both a navy and an army as dangers to liberty. Hamilton dissented from the consensus, always retaining a Harringtonian rather than a Bolingbrokean sense of power.

For a broader justification for foreign policy goals, Americans turned to the relatively new science of the law of nations. The law of nations was the lingua franca of diplomacy; it often served as the diplomatic voice of the republicanism of the English Opposition. Ideas expressed at home in the language of Bolingbroke or "Cato" were argued abroad in the language of Grotius and Vattel. The law of nations emerged as a coherent body of thought in the century after the Thirty Years' War. The idea of a "universal monarchy" as a secular counterpart to a universal church gave way to recognition of multiple religions in the wake of the Reformation and a corresponding system of balanced power among competing nation-states, no one of which could be allowed to predominate. The survival of each nation depended on the maintenance of a balance-of-power system, and presumably no nation would risk upsetting this system for fear of reprisal from other nations. The Treaty of Utrecht, by separating the French and Spanish Bourbons, codified the new system and replaced transnational dynasties with discrete nations as the fundamental diplomatic units.[44]

The law of nations that Americans read was the product of many hands and minds working in both theory and practice. Most commentators, including Madison, called the Dutch lawyer and diplomat Hugo Grotius (1583–1645) the father of the law of nations, based on his 1625 work *The Rights of War and Peace*. Samuel von Pufendorf (1632–1694), the Saxon philosopher and diplomat, followed Grotius and later influenced the Genevans Jean Jacques Burlamaqui and Jean-Jacques Rousseau. The dominant figure in framing the law of nations was the Swiss jurist Emmerich de Vattel (1714–1767). Vattel was a native of Neuchâtel, a Swiss canton later praised by Adams for its balanced constitution. Vattel served as Saxony's minister to Bern and later as a member of the Saxon privy council. His crowning achievement was his 1758 work *The Law of Nations*, which transformed Christian Wolff's *The Law of Nations treated according to a Scientific Method* into a handbook for diplomatic practice. The law of nations was not an exclusively republican science; Vattel's *Law of Nations* went through dozens of editions in every major language in western Europe. The law of nations was compatible with American republicanism in two ways. First, the two shared a similar theoretical basis, with an emphasis on natural equality and contractual association. Second, the law of nations protected the interests of small, neutral powers and provided a justification for many American foreign policy goals.[45]

The law of nations was built on the idea of natural law, which formed the basis for both individual and national rights. Because nations recognized no superior authority, they could therefore be said to exist in a state of nature, which gave each nation the right to pursue its own ends. In *The Law of Nations,* Vattel wrote that "nations are *free, independent* and *equal,*" and each holds the right to judge its own actions. The state, Jean Jacques Burlamaqui argued, is a "moral person."[46]

Given that nations began in a state of nature, the next question concerned the natural relationship among them. In *Leviathan,* Thomas Hobbes took the pessimistic view that the natural state of both individuals and nations was war, or at least potential war. Without a central organ of control, there were no moral or legal limits to any state action. Most theorists, including Burlamaqui, Grotius, and Pufendorf, took the more optimistic stand that the state of nature was a state of peace and that, although no positive law of a world community governed nations, natural law and morality did. Republican government and natural law sprang from the same roots, the free association of individuals. Locke's argument that men in a natural state formed societies for mutual safety found its counterpart in Vattel, who went so far as to call the European system "a kind of republic."[47]

The law of nations provided a theoretical basis for many American foreign policy goals, particularly concerning freedom of trade. "It is necessary that there should be some law among nations to serve as a rule for mutual commerce," wrote Burlamaqui. The first rule was that the sea was free to all. Grotius argued that the sea was too large for any one nation to control and was therefore the common property of all. According to Vattel, "the nation that attempts to exclude another from that advantage [free navigation] does her an injury, and furnishes her with sufficient grounds for hostilities." Vattel extended natural freedom of trade to cover the complete freedom of neutrals to trade in non-contraband goods. The natural right to trade was not a specifically republican idea, but it was congenial to republican government and became a cornerstone of American foreign policy.[48]

Enlightenment thought generally celebrated economic freedom as an expression of natural law. The French Physiocrats (whose name meant "rule of nature") called for free trade in reaction to feudal and noble restrictions on the French economy. The Physiocrats held that private landed property and agricultural production were the source of all wealth. Although the Physiocrats advocated an absolutist royal government to protect free trade from noble interference, Physiocratic economic thought was compatible with that of Harrington, and later that of Jefferson and Madison. A century later, on the eve of American independence, the Scottish philosopher Adam Smith in *An Inquiry into the Nature and the Causes of the Wealth of Nations*

called for complete economic freedom in all fields. "To prohibit a great people . . . from making all that they can out of every part of their own produce, or from employing their own stock and industry in the way that they
judge most advantageous to themselves," Smith wrote, "is a manifest violation of the sacred rights of mankind."[49]

Smith took aim at three hundred years of British and European economic policy, which he labeled "mercantilism." Mercantilism was not a set
policy but rather a cluster of accumulated policies and assumptions regarding trade and national power. Mercantilism assumed that world politics was
a zero-sum game, which no nation could win without another losing. Win-
ning was defined as maintaining a favorable balance of trade by hoarding
and preventing the export of gold; by preventing the export of raw materials, such as wool, that were needed for domestic industry; and by encouraging exports and discouraging imports. Colonies in the mercantile system
existed to serve the mother country by providing raw materials and an exclusive market for exports. Smith attacked mercantilism in each of its assumptions and argued that free trade was a surer way to wealth. At a certain
point, the amount of gold stockpiled would exceed demand, he argued,
and nothing could prevent its export. Similarly, taxes designed to prevent
importation were counterproductive. Smith criticized the mercantile conception of empire and wrote that the expense of defending colonies far outweighed the economic benefit of their markets. The British national debt
incurred in defense of the colonies, which spawned the Stamp Act and the
Townshend Duties, proved Smith correct.[50]

Economic theory was a part of the broader mid–eighteenth century inquiry into the nature of human society. Scottish thinkers such as David
Hume, Adam Ferguson, and Adam Smith believed that human society
passed through four stages—hunting, pasturage, agriculture, and commerce. At each stage virtue consisted in the full use of natural talents, with
commerce as the highest and most virtuous stage of society. David Hume
argued that the development of commerce and manufacturing, including
luxury goods, promoted wealth, happiness, refinement, and the spirit of
improvement. Adam Ferguson argued in 1767 that competition among nations improved societies, as economic competition improved individuals.
The Scottish analysis of societal evolution held tremendous implications
for American diplomacy, which centered on trade. The nature of American
contact with the world would be in part determined by the nature of American society.[51]

Free trade brought the danger of luxury, which the revolutionary era
supposed to be incompatible with republicanism. Montesquieu argued that
"a soul depraved by luxury has many other desires [than the public good]
and soon becomes an enemy to the laws that confine it." The central problem for Americans was determining the stage at which republican government was possible. American agrarians such as Jefferson and Madison believed that the third stage, as the Common Sense thinkers defined it, was

best suited to republicanism, and they saw extensive manufactures as a sign of old age and decay. The mercantile system and the Navigation Acts were devices whereby a dying system prolonged its life at the expense of a younger, more vigorous society. Land was relatively widely distributed in America, making manufacturing inappropriate. The commerce of the new nation would be based on agricultural exports. Thomas Jefferson summed up the agrarian creed in his *Notes on the State of Virginia:* "Those who labor in the earth are the chosen people of God, if ever he had a chosen people, whose breasts he has made his peculiar deposit for substantial and genuine virtue." As for manufacturing, Jefferson proposed to "let our work-shops remain in Europe." Jefferson and Madison would use free trade to keep the United States an agrarian nation.[52]

ENGLISH OPPOSITION WRITERS AND NATURAL LAW THEORISTS formed what Bernard Bailyn called the "intellectual switchboard" of the revolutionary generation. Americans believed that a spirit of opposition to liberty was the determining factor in colonial policy and evidence of British decay. The Stamp Act and Townshend Duties were an attempt to create a Walpolean fiscal machine in America. The army sent to America, which many feared would be quartered in American homes, provided a variety of constitutional horrors and completed the Walpolean machine. Americans who were well read in the Real Whig works believed that an army designed to combat a foreign adversary (in this case the Indians on the western frontier) would inevitably be turned against domestic liberty. The Boston Massacre in 1770 served to confirm those fears.[53]

Opposition writers taught the colonists to oppose the new parliamentary actions and, without directly recommending a course of action, suggested a power Americans might possess, inasmuch as Bolingbroke, "Cato," and other writers emphasized the colonial contribution to British power. The colonists hoped to force repeal of the Stamp Act by exploiting a supposed British dependence on American markets through non-importation. Non-importation seemed to solve a number of constitutional problems. It allowed Americans to strike a significant blow without committing treason. Also, ostentatious self-sacrifice increased the Americans' sense of their own superior virtue. The success of the resistance in securing the repeal of the Stamp Act convinced many American leaders that the colonies were the linchpin of the empire. By the eve of the revolution, some Americans saw all British regulations as attempts to stunt American growth. Boston merchants began calling for complete free trade by 1772, and after the outbreak of war, American writers lumped the Navigation Acts with all other forms of British taxation.[54]

Non-importation was not the cure-all that many Americans believed it to be. British politicians generally agreed that America should be taxed in some fashion, even if they disagreed on exactly how to do it. The British merchants who traded with America were too few in number to form an effective lobby. Caution by merchants on both sides of the Atlantic assured that non-importation would be less effective against the Townshend Duties. In 1775 non-importation failed to prevent armed conflict. Adams and Hamilton gave up on economic coercion by the end of the revolution. However, Jefferson and Madison continued to believe that commerce could secure American goals without recourse to large military establishments. Most saw commercial diplomacy as particularly suited to republican government. Trade was not just a lure, as Bolingbroke depicted it, but the ultimate weapon. Americans held the upper hand, Thomas Paine wrote, "while eating is the custom of Europe."[55]

A commitment to republican government shaped the way Americans viewed the world, and consequently the course of American foreign policy. When the Continental Congress took up the question of foreign policy in 1775, its members looked for guidance to the political thought and experience that had led them to rebellion. Over the next forty years, changing circumstances and differing experiences led John Adams, Thomas Jefferson, James Madison, and Alexander Hamilton to different conclusions about the relationship between republican government and foreign policy.

CHAPTER TWO

The Arc of Virtue

In his retirement, John Adams's favorite topic was the age of the American Revolution. "You ask how different were our Feelings and Conduct in 1774? Different indeed," he wrote to Benjamin Rush in 1808. "We then loved Liberty better than Money. Then Liberty meant security for Life, Liberty Property and Character."[1] Adams's statement reflects the tension between classical and whig virtue, between selfless devotion to the republic and the desire to trade, between Harrington and Bolingbroke. A fear of power (requiring a balanced government) and the promotion of commerce without political connections coexisted uneasily in Adams's thought and diplomacy with an ethic of self-sacrifice, often taking the form of a martial ethic, and a zeal to promote liberty on an international scale.

Young Adams had a Harringtonian sense of American power. According to legend, the pilgrims carved the words "The eastern nations sink, their glory ends / An empire rises where the sun descends" on Plymouth Rock. Adams believed the sentiment, if not the legend. He accepted Benjamin Franklin's 1751 theory that the American population would double every twenty years. In 1755 he observed that Rome and Great Britain rose to power from humble origins, and he speculated that "the great seat of Empire" might cross the Atlantic to America. "For if we can remove the turbulent Gallicks, our own people according to the exactest computations, will in another Century, become more numerous than England itself," he wrote. "Should this be the Case, since we have (I may say) all the naval stores of the Nation in our hands it will be easy to obtain mastery of the seas, and then the united force of all Europe will not be able to subdue us."[2]

Yet Britain's triumph meant the end of American freedom. Adams dated the conflict with Great Britain from the American articles of the 1763 Treaty of Paris—"The Cession of Canada, Louisiana, and Florida to the English." More specifically, the fall of Canada led the British government to devour its young in order to maintain power. "Suffice to it say, that immediately upon the Conquest of Canada from the French in the Year 1759, Great Britain Seemed to be Seized with a Jealousy against the Colonies," Adams wrote in 1780, "and then concerted the Plan of changing their forms of Government, of restraining their Trade within narrower Bounds, and raising a Revenue within them by Authority of Parliament, for the avowed or Pretended purpose of protecting, Securing and defending them."[3]

Adams addressed the crisis with Great Britain from a whig standpoint, focusing on the fear of uncontrolled power. To maintain liberty, both within a state and among nations, power must be dispersed as widely as possible. In *A Dissertation on the Canon and Feudal Law,* Adams described power as the "Desire for Dominion, that encroaching, grasping, restless, and ungovernable Principle in human Nature, that Principle which has made so much Havock and Desolation."[4]

When resistance to Great Britain turned to war, Adams turned to classical virtue, meaning a selfless devotion to the republic and to liberty, for his model citizen. In January 1776, he wrote, "I am so tasteless as to prefer a Republic" that would "produce Strength, Hardiness Activity Courage Fortitude and Enterprise. . . . Under a well regulated Commonwealth, the people must be wise and virtuous and cannot be otherwise." In April 1776, he explained that the enemy of republican virtue was the "Spirit of Commerce," meaning private interest, which was "incompatible with that purity of Heart, and Greatness of Soul, which is necessary for a happy Republic."[5]

At the same time, Adams shared the common belief, suggested by the Opposition school, that by denying trade to Great Britain and offering it to the rest of the world, Americans could manipulate the European balance of power for their own ends without any political involvement. On September 30, 1774, the Continental Congress banned the importation of British and Irish goods, as of December 1, 1774, and banned exports to Great Britain, Ireland, and the British West Indies, as of September 10, 1775. At heart Adams was a free trader. "I am against all shackles upon Trade," he wrote to James Warren in 1777. "Let the Spirit of the People have its own Way, and it will do something." Adams feared that non-exportation would hurt America more than Great Britain. "Can the Inhabitants of North America live without foreign trade?" he asked. However, Adams did recognize that commerce was the only real weapon America had, and in October 1775 he called the non-importation and non-exportation agreements a "formidable Shield of Defense."[6]

In his autobiography Adams wrote, "The Battle of Lexington on the 19th of April, changed the Instruments of Warfare from the Penn to the Sword." To a seventeenth-century republican, the best defense was a good offense. In this spirit, Congress authorized an attack on Canada, which Adams supported. He recalled that he was "wholly occupied" by it. The Canada expedition falls into a gray area between military and foreign policy. Radicals in

Congress saw the Canadians as fellow victims of British oppression, theoretically no different from residents of Massachusetts. Partially at Adams's insistence, the congressional committee that drafted a list of grievances cited the Quebec Act, "establishing the Roman Catholick Religion in the Province of Quebec, abolishing the equitable system of English laws, and erecting a tyranny there." In his own notes, Adams described the Quebec Act as "Danger to us all. An House on fire." In practice, the invasion was a measure of foreign policy. Unlike Massachusetts, Canada did not ask—or want—the Continental Army to come to its aid. Two different and uncoordinated American forces, under General Richard Montgomery and Colonel Benedict Arnold, entered Canada in 1775. They jointly attacked Quebec on December 30 but failed to take the city.[7]

At the same time the Continental Congress learned of the military failure in Canada, it began to consider what Adams later called "three Measures, Independence, Confederation and Negotiations with foreign powers [which] ought to go hand in hand."[8] Adams was a central figure in all three measures. He wrote *Thoughts on Government* in April 1776 to guide the formation of new colonial governments, which he saw as the precondition for independence and confederation. He drafted the Model Treaty as the basis for American relations with the world. Both the foreign and domestic halves of Adams's plan of 1776 proceeded from the same principles and drew on a combination of classical and whig republicanism.

On constitutional matters, Adams's suspicion of human nature led him to advocate a bicameral legislature. "A single assembly is liable to all the vices, follies and frailties of an individual," he wrote. Like Harrington, Adams believed that properly balanced government could produce virtue. He advocated laws to promote education, and sumptuary laws to keep the spirit of luxury under control. "Frugality is a great revenue," he wrote, "besides curing us of vanities, levities, and fopperies which are antidotes to all great, manly and warlike virtues." A constitution, he concluded, could "make the common people brave and enterprizing. That ambition which is inspired by it makes them safer, industrious and frugal." Adams knew that men often acted on their passions and interests rather than for the public good. A balanced constitution could force people to act virtuously. The desire for fame and honor required some contribution to the public good, regardless of motive. "Ambition in a Republic, is a great Virtue, for it is nothing more than a Desire, to Serve the Public, to Promote the Happiness of the People, to increase the Wealth, the Grandeur, and Prosperity of the Country," Adams later wrote.[9]

The second half of Adams's plan of 1776, the question of foreign alliances, also came in the midst of the Canada debacle. Great Britain forced the issue when Parliament passed the American Prohibitory Act, which declared American ships subject to capture and declared the colonies beyond the protection of the law. The act arrived in the Continental Congress on February 27. In response, Congress opened American ports to the world on April 6, 1776.[10]

Both moderates and radicals recognized that formal alliances with foreign powers presupposed independence. Opponents of independence naturally opposed alliances. "When We have bound ourselves to an eternal Quarrel with G.B. by a Declaration of Independence," John Dickinson argued on July 1, 1776, "France has nothing to do but hold back and intimidate G.B. till Canada is put into her hands, then to intimidate Us into a disadvantageous Grant of our Trade." Even radicals such as Patrick Henry shared Dickinson's concerns that an alliance should come first. Henry opposed resolutions in the Virginia Assembly calling for independence, as he believed that confederation and foreign alliances should precede independence.[11]

Instead of needing foreign alliances first, Adams argued, America needed to declare independence before any nation would sign an alliance. Merely opening the ports was not enough. "Foreign powers could not be expected to acknowledge Us till We had acknowledged ourselves and taken our Station, among them as a sovereign Power, and an Independent Nation." Adams dismissed Dickinson's fears of French domination because America did not seek a political or military alliance. He would not give France the opportunity for political interference. "I wish for nothing but Commerce," he wrote. In March 1776, he argued in Congress, "is any Assistance attainable from F[rance]? What Connection may We safely make with her? 1st. No Political Connection. Submit to none of her Authority—receive no Governors, or Officers from her. 2d. No Military Connection Recieve no Troops from her. 3d. Only a Commercial Connection." A treaty based on trade, Adams believed, would gain French support without violating the principle of separation from European politics. His policy temporarily matched that of the moderate-dominated Committee of Secret Correspondence, which instructed the commissioner to France Silas Deane, posing as a private merchant, to emphasize to the French that British wealth came from American trade.[12]

Adams believed that American commerce could dictate terms to other nations, exploit a balance between Great Britain and France, and reorder the world. The constant demand for grain on the European continent, aggravated by endemic warfare, would guarantee American independence and commerce without political commitments. "We have always said in America," Adams wrote in 1781, "'By and by will come a scarce year for grain in Europe, and then the nations there will begin to think us of some consequence.'" Furthermore, American commerce forced other nations to change their behavior and strike a blow for the principle of freedom of the seas, as set down by writers on the law of nations and endorsed by American republicans. "Every body throughout the world sees, that a renewal of the English monopoly of the American trade, would establish an absolute tyranny upon the ocean, and that every other ship that sails would hold its liberty at the mercy of these Lordly Islanders," Adams wrote in 1780. He wanted to break the British monopoly on American commerce and to open markets to France and other countries, giving each nation an incentive to respect American independence. Adams later recalled that the Americans hoped to "annihilate all Domination at Sea, and establish a universal and perpetual Liberty for all Nations Neutral and belligerent on that element."[13]

Adams presented his draft of the Model Treaty in July 1776. He was influenced in framing it by the Anglo-French articles of the 1713 Treaty of Utrecht, which gave France and Great Britain limited most-favored-nation status and established free navigation in each other's European possessions. Lord Bolingbroke attempted to use trade as a prelude to a political alliance, but Adams intended to use trade as a substitute for one. The Model Treaty's thirty articles guaranteed reciprocal trade, protection for each signatory's ships in the other's ports, and by excluding food and ships' stores in the definition of contraband it took a step toward the principle of "free ships, free goods" (the principle that goods belonging to a belligerent but carried in a neutral vessel are to be considered neutral). The only military concessions included merely a commitment that the United States would remain neutral (rather than ally with Great Britain) if Great Britain declared war on the allied nation and that in the present conflict the United States would not seek a separate peace with Great Britain. Furthermore, the treaty barred a signatory from taking over any British colonies in North America. Congress adopted a slightly modified version on September 17, 1776.[14]

The Model Treaty revealed the connection between ideology and diplomacy, particularly a fusion of classical and whig theories. It reflected the fear of foreign engagements and the primacy of commerce inherited from the English Opposition, and it made a careful distinction between commercial and political treaties. The treaty showed that Adams viewed the European balance of power as Bolingbroke had, as an external system that could preserve national liberty without political or military commitments. The classical element came from the belief that American virtue could use Europe's sins against it. Adams believed that the "Spirit of Commerce"—the pursuit of self-interest rather than a common good, which he deplored in domestic politics—was the organizing principle of international relations. Like his domestic system, Adams's diplomatic system depended on the American people's classical virtue, especially in its martial aspect. Americans could hold out despite personal hardship while Great Britain choked on its own luxury. Adams believed that a combination of divine favor, American virtue, and British corruption would bring a quick victory, making permanent foreign alliances unnecessary. "My toast is a short and violent War," Adams wrote in 1777.[15]

Military collapse in December led Congress to abandon the Model Treaty and authorize the envoys in Paris to agree to whatever was necessary to bring France into the war. The Comte de Vergennes, the French foreign minister, intended to use the United States to increase French power relative to Great Britain. He would not openly commit France without greater assurances that the Americans would continue to fight.[16]

On November 7, 1777, Congress appointed Adams to replace Deane as a commissioner to France. He arrived on April 1, 1778, and learned that Benjamin Franklin, Silas Deane, and Arthur Lee had signed two treaties on February 6: a commercial treaty based on the Model Treaty, and a military alliance that the Model Treaty had been designed to prevent. Adams did not believe a political commitment to France was either desirable or necessary. He supported the treaties for two practical reasons. First, the United States would need French support as long as Great Britain occupied ground in North America. "Will it ever do to think of Peace, while G. Britain has Canada, Nova Scotia and the Floridas, or any of them?" he asked James Warren in July 1778. Second, if the United States did not fulfill its obligations, it could expect no further help from Europe. "This faith [in upholding the treaty] is our American Glory, and it is our Bulwark," Adams wrote Warren in August, "it is the only Foundation on which our Union can rest secured, it is the only Support of our Credit both in Finance and Commerce, it is our only Security for the Assistance of Foreign Powers."[17]

Once in Europe, Adams had to translate republican theory into diplomatic practice. The problem fell into three overlapping questions. The first question was whether there was a specifically republican style of diplomacy and diplomatic conduct. The second question was what military strategy was best suited to a republic. The third question was the degree to which the United States shared a common interest with other republics, or with other nations sharing similar diplomatic goals.

Adams first dealt with the question of diplomatic conduct. Soon after Deane's recall, Lee accused Deane of using his position to further his commercial interests. In 1776 Pierre-Augustin Caron de Beaumarchais had organized the trading firm Rodrigue Hortalez et Cie to serve as a vehicle for sending military supplies to America. Louis XVI had given the company starting capital, which led Lee to believe the company was a front. The king had authorized the company to sell stock, and both Beaumarchais and Deane treated the company as a legitimate business. Deane invested heavily, often mixing his private and official financial accounts. The suspicious-minded Lee accused Beaumarchais and Deane of fraud. Deane responded by charging the Lee family with disloyalty to the alliance and with outright treason. The story reached Paris in February 1779 and caused an immediate rift between Adams (a Lee family ally) and Franklin, who believed Deane innocent of any wrongdoing. Adams wrote in his diary, "that there appeared to me no Alternative left but the Ruin of Mr. Deane, or the Ruin of his Country. That he appeared to me in the light of a wild Boar, that ought to be hunted down for the Benefit of Mankind."[18]

The Deane affair was to Adams a fairly straightforward case of corruption triumphing over virtue, and the commercial over the public spirit. Franklin's conduct was a more complicated problem. Adams, a self-described "stern and haughty Republican," called Franklin's lifestyle "a

Scene of continual dissipation." Franklin's diplomacy seemed to place the United States in a subservient position; he seemed to base his diplomacy on his personal relationship with the French more than on mutual interest. Franklin expressed his gratitude toward France for its help in public displays that Adams found distasteful for a republican. "Franklin, while in France, was very French," according to one Franklin biographer. Unlike Adams, Franklin did not conceive of a republican style of diplomacy. For Adams, this was the problem. "He [Adams] thinks . . . that America has been too free in Expressions of Gratitude to France," Franklin wrote in 1780, believing "that this Court is to be treated with Decency & Delicacy." Adams believed the American cause needed no embellishment. "The dignity of North America does not consist in diplomatic ceremonials or any of the subtleties of etiquette," he wrote to Vergennes in 1781, "it consists solely in reason, justice, truth, the rights of mankind and the interests of the nations of Europe, all of which, well understood, are clearly in her favor."[19]

Congress reorganized the diplomatic corps on September 14, 1778, naming Franklin the sole minister. Adams received the news on February 12, 1779, and learned he had not been sent even a formal letter of recall. Adams returned to the world of diplomacy later in 1779, as part of a radical effort to curb French influence. Conrad-Alexandre Gérard, the French minister to the United States, used the divisions in Congress to make American peace demands more acceptable to Spain so that Spain would enter the war. Initially, the United States presented an ambitious list of demands. On February 23, 1779, a committee recommended that the United States demand absolute independence (with the Mississippi River as the western boundary), British evacuation, complete access to the Newfoundland fisheries and the entire length the Mississippi, and either the cession or the independence of Nova Scotia. Gérard sought to make these demands more acceptable to Great Britain and less threatening to Spain, which entered the war as a French (but not American) ally on April 12, 1779. Gérard influenced Congress to drop the fisheries, and on August 14 Congress settled on its demands: absolute independence and control of territory west to the Mississippi and south to 31° north latitude. Gérard lobbied for John Jay, then linked with pro-Deane forces, to be peace commissioner and minister to Spain. Pro-Lee members, led by Samuel Adams, abandoned Lee in favor of John Adams, whose election would secure the fisheries even without specific instructions. Congress deadlocked until both sides agreed to divide the two jobs, electing John Adams peace commissioner and Jay minister to Spain on September 27.[20]

Adams's second tour concerned the second great question he faced in Europe, as to what military strategy was appropriate to a republic. In the process, he began to shift his support from classical toward whig virtue. He began to see the American advantage as lying in its geographic position rather than in the spirit of its people.

In April 1780 Adams read former Massachusetts governor Thomas Pownall's pamphlet *A Memorial, Most Humbly Addressed to the Sovereigns of Europe, on the Present State of Affairs, Between the Old and New World.* "Gov.
Pownal Speaks like an oracle," Adams remarked early in the edited version
he sent to Congress. No doubt he considered Pownall's work brilliant for its
agreement with his own thinking on many points. Pownall wrote that the
Seven Years' War created a system dominated by the "Spirit of Commerce"
and centered on Great Britain. The creation of an independent America forever changed this system. America's strength lay in its domination of a continent and separation from Europe. Pownall considered America an "Infant
Hercules." Pownall believed that America would become "a free Port to all
Europe," and all Europe would have a stake in keeping America open and
independent. To fulfill this destiny, Pownall counseled America to avoid
foreign alliances and Europe's wars.[21]

Adams had previously argued all of Pownall's main points. Agreement
from a former British official with extensive American experience certainly
suggested that Adams was right all along. Pownall's arguments coincided
with a trend in Adams's own thought that led him to locate America's
diplomatic advantages in natural resources and in distance from Europe
rather than merely in form of government. In Adams's strategic thinking,
the whig element began to predominate.

English Opposition thought and his own experience taught Adams that
a navy was the means of defense best suited to a republic; for him a navy
was "our Natural and our only adequate Defence." With a tiny navy itself,
the United States had to rely on France. Like many Americans, Adams believed that French sea power would prevent the resupplying of British
troops in America, which would allow the United States to win without relying on French ground troops. This belief supplied the strategic assumptions of the Model Treaty.[22]

The United States needed the French and Spanish navies in American
waters in order to enforce separation from Europe. Instead, France and
Spain collaborated on an abortive invasion of Great Britain in the summer of 1779. Adams felt obliged to tell France and Spain how to run the
war. "It is not by besieging Gibraltar nor invading Ireland, in my humble opinion, but by sending a clear Superiority of naval Power into the
American Seas," he wrote to Benjamin Rush. After Adams learned of Admiral Rodney's victory over the Spanish at Gibraltar on January 16,
1780, he complained that vast fleets were wasted on Gibraltar, "which is
but a Trifle," while even a smaller fleet would triumph off America. On
July 13, Adams advised Vergennes that a show of naval force in American waters would reassure the country and force the British out of
Philadelphia, isolating them in New York City. Vergennes—with a
smaller fleet than the British, and a reluctant ally in Spain—could not
accommodate Adams, who concluded that Vergennes wanted to see
America independent of Great Britain, but not of France.[23]

On July 27, 1780, Adams left for the Netherlands to deal with the third question regarding diplomacy and republicanism. To what degree were American fortunes linked to other republics and maritime states? On September 16, Adams temporarily replaced the captured Henry Laurens as minister to the Netherlands. While Adams was there, American interests seemed to coincide with possible Dutch entry into the Armed Neutrality. Catherine II of Russia, hoping for an agreement of the neutral powers of northern Europe, issued the Declaration of Armed Neutrality on February 28, 1780. Of the five principles of the Armed Neutrality, the first three—freedom of neutrals to trade with belligerents, the idea that "free ships make free goods," and a limited definition of contraband—appeared in the Model Treaty. The fourth principle stated that only an effective blockade could be legal; the fifth set the first four as the basis for judging the legality of prizes.[24]

Adams believed the United States could alter the structure of European diplomacy, and he took partial credit for the agreement, calling it "one of the most brilliant events which has yet been produced by the American Revolution." He hoped that the northern powers could tie up the British fleet in Europe and make up for the lack of French naval cover. Adams reported that "either the War will be pushed this year with more vivacity than ever, both by Land and by Sea, or that Peace will be made without delay." Congress shared Adams's enthusiasm and sent Francis Dana, Adams's secretary, to apply for membership in the Armed Neutrality.[25]

The Dutch joined the Armed Neutrality for their own protection on November 20, 1780, and the British authorized attacks on Dutch shipping on December 20. The Dutch appealed to Russia for help on January 12, 1781. Adams hoped that Armed Neutrality would then join the war, forcing Great Britain to negotiate for peace and reducing American dependence on France. Adams's hopes, along with the Armed Neutrality itself, all collapsed when Russia refused to go to war for the Dutch.[26] Adams's hopes for the Armed Neutrality reflected his belief that all maritime powers formed a natural common interest with the United States.

Like his Opposition forebears, Adams believed that the Netherlands was the only modern continental nation that had achieved liberty, resulting in part from its maritime nature. He assumed that, in addition to a common maritime interest with the Armed Neutrality, America had a common political interest with the Netherlands, the sole republican member of the League. This assumption shifted the basis of his diplomacy from an emphasis on strategic interest (the foundation of the American appeal to France and Spain) to an ideological consideration, the common interest of republics. Adams opened a question that would resurface during the French Revolution: to what degree does a similarity in form of government, real or perceived, dictate relations among nations?

Adams wrote to Franklin in June 1782 that "The permanent friendship of the Dutch may be easily obtained." The basis for this friendship was to be republicanism and commerce. On April 19, 1781, Adams presented a memorial to the States-General of the Netherlands outlining the interest the Dutch should take in the American cause: "If there ever was among nations a natural alliance, one may be formed between the two republics," Adams wrote. He went on to discuss the Pilgrims' residence at Leyden and parallels in the origins of both countries, as well as similarities in religion, government, and commerce. Adams concluded that "in all the particulars the union is so obviously natural that there has seldom been a more distinct designation of Providence to any two distant nations to unite themselves together." Unfortunately for Adams, republicanism was not a sufficient bond. The Dutch simply wished to trade with all the belligerents and were not interested in schemes to remake the law of the sea.[27]

Adams's Dutch negotiations reflected his general approach to diplomacy, that the United States should not become dependent on any power. "It seems to me of vast importance to us to obtain an acknowledgement of our independence from as many other sovereigns as possible, before any conferences for peace should be held," he wrote to Franklin. Adams's general appeal for aid conflicted with Franklin's more cautious approach. Like Adams, Franklin wished to keep the United States as much as possible out of European politics. Franklin wrote in 1777 that the United States should not "go suitering for Alliances, but wait with decent Dignity for the applications of others." Once the alliance with France was signed, Franklin believed that France could offer the most help and that American interests would be best served by relying on France rather than by introducing more powers and deeper American commitments to European nations. Adams certainly agreed that "France deserves the first Place, among those Powers with which our Connections will be the most intimate." In Adams's mind, Franklin's system rested on two things that Adams did not trust: Franklin's personal relationship with Vergennes and the basic goodwill of the French.[28]

Vergennes naturally preferred to deal with Franklin, and he always considered Adams a nuisance. Military failure and congressional panic gave Vergennes the chance to have Adams recalled. In the spring of 1781, the new French minister, the Chevalier de la Luzerne, complained about Adams's conduct and asked Congress to restrain him. In a show of anti-Adams and anti–New England sentiment, Congress revoked Adams's peace commission on June 15 and instead named a delegation comprised of Adams, Franklin, Jay, Laurens, and Thomas Jefferson, which it instructed to be guided by France in negotiating peace. Congress delivered the coup de grace on July 15 by revoking Adams's commission to negotiate a commercial treaty with Great Britain.[29]

Adams received his new commission on August 24, 1781, and saw a clear sign of the decay that eventually came to all republics. The instructions were both a personal insult and a dereliction of duty, a symbol of Congress's abandonment of its agents comparable to its seeming abandonment of the army at Valley Forge, when Congress left the army underfed and poorly clothed during the winter encampment of 1777–1778. Adams wrote Franklin, "I am very apprehensive that our new commission will be as useless as my old one." His optimism of 1776—based on a belief in the classical virtue, that is, the spirit of self-sacrifice, of the American people—had faded, and after years of disappointment Adams warned his wife "not to flatter yourself with hopes of Peace. There will be no such thing for several years." Not even the British surrender at Yorktown changed his mood. Adams wrote to Robert R. Livingston, the secretary of foreign affairs, that "I cannot be of your opinion, that, great as it [Yorktown] is, it will defeat every hope that Britain entertains of conquering a country so defended." He was thus surprised when on September 28, 1782, Jay informed him that Great Britain was prepared to negotiate and that he should come to Paris.[30]

Jay and Franklin began the peace process, meeting with Vergennes on August 10, 1782. Vergennes considered the American claim of territory as far west as the Mississippi extravagant. The meeting convinced Jay that the Americans might have to violate their instructions and sign a separate peace. Great Britain was more willing to make a generous peace. The British prime minister, the Earl of Shelburne, believed the territory north of the Ohio River was lost. Better to give it to the Americans, who would continue to trade with Great Britain, than to France or Spain.[31]

Jay's draft treaty on October 5, 1782, called for recognition of American independence and British evacuation of American territory. It set American boundaries at the Mississippi on the west, 31° north latitude on the south, the St. Lawrence River and 45° north latitude on the northwest, and the St. John's River to the Bay of Fundy on the northeast. The draft gave the United States the right to catch and dry fish off Newfoundland, and it granted the United States and Great Britain free navigation of the Mississippi. The British negotiator, Richard Oswald, approved the treaty, but the British cabinet rejected it on October 17. The cabinet wanted to exclude the Americans from the fisheries, establish a more advantageous Maine boundary, and make some provision for American Tories. Adams arrived in Paris on October 26. He was still suspicious of Franklin but discovered that Jay, previously connected with the pro-Deane moderates, was now fully anti-French. "Mr. Jay likes Frenchmen as little as Mr. Lee and Mr. Izard did," Adams noted with some satisfaction in his diary. "Our Allies dont play fair, he told me."[32]

Adams's main contributions to the treaty came in the last sessions, which began on November 25, 1782. The fisheries were the final problem. Adams considered the fisheries vital "both to the commerce and the Naval Power of this Country," Adams wrote in his autobiography. The sessions were a triumph for whig diplomacy, which based American security on a navy. To achieve his end, Adams put forth the argument that all nations should see their interest in American success. It was an argument that Adams himself believed less and less. Adams connected access to the fisheries to the survival of republican government in two ways. First, both the

origins of the republic and its right to the fisheries rested on the same principles of natural law. Second, Adams believed that his nation was destined
to be a great naval power, and the fisheries formed the training ground for
the sailors. He argued that acknowledging American rights to the fisheries
was safer for Britain than making concessions to France. It was safer to allow the United States to add to its navy than to let the French add to theirs.
The fisheries were a source of great profit. If the Americans shared in the
fisheries, much of their profits would end up in London in trade. The
British could not expect the same from the French. The fisheries were a potential source of naval conflict, and it was in Britain's interest to remove
sources of Anglo-American conflict rather than drive the Americans closer
to France. Adams presented a draft article on November 28 that gave the
United States the right to fish on the Grand Banks and wherever else Americans traditionally fished. Americans would also have the liberty to dry fish
on Cape Sable and the unsettled parts of Nova Scotia.[33]

On November 29, 1782, Adams reasserted a natural if not a divine right
to the fisheries. "When God Almighty made the Banks of Newfoundland at
300 Leagues Distance from the People of America and at 600 Leagues distance from those of France and England, did he not give as good a Right to
the former as to the latter," Adams thundered at Oswald. "If Heaven in the
Creation gave a Right, it is ours as much as yours. If Occupation, Use, and
Possession give a Right, We have it as clearly as you." Allyne Fitzherbert,
Oswald's secretary, conceded the point but saw no way around Oswald's instructions, which prohibited any such agreement. Adams vowed that he
would never sign a peace that kept the Americans out of the fisheries, and
Laurens and Jay quickly agreed. To prevent the negotiations from collaps-
ing, Oswald proposed reducing the Americans' claimed "right" to the
coastal fisheries to a "liberty" and yielded on drying privileges but only in
uninhabited areas. The Americans agreed to the compromise and signed
the Provisional Treaty on November 30, 1782.[34]

Adams was pleased with the treaty, even though the American commissioners had to violate their instructions to obtain it. "The great Interests of our Country in the West and in the East are secured, as well as her
independence. St. Croix is the boundary against Nova Scotia. The Fisheries are very safe, the Mississippi and the Western Lands to the middle
of the Great Lakes are as well secured to Us as they could be by England,"
Adams wrote to James Warren. "All these Advantages we could not have
obtained if we had literally pursued our Instructions." Livingston sent a
letter to the commissioners on March 25, 1783, praising the treaty but
criticizing the commissioners for not consulting the French. The commissioners defended their stroke for independence in violation of their
instructions of June 15, 1781. "Since we have assumed a Place in the Political System of the World, let us move like a Primary and not a Secondary Planet," they averred. "It is a Glory to have broken such infa-
mous Orders," Adams wrote in his diary.[35]

Diplomatic experience confirmed for Adams many English Opposition theories on foreign policy and strengthened his conviction that the United States was well rid of any political connection with Europe. "For my own Part I thought America had been long enough involved in the Wars of Europe. She had been a Football from the Beginning, and it was easy to see that France and England both would endeavour to involve Us in their future Wars," Adams wrote in his diary; "I thought [it] our interest and Duty to avoid [them] as much as possible and to be completely independent and have nothing to do but in Commerce with either of them." Adams hoped to expand commercial connections all over Europe in order to avoid dependence on France. Only by an impartial conduct toward all nations could the United States preserve the balance of power. "If We give exclusive priviledges in Trade, or form perpetual Alliances offensive and defensive with the Powers in one Scale," he warned James Warren, "We infallibly make enemies of those in the other." Adams argued in his diary that "it was not in our interest to hurt Great Britain any further than was necessary to support our Independence and our Alliances." By the end of the war, Adams had abandoned the idea of manipulating the international balance of power and merely sought shelter within that balance.[36]

Adams also came to believe that republican theory did not, and perhaps should not, dictate diplomatic style. "It may be said that Virtue, that is Morality applied to the Public is the Rule of Conduct in Republicks, and not Honor," Adams wrote his wife, "True. But American Ministers are acting in Monarchies, and not Republicks."[37] This opinion was a subtle but significant shift in Adams's thought. He did not follow it to the logical conclusion that Franklin had been right about how to approach the French. In later diplomacy, however, particularly during the Quasi-War with France, Adams accepted European practices that he had not accepted during the revolution.

Adams's program gradually ceased to define republican virtue in classical and martial terms. He remained in Europe for five years after the end of the American Revolution, and during that time he dropped two key assumptions at the center of the system of diplomacy he had previously based on classical virtue. First, he came to see that the American people were not more virtuous than any other people. His doubts festered after his recall in 1779, they grew worse in 1781, and by the time he went home in 1788 he had lost all faith in the classical virtue of the American people. Failures in diplomacy, specifically the American failure to combat British trade restrictions, contributed to his disillusionment.

The second assumption, which Adams held throughout the revolution, was that the United States could use trade to manipulate the European balance of power. Balanced government, as in 1776, was the solution to a lack of virtue. By the 1780s, Adams had come to see balanced government as a replacement for the virtue Americans did not possess. Such a belief mirrored his view of diplomacy, in which he expected balance and interest rather than virtue to restrain nations. In diplomacy, Adams turned to the republican realpolitik of the English Opposition school: neutrality from European politics and aloofness from the balance of power defended by a navy.

From 1776 onward, Adams based his diplomacy on the premise that all nations would open trade with the United States because it was in their interest to do so. Like most Americans, he tended to view British interest in terms of American interests and expected the two to coincide; he tended to prompt Great Britain to allow the United States back into the West Indian trade as if no war had occurred. "The commerce of the West Indies is part of the American system of commerce," he wrote to Livingston. "They can neither do without us, nor us without them." Chancellor of the Exchequer William Pitt was prepared to offer such trade, until a severe nationalist backlash in Parliament, bent on punishing the United States for its independence, forced the Fox-North ministry to act otherwise. On July 2, 1783, the Privy Council approved an order barring American ships from the British West Indian trade. The normally powerful West Indian lobby, who like the United States favored a quick return to normalcy, assumed that the measure was temporary and did not protest. The impasse made the final treaty of September 3, 1783, "a Simple Repetition of the provisional Treaty."[38]

The order became permanent with the Limiting Act of 1788. British shipping replaced American ships in the West Indian carrying trade, and the British government groomed Nova Scotia as the new focal point of trade. To Adams, the new policy sacrificed British interest to wounded pride. "The liberal sentiments in England, respecting the trade, are all lost for the present," he warned Livingston. When he learned of the July 2 order, he wrote Livingston that "a jealousy of American ships, seamen, carrying trade, and naval power, appears every day more and more conspicuous." Four days later, Adams added that "the present ministry swerve more and more from the true system, for the prosperity of their country and ours."[39]

The Earl of Sheffield's *Observations on the Commerce of the American States* appeared just before the Orders-in-Council and explained British policy most clearly. Sheffield first reminded his readers that, "it is in the light of a foreign country that America must henceforth be viewed." To preserve British shipping and the rest of the empire, the Americans could not be allowed back into the West Indies. Sheffield advocated developing Nova Scotia and Newfoundland as substitute granaries and using only British ships to carry the merchandise. "Rather than give up the carrying trade of our islands, surely it would be better to give up the islands themselves," Sheffield wrote. "It is the advantage to our navigation which in any degree, countervails the enormous expense of their protection." Great Britain need not fear American retaliation. The American government was weak, and Americans would buy British goods regardless of British policy.[40]

Adams had two goals as minister to Great Britain: to sign a commercial treaty and to ensure British adherence to the peace treaty, especially regarding British evacuation of the northwestern forts. Adams feared that the British anger, demonstrated in Sheffield's book, that blocked a commercial treaty in 1783 would continue to shape British policy. "The popular pulse seems to beat high against America," he observed early in the mission. "The people are deceived by numerous falsehoods industriously circulated in the gazettes and in conversation, so that there is much reason to believe that, if this nation had another hundred millions to spend, they would soon force this ministry into a war against us." Adams's first meeting with the foreign secretary, Lord Carmaerthen, on June 17, 1785, set the tone for Adams's three-year mission. Adams brought up British violations of the peace treaty, and Carmaerthen responded with complaints about American violations, specifically interference with the collection of prewar debts and the return of confiscated estates.[41]

Adams's hope of signing a commercial treaty soon vanished. He wrote to Secretary of Foreign Affairs Jay on June 26, 1785, that "we shall have no treaty of commerce until this nation is made to feel the necessity of it." Little over one month later, he reported that "the boast is that our commerce has returned to its old channels, and that it can follow no other." Adams believed British policy to be rooted in the fear that a trade treaty would build American maritime power at Britain's expense. "This nation is strangely blinded by prejudice and passion," Adams wrote in November. Although Adams was mistaken in seeing British policy as rooted in anger alone, he was correct in believing that maritime power was the central issue. Adams gave up on a commercial treaty in December 1785, informing Jay that the king and ministry were completely committed to the present navigation system and had no fear of American retaliation.[42]

Adams believed that the United States had justice on its side in pursuing a commercial treaty. The issue of violations of the peace treaty was not as clear-cut, as both sides were in the wrong. Whenever Adams asked when the British planned on evacuating the forts, the British asked when prewar debts would be paid. Adams met with Pitt on August 24, 1785, and the prime minister told him that the problems of the debts and posts were linked and would have to be solved together. Carmaerthen informed Adams on October 20 that nothing could be done regarding posts until debts were repaid. Adams protested that the treaty did not require the debts to be paid, only that the United States place no legal impediments on their collection.[43] The distinction was for all practical purposes meaningless. On February 28, 1786, Lord Carmaerthen presented Adams with a report showing that eight states had passed laws interfering with the collection of debts. Secretary Jay conducted his own study and concluded that "there has not been a single Day since it [the peace treaty] took Effect on which it has not been violated in America by one or other of the States."[44] Adams believed that the British used the debt issue merely as a pretext to hold the forts, yet it was a pretext provided by the

United States. He criticized the Massachusetts action against debt collection as "a direct Breach of the Treaty."[45] The only solution was a stronger union. Adams wrote Jay that "it is now with the states to determine whether there is or is not a union in America. If there is they may easily make themselves respected in Europe, if there is not, they will be little regarded."[46]

Adams saw the Eden Treaty, concluded between Great Britain and France on September 26, 1786, as further evidence that the United States was little respected in Europe. The treaty granted each nation most-favored-nation status in Europe. Both France and Britain hoped the treaty would encourage trade and ease domestic fiscal problems. Since 1782, Adams had argued that American trade was more valuable to Britain than French trade, and he could not believe that the Eden Treaty was economically motivated. In reality, it was a hostile move against the United States. "The time may not be far distant, however, when we may see a combination of England with the house of Bourbon against the United States," Adams warned Jay in 1786. Adams expected no settlement with Great Britain concerning the posts and told Jay in 1787 that the United States "had never more reason to be upon their guard." Before his departure in 1788, Adams observed that he, and by extension his nation, had been treated with "dry decency and cold civility."[47]

Adams's failed mission led him to abandon one of the key assumptions of the plan of 1776, that the United States could use national interest (the European desire for American trade) to manipulate the European diplomatic system to work in the American interest. Adams believed that the promise of trade would shield the United States from the effects of European diplomacy. His vision of free trade assumed that American navigation as well as agriculture would be protected. Yet no one nation could carry out a policy of free trade in a mercantilist world. "We have hitherto been the bubbles of our own philosophical and equitable liberality," Adams warned Jay in August 1785. Six months later Adams issued a direct attack on the French Physiocrats, writing Jay that a policy of free trade would eliminate the need for diplomacy. This would not be the only effect. "The consequence nevertheless would be the sudden annihilation of all their manufactures and navigation," Adams wrote. "We should have the most luxurious set of farmers that ever existed, and should not be able to defend ourselves against the insults of a pirate."[48]

Wisdom, to Adams, clearly meant building a navy, the politically safest method of protection, and passing commercial legislation to match British policy. "I hope our Countrymen will learn Wisdom, be frugal, encourage their own Navigation and Manufactures and Search the Globe for a Substitute for British Commerce," Adams wrote his son. To the Marquis de Lafayette he wrote that "our Timber and Masts will very soon, vindicate themselves from all English slanders." He advised Rufus King, "the United States have nothing to do but go on with their Navigation Acts." Furthermore, as the French had been no more friendly than the British to American shipping, Adams advocated a strict neutrality.[49]

Adams cheered congressional attempts to pass an impost aimed at British ships. He wrote that such a measure would "instantly raise the United States in the consideration of Europe, and especially England." On the tenth anniversary of independence, he wrote that the United States had passed from their youth to an early decline, and he observed that the United States had failed to carry out its end of the 1783 peace treaty or make any move to defend themselves against British commercial attacks. "Our Country is grown, or at least it has been dishonest," he lamented to a family friend. "She has broke her faith with Nations & with her own Citizens." For Adams, failure to strengthen the national government and stand up to Great Britain showed the same lack of national character that led Congress to give France control of the peace negotiations. Americans had retreated from a commitment to the public good and allowed private interest to predominate. If Adams had any faith in American classical virtue after 1781, it was gone by 1788.[50]

Adams's frustrations in London brought him to a final disillusionment regarding the virtue of the American people. He realized that the United States could not have declined from the height of virtue to the depths of depravity in only ten years. The Americans could not have been especially virtuous to begin with. As he had suspected in 1776, the war created virtues the Americans would not always possess. Whatever Americans were, Adams concluded, they were not Spartans, and perhaps this was for the best. "It is most certain that our Countrymen, are not and never were, Spartans in their Contempt of Wealth, and I will go farther and say they ought not to be," Adams wrote Warren. "Such a Trait in their character would render them lazy Drones, unfit for the Agriculture Manufactures Fisheries, and Commerce, and Population of their Country; and fit only for War." This admission resolved the contradiction of holding a political belief that feared commerce and pursuing a foreign policy that encouraged it.[51]

Adams could portray the United States as a simple agrarian nation to Europeans who might be threatened by a commercial and manufacturing nation. "Agriculture ever was and ever will be the dominant Interest in America," he wrote a Dutch sympathizer in 1780. The American reality was different. Adams need look no further than his native New England and its diversified economy to see the future course of economic development. "Agriculture, Manufactures and Commerce with one another will soon make us flourish," he wrote in 1786.[52] In the mid-1780s Adams moved the "Spirit of Commerce" from the fringe of his political philosophy, as a side effect of liberty mitigated by a balanced constitution, to the center, as the mainspring of human action, to be channeled for the good of all in a balanced government. Luxury was a part of the American future, and American thinkers had to fit it into their systems of republican government. "It is in vain, then to amuse ourselves with the thought of annihilating commerce, unless as philosophical speculations," Adams wrote to Jay. "We are to consider men and things as practical statesmen, and to consider who our constituents are and what they expect of us."[53]

Adams's three-volume work, *A Defence of the Constitutions of Government of the United States of America,* appeared in 1787 and 1788. It represents his attempt to come to terms with a republic not founded on classical virtue. Adams's ode to bicameralism was a response to the French philosopher Anne Robert Turgot, who attacked the Americans for copying British forms too closely. Adams went beyond this goal, moving into an analysis of human motivation as well. J. G. A. Pocock has called Adams's *Defence of the Constitutions* the last major work of classical republicanism.[54] From the beginning, however, Adams noticed the gap between classical and modern worlds. "The inventions in the mechanic arts, the discoveries in natural philosophy, navigation and commerce, and the advancement of civilization and humanity," Adams wrote, "have occasioned changes in the condition of the world, and the human character, which would have astonished the most refined nations of antiquity." Adams wrote later in the work that "love of poverty is a fictitious virtue, that never existed," adding that "frugality . . . is admired and esteemed more than beloved." A free people was inevitably drawn to luxury. "In a country like America, where the means and opportunities for luxury are so easy and so plenty," Adams wrote, "it would be madness not to expect it, be prepared for it, and provide against the dangers of it in the constitution." With a balanced constitution at home, Adams could fully accept a diplomacy centered on commerce.[55]

The love of distinction was another theme in Adams's book. "Every man hates to have a superior, but no man is willing to have an equal," Adams wrote, as "every man desires to be superior to all others." Natural inequalities in wealth, ability, appearance, intelligence, and the like led some to seek social or legal distinction. Americans were as likely to seek honors and awards as Europeans. "Are there not distinctions as earnestly desired and sought, as titles, garters, and ribbons are in any nation in Europe?" Adams asked. "We may look as wise, and moralize as gravely as we will; we may call this desire of distinction childish and silly," Adams wrote, "but we cannot alter the nature of man; human nature is thus childish and silly."[56]

In surveying the historical wreckage of republican governments, Adams found two that worked, Great Britain and the United States. His definition of a republic was fairly loose. "A limited monarchy therefore, especially when limited by two independent branches, an aristocratical and a democratical power in the constitution, may with strict propriety be called by that name [republic]." Adams explained in 1814 that he used the word "monarch" in the strict sense of "one who rules." Montesquieu used the same definition. With a clear conscience, Adams could argue that the British constitution was, "both for the adjustment of the balance and the prevention of its vibrations, the most stupendous fabric of human invention; and that the Americans ought to be applauded instead of censured for imitating it as far as they have done." Adams went on to argue that the British constitution "has still preserved the power of the people by the equilibrium we are contending for, by the trial by jury, and by constantly refusing a standing army." That is, Great Britain had prevented the tools of foreign policy from turning against domestic liberty. Of course, the American version of the balanced government differed from the British, especially regarding elected senates and executives. "Here they differ from the English constitution, and with great propriety," Adams wrote, adding that sovereignty "must reside in the whole body of the people." Adams observed that "In America, there are different orders of *officers,* but none of *men.*"[57]

The outward form of Adams's republicanism as outlined in *Defence of the Constitutions* was not new. He had classified Great Britain as a republic in the "Novanglus" letters in 1775, and his conception of balanced government was central to *Thoughts on Government.* He had previously discussed the use of medals and rewards to encourage virtue. The true change in Adams's thought was in his view of the American people. He never had absolute faith in American virtue, but by 1787 his view of the American people had darkened. He concluded from the political and diplomatic failures of the 1780s that Americans lacked classical republican virtue, and he shaped his conception of republicanism accordingly. In 1787 he formed a theory of republicanism around the reality of a non-Spartan American people. In doing so, he replaced classical virtue with the "Spirit of Commerce" that he had attacked in 1776.[58] "The best republics will be virtuous, and have been so; but we may hazard a conjecture that the virtues have been the effect of a well-ordered constitution, rather than the cause," Adams wrote near the conclusion of his work. "And perhaps it would be impossible to prove that a republic cannot exist even among highwaymen, by setting one rogue to watch another; and the knaves themselves may in time be made honest men by the struggle."[59] When Adams decided that martial virtue was not needed to found a republic, he left the classical world behind. The proper constitution may lead people into virtuous behavior, but one could not take classical virtue for granted. Adams then based his political philosophy on whig virtue, which meant supporting balanced government.

Adams did not discuss diplomacy in *Defence of the Constitutions.* However, it is clear that his mission to Great Britain played a significant role in his thinking. Adams had seen that nations, like men, lust after distinction and are governed as much by pride as by interest, by emotion as by reason. His descriptions of human characteristics in *Defence of the Constitutions* and of British actions in his dispatches to Jay are strikingly similar. Adams had long accepted the idea that the clash of interests could create a common good where none existed as the organizing principle of diplomacy; it was a key assumption of the Model Treaty (only later did Adams apply the principle as vigorously to domestic constitutions). The balance of power that controlled men and channeled their energies could also be used to control nations. Adams already believed that the international system set one rogue to watch another, with little hope of complete success. By 1788 diplomatic experience helped bring his political thought to the same conclusions.

CHAPTER THREE

Tillers of the Earth

At first, there was little operational difference between classical and yeoman virtue. However, Jefferson and Madison never held out a classical model of virtue. Without classical virtue, there was no disillusionment, and hence no change in thought. The spirit of the people was never the problem. Rather, the problem was to create institutions that preserved the yeomanry and harnessed its economic power for diplomatic purposes. The yeoman farmer, the central figure in the thinking of Jefferson and Madison, wielded the plowshare rather than the sword, providing "another umpire than arms."[1] The yeoman's agricultural production could bend the world to the American will and secure the two central foreign policy goals of yeoman diplomacy: free trade and the free navigation of the Mississippi River. Both goals were necessary to a republican political economy and were couched in terms of natural right. Following Harrington, the emphasis on natural right held out the possibility for liberty in other nations, regardless of historical or constitutional circumstances. Yeoman virtue fused Harrington's agrarianism with the Opposition's fear of power and paper wealth. In fact, Jefferson and Madison went further and condemned a large navy as being just as dangerous as a standing army. Paradoxically, a diplomacy based on the independence of the yeoman farmer depended on conditions beyond American control. Jefferson and Madison assumed that Great Britain would recognize its own economic weakness, that France would act as a friend to the United States, and that Spain would realize it could not resist American expansion. If these assumptions were false, the United States could not depend on trade for its defense and would have to resort to military establishments that the Opposition deemed dangerous to liberty. Jefferson and Madison were conscious of the theory under which they acted, and they raised it almost to the level of a religious faith.

Madison so respected the yeoman farmer that it cost him a House of Delegates seat in 1777. Virginia freeholders traditionally gathered in the county courthouse and voted orally. Candidates were expected to "treat" the voters, keeping open house and offering hospitality to all, supporters and opponents, to avoid the appearance of corruption. Madison refused to treat, on the ground that treating was incompatible with republicanism. "The consequence was that the election went against him," Madison later recalled, "his abstinence being represented as the effect of pride or parsimony."[2]

Jefferson's first foray into continental politics was his 1774 pamphlet *A Summary View of the Rights of British America,* which began as instructions to the Virginia delegates to the Continental Congress. Jefferson argued for a natural right to "a free trade with all parts of the world" and condemned the Navigation Acts as a violation of that right. Jefferson expanded on the yeoman vision in his only book-length work, *Notes on the State of Virginia,* written in 1781 and published six years later. He reasserted the primacy of natural right and argued that when a government collapsed the power devolved back on the people who granted it. Jefferson considered the farmer the model republican citizen and opposed any attempts to turn farmers into merchants or manufacturers. He dismissed the idea that every country should manufacture for itself, as such a policy would plant large cities in America, which Jefferson considered sores on the body politic. "Our interest will be to throw open the doors of commerce, and knock off all its shackles, giving perfect freedom to all persons for the vent of whatever they may chuse to bring into our ports, and asking the same in theirs," he wrote.[3]

Jefferson preferred that Americans not turn to the sea either. "And perhaps, to remove as much as possible the occasions of making war, it might be better for us to abandon the ocean altogether, that being the element whereon we shall be principally exposed to jostle with other nations," he wrote, "to have others bring what we shall want, and to carry what we can spare." Yet he conceded that "the actual habits of our countrymen attach then to commerce," making occasional wars inevitable (in which case, the United States had to find a defense against European nations that was compatible with republicanism). Jefferson dismissed a land army as "useless for offence, and not the best or safest instrument of defence." Fortunately, he argued, "Providence has placed their richest and most defenceless possessions at our door," making a small navy sufficient for national defense without accumulating a national debt.[4]

The partnership of Jefferson and Madison began when they met in 1776. They began to work closely together in 1779, when Jefferson became governor and Madison a member of the Council of State. By 1783 Madison was "Jefferson's favorite political companion."[5] Politically they grew closer together, and by 1793 they had become very similar. In the 1780s Madison had been more nationalistic in constitutional matters, favoring a stronger central government than Jefferson did. Jefferson was more nationalistic in foreign relations, willing to sacrifice his preference for a purely agrarian political economy to his role as a representative of the whole nation. For example, Madison did not see the Newfoundland fisheries as anything more than the sectional interest of New England, but Jefferson considered them a national benefit.[6]

Madison generally concurred with Jefferson on issues of political economy. Free trade, liberated from colonial shackles, would preserve a republican political economy by promoting agriculture and discouraging domestic manufactures. "The general policy of America is at present pointed at the encouragement of Agriculture, and the importation of the objects of consumption. The wid[er] therefore our ports be opened and the more extensive the priviliges of all competitors in our Commerce the more likely we shall be to buy at cheap & sell at profitable rat[es]," he wrote Edmund Randolph in 1783; "But in proportion as our lands become settled, and spare hands for manufactures & navigation multiply, it may become our policy to favor these objects." In the late 1780s, Madison opposed protective tariffs and discounted the idea that a lack of domestic manufactures would leave the United States dependent on other nations. Madison believed that European desire for American agricultural products would overcome all obstacles to trade, including war. "Neutral nations, whose rights are becoming every day more & more extensive," he wrote Edmund Pendleton, "would not now suffer themselves to be shut out of our ports."[7]

Both Jefferson and Madison believed the United States could manipulate the European balance of power to their own advantage. Trade gave the United States a strategic invulnerability that would remove the need for a dangerous and unrepublican military establishment. Their view was similar to Adams's while he was drafting the Model Treaty, but whereas Adams gave up on economic coercion in the 1780s, Madison and Jefferson never did. They unwittingly staked the survival of republican government on the actions of other nations. Their system demanded that European nations see their interests as they saw them, in making equitable trade arrangements and recognizing an American claim to navigate the Mississippi. Jefferson and Madison's great fear was not so much that European nations would act other than they supposed they would but that diplomats from the eastern states would act in ways that were incompatible with the yeoman vision.

As governor of Virginia, Jefferson's main foreign policy activity was to attempt to open up the Mississippi. In 1779 he informed Bernardo de Galvez, governor of Louisiana, that Americans were beginning to settle along the Ohio and Mississippi valleys and that Spain would reap great profits if it opened New Orleans to American trade. The following January, Jefferson armed George Rogers Clark with three hundred land warrants and instructed him to build a fort and a town near the junction of the Mississippi and Ohio rivers. At the end of the year, he instructed Clark to take Detroit, to keep the British from expanding Canada and to "add to the Empire of Liberty."[8]

Madison agreed that navigation of the Mississippi was vital to American independence and the preservation of republican government. When he entered the Continental Congress in 1780, he became one of the more vocal defenders of American claims on the Mississippi. He argued that under natural law, usage and mutual benefit gave the United States a natural claim to the right to navigate the entire course of the Mississippi. In a long letter to Jay concerning Jay's instructions as minister to Spain, Madison listed five reasons why the United States should insist on its rights on the Mississippi: the Mississippi formed a natural boundary, the United States could not prevent western settlement, the territory east of the Mississippi fell within the colonial charters, the territory already included American citizens, and the United States needed the river more than Spain did. "An *innocent passage* (says Vattel) is due to all nations with whom a state is at peace," Madison continued, "and this duty comprehends troops equally with individuals." The Virginia delegates in Congress advised Governor Jefferson to instruct the delegation not to give up the right to the lower Mississippi in exchange for a Spanish alliance unless it was absolutely necessary.[9]

In defending the American claim to the Mississippi, Madison acted (to use Lance Banning's term) as a "Virginia Continentalist." He sought the Mississippi as a Virginia interest but also as an interest of the whole nation. In November 1780, Madison attacked the notion that the United States should give up the Mississippi to gain peace and implicitly criticized the idea that the Mississippi and the fisheries were equivalent interests. "Obsticles enough will be thrown in the way of peace, if [it] is to be bid for at the expense of particular members of the Union," he wrote. "The Eastern States must on the first suggestion take alarm for their fisheries. If they will not support the other States in their rights, they cannot expect to be supported themselves when theirs come into question." Unlike Adams, Madison believed a navy and a large merchant marine were incompatible with republican government, and he was at first more doctrinaire on this point than Jefferson. Madison considered the fisheries merely the special interest of New England, rather than a national interest. Madison advocated southern participation in a navy only as a hedge against disunion, which would leave a well-armed North to prey on a rich and defenseless southern commerce.[10]

Madison's faith in French friendship was greater than his faith in American diplomats. Fear of defeat and fear that Adams would prolong the war over the fisheries led Madison to support the instructions of June 15, 1781, that revoked Adams's peace commission. Madison himself sponsored the motion of July 12, 1781, to strip Adams of his power to negotiate a commercial treaty with Great Britain. To Madison, the new instructions were a concession to military necessity. "It is impossible to expect that France should maintain the war by her own treasury," the Virginia delegation informed Governor Thomas Nelson in October 1781. More than a year later, Madison continued to defend the instructions of June 15, 1781. On July 24, 1782, he opposed a motion to reconsider those instructions. On August 8, he conceded that the instructions were "a sacrifice of national dignity," but he defended them as "a sacrifice of dignity to policy." He considered the "situation of our affairs and circumstances of that time rendered this sacrifice necessary." Madison dismissed any suspicions of France, arguing that "our interests are as safe in her hands now as they were before or as if the ministers were left wholly to their own discretion."[11]

With the conclusion of the war, the United States hoped to resume trade with Great Britain as quickly as possible, but on a more equal level than in the colonial era. On May 6, 1783, Secretary Livingston submitted a draft treaty that reestablished direct trade between the United States and the British West Indies and allowed the United States into the carrying trade between the British West Indies and Europe. In exchange, British merchants were allowed to trade in the United States on an equal footing with Americans. Madison believed the price for the West Indian trade was too high, warning Jefferson that the result would be a relapse into a state of dependency on Great Britain and revival of the "scotch monopoly." In the absence of a central government capable of making a better agreement, Madison suggested that the southern states encourage their own shipping. "The monopoly which formerly tyrannized over it [Virginia's commerce] has left wounds which are not yet healed," Madison wrote to Edmund Randolph on May 20, 1783. Four days later, Randolph replied to Madison, "our ports are fully open to British ships: and I am sorry to see a general ardor after those commodities which public acts have so lately proscribed." Two years later, Madison complained to James Monroe that "our trade was never more completely monopolized by G.B. when it was under the direction of the British Parliament than it is at this moment."[12]

The "scotch monopoly" that Madison referred to was the Scottish factor system, which controlled the Virginia tobacco trade. Virginia planters considered the system a part of the general plot against liberty. The 1707 Act of Union admitted Scottish merchants into the colonial trade. As Virginians moved into the Piedmont, resident factors of Scottish mercantile houses followed them, selling goods on credit. Large Tidewater planters dealt directly with Glasgow and Edinburgh. The net effect was that all planters, large and small, were deeply in debt, amounting to two million pounds sterling by the eve of the revolution. The credit collapse of 1772 and a glut on the tobacco market drove Virginians deeper into debt. The crash of 1772 reemphasized the dangers of debt and luxury, which, according to yeoman thought, undermined the personal independence required for republican citizenship.[13]

Jefferson too feared the reestablishment of British commercial hegemony. In 1784 he replaced Jay as a commissioner to negotiate trade treaties with European powers. Like Adams, Jefferson sought as many trade partners as possible. In the 1790s, Jefferson soured on the idea that diplomacy was necessary to promote trade, but in the 1780s he had accepted the need for diplomats. As a member of Congress, Jefferson co-wrote a report advocating treaties with most European nations, and he submitted a treaty plan similar to the Model Treaty of 1776. Jefferson took particular interest in the Mediterranean trade as a replacement for lost British trade and as an opportunity to start a navy. A secure trade demanded war against the Barbary pirates, which would gain free ports in Spain, Portugal, Naples, and Venice in addition to enhancing the international reputation of the United States. "We ought to begin a naval power, if we mean to carry our own commerce," he wrote to James Monroe. "Can we begin it on a more honourable occasion or with a weaker foe?" The weaker foe was the key to Jefferson's plan. He wanted to defeat the pirates in order to give the United States the reputation for being willing to build and use a navy. Ideally, defeating the Barbary pirates would give pause to stronger naval powers such as Great Britain. Yeoman military strategy in the 1780s and beyond rested on a large amount of bluff.[14]

British stubbornness and a weak Congress made Jefferson's task more difficult. "Their hostility towards us has attained an incredible height," Jefferson wrote Madison. Britain expected to dominate the American trade without any fear that the United States could or would retaliate. In response, Jefferson fell back on the theory that underpinned not only the Model Treaty but also the non-importation movements of the 1760s and all of yeoman diplomacy through the War of 1812: that Britain needed America far more than America needed Britain. Jefferson agreed with Adams that Great Britain indulged its wounded pride at the expense of its material interests. "Nothing will bring them to reason but physical obstruction, applied to their bodily senses," Jefferson explained to Madison. With Great Britain shut out, the other commercial nations would compete to "supply us with gew-gaws" and "buy our tobacco." If the British persisted in an exclusionary policy, American shipping would increase, and the Dutch would capture what was left of the market.[15]

On August 23, 1785, Jefferson wrote what he considered a private letter to Secretary Jay, in response to Jay's asking if the United States should carry its own goods to market, in which he restated the answer he gave in *Notes on the State of Virginia* and other private correspondence. In theory, Jefferson preferred that Americans remain farmers rather than turn to other professions. "They are the most vigorous, the most independant, the most virtuous, and they are tied to their country and wedded to it's [sic] liberty and interests by the most lasting bands." If forced to choose, Jefferson would prefer to turn farmers into sailors rather than manufacturers. "I consider the class of artificers as the panders of vice and the instruments by which the liberties of a country are generally overturned."[16]

Jefferson lamented that "we are not free to decide this question on principles of theory alone," and he recognized that "Our people are decided in the opinion that it is necessary for us to take a share in the occupation of the ocean, and their established habits induce them to require that the sea should be kept open to them, and that that line of policy be pursued which will render the use of that element as great as possible to them." Jefferson considered it his duty to carry out the will of his constituents. Yet commerce placed American lives and property in harm's way, and he expected that "our commerce on the ocean and in other countries must be paid for by frequent war." In the event of war with Great Britain, Jefferson would "abandon the carrying trade because we cannot protect it." He advocated a small naval force for coastal defense and to threaten British possessions in the Western Hemisphere. "Our vicinity to their West Indian possessions and to the fisheries is a bridle which a small naval force on our part will hold in the mouths of the most powerful of those countries."[17]

Jefferson's tepid support of an American carrying trade and navy must be seen in the context of his primary goal in Europe, to force open the European and colonial trades. Jefferson never gave up on the belief that, presuming Congress had the power to act, the United States could use trade to bend other nations to its will. Even Great Britain would come around eventually, as "her interest is her ruling passion. . . . When they shall see decidedly that without it [a treaty] we shall suppress their commerce with us, they will be agitated by their avarice on one hand, and their hatred and their fear on the other." Jefferson had no fear that the United States would develop either a carrying trade that would rival agriculture or a large-scale navy. Jefferson believed that Britain feared American maritime potential and that it would do anything, even open the West Indies, to prevent the United States from growing into a true maritime rival. Yeoman diplomacy contained a built-in fail-safe mechanism: Britain would see reason before the United States could endanger its agrarian political economy. Also, American friendship with France would prevent Britain from sending its whole navy to the West Indies. According to Merrill Peterson, Jefferson "never let the dreamy ideal control his search for a viable system of political economy." This was true in 1785, at the height of Jefferson's nationalist phase. By the 1790s the dreamy ideal began to take over, however.[18]

In the absence of British concessions that would allow free trade on American terms, Madison also saw the need to force Great Britain into a new relationship. He did not wish to restrict trade but to put it on a more equal footing. His system also required that the British and other nations bid for American trade. Without national commercial regulations, Madison believed that Virginia would have to act on its own. On June 8, 1784, the Virginia House of Delegates took up the "Bill Restricting Foreign Vessels to Certain Virginia Ports," better known as the Port Bill. The bill began, "Whereas the Trade and Commerce carried on between the Citizens of this Common Wealth and forreign Merchants would be placed on a more equal foundation, and expedition & dispatch thereby the better promoted if the Vessels of forreign Merchants trading to this State be restricted to certain Ports." The bill stated that all ships other than Virginian ships would be restricted to Norfolk, Alexandria, York, Tappahannock, and Bermuda Hundred. "We made a warm struggle for the establishmt. of Norfolk & Alexandria as our only ports," Madison informed Jefferson, "but we were forced to add York, Tappahannock & Bermuda Hundred in order to gain anything & to restrain to these ports foreigners only." Jefferson applauded the bill. He had hoped foreign trade would be confined to fewer ports, but he assumed most of it would wind up in Norfolk and Alexandria regardless of how many ports were established.[19]

Madison hoped to end the British monopoly that subverted a republican political economy by inviting in competitors and by denying British merchants direct access to the planters, in the hope of replacing British middlemen with Virginians. He "meant to reduce the trade of G.B. to an equality with that of other nations" and would not discriminate against merchants from other states. Only then could Virginia turn its supposed economic advantages over Europe into an effective diplomatic tool. Madison preferred free trade, but this did not mean unregulated trade. He believed that before free trade could be established the United States had to be out of debt, and all other nations had to adopt a free system. He did not make the encouragement of Virginia shipping a priority. Madison wrote to James Monroe that if the southern states "are not their own carriers I shod. suppose it no mark either of folly or of incivility to give our custom to our brethren [in the eastern states] rather than to those who have not yet entitled themselves to the name of friends." Revisions of the Port Bill in 1786 and 1788 expanded the number of ports of entry for foreign and domestic shipping, essentially defeating the purpose of the original bill. Virginia's ratification of the Constitution in 1788 made the Port Bill unconstitutional.[20]

As Madison pressured Great Britain from Richmond, Jefferson did the same from Paris. In May 1785, Jefferson had replaced Franklin as the American minister to France. Jefferson traveled in the same pro-American circles as had Franklin and, like Franklin, sought to translate goodwill into tangible benefit. He captured the essence of the problem early in his mission. "The body of the people of this country love us cordially," he wrote John Langdon; "But ministers and merchants love nobody." In his efforts to expand American trade with France, Jefferson encountered a thicket of regulations and customs seemingly impervious to outside influence.[21]

The most formidable obstacle to closer trade relations was the tobacco monopoly held by the Farmers-General. This episode may be seen as a yeoman morality play, and it best illustrates Jefferson's approach to diplomacy in the 1780s and beyond. Tobacco was the single most important article in Franco-American trade, accounting for 76.4 percent of American exports to France from 1786 to 1788. Jefferson condemned the monopoly on both practical and ideological grounds. "The monopoly of the purchase of tobacco in France discourages both the French and American merchant from bringing it here, and from taking in exchange the manufactures and productions of France," Jefferson complained to Vergennes; "It is contrary to the spirit of trade, and to the dispositions of merchants to carry a commodity to any market where but one person is allowed to buy it, and where that person fixes the price, which the seller must receive, or re-export his commodity, at the loss of his voyage thither." He argued that ending the monopoly would increase the king's revenue and draw the United States and France closer together. The United States sold "rice, tobacco, furs, ship-timber," and France sold "wines, brandies, oils and manufactures." As a result "no two countries are better calculated for the exchanges of commerce."[22]

Dumas Malone argued that Jefferson's memoir was "practical, not theoretical." In a sense it was, in that France presented a large market for tobacco, the United States' most valuable cash crop. Yet at the same time, Jefferson assumed that the prospect of taking a profitable trade from Great Britain would lead the French to dismantle overnight a mercantile system that had been in place for more than a hundred years. Indeed, the success of yeoman diplomacy depended on the American ability to force such changes. Jacob Price wrote that Jefferson's memoir of August 15 "was more that of a *philosophe* than that of a diplomat." Rather, the memoir reflected two key tenets of yeoman diplomacy: the expectation of French friendship and the power of American commerce to remake the world.[23]

Before Jefferson took office as minister, the Farmers-General awarded the tobacco contract to Robert Morris, the former minister of finance. This arrangement remained secret until October 1785. The resulting criticism from other Frenchmen, including the Marquis de Lafayette, led comptroller-general Charles-Alexandre de Colonne to form a committee to review the contract. The committee met at Colonne's country seat at Berni on May 24, 1786, and agreed that the contract not be renewed after its expiration in 1787 and that France should purchase an additional twelve or fifteen thousand hogsheads per year.[24]

Jefferson sought the abolition rather than any modification of the monopoly. Only a free trade could secure the full value of the tobacco crop to American growers, secure Franco-American friendship, and divert American wealth from Great Britain. Lafayette kept Jefferson current on the activities of the special committee. "Various palliatives were proposed from time to time," Jefferson wrote to Jay in May 1786; "I confess that I met them all with indifference, my object being a radical cure of the evil by discontinuing the farm, and not a mere assuagement of it for the present moment which, rendering it more bearable, might lessen the necessity of removing it totally, and perhaps prevent that removal." By October Jefferson had abandoned the hope, at least in the short term, of eliminating the monopoly. He revisited the issue with Vergennes's successor, the Compte de Montmorin, in 1787, calling the Berni agreement a "temporary relief. The radical evil will remain."[25]

In practice, the tobacco contract did benefit the Chesapeake trade in particular and American trade in general. The contract accomplished one of Jefferson's goals, to shift American commerce to France. Under the Berni agreement, France bought far more tobacco than it consumed. The purchase created a scarcity of Chesapeake tobacco that drove up the price in London.[26] Yet Jefferson displayed a tendency toward ideological rigidity during the tobacco negotiations that would resurface in later diplomacy, particularly in questions regarding the British maritime system. He would never accept a beneficial practice if it left a noxious theory in place. He demanded that nations act according to his republican principles as well as in their own interests. In so doing, he overvalued the power of American commerce as a punishment or reward.

Jefferson never considered that the yeoman theory was wrong but concluded that other factors had prevented its success. He believed that the "friendship of the people of this country" would force the ministers to act for the benefit of the United States. The greed of the Farmers-General and Robert Morris already counteracted French friendship. Lafayette was a tremendous help, but the French government was not run by men of Lafayette's mindset. Vergennes might have been more help, but he had *"imperfect ideas"* of American affairs. "His *devotion to* the principles of *pure despotism* render him *unaffectionate* to *our governments, but his fear* of *England makes him value us* as a *make weight,"* Jefferson wrote to Madison in January 1787. Vergennes's successor was no better; Jefferson described Montmorin as *"weak tho a worthy character,"* who was *"indolent and inattentive too in the extreme."*[27]

Jefferson believed that war might create opportunities for American trade. In June 1787, Great Britain put its fleet to sea when the States-General of the Netherlands called on France to mediate its internal disputes. For months Great Britain and France hovered near war. "If we remain neutral our commerce must become considerable; and particularly the carrying business must fall principally in our hands," Jefferson wrote to Alexander Donald, a Richmond merchant; "The West Indian islands of all the powers must be opened to us." Jefferson did not believe that a war in Europe would drag in the United States under the 1778 treaty. France would benefit more by letting the United States remain a neutral carrier.[28]

Securing the right to navigate the Mississippi was no easier than securing a trade treaty. In fact, Congress's inability to act may have made Spain more intransigent. In the summer of 1785, Spain sent Don Diego de Gardoqui to the United States to negotiate with Jay. The Count de Floridablanca, the Spanish foreign minister, forbade Gardoqui from making any concessions on Spain's claim of absolute control over the navigation of the lower Mississippi. However, Gardoqui could offer commercial concessions, including most-favored-nation status, and he was willing to give up Spanish claims to territory north of 31° north. Gardoqui even offered Spanish naval protection against the Barbary pirates. Jay, almost desperate to find a way out of a commercial depression, was anxious to bargain. By 1786 Jay was prepared to compromise on the Mississippi, which he had refused to do five years before. He would not give up the right to the lower Mississippi but would agree to forbear the use for twenty-five years, enough time for the West to fill up with Americans. On August 3, 1786, Jay asked Congress to approve his actions, putting the choice as one between accommodation, war, or disgrace.[29]

In the West, settlement continued, with or without an agreement with Spain. In the early 1780s, Virginians and non-Virginians alike poured into Kentucky. By 1784 all political groups within Kentucky agreed on separation from Virginia. Virginia leaders generally approved, but they set conditions ensuring that Kentucky would pay its share of the Virginia public debt. The Jay-Gardoqui negotiations complicated matters, leading some Kentuckians to favor independence from the United States as well as from Virginia. General James Wilkinson met secretly with Spanish officials and urged them to hold the line against the United States, promising that Spain could reach an agreement with an independent Kentucky.[30]

To the yeoman vision, the use of the Mississippi was central to the preservation of the republic. Free access to the Mississippi would promote the settlement of the West, which in turn would prevent the development of American manufactures while producing a large market for foreign manufactures. In May 1786, James Monroe informed Madison of the progress of the Jay-Gardoqui negotiations, warning that Jay might agree to the closure of the lower Mississippi. Madison replied that it was a "dishonorable policy" to sell the *"affection of our ultramontane brethren"* in a treaty with a nation, *"whose government religion & manners* unfit them, of all the *nations in Christiandom* for a coalition *with this country."* Monroe had worse news in August. "It is manifest here that Jay & his party in Congress are determin'd to pursue this business as far as possible, either as the means of throwing the western people & territory without the Govt. of the U.S. and keeping the weight of population & govt. here, or dismembering the govt. itself, for the purpose of a separate confederacy." In response to the negotiations, Madison submitted a resolution to the House of Delegates, claiming a natural right to the Mississippi and calling on the Virginia delegates in Congress to reject any attempt to surrender it. Madison returned to Congress in January 1787 and on April 18 proposed that negotiations with Spain be moved to Madrid and entrusted to Jefferson.[31]

Jefferson already knew that France was unlikely to help the westward expansion of the United States. In January 1786, Jay wrote to Jefferson asking if France would help enforce the surrender of the western forts promised in the peace treaty. In May Jefferson raised the subject with Vergennes, who "said that surely we might always count on the friendship of France, & added that by the treaty of Alliance, she was bound to guarantee our limits to us, as they should be established at the moment of peace." Yet, Vergennes claimed, no one knew where the boundaries were. Jefferson reminded Vergennes that the peace treaty indicated exactly where the boundaries were. Jefferson then dropped the subject for fear that Vergennes would press him on the American promise to protect the French West Indies.[32]

Jefferson certainly considered the Mississippi a vital national interest. He did not believe that the United States was too large for a republic, and he considered the United States "as the nest from which all America, North and South is to be peopled." His main concern was that Spain was "too feeble" to hold its territory "till our population be sufficiently advanced to gain it from them peice by peice. . . . The navigation of the Mississippi we must have." He continued, "This is all we are as yet ready to receive."[33]

When Jefferson learned of Jay's negotiations, he shared Madison's concerns about—but not Monroe's suspicions of—Jay's motives. Jefferson considered the abandonment of the Mississippi "an act of separation between the Eastern and Western country." "It is a relinquishment of five parts out of eight of the territory of the United States," he wrote Madison, "an abandonment of the finest subject for the paiment of our public debt, and the chaining those debts on our own necks in perpetuum."[34]

The Mississippi question led Madison to rethink the nature of the union. Madison believed access to the Mississippi vital to an agrarian political economy. A stronger central government was necessary to force open the Mississippi. Therefore, Madison had to construct a theory that accommodated a large republic. On March 20, 1785, Madison wrote to the Marquis de Lafayette concerning the Mississippi, in a letter that reveals his thinking on the problem and that stands at the beginning of a line of argument he would complete in Federalist no. 10. Madison agreed with Jefferson that control of the Mississippi would allow the United States to sell public land and liquidate the national debt. Madison again asserted a natural right to the Mississippi. "If the United States were to become parties to the occlusion of the Mississippi they would be guilty of treason against the very laws under which they obtained and hold their national existence." He joked that Spain had its policy backward. If Spain wanted peace, it should allow the Americans to cultivate their lands and use the Mississippi. Otherwise, the Americans who would have gone west would instead go to sea, where they could do Spain the most harm. "As these [settlements] become extended the members of the Confederacy must be multiplied, and along with them the Wills which are to drive the machine," he explained. "In the multiplicity of our Counsellors, Spain may be told, lies her security," he wrote, no doubt thinking of Kentucky as he did so. Here is an early indication of Madison's thinking on a large republic. If the wills multiplied, the machine must be rebuilt to harness them. He then restated the value of American commerce, as a supplier of agricultural goods to Europe and a market for finished goods. Europe would lose the value of this commerce if Spain closed the Mississippi. He pointed out that such an event would harm France, and surely France would act to prevent it.[35]

Whereas Adams's writings on the failures of the 1780s turned on the virtue of the people as reflected in the state governments, Madison's writings turned on the power of the states relative to the union. The American people, in Madison's view, had sufficient yeoman virtue (rather than classical virtue) to sustain the republic. The Americans did not have effective institutional supports for yeoman virtue, however. The weakness of the government limited American use of the Mississippi and threatened to force the United States prematurely into large-scale domestic shipping and manufactures. The problems of the United States could only be solved by a stronger national government that could submerge local interests into a general good. State solutions, such as the Port Bill, were no longer sufficient, if indeed they ever had been. "The states are every day giving proofs that separate regulations are more likely to set them by the ears than to attain the common object," Madison wrote Jefferson; "When Massts. set on foot a retaliation of the policy of G.B. Connecticut declared her ports free." Jefferson agreed that the confederation's problems were institutional rather than moral. As early as 1783, Jefferson had spotted "the pride of independance taking deep and dangerous hold on the hearts of individual states." By 1785 Jefferson concluded that only by giving Congress the full power to regulate commerce could the United States escape its diplomatic embarrassments.[36]

Unlike Adams, Jefferson did not take time out of his mission to write any volumes on political theory. He did send crates full of books to Madison, and Madison searched the history in those books for answers. Between April and June 1786, Madison composed his "Notes on Ancient and Modern Confederacies," intended for his private use. After surveying the history of confederacies, Madison came to one inescapable conclusion, that all confederacies fail. Weak national institutions allow other nations to play members of a confederation against one another. The weakness and the population imbalance of the Helvetic Confederacy invited foreign influence. The Achaean League fell when "the Romans seduced the members of the League by representing that it violated their sovereignty." Madison devoted the longest section of his "Notes" to a discussion of the United Netherlands, which seemed to offer the most lessons for the United States. The Netherlands' problems included jealousy among the provinces and extreme difficulty in getting anything accomplished. The United States had experienced both of these. Madison also noted that "Grotius has sd. that the hatred for his Countrymen agst the H. of Austria kept them being destroyed by the vices of their Constitution." Madison no doubt was thinking that war with Great Britain had overshadowed the defects of the Articles of Confederation. Peace had made those defects all the more obvious.[37]

Madison attended the Annapolis Convention in September 1786, one of only twelve delegates to appear. The convention merely issued a call for another convention to meet at Philadelphia in May 1787, which the Virginia legislature unanimously approved. Madison's mood worsened as the Philadelphia convention drew near. "Indeed the present System neither has nor deserves advocates; and if some strong props are not applied will quickly tumble to the ground," he complained to Pendleton. "The bulk of the people will probably prefer the lesser evil of a partition of the Union into three or more practicable and energetic Governments."[38]

However, partitioning the union would only invite foreign interference and endanger republicanism. For Madison, the only acceptable solution was to create a balanced national government that would unify the country and secure access to the Mississippi. He suggested two remedies to Jefferson: proportional representation and a veto over state laws. Both would free the central government from dependence on the states and prevent the states from "thwarting and molesting each other."[39]

In April 1787, Madison prepared a memorandum entitled, "Vices of the Political System of the United States," which he used in his speeches and copied for other members of the Constitutional Convention. Madison blamed most of the nation's problems on the unchecked power of the states. The states passed laws preventing the execution of the peace treaty of 1783. So far the United States had not been called to account for its misdeeds, but this would not last forever. People and elected officials acted out of private interest rather than the public good. "Is it to be imagined that an ordinary citizen or even an assembly-man of R. Island in estimating the policy of paper money, ever considered or cared in what light the measure would be viewed in France or Holland; or even in Massts or Connect.?" The only solution was to increase the number of interests that the central government acted upon, or rather to increase the scope of the government to contain the interests that already existed. "If an enlargement of the sphere is found to lessen the insecurity of private rights, it is not because the impulse of a common interest or passion is less predominant in this case with the majority," Madison wrote, "but because a common interest or passion is less apt to be felt and the requisite combinations become less easy to be formed by a great than a small number."[40]

Like Adams, Madison was willing to substitute a balance for classical virtue. Madison was no doubt influenced by David Hume's 1752 essay, "Idea of a Perfect Commonwealth." Hume had also recognized the inevitability of faction and opposing interest, and he proposed that the people be divided into as many smaller divisions as possible. However, Madison's and Hume's solutions were slightly different. Hume hoped to reorganize Parliament for more equal representation, but he could assume the existence of a national government. Madison had to create one.[41]

Both whig and yeoman diplomacies shared the desire to remain separate from Europe and at least a grudging acceptance of the modern world. These similarities, however, mask a large gap between the two. Both were prepared to abandon the need for classical virtue as the theoretical basis of the republic. However, Jefferson and Madison clung to the belief that republican foreign policy could manipulate the conduct of other nations, whereas Adams did not. Jefferson and Madison did not share Adams's whig vision of a republican realpolitik based on naval power; instead, they embraced a commercial diplomacy that represented a combination of Opposition fear of military power and an absolute faith in commercial power.

CHAPTER FOUR

Extending the Sphere

J ames Madison and Alexander Hamilton were the two statesmen most connected with drafting, defending, and implementing the Constitution. Madison was an architect of the yeoman vision, but Hamilton, like Adams, made the journey from classical to whig virtue. By the 1780s, Hamilton had shifted his belief from personal to institutional virtue as the basis for the republic. He no longer believed that the United States could rely on economic power as a weapon in diplomacy. The chief difference between Adams's and Hamilton's versions of whig virtue was that Adams retained some of the Opposition's fear of power, and of the Walpolean system, whereas Hamilton did not.[1]

When Hamilton arrived on the political scene in 1774, his political philosophy was more similar to those of Adams, Jefferson, and Madison than at any other point. In *A Full Vindication of the Measures of Congress,* Hamilton placed American rights on the twin pillars of natural right and the English constitution. He denounced Great Britain as a nation sunk in luxury and "oppressed with a heavy national debt," which marked its decline and its hostility to liberty. Hamilton firmly believed in the power of American economic coercion. He took the Spartan view that America "can live without trade of any kind," but Great Britain depended on America for its wealth, as did the West Indies for its food. To Hamilton, vice produced tyranny and virtue freedom. Only a lack of virtue could retard the cause of freedom in America.[2]

Hamilton expanded on these ideas in his February 1775 pamphlet, *The Farmer Refuted.* Following Locke, Hamilton portrayed civil government as "a voluntary compact, between the rulers and the ruled." Great Britain had determined to break that contract and enforce its will with a standing army, "maintained out of our own pockets to be at the devotion of our oppressors. This would be introduced under pretence of defending us," Hamilton continued, "but in fact to make our bondage and misery complete." Hamilton shared Adams's confidence that "in fifty or sixty years, America will be in no need of protection from Great-Britain. She will be able to protect herself, both at home and abroad. She will have a plenty of men and a plenty of materials to provide and equip a formidable navy." Free of the restraints Great Britain placed on trade, America would establish its own stable economy. "If we were to turn our attention from external to internal commerce, we should give greater stability, and more lasting prosperity to our country, than she can possibly have otherwise. We should not then import the luxuries and vices of foreign climes; nor should we make such hasty strides to public corruption and depravity."[3]

Hamilton's faith in American virtue was never complete. When the New York Sons of Liberty destroyed loyalist printer James Rivington's press, Hamilton warned Jay that it was "not safe to trust the virtue of any people." Hamilton became more pessimistic during the winter of 1777–1778 at Valley Forge. He lamented that the great men had left Congress, leaving inferiors to guide the nation. "Folly, caprice a want of foresight, comprehension and dignity, characterize the general tenor of their actions," he wrote George Clinton. He believed Congress had abandoned the army: "we are reduced to a more terrible situation than you can conceive."[4] Hamilton blamed local attachments for the nation's and the army's problems, and he considered the tendency to put local interest ahead of national interest "a most pernicious mistake." Hamilton's mood worsened with American military misfortune. By 1780 he believed "our countrymen have all the folly of the ass and all the passiveness of the sheep in their compositions" and that only the intervention of France and Spain would save the republic.[5]

Hamilton and Adams became disillusioned with the virtue of the American people at about the same time and for roughly the same reasons. Hamilton seems to have been more surprised than Adams that Americans were not always selflessly devoted to the republic. Forrest McDonald described Hamilton as a romantic, which probably exaggerates the highs and lows of Hamilton's wartime experience.[6] Adams certainly cannot be described as a romantic. Furthermore, Hamilton was either eighteen or twenty years younger than Adams, who already had a significant adult career behind him at the outbreak of the American Revolution and could view events with a more experienced eye.

In his private correspondence during the 1780s, Hamilton pounded on one theme: Congress was too weak and this weakness would doom the nation. In a letter to James Duane he blamed "an excess of the spirit of liberty," which prevented "the development of central power." He continued, "Congress should have complete sovereignty in all that relates to war, peace, trade, finance, and the management of foreign affairs, the right of declaring war and raising armies." To Robert Morris, he demonstrated his shift from classical to whig virtue, describing the United States as a modern commercial nation, in which the benefits of commerce and trade far outweighed the dangers of luxury and corruption.[7]

Hamilton returned to the world of polemics with a series of essays, *The Continentalist*, published in 1781 and 1782. These essays reflect the impact of his military service on his thinking, and they foreshadow the line of argument he would take in *The Federalist*. Like Adams, he abandoned the idea that classical virtue would or should be the ethos of the new republic. "We may preach till we are tired of the theme, the necessity of disinterestedness in republics," he wrote, "without making a single proselyte." He dismissed the idea, also prevalent at the start of the revolution, that American trade would flourish without political or diplomatic intervention. Hamilton called the idea that trade would regulate itself "one of those wild speculative paradoxes, which have grown into credit among us, contrary to the uniform practice and sense of the most enlightened nations." He noted that England prospered when Elizabeth promoted its commerce and that Jean-Baptiste Colbert, as finance minister, laid the foundations for French commerce. Unlike Jefferson and Madison, Hamilton saw no conflict between promoting agriculture and shipping, "for the truth is they are so inseparably interwoven, that one cannot be injured without injury, nor benefitted, without benefit to the other."[8]

At bottom, Hamilton believed a misplaced fear of power had fatally weakened the confederation. Students of Hamilton's career generally focus on his personality as the source of his attitudes toward power. Karl-Friedrich Walling suggests that the idea of responsibility triumphed over jealousy. Forrest McDonald posits a psychological explanation, that "Hamilton trusted Hamilton, and Madison did not trust Madison." Hamilton's attitude toward power was more that of a seventeenth-century republican such as Harrington or Sidney, willing to put great power in the hands of a properly constituted government, than that of the eighteenth-century Opposition. "History is full of examples," Hamilton observed, "where in contests for liberty, a jealousy of power has either defeated the attempts to recover or preserve it in the first instance, or has afterwards subverted it by clogging government with too great precautions for its felicity, or by leaving too wide a door for sedition and popular licenciousness." The only solution to the problems of the confederacy was to overcome the fear of power and give Congress the power to regulate trade, tax land and people, sell public lands, and appoint all army and navy officers.[9]

Hamilton and Madison came to Philadelphia with a disdain for the Articles of Confederation. Madison arrived on May 3, 1787, and after nearly two weeks of anxious waiting, the Constitutional Convention met at the Pennsylvania State House (later Independence Hall) on May 14. The Virginia Plan, submitted to the convention by Edmund Randolph on May 29, proposed a new government containing a bicameral legislature, with the lower house elected by the people and the upper house by the lower house, and each branch elected in proportion to each state's population. The national legislature would choose an executive who would act with a national judiciary as a council of revision.[10]

The foreign policy questions of the convention centered on the power to make war and the power to regulate commerce, and they reflected the Opposition Whig fear that war augmented executive power. The debate over war powers directly involved the relationship between the executive and the legislature. On June 1, the Committee of the Whole began discussing the composition and powers of the executive. Charles Pinckney of South Carolina "was for a vigorous Executive" but feared that its powers "might extend to peace & war &c which would render the Executive a Monarchy." Roger Sherman of Connecticut added that he "considered the Executive magistracy as nothing more than an instrument for carrying the will of the Legislature into effect, that the person or persons ought to be appointed by and accountable to the Legislature only." Rufus King noted that Madison, along with James Wilson of Pennsylvania, argued that the executive powers "do not include the Rights of war & peace &c." On June 4, the convention approved a single executive with a partial veto over legislation. The next day the convention rejected the idea of legislative appointment.[11]

Hamilton staked out a position as the most extreme proponent of copying the British constitution. He did not speak until June 18, and then he spoke out of a dislike of both the Virginia and the New Jersey Plans. Many sensed that a republicanism was a disadvantage in conducting diplomacy, but Hamilton was the only one to voice that doubt in public. He believed that a functioning executive could not be "established on Republican principles." A republic was vulnerable to foreign influence, and only a hereditary monarch such as the British king, for example, could be above corruption. As a remedy to the weakness of republics, Hamilton advocated that the executive and one house of the legislature serve for life or during good behavior. "But is this a Republican Govt., it will be asked? Yes, if all the Magistrates are appointed, and vacancies are filled, by the people, or a process of election originating with the people." On June 22 Hamilton defended the practice of members of the legislature serving simultaneously in executive offices, which most American observers and Opposition writers considered a form of corruption. Hamilton believed such inducements were necessary to ensure a supply of public servants at the national level.[12]

Hamilton's view of the executive found no defenders. Madison, like many Americans of the revolutionary era shared the Opposition Whig fear of executive power, which influenced his thinking on the war powers of the new government. "In time of actual war, the great discretionary powers are constantly given to the Executive Magistrate," Madison told the convention on June 29. "Constant apprehension of War has the same tendency to render the head too large for the body. A standing military force, with an overgrown Executive will not long be safe companions to liberty." Madison concluded with the classic Opposition Whig thesis, that the "means of defence agst. foreign danger have always been the instruments of tyranny at home." In Great Britain the power to make war, to decide on war and to wage it, rested with the king although Parliament gained greater influence over foreign policy during the eighteenth century. On August 17, Madison and Gerry divided the two aspects of the war power. Congress would hold the power to declare war, and the executive branch would hold the power to repel sudden attacks. The motion passed 7–2.[13]

Hamilton's debate with Charles Pinckney of South Carolina further illuminates Hamilton's attitudes toward power and diplomacy. On June 25, 1787, Pinckney gave a speech that might well have come from Jefferson, arguing that the Americans were not a Spartan people. The United States was "a new extensive Country containing within itself the materials for forming a Government capable of extending to its citizens all the blessings of civil & religious liberty—capable of making them happy at home." Pinckney cautioned against establishing a government "to make us respectable abroad." Hamilton responded four days later. Pinckney had drawn an "ideal distinction," and a government that could not make the United States respectable abroad would invite foreign influence. Gerald Stourzh places this debate in terms of realism against idealism; it is a better example of yeoman virtue against Hamilton's version of whig virtue. Pinckney's argument suggested that the United States could turn away from diplomacy and that the power to conduct foreign relations was inherently dangerous. Hamilton's response showed no fear of power and no hope that the United States could escape diplomacy.[14]

The debate over commercial regulations threatened to stir up sectional conflict. Madison opposed a prohibition on export duties, arguing on August 21 that one day they might be necessary to raise revenue or to force "equitable regulations from other nations." However, a solid bloc of southern states combined with two shipping states, Massachusetts and Connecticut, in the vote to prohibit export duties. The debates also developed how the new government could contain sectional disputes. General Charles Cotesworth Pinckney of South Carolina captured the spirit of mutual concessions best when he told the convention that it was not in the southern interest to have any regulation of commerce, but northern concessions on the slave trade demanded a generous response. The rich—but weak—southern states needed the support of the northern states, and Pinckney was willing to give Congress complete control of commercial policy in order to get this support. Madison also noted that a navigation act would harm the South by raising shipping rates, but congressional power to regulate commerce would remove a major source of interstate conflict.[15]

Madison intended the Constitution to solve several problems. First, it would create a government that would protect national interests. Second, it could achieve the two foreign policy goals he believed vital to the survival of republican government. The Constitution would form a government strong enough to keep open the Mississippi, thereby keeping the West in the union, preventing European interference in American politics, and preserving a republican political economy. The new government could also more fully regulate commerce and pass laws designed to force Great Britain into a more equitable trade relationship. By preserving an outlet for western products through the Mississippi and creating a freer trade system on the Atlantic, the United States could preserve and exploit its agriculture as a diplomatic tool. Therefore, Madison believed that the Constitution prevented the United States from being driven into domestic manufactures. It would create a government that would protect sectional as well as national interests. Madison helped create what Gordon Wood calls "a new and original sort of republican government," one that did not require virtue for its success. He intended that yeoman virtue would replace classical virtue. Madison, like Adams and Hamilton, reached the conclusion that balance could be substituted for classical virtue as the theoretical basis for the American republic.[16]

Madison, Hamilton, and Jay combined to write *The Federalist* in order to secure ratification in New York, although Jay fell ill and was forced to leave most of the task to Hamilton and Madison. Hamilton's perception of the new Constitution was shaped less by Opposition's fear of power than by a seventeenth-century concern with the proper framework of government. Madison, his partner in "Publius," had the opposite concern, that of limiting power. Under cover of a common goal (the ratification of the Constitution), these differences were not as apparent as they would become in 1789. Hamilton's "Publius," unlike Madison's, was more concerned with creating a national government that could exert great power than with placing limits on that power.[17] In Federalist no. 1, Hamilton made a direct assault on the idea that an energetic government and a free government were incompatible, and he attacked the fear of power that characterized the Opposition thought of the eighteenth century. "An overscrupulous jealousy of danger to the rights of the people, which is more commonly the fault of the head than of the heart will be represented as mere pretence and artifice; the bait for popularity at the expense of the public good," he promised. Later, he argued that the events feared by the Anti-Federalists, such as the establishment of a standing army, came from the current government rather than from the proposed Constitution.[18]

Hamilton listed the conduct of war and of foreign negotiations as the chief diplomatic functions of the central government, and those powers required a substantial grant of power. "Every view we may take of the subject, as candid enquirers after truth, will serve to convince us, that it is both unwise and dangerous to deny the Foederal Government an unconfined authority, as to all those objects which are intrusted to its management," Hamilton wrote in Federalist no. 23. In no. 31, he argued that the central government should be "free from any other control, but a regard to the public good and to the sense of the people." In no. 70, he stated that a strong president was essential to the new government. "Energy in the executive is a leading character in the definition of good government," Hamilton believed.[19]

Hamilton concentrated on foreign affairs in the sixth, seventh, eighth, and eleventh Federalist papers. He believed that distance from Europe would provide a measure of security, but only under a strong union. A weak confederacy or a mere alliance would invite European interference and draw the United States into "all the pernicious labyrinths of European politics and wars." He did not believe separate confederacies would be long at peace, and he discounted two key beliefs of the yeoman school: that republics were peaceful by nature and that trade promoted peace. He noted that "the causes of hostility among nations are innumerable," whether from perceived national interest or from the personal ambition of rulers. Turning to commercial republics, he noted that all commerce did was "change the objects of war," and he observed that Rome, Sparta, Athens, and Carthage were perpetually at war. Modern republics were no different. The Netherlands "had furious contests with England for the dominion of the sea; and were among the most persevering and most implacable of the opponents of Louis XIV." Great Britain was also a commercial nation often embroiled in war. Although Britain was a monarchy, Hamilton argued that the British people, more so than the king, were often the driving force for war. In Federalist no. 7, he observed that the main conditions for war, jealousy over territory and trade, existed among the American states.[20]

Hamilton turned to the tools of foreign policy in the seventh, eighth, and eleventh papers. In Federalist no. 11, he observed that only a strong union could allow the United States to effectively marshal its commercial resources. "Suppose, for instance, we had a government in America capable of excluding Great-Britain (with whom we have at present no treaty of commerce) from all our ports, what would be the probable operation of this step upon her politics?" Hamilton asked. "Would it not enable us to negotiate with the finest prospect of success for commercial privileges of the most valuable and extensive kind in the colonies of that kingdom?" Without a powerful central government, the United States would lose its potential commercial wealth and would be unable to protect it by negotiation or force. Hamilton went on to suggest that the Constitution would allow the United States to reform the maritime code of Europe. "It belongs to us to vindicate the honor of the human race, and teach that assuming brother moderation," he wrote.[21]

Hamilton, like Madison after him, would occasionally make arguments that aimed at a particular constituency but that were not representative of his own thought. He never again raised the possibility of commercial warfare. Such an argument would be calculated to win the approval of southern staple-exporters that might be leaning against the Constitution. Similarly, Hamilton had no real hope that the United States could force European nations to change their ways.

Hamilton addressed the issue of a standing army in Federalist no. 8. First, he answered the objection that the Constitution did not prohibit standing armies. Hamilton agreed that, in Europe, standing armies "bear a malignant aspect to liberty and oeconomy." Yet under the Constitution various political, cultural, and geographic factors would prevent a similar scene in the United States. The habits of the American people, "absorbed in the pursuits of gain, and devoted to the improvements of agriculture and commerce are incompatible with the condition of a nation of soldiers." Hamilton had learned this lesson the hard way at Valley Forge. Furthermore, the United States was at a great distance from Europe. Hamilton compared the United States to Great Britain, in an "insular situation" that, combined with a navy, prevented invasion and the need for an army. "If we are wise enough to preserve the Union, we may for ages enjoy an advantage similar to that of an insulated situation."[22]

Hamilton did not share the generalized fear of power that fed into a fear of standing armies. His own experience in the Continental Army had led him to dismiss the idea "that the Militia of the country is its natural bulwark," adding that this notion "had like to have lost us our independence." Later, in Federalist no. 26 he noted that England in 1688, having settled its constitutional problems, was in a similar situation as the United States in 1787, and he saw no need to prohibit standing armies. Ultimately, Hamilton believed that if the power to raise and regulate armies rested in the hands of the people's representatives, it could not result in tyranny. He considered constitutional safeguards against standing armies in peacetime unnecessary. "The power of raising armies at all, under those constitutions, can by no construction be deemed to reside any where else, than in the legislatures themselves; and it was superfluous, if not absurd, to declare that a matter should not be done without the consent of a body, which alone had the power of doing it," he wrote. In Federalist no. 28, Hamilton added that government in the hands of the people "is the essential, and after all the only efficacious security for the rights and principles of the people which is attainable in civil society." In Federalist no. 29, he asked, "Where in the name of common sense are our fears to end if we may not trust our sons, our brothers, our neighbours, our fellow-citizens?"[23]

Madison's first effort, Federalist no. 10, appeared on November 22, 1787, and can be read as a summation of the influence of the Mississippi on his thinking, which specifically forced him to explain how an extended republic would work. It is generally seen as the most important among the essays and is the most prone to conflicting interpretations. William Appleman Williams, for example, has argued that Madison used the term "extend the sphere" in the literal sense of physical expansion and that continental expansion was the only way to preserve republican government. Portraying Federalist no. 10 as a forward-looking document takes it out of its political context. It was a defense of past expansion rather than a call for future expansion.[24]

Madison began with what had become his standard analysis of faction. "By a faction I understand a number of citizens whether amounting to a majority or a minority of the whole, who are united and activated by some common impulse of passion, or of interest, adverse to the rights of the other citizens, or to the permanent and aggregate interests of the community." Madison learned from the Scottish Common Sense school that factionalism was an inevitable and unchanging feature of human behavior. Factions sprang from any number of causes. "But the most common and durable source of factions, has been the various and unequal distribution of property," Madison wrote. "The regulation of these various and interfering interests forms the principle task of modern Legislation, and involves the spirit of party and faction in the necessary and ordinary operation of the Government," he continued.[25]

Next, Madison moved on to the advantage of a republic over a democracy. Arguing against Montesquieu's theory that a republic could exist only in a small territory, Madison wrote that the chief advantage of a republic was "the greater number of citizens, and greater sphere of country, over which the latter may be extended." In a simple democracy, which would necessarily be a smaller society, it would be easier to form a majority that could control the government. "Extend the sphere, and you take in a greater variety of parties and interests," Madison wrote; "you make it less probable that a majority of the whole will have a common motive to invade the rights of the other citizens."[26] Again, the Mississippi question was the backdrop. The threats of division accompanying the Jay-Gardoqui negotiations forced Madison to explain how a republic could exist over a territory that some already considered too large. The only way was to split the thirteen state interests into a myriad of individual interests by creating a government that both acted directly on those individual interests and contained them within a balanced structure. The need to use the Mississippi forced Madison to reinvent the republic.

Two later Federalist essays shed further light on Madison's thinking in Federalist no. 10. Madison returned to the size of the republic in Federalist no. 14 and argued that the natural limit of the republic was the furthest distance a representative could travel. The thirteen original states clearly fell within those limits. The average distance from the Atlantic to the Mississippi was 750 miles, which still fell within the natural boundaries of a republic. Madison revisited the problem of faction in Federalist no. 51, specifically addressing the issue of religious freedom. He compared political and religious liberty, arguing that "the degree of security in both cases will depend on the number of interests and sects." The number of interests and sects, in turn, "may be presumed to depend on the extent of country and number of people comprehended under the same government." Madison certainly did not rule out future expansion. However, Federalist no. 10 did not demand it. Madison wrote primarily to defend expansion that had already taken place.[27]

Federalist no. 41 is another key to Madison's conception of a republican foreign policy. Like the English Opposition writers, he believed a large peacetime military establishment was incompatible with liberty at home.

Madison wrote that "the liberties of Rome proved the first victim of her military triumphs, and that the liberties of Europe, as far as they ever existed, have with few exceptions been the price of her military establishments." He believed that the proper form of government, provided by the Constitution and combined with a physical separation from Europe, would ensure all the protection necessary against foreign invasion and would eliminate the need for a large military. "America united with a handful of troops, or without a single soldier, exhibits a more forbidding posture to foreign ambition, than America disunited, with an hundred thousand veterans ready for combat." Furthermore, the union "will be the only source of our maritime strength."[28]

Madison's public enthusiasm for a navy fluctuated, depending on his audience. As he wrote *The Federalist* to sway New York, he played up the naval angle more than usual. In addition, he doubtless realized that within a few days his essay would appear in the Boston newspapers, where the Massachusetts convention was at that moment considering ratification.[29] The bedrock of Madison's diplomacy was not a navy, but a strong union that would prevent foreign powers from playing one state off another and that would effectively regulate commerce. This way, the United States could avoid the fate of continental Europe.

In considering the powers of the House of Representatives, Madison wrote in Federalist no. 53 that, although the House did not directly participate in foreign negotiations, "from the necessary connection between the several branches of public affairs, those particular branches will frequently deserve attention in the ordinary course of legislation, and will sometimes demand particular legislative sanction and cooperation." He did not elaborate on this point, but his actions in the 1790s suggest that the "ordinary course of legislation" most likely included commercial regulations and war.[30]

THE DIFFERENCES BETWEEN HAMILTON and Madison became more evident when they began to put the theories of the Federalist into practice in the new government in 1789. They both counted on a high level of British trade as the basis for their policies. As a member of the House of Representatives, Madison immediately planned to use the new government to raise a public revenue and free American trade from British domination. He introduced a proposal on April 8, 1789, to revive the impost of April 18, 1783. He proposed higher duties on such items as rum, wine, molasses, sugar, coffee, and tea and called for staggered duties on tonnage. He proposed that American-built and -owned ships pay the lowest tonnage duties, followed by ships from nations in a commercial treaty with the United States, specifically French ships. Ships from other nations (especially Great Britain) would pay the highest duties.[31] Madison had learned from the French Physiocrats and the Scottish Common Sense school to oppose commercial restrictions in principle, telling the House of Representatives that, "if industry and labor are left to take their own course[,] they will be directed to those objects which are the most productive, and this is a more certain and direct manner than the wisdom of the most enlightened legislature could point out." However, American ships would disappear from the sea if the United States kept its ports open while other nations maintained closed systems. Furthermore, the United States could not afford free trade as long as American trade to foreign ports was "restrained to an artificial channel."[32]

Madison's plan for commercial discrimination—and the yeoman program through the War of 1812—rested on his almost unshakable faith in the power of American commerce, and specifically the export of agricultural goods, to break down the British mercantile system. Economic power as tool of diplomacy avoided the use of a military and would prevent the means of diplomacy from turning against domestic liberty. "It would be proper to consider the means of encouraging the great staple of America, I mean agriculture," Madison told the House of Representatives on April 9, 1789; "other nations can and do rival us [in manufactures] but we may be said to have a monopoly in agriculture." On April 25 he added, "The produce of this country is more necessary to the rest of the world than that of other countries is to America." Great Britain needed the United States as an export market, and the British West Indies were virtual economic hostages to America. "The supplies of the United States are necessary to their existence, and their market to the value of her islands," he explained to Jefferson. Trade also gave the United States a military advantage. "In time of war, which is generally decided in the West Indies, friendly offices not violating the duties of neutrality might effectually turn the scale in favor of an adversary." A year later, he argued before the House of Representatives, "As to the British West-Indies, it had been fully shewn, that they could neither prosper nor subsist without the market of the United States: they were fed from our granaries."[33]

Madison sought to break the British stranglehold on American trade by encouraging other nations to compete in buying American exports and selling the United States their manufactured goods and shipping services. Commercial discrimination would preserve the yeoman republic by preventing the development of domestic manufacturing industries and a large-scale shipping industry existing independently of agricultural production. Also, commercial diplomacy would secure American diplomatic goals without war, which Madison believed was republicanism's greatest enemy.[34]

New England congressmen opposed his proposals, which forced Madison to shift his argument to appease them, by emphasizing results that he believed New Englanders would favor. Madison told the House of Representatives on April 21, 1789, that his proposals were needed "to form a school for seamen, to lay the foundation for a navy." On May 4, Madison declared himself "a friend to the navigation of America," who would "be always ready to go as great lengths in favor of that interest as any gentlemen on this floor." Speaking on trade regulations a year later, he argued that if the British maintained their trade practices, "our own navigation and manufactures would in the meantime be encouraged."[35]

Madison certainly believed that shipping and manufactures could increase as a result of commercial discrimination, but he left the New Englanders with the false impression that he himself favored those ends. Madison hoped and believed that Great Britain would alter its navigation system first. Throughout the 1780s, Madison argued against encouraging manufactures as they were incompatible with a republican political economy. In "Fashion," written in 1792, Madison used the plight of Great Britain's shoe-buckle manufacturers, left destitute by the increased use of laces, as a cautionary tale. "The condition of those who receive employment and bread from the precarious source of fashion and superfluity, is a lesson to nations as well as individuals," he wrote. "In proportion as a nation consists of that description of citizens, and depends on external commerce, it is dependent on the consumption and caprice of other nations." Madison agreed with Thomas Paine that food never went out of style.[36]

Neither did Madison view shipping as an unquestioned good. In his March 3, 1792, *National Gazette* article, "Republican Distribution of Citizens," Madison wrote that the "life of the husbandman is pre-eminently suited to the comfort and happiness of the individual." On the other hand, "the condition to which the blessings of life are most denied is that of the sailor." "How unfortunate, that in the intercourse, by which nations are enlightened and refined, and the means of safety extended," Madison continued, "the immediate agents should be distinguished by the harshest condition of humanity." It seems unlikely that Madison would have actively supported the expansion of a class he clearly believed to be unfit for republican government. He saw shipping as beneficial only if it were kept subordinate to agriculture. He did not seek to create an American shipping monopoly or, in contrast to his New England colleagues, encourage the carrying trade as a separate endeavor. Madison believed that commercial discrimination would promote American shipping to the point of breaking the British hold on the American economy without creating a domestic rival to agriculture.[37]

Europe would, despite itself, help Madison and Jefferson to preserve the yeoman republic. In the summer of 1790, Spain and Great Britain nearly went to war over possession of Nootka Sound (modern Vancouver). Secretary of State Jefferson recommended that the United States remain neutral and use the crisis to force other nations to bid for American trade. The "Nootka Sound doctrine," as Doron Ben-Atar describes it, was the same idea that spawned the Model Treaty—that the United States could use trade as a weapon.[38]

Like Jefferson and Madison, Hamilton saw the Constitution as a vehicle to harness the economic potential of the United States. However, Hamilton did not see the possibility or the need of forcing changes in the British mercantile system. "I have always preferred a Connexion with you, to that of any other Country," he told George Beckwith, an unofficial British agent. "*We think in English,* and have a similarity of prejudices, and of predilections." Hamilton added that although the United States was an agricultural nation and would remain so for some time, it would also be a manufacturing nation. In a sense, Hamilton expected that Great Britain would fund America's rise to power. He did not believe that commerce could be completely separated from politics. In 1791 he cautioned Jefferson against any commercial policy "which may lead to commercial warfare with any power; which as far as my knowledge of examples extends is commonly productive of mutual inconvenience and injury and of dispositions tending to a worse kind of warfare."[39]

Unlike Jefferson and Madison, Hamilton did not have an idea of a republican political economy, in the sense that he did not believe one form of economic activity more compatible with republican government than another. Hamilton's reports on the debt-funding system, on excise, on the Bank of the United States, and his encouragement of manufactures focus on economic utility. In his Report on Public Credit, he recommended the establishment of a sinking fund, an annual appropriation that would be earmarked to make payments on the $52 million in national debt and to assume $25 million in state debt. Such a measure would restore the nation's international reputation and credit; it would increase the stock of capital and create a substitute for paper money. The last provision required that current holders of securities be paid in full irrespective of whether they were original buyers.[40] Hamilton expected a flood of foreign trade and investment, but he knew that external sources of revenue were not always secure. To provide an internal source, he proposed an excise on distilled spirits. The capstone of the fiscal system was the Bank of the United States. "It is a fact well understood, that public Banks have found admission and patronage among the principal and most enlightened commercial nations," Hamilton wrote. The bank would serve a number of functions, which would include increasing capital, easing tax payments, and providing the government with a stable source of loans in emergencies. The value of bank certificates would be more stable than government-issued paper, and the market would determine the value of bank notes. Hamilton saw no reason for a constitutional justification until Washington asked him for one in February 1791. Hamilton provided a broad interpretation of the meaning of "necessary and proper," arguing that "*necessary* often means no more than *needful, requisite, incidental, useful,* or *conducive to.*"[41]

The last report, on manufactures, struck at the heart of the yeoman vision. Hamilton proposed to turn farmers into manufacturers, an idea Jefferson had denounced in *Notes on the State of Virginia*. "The expediency of encouraging manufactures in the United States, which was not long since deemed very questionable, appears at this time to be generally admitted," Hamilton began, perhaps with more confidence than warranted. He dethroned agriculture as "the only productive species of industry" and went on to speculate that "there is no natural difference between the aggregate productiveness of one, and of the other kind of industry." Hamilton saw no conflict between manufactures and agriculture. Each would provide a market for the other's goods, thus tying North and South closer together.[42]

Above all, domestic manufactures would secure American independence. Here Hamilton was similar to Adams and differed from Madison and Jefferson in his belief that independence consisted in being able to produce all the nation's necessities without depending on other nations. Hamilton went further, in seeking to ensure a stable fiscal system through the use of foreign capital. Imports sent American capital to Europe. By encouraging manufactures, the reverse would happen. In language reminiscent of Federalist no. 10, Hamilton urged Congress to "enlarge the sphere" in which foreign capital would be employed. Manufactures were also necessary for national defense, given that the United States did not have an effective navy to protect overseas commerce.[43]

To Madison it seemed Hamilton's fiscal plans represented an attempt to impose a Walpolean system on the United States, inevitably leading to corruption and tyranny. In addition, he saw a threat to Virginia's interests from northern states replacing the prewar obstacles posed by Britain to managing Virginia's credit. Madison objected to the assumption of state debts on the grounds that, using its great holdings in western lands, Virginia had already paid its public debt and that, by increasing the national debt, assumption forced Virginia to pay toward the other states' debts. More important, he believed that debt itself was a political evil. "I am of the opinion also that the measure is not politic," Madison told the House of Representatives on April 22, 1790, "because, if, the public debt is a public evil, an assumption of the state debts will enormously increase, and, perhaps, perpetuate it."[44]

Madison saw Hamilton's proposals for a bank and for American manufactures as additional threats to republicanism. "The constructions of the constitution which have been maintained on the occasion [of introducing the proposal for a bank], go to the subversion of every power whatever in the several States," Madison argued on February 8, 1791. "If Congress can do whatever in their discretion can be done by money, and will promote the *general welfare,* the Government is no longer a limited one possessing enumerated powers," he complained privately to Edmund Pendleton, "but an indefinite one subject to particular exceptions." Madison attacked Hamilton's reports on the bank and manufactures publicly in a series of articles in the *National Gazette.* Under the topic "Consolidation," he criticized Hamilton's attempts to increase the power of the central government: "Let it be the patriotic study of all to maintain the various authorities established by our complicated system, each in its own respective constitutional sphere." Under the title "Fashion," he specifically attacked Hamilton's Report on Manufactures, arguing that "the mutability of fashion" made manufacturing an unsuitable and unrepublican occupation for Americans. In "The Union. Who Are its Real Friends?" Madison denounced the Hamiltonian program as a whole. "In a word," he wrote, "those are real friends to the Union who are friends to that republican policy throughout, which is the only *cement* for the Union of a republican people in opposition to a spirit of usurpation and monarchy."[45]

As secretary of state, Jefferson was forced to fight a rearguard action against Hamilton's reports. Jefferson reported to Washington that Congress had no constitutional authority either to establish a bank or to encourage manufactures. In private Jefferson denounced Hamilton and his supporters as "a sect" determined to use the new Constitution as a way station to a British model, complete with hereditary monarchy and aristocracy. Jefferson lamented that Congress was now filled with "stock jobbers and king-jobbers." The most disturbing element was that Washington, a fellow Virginia planter, sided with Hamilton. Washington "said not a word on the corruption of the legislature, but took up the other point, defended the assumption, and argued that it had not increased the debt, for that all of it was honest debt." Jefferson, realizing that the last defense against the funding system had fallen, "avoided entering into any argument with him on those points."[46]

The fiscal system shattered the coalition that had produced the Constitution. Debate was never confined to the merits of the system, as Hamilton might have hoped, but always returned to the nature of the republic. In 1818 Jefferson recalled that Hamilton intended to confuse the public and corrupt the legislature, and he charged that "Hamilton was not only a monarchist, but for a monarchy bottomed on corruption." Hamilton was shocked by the reaction and was surprised that Madison would join with Jefferson "to narrow the Federal authority."[47] The charges of monarchist against republican and disunionist against the Constitution transcended domestic and foreign policy, and they intensified when the French Revolution became an issue in American politics.

CHAPTER FIVE

The Cause of Liberty

When the French Revolution spilled onto the Atlantic in 1793, theoretical debates over the nature of the revolution became a concrete debate about its effects on American foreign policy. The yeoman and whig camps (roughly corresponding to the Republican and Federalist parties) agreed on one thing—the United States should stay out of the war. Jefferson and Adams set out the yeoman and whig division over the nature of the revolution. Yeoman republicanism saw France as a fellow republic and believed not only in the possibility of universal republicanism but also in the idea that the sister republics would rise or fall together. Adams put forth the whig view that the French Revolution was not the cause of liberty and was doomed to failure. Republicanism was not suited to all nations. As a cabinet officer, Hamilton was more responsible for policy than Adams, and he established the whig stand that the United States could not involve itself in the crusades of other nations and that the fate of the United States hung only on its own efforts.

On May 4, 1789, the Estates-General met for the first time in 175 years, in an attempt to rebuild French finances. The Third Estate proposed that the three estates—commons, nobles, and clergy—meet together, which gave the Third Estate the numerical advantage. The nobles responded by locking the Third Estate out of Versailles, forcing it to meet in the tennis court and proclaim itself the National Assembly of France. Revolt spread to the people at large. On July 14, 1789, the Paris mob stormed the Bastille in a show of defiance to royal authority. On August 4, the National Assembly abolished the last vestiges of feudalism and cut ecclesiastical ties with Rome. On August 26, the National Assembly issued its Declaration of the Rights of Man and Citizen, which stated that "men are born and remain free and equal in their rights."[1]

Jefferson had the closest view of any American to the outbreak of the French Revolution. He consulted with Lafayette and other members of the National Assembly and shared the general American enthusiasm for the event and confidence in the result. "The National assembly now have as clean a canvas to work on here as we had in America," Jefferson observed to Trondin-Diodati; he expected that France would adopt the British model "in it's outlines, but not it's defects," retaining a hereditary king and adding a representative body elected from equal districts. The natural consequence of the change in the French government would be closer relations between the two republics. "It is impossible to desire better dispositions toward us, than prevail in this assembly," Jefferson reported to Madison from Paris. "Our proceedings have been viewed as a model for them on every occasion; and tho' in the heat of debate men are generally disposed to contradict every authority urged by their opponents, ours has been treated like that of the bible, open to explanation but not to question."[2]

Vice president Adams did not share Jefferson's optimism. He took one look at the National Assembly, a government consisting of a unicameral legislature, and concluded that the revolution was doomed to failure. "My opinion of the French Revolution has never varied from the first assembly of the Notables to this day," Adams wrote in 1805; "I always dreaded it and never had any faith in its success or ability." Senator William Maclay noted that Adams despised all of the pamphlets written on the French Revolution, except for Edmund Burke's *Reflections on the Revolution in France*, "and this same Mr. Burke despises the French Revolution."[3]

Adams attacked the French Revolution in his last theoretical work on politics, *Discourses on Davila*, published in 1790 and 1791. It began as a critique of Henrico Davila's *History of the Civil Wars of France* but quickly became an exposition of Adams's two favorite political topics, the human desire for distinction and the need for balanced government to control it. "There is in human nature, it is true, simple *Benevolence*, or an affection for the good of others, but alone it is not a balance for the selfish affections," Adams wrote. "As no appetite in human nature is more universal than that for honor, and real merit is confined to a very few," he continued, "the numbers who thirst for respect are all out of proportion to those who seek it only for merit." Nations were no different from individuals. "As long as there is patriotism, there will be national emulation, vanity and pride," he went on, making no distinctions between republics and monarchies; "It is national pride which commonly stimulates kings and ministers."[4]

Having restated the basic tenets of his political philosophy, Adams went on to consider the progress of the French Revolution. "We are told that our friends the National Assembly of France have abolished all distinctions," he wrote. "But be not deceived, my dear countrymen. Impossibilities cannot be performed." A government in a single assembly was doomed to end in tyranny, Adams argued, and he praised Americans for establishing a balanced government instead of resorting to "whimsical and fantastical projects." Adams ended with a ringing defense of balanced government. "If the people have not the understanding and public virtue enough, and will not be persuaded of the necessity of supporting an independent executive authority, an independent senate, and an independent judiciary power, as well as an independent house of representatives," he concluded, "all pretensions to balance are lost, and with them all hopes of security to our dearest, and all hopes of liberty."[5]

To Jefferson, Adams's beliefs were, literally, "political heresies." Jefferson's central dispute with Adams and Hamilton was over whether other nations could replicate the American experiment. The dinner party of April 1791 should be seen in this light. (Washington, when he left for Mount Vernon in April 1791, instructed Jefferson to consult with the cabinet and vice president Adams. Jefferson invited them to dinner, and this dinner was the event when he, Hamilton, and Adams got into their discussions of forms of government). When Adams and Hamilton praised the British constitution, they recognized, with Montesquieu and the eighteenth-century whigs, that a government had to match the spirit of its people. To Jefferson, neither republicanism nor its opposition knew any boundaries. He believed that France would soon spread republican government all over Europe. If France failed it would give enemies of republicanism at home an excuse to establish a British-style monarchy.[6]

Once Jefferson decided that the French Revolution represented the spirit of liberty, there was no turning back. He made support for the French Revolution a test of republican orthodoxy. He identified the Jacobins, the most radical party in the National Convention, as "representing the true revolution-spirit of the whole nation." Jefferson would hear no criticism of France. William Short, Jefferson's protégé and chargé d'affaires in Paris, condemned as "unquestionable evils for humanity" the French conquests along the Rhine. "The liberty of the whole earth was depending on the contest, and was ever such a prize won with so little innocent blood?" Jefferson retorted; "My own affections have been deeply wounded by some of the martyrs to the cause, but rather than it should have failed, I would have seen half the earth desolated." Even the execution of Louis XVI did not faze Jefferson, for he believed the event would "produce republics everywhere," or at least "soften the monarchical governments."[7]

What had been a parlor debate in 1791 became a more immediate influence in American politics in 1793. The Girondins, young and idealistic republicans, came to dominate the French National Convention and abolished the monarchy on September 22, 1792. The National Convention executed Louis XVI on January 21, 1793, as punishment for his attempted flight to Austria. On February 1, 1793, France declared war on Great Britain. The Girondins assumed they would have American support because of their ideological sympathy and the 1778 treaties. On February 20, 1793, Edmond Genet set sail as the new republic's first minister to the United States. Genet was barely thirty years old and something of a boy wonder in both the royal and republican diplomatic corps. Genet's main goal was to secure American aid against Great Britain, and he tried to stir up public support as a counter to the official neutrality of the Washington administration. He landed at Charleston on April 8, 1793, and began stirring up crowds and handing out blank military commissions. He worked his way slowly north, arriving in Philadelphia in May.[8]

Adams did not think the blustery young man fit for his office. "A declamatory Style, a flittering, fluttery Imagination, an Ardour in his Temper, and a civil Deportment are all the Accomplishments or Qualifications I can find for his place," Adams wrote his wife after Genet concluded his mission. More important, Adams resisted any attempt to bring the United States into the war. Having renounced any ideological community with France in *Discourses on Davila,* Adams went on to deny any strategic connection. While most of the debate over policy took place in terms of the law of nations, the law of nations was more a source of justification than inspiration. Adams recognized this with more clarity than most. "A Neutrality absolute total neutrality is our only hope," Adams wrote to Tench Coxe; circumstances absolved the United States of its obligations to defend the French West Indies. One could find justification in Vattel, but "reading is not necessary to instruct us what to do."[9]

Hoping to have policy set before Genet arrived, Washington asked the cabinet for their opinions and received diametrically opposed answers. Hamilton believed that the 1778 treaties died with Louis XVI and recommended that Washington suspend them; Jefferson believed the treaties were still in force. Washington did not want to repudiate the treaties outright, but he did not have any intention of adhering to the articles pledging American defense of the French West Indies. Hamilton gained only a tactical advantage when Washington issued the Proclamation of Neutrality on April 22, 1793. The president did not use the word "neutrality" in the brief statement but rather said that "the duty and interest of the United States require that they should with sincerity and good faith adopt and pursue a conduct friendly and impartial toward the belligerent powers." Jefferson complained to Madison that Hamilton wanted to nullify the French treaty based on what Jefferson called "an ill-understood scrap in Vattel," which appeared to support the idea that a change in government voided treaties concluded by the previous government. He considered the Proclamation of Neutrality unconstitutional, as Congress had the power to decide on war or peace. He also believed the United States should force the warring powers to offer concessions in exchange for American neutrality.[10]

What relations, if any, the United States would have with the French republic depended on whether the 1778 alliance was still valid. The validity of the alliance in turn depended on a set of deeper philosophical questions: whether France was a republic as Americans understood the term, and whether similarity in form of government created a community of interest. Jefferson answered an emphatic yes to the first question and a qualified yes to the second. Hamilton answered no to the first, but he ignored this question in his public arguments and focused instead on an unequivocal negative to the second.

Jefferson began by restating the theory of the Declaration of Independence. "I consider the people who constitute a society or nation as the source of all authority in that nation, as free to transact their common concerns by any agents they think proper, to change those agents individually, or the organization of them in form or function whenever they please," he argued. Under this formulation, Jefferson considered that the king signed the treaties as the agent of France, and he concluded that the treaties did not die with the king.[11] Jefferson was guided more by his approval of the French Revolution and his faith in French friendship with the United States than by abstract considerations of the law of nations.

Neither did Jefferson consider either the potential danger of fulfilling the mutual guarantee of territory in the alliance or the provision for outfitting French privateers in the commercial treaty as grounds for renouncing the treaty. He did not believe that France would call for the territorial guarantee or that the United States would be in a position to execute it. In fact, Jefferson saw a greater danger in abrogating the treaty. If the United States renounced its treaty obligations "without just cause or compensation, we give to France a cause of war, and so become associated in it on the other side. . . . An injured friend is the bitterest of foes, and France has not discovered either timidity, or over-much forbearance on the late occasions." Jefferson concluded with a defense of the idea of a community of republics. The United States signed an alliance with "A despotic government," and the case was stronger for friendship with a French republic: "Who is the American who can say with truth that he would not have allied himself with France if she had been a republic?"[12]

Dumas Malone argued that Jefferson put his tilt toward France in terms of national interest rather than ideology. Jefferson would not have drawn as sharp a dichotomy. Furthermore, in his private correspondence, Jefferson seemed as caught up in the enthusiasm for Genet as any of Genet's supporters along the coast. Jefferson wrote Madison that he favored the warm popular greeting over the "cold caution" of the administration. When the crowds cheered Genet, Jefferson cheered with them. "All the old spirit of 1776. is rekindling," he told James Monroe. When a French frigate seized a British ship, "the *yeomanry* of this city [Philadelphia] crowded and covered the wharfs." Jefferson applauded the spirit but hoped it would stay "within the limits of a fair neutrality." Jefferson believed that American neutrality, not to mention the survival of the American republic, depended on the French staving off Great Britain. In a letter to Harry Innes, he wrote that if "the arms of kings" subdued France "it is far from being certain they might not chuse to finish their job completely, by obliging us to change in the form of our government, at least, a change which would be grateful to a party here, not numerous, but wealthy and influential."[13]

When Genet presented his letters of credence, he seemed too good to be true. He told Jefferson that France did not intend to demand the territorial guarantee. Rather, Genet offered a new commercial treaty, including an open trade with the French West Indies. Like Jefferson, Genet emphasized the natural friendship of republics. "It is impossible for any thing to be more affectionate, more magnanimous than the purport of his mission," Jefferson told Madison. "In short he offers every thing and asks nothing."[14]

Yeoman diplomacy, as practiced by Jefferson and Madison, presumed that other nations would act in such a way as to allow the United States to defend itself and achieve its diplomatic goals without recourse to military force. Furthermore, Jefferson and Madison presumed the friendship of France, especially when France was a republic. The French Revolution removed cold royalists like Vergennes who did not seem to truly appreciate the value of American friendship. Both Jefferson and Madison displayed a career-long tendency to accept at face value statements from diplomats that fit into their general theory and either to ignore or to explain away all the rest. Jefferson displayed this trait from the outset of the Genet mission.

Of course Genet's initial conversation with Jefferson was too good to be true. Genet and his patrons in France depended on American friendship, but as a weapon to use against Great Britain. Genet was seeking to preserve American neutrality in order to provide a safe haven for French privateers. France opened the trade to the West Indies because of the destruction of its own merchant marine. As a neutral, the United States might be able to aid France and stay out of the British line of fire; as a combatant, the United States would be of little or no use.[15]

Left unchecked, Genet might drag the United States into war, and his actions highlighted the dangers that Jefferson downplayed in his opinion of April 28, 1793. Jefferson had already informed Genet's predecessor that France could not outfit privateers or sell prizes in American ports. The *Grange,* whose capture was celebrated by Jefferson and the yeomanry of Philadelphia, must be returned to Great Britain. Genet accepted the specific request but denied the theory, asserting that an ally ought to have the right to use a friend's ports as bases for privateers. On June 5 Washington made the privateering ban official.[16]

Genet took the ban badly, and his conferences with Jefferson degenerated into long denunciations of the president. "I do not auger well the mode of conduct of the new French minister," Jefferson told Monroe at the end of June. "I fear he will enlarge the circle of those disaffected to his country." Jefferson went on to describe his efforts to convince Genet of the futility of his attempts to drive a wedge between the people and the government. Genet, however, did not let such a minor matter as Washington's opposition prevent him from using American ports as French bases. In June Genet began outfitting the captured British ship *Little Sarah,* renamed the *Petite Democrate,* in Philadelphia. The crew included several Americans. On July 6, 1793, Pennsylvania Governor Thomas Mifflin informed the administration of Genet's activities.[17]

Once again, Jefferson was in the position of trying to keep peace with France while engaged in a verbal war with the French minister. In private, Jefferson railed against Genet. "Never, in my opinion, was so calamitous an appointment made, as the present minister of F. here," he complained to Madison. "Hotheaded, all imagination, no judgment, passionate, disrespectful and even indecent towards the P. in his written as well as his verbal communications, talking of appeals from him to Congress, from them to the people, urging the most unseasonable and groundless propositions, and in the most dictatorial style, &c.&c.&c." At the same time, Jefferson hoped to derail a proposal by Hamilton and Knox to mount a battery at Mud Island and hold the ship by force. Jefferson perceived an imbalance in American policy, which seemed ready to attack an ally over recent troubles, while the United States "has been patiently bearing for ten years the grossest insults and injuries from their late enemies." Jefferson placed his objection in terms of a now nearly discredited idea of a unity of republics, arguing, "I would not gratify the combination of kings with the spectacle of the two only republics on the earth destroying each other for two cannon." The *Petite Democrate* escaped to Chester on July 9. A few days later Washington asked the Supreme Court for an advisory opinion. The delay allowed the privateer to sail unnoticed to the Atlantic.[18]

On August 3, Jefferson announced to Madison that the cabinet had decided to ask for Genet's recall. *"He will sink the republican interest if they do not abandon him."* Several weeks of open defiance of American neutrality and flagrant disrespect toward the administration could no longer be ignored. To the end, Jefferson hoped to separate reaction to Genet's conduct from policy toward France. In his formal letter requesting Genet's recall, Jefferson wanted to express the hope that Franco-American difficulties would not produce the spectacle of *"liberty warring on herself."* Hamilton objected on the grounds that the statement would cause a rift with the other powers at war with France, that it was not the duty of the United States to declare the cause of France to be the cause of liberty, and finally that he did not believe France was fighting for liberty. Knox and Randolph joined with Hamilton. Washington was willing to leave the phrase in, but he left it up to the cabinet, which voted against Jefferson. What Jefferson considered a backlash against republicanism at home and abroad was in part Genet's fault. "His conduct has given room to the enemies of liberty and France to come forward in the stile of acrimony against that nation which they never would have dared to have done," Jefferson explained to Madison; "The disapprobation of the agent mingles with the reprehension of his nation and gives tolerable to that which it never had before."[19]

Genet's country abandoned him as well. The Jacobins, led by Maximilien Robespierre, took control of the National Convention on June 2, 1793. Beginning in the fall, the new government sent its opponents—including Genet's political patrons—to the guillotine. The Jacobins feared that Genet had alienated the United States, and on November 17 Robespierre denounced

Genet and accused the Girondins of treason. Jean Fauchet arrived at Philadelphia as the new French minister on February 21, 1794. Genet knew the guillotine awaited him in Paris. He married a daughter of New York governor George Clinton and retired to the life of a gentleman farmer in New York.[20]

Jefferson's conduct during the Genet mission reflects two tenets of the yeoman vision of republican diplomacy: the belief that other nations regardless of historical circumstances could create republics and the belief that France would act as a friend of the United States. French friendship would be strengthened under a French republic. The yeoman vision tended to be more doctrinaire than its whig counterpart, and if one part was untrue, then the entire structure would crumble. Troubles with France, therefore, must be the result of Genet's intemperate actions and Federalist efforts to discredit France, not from any failure of French republicanism.

Worn out after three years of a losing battle with Hamilton, Jefferson left office at the end of 1793 and formally joined Madison in the opposition. Jefferson's last state paper, the *Report on Commerce,* dated December 16, 1793, reflected the yeoman vision of commerce as a means to coerce European nations. His commercial vision in 1793 was consistent with what he had outlined in *Notes on Virginia* and his dispatches to Jay. Jefferson was willing to put aside philosophical misgivings about a merchant marine. Of course, he had no doubt that shipping would remain in proper proportion to agriculture. Unlike Madison, he did not yet see shipping as a mainly sectional interest.

Jefferson began with the central assumption that Europe needed the United States far more than the United States needed Europe. "The Commodities we offer, are either necessaries of life; or materials for manufacture; or convenient Subjects of Revenue," in exchange for which the United States purchased "mere Luxuries." The United States preferred—and had every right to expect—a free trade with all of Europe. Yet if other nations continued with "Prohibitions, Duties and Regulations," the United States would have no choice but to respond in kind. "Free commerce and navigation are not to be given in exchange for Restrictions, and Vexations: nor are they to produce a relaxation of them."[21]

"Our Navigation involves still higher consideration," Jefferson continued. "As a Branch of Industry, it is valuable; but, as a means of Defence, essential." If the United States was to have a seaborne commerce, it had to be protected. The United States had "nothing to fear on their land-board," but at sea "they are open to injury." To protect commerce, the United States needed "a respectable Body of Citizen-Seamen" and the means to build and maintain ships.[22] As with navigation, Jefferson no doubt believed that need for a navy would be naturally limited by the power of American commerce. Jefferson presumed that American commerce was so valuable that other nations would not risk it being denied to them, making the navy a secondary line of defense. Jefferson was not a navalist in the sense that Adams was, and his reference to "Citizen-seamen" foreshadowed the "naval militia" of the Jefferson administration. Jefferson's *Report* turned out to be the end of the yeoman vision within the Washington administration, rather than a guide to future policy. With Jefferson's departure, Hamilton's version of the whig vision, less optimistic about international republicanism, less confident in economic coercion, and less fearful of power, triumphed.

HAMILTON SERVED IN THE CABINET for only thirteen months after Jefferson's resignation. Yet Hamilton's career-long relationship with Washington made him the most influential figure in American foreign relations, short of the president himself, from the Proclamation of Neutrality to the Farewell Address. Hamilton's vision of whig diplomacy was naturally opposed to Jefferson's yeoman diplomacy in its key points. Where Jefferson saw a community of interest with France, strengthened by its turn to a republic, Hamilton believed "the interest of every nation is to every other always distinct, frequently rival." Jefferson's way led to foreign influence, "the GRECIAN HORSE to a republic." Jefferson believed the United States had the power to coerce other nations with trade without risk of war, but Hamilton had no such conceit. Hamilton considered the United States "a Hercules in the cradle."[23] The key word in 1793 was "cradle." One day the United States would take its place as a great power, but this day had not yet arrived. War would unhinge the new nation's finances, and by extension the Constitution and the union. Jefferson, on the other hand, feared war for its tendency to add to executive power and create armies that would destroy liberty. Hamilton did not fear power if it was exercised by a properly constituted government, and he favored giving the president more latitude in initiating policy.

Hamilton preferred not to receive Genet at all, or at least to receive him only provisionally "reserving to ourselves a right to consider the applicability of the Treaties."[24] After President Washington had submitted a list of questions to the cabinet on April 18, 1793, Hamilton answered that the treaty of 1778 was signed by Louis XVI and had died with him. Hamilton agreed with Jefferson that any nation had the right to change its form of government, but he added that such a change at least suspended any treaties with other powers. While Jefferson saw France as a sister republic, Hamilton saw no such relationship. There was no guarantee that France would remain a republic at the end of the present war, or that France was even a republic at all. "The character of the United States may be also concerned in keeping clear of any connection with the Present Government of France in other views," Hamilton warned. In his public and official capacities, Hamilton tended to avoid a direct answer to the question as to whether France represented the cause of liberty. "A struggle for liberty is in itself respectable and glorious," Hamilton argued. "But if sullied by crimes and extravagancies, it loses its respectability." He went on to note that "the pending revolution in France has sustained some serious blemishes."[25]

In another letter written the same day, Hamilton answered Washington's eighth question, whether the war was offensive or defensive. To Hamilton, this was an easy question and offered the best way out of the alliance. "The War is plainly an *offensive war* on the part of France," he argued. He noted that France "was the first to declare war against every one of the Powers with which she is at War." France threatened to extend its war as far as possible, promising aid to the oppressed peoples of Europe against their governments on November 19, 1792. Such actions forced France's enemies to join together. "The *casus foederis* of the guarantee of the treaty of Alliance between the UStates and France cannot take place, though her West Indian Islands should be attacked," he concluded.[26]

To Hamilton, the preservation of the republic lay in absolute neutrality, and he forcefully opposed Genet's attempts to subvert it. Genet's efforts to recruit American soldiers and sailors were a direct violation of American sovereignty, "an injury and affront of a serious kind," Hamilton wrote to Washington. If the United States acquiesced, he went on, "such nation becomes an Associate, a Party." Genet's actions also constituted "an offence against the law of Nations—the law of Nations is a part of the law of the land," he told Richard Harrison. Hamilton supported all measures to block Genet, including mounting a battery to fire on the *Petite Democrate*.[27]

Perhaps the most dangerous part of Genet's mission was his open participation in American politics, eating away at neutrality from within. Hamilton described Genet's reception in Philadelphia to an unidentified correspondent and observed that Genet's supporters "were the same men who have been uniformly the enemies and disturbers of the Government of the Ustates." In private, Hamilton saw no comparison between the American and French Revolutions. "Would to heaven that we could discern in the Mirror of French affairs, the same humanity, the same solemnity, which distinguished the cause of the American Revolution." Hamilton was pleased that "there is no real resemblance between what was the cause of America & what is the cause of France." He concluded "that the difference was no less great than that between Liberty & Licentiousness." Hamilton feared that such celebrations for Genet would cause "jealousy and resentment" in the nations at war with France and would drag the United States into the war.[28]

In June 1793, Hamilton launched a defense of the Proclamation of Neutrality, and Washington's policy generally, in a series of essays signed "Pacificus." He defended Washington on two grounds, the power of the president to proclaim neutrality and the wisdom of the policy itself. Hamilton did not discuss the specifics of the Genet mission or even mention Genet's name, and he rejected the polemical approach he had earlier considered. In an unpublished defense of neutrality, Hamilton attacked a "dangerous combination" of politicians "who for some time past have been busy in undermining the constitution." These same people sought "to inflame the zeal of the people for the cause of France," he continued, "and to excite their resentments against the powers at war with her."[29] As "Pacificus," Hamilton took a higher tone than in private.

First, Hamilton placed the Proclamation of Neutrality squarely within the president's constitutional authority to conduct foreign relations. "The Legislature is not the *organ* of intercourse between the UStates and foreign nations," he wrote. "It is charged neither with *making* nor interpreting Treaties." A treaty fell under the same category as a domestic law, whose enforcement fell to the executive branch. The Proclamation of Neutrality changed no law but merely expressed the president's interpretation of the status of the 1778 treaties. In the final essay, Hamilton defended the timing of the proclamation, explaining that a war between France and Prussia would not affect the United States, but war with Atlantic powers such as Great Britain and the Netherlands would.[30]

Next, Hamilton moved on to a defense of neutrality itself. In doing so, he reused much of the material from his May 2, 1793, letter to Washington. Hamilton observed that the 1778 alliance was defensive. France was the first to declare war on each of its enemies. The National Convention's November 19, 1792, declaration that France would help the "oppressed" peoples of Europe was further evidence of French aggression. Therefore, the clause pledging the United States to defend the French West Indies was not activated by the present war.[31]

Even if the Washington administration wanted to defend the French West Indies (and Hamilton certainly did not), it was in no position to do so. "It is certainly known that we are wholly destitute of naval force," Hamilton observed, noting that France was at war with "all the great maritime Powers." Fulfilling the guarantee would sink the United States into an unwinnable war. With the United States flanked on land by Spain and Great Britain and hopelessly outgunned at sea, "it is impossible to imagine a more unequal contest, than that in which we should be included in the case supposed." Furthermore, the war was not a mere territorial or commercial dispute, but about the nature of the French government, an object far beyond the scope of the alliance.[32]

In the fourth "Pacificus," Hamilton moved from a discussion of the concrete provisions of the alliance to the more nebulous idea of gratitude as a basis for national policy. "Faith and Justice between nations are virtues of a nature sacred and unequivocal," Hamilton wrote. Yet gratitude could not be as easily measured or applied to policy. Hamilton did not "advocate a policy of absolutely selfish or interested in nations" but rather "a policy regulated by their own interest, as far as justice and good faith will permit." He rejected a policy based on a "self-denying or self-sacrificing gratitude."[33]

In the fifth and sixth essays, Hamilton allowed himself to score some political points off the Republicans. He noted that the argument for a policy based on gratitude came from "those *who love France more than the United States.*" He noticed a certain inconsistency in the gratitude rationale. Those to whom the United States should be grateful had either been executed or exiled. "The preachers of gratitude are not ashamed to brand *Louis* the XVI as a tyrant, and *LaFayette* as a Traitor." Hamilton briefly raised the argument "that the cause of France is the cause of liberty: and that we are bound to assist the nation on that score in their being engaged in the defence of that cause," but he then deferred discussion to a future essay.[34]

Hamilton ultimately concluded that the preservation of the republic rested on an absolute neutrality, and he urged avoiding even the hint of an ideological crusade. The United States could not, for reasons other than its own, "expose itself to the jealousy illwill or resentment of the rest of the world." The best way to avoid being dragged into war was to prevent foreign influence, which Hamilton considered the greatest danger to a republic. In language later used in Washington's Farewell Address, Hamilton cautioned Americans "not to over-rate our *foreign friendships*—to be on our guard against *foreign* attachments. The former will generally be found hollow and delusive; the latter will have a natural tendency to lead us from our own interest, and to make us the dupes of foreign influence."[35]

Hamilton turned to the specifics of the Genet mission in a series signed "No Jacobin," written in response to charges that the United States had violated the 1778 treaties. Hamilton asserted an absolute right to "prevent a violation of its jurisdiction," which included the right to prohibit privateering. Furthermore, Genet's conduct was a continuous insult to the United States government. "The history of diplomatic enterprize affords no parallel to this," Hamilton wrote; "We should look in vain for a precedent of a foreign minister, in the country of his mission, becoming the declared head, or even the acknowledged member of a *political Association*." The lesson, as in "Pacificus," was "to dread and to shun the treacherous and destructive embraces of foreign influence, more than war, pestilence or famine."[36]

In January 1794, Hamilton returned to the Proclamation of Neutrality in the "Americanus" essays, the belated conclusion to the "Pacificus" series. He opened with the topics he had promised to cover in the sixth "Pacificus": whether the French Revolution was the cause of liberty and whether the United States should aid France as a result. Hamilton concentrated on the actions of the French government rather than the underlying theory of the revolution. He believed there was "no adequate apology for the horrid and distressing scenes which have been and continue to be acted." Hamilton noted that observers of the French Revolution could see its leaders as "assassins still reeking with the blood of murdered fellow Citizens," and they could conclude that the revolution itself would end in the rule "of some victorious Scylla or Marius or Caesar."[37]

In his unpublished drafts, Hamilton was much more critical of the French Revolution. "Theories of Government unsuited to the nature of man, miscalculating the force of his passions, disregarding the lessons of experimental wisdom, have been projected and recommended," he wrote in 1794. The same Hamilton proclaimed that the French Revolution was "not the cause of Liberty, but the cause of Vice Atheism and Anarchy." Hamilton came to dismiss the idea that the United States owed any gratitude toward France, as France had acted against American interests in 1782 by failing to support American claims to the Mississippi and the cod fisheries.[38]

Hamilton toned down his private condemnation of the French Revolution because his newspaper essays, like the *Federalist* essays, were not merely an exposition of his own political philosophy. He was defending Washington's policies (which he had helped craft), and he had to write in accordance with those policies. Washington himself had not condemned the French Revolution in toto; therefore, neither could Hamilton. Furthermore, in the nation as a whole, a defense of the Proclamation of Neutrality as a hedge against a destructive war or an attack on the excesses of the French government was politically safer than a frontal assault on the revolutionary movement.

Hamilton did not believe the United States could help France in any case. It had no navy to defend the French West Indies or to attack the British islands. War would destroy American navigation, taking agriculture and 90 percent of the public revenue with it. Hamilton dismissed the idea that American liberty was tied up in the success of the French Revolution, for geographic reasons if nothing else. The victorious powers would not cross the Atlantic and stamp out the American republic. "To subvert by force republican Liberty in this Country, nothing short of entire conquest would suffice," Hamilton argued. "This conquest, with our present increased population, greatly distant as we are from Europe, would either be impracticable or would demand such exertions, as following immediately upon those which will have been requisite to the subversion of the French Revolution, would be absolutely ruinous to the undertakers."[39]

As the crisis with France faded, a crisis with Great Britain rose to take its place. The British government sought to prevent goods from the French West Indies from reaching their markets and passed an Order-in-Council on November 6, 1793, authorizing the capture of any ships carrying goods to or from the French islands. An order of January 8, 1794, relaxed regulations and allowed direct trade between the United States and French possessions. The new order reaffirmed the Rule of 1756, which stated that trade illegal in peacetime cannot be made legal in wartime. The new order made the neutral trade between France and its islands subject to capture and sale in prize courts.[40]

British regulations threatened to reignite the smoldering American hatred for the mother country. To Hamilton the great danger to the republic was that such hatred could easily turn to war. Great Britain was a far more dangerous open enemy than France. France could not materially hurt the United States, but it could subvert the American political system and turn the United States to its own purposes. Great Britain neighbored the United States on land, dominated the seas, and made up the bulk of American foreign trade. Great Britain could cripple the United States, and Hamilton did not believe the United States had power to fight Great Britain on equal terms. This was the conceptual framework Hamilton used to shape his response to the British crisis.

Hamilton advised Washington to seek an accommodation with Great Britain. He saw three schools of thought on how to approach the crisis. The first, in which Hamilton included himself, proposed preparing for war while making one last effort to avoid it. The second school of thought wanted to whip up public fervor against Great Britain as a prelude to war. The third "weakly hope that they may hector and vapour with success— that the pride of Great Britain will yield to her [commercial] interests—and that they may accomplish the object of perpetuating animosity between the two countries without involving War."[41]

Hamilton never shared Jefferson and Madison's faith that commerce could be entirely separated from politics or used as a weapon. "A proper estimate of the question of the human passions must satisfy us that she [Great Britain] would be less disposed to receive the law from us than from any other nation," Hamilton wrote. The measures proposed by the Republicans— sequestering British debts and cutting off trade—were likely to cause war and to backfire on the United States. The United States would suffer far more than Great Britain from Republican measures. "'Tis as great an error for a nation to overrate as to underrate itself," Hamilton warned. "We forget how little we can annoy and how much we may be annoyed." Hamilton recommended a final diplomatic effort to avert war, and he recommended John Jay as the envoy. To argue, as Jerald Combs does, that ideology and calculations of available power played separate roles in Hamilton's thinking is to draw a false distinction. With Hamilton, as with Jefferson, Madison, and Adams, the two were always intertwined.[42]

On April 21, 1794, Hamilton met with John Jay, Oliver Ellsworth, Rufus King, and George Cabot to plan Jay's mission. They agreed to ask the British for payment for seized slaves and the cession of the western posts as provided for in the 1783 peace treaty. They sought compensation for shipping losses, or at least for the goods lost. Jay was to seek the admission of American vessels of from sixty- to eighty-tons burden into the British West Indian trade. The recommendations of this meeting formed part of the official instructions from Secretary of State Randolph.[43]

Secretary Randolph included in the instructions the possibility of appealing to a revived Armed Neutrality, consisting of Denmark and Sweden. Hamilton held out little hope or desire for an international agreement on neutral rights. "The United States have peculiar advantages from their situation which would thereby be thrown into common stock without an equivalent," Hamilton wrote to Randolph. If the United States went to war with Great Britain, common interest would draw neutral powers together without a formal alliance. About the same time, Hamilton told British minister George Hammond that "even in the event of an open contest with Great Britain," the United States would "avoid entangling itself with European connexions." Hamilton was not telling Hammond anything he did not already know. Hammond had already noticed Hamilton's desire to keep out of European politics. Furthermore, an armed neutrality without active Dutch or Russian participation was worthless.[44]

Jay arrived in Great Britain in July and concluded the Treaty of Amity, Commerce and Navigation, commonly known as the Jay Treaty, on November 19, 1794. Jay was forced to abandon "free ships, free goods," and he made no headway on the impressment of American seamen—one aspect of the British practice of seizing American ships to remove suspected deserters. Jay did secure the cession of the western forts, compensation for seized ships, and a limited entry into the West Indian trade. Jay agreed to bar the sequestration of British debts, and he also agreed to a commercial treaty on the basis of most-favored-nation status for twelve years. Above all, the treaty kept the peace.[45]

The treaty was not entirely to Hamilton's liking. He objected to article 12, which prohibited the reexport of most West Indian products, but he believed it better to remove the article than to restart negotiations. He wrote to William Bradford:

> I expect the treaty will labour. It contains many good things but there is one ingredient in it which displeases me—of a commercial complexion. I am however of opinion on mature reflection that it is expedient to ratify accompanied by a declaration that it is our intention till there be a further explanation & modification of the article to forbear the exercise of a certain privilege & consequently the performance of the condition of it—or something equivalent.

Hamilton prepared an examination of the treaty for Washington, reiterating his support. "The truly important side of this Treaty is that it closes and upon the whole as reasonably as could be expected the controverted points between the two Countries," he asserted. Washington submitted the treaty to the Senate in June 1795. In secret session, the Senate eliminated article 12 and ratified the treaty 20–10.[46]

Stiff Republican opposition to the treaty led Hamilton to once again take to the newspapers. "The Defence," written under the pseudonym "Camillus," appeared in the *New York Argus* from July 1795 to January 1796. Hamilton restated the tenets of the whig diplomacy that he articulated in his advice to Washington. The United States was not in a position to demand that Great Britain dismantle its maritime system. "War, or disgrace" were the only possible results of Republican measures in Congress. War would be the solvent of the union. "Few nations have stronger inducements than the U States to cultivate peace. Their infant state in general—their want of a marine in particular to protect their commerce would render war in an extreme degree a calamity." War with Great Britain would destroy American trade, damage agriculture, and increase debts and taxes. Hamilton cautioned the United States against "dangerous mistakes" brought by overestimating its own power. "If we can avoid War for ten or twelve years more, we should then have acquired a maturity, which will make it no more than a common calamity and will authorise us on our national discussions to take a higher & more imposing tone."[47]

Hamilton pointed out that the chief benefits from the treaty came in the West. The British evacuation of the western forts permitted the free navigation of the Mississippi, uniting the West and the East. Jay "conformed to the general spirit of our Country and to the general policy of our laws" by opening a free trade in the Northwest. The articles on the West were a permanent benefit, whereas the commercial provisions expired after twelve years.[48]

Hamilton doubtless recognized that the Republicans found the commercial articles of the treaty the most objectionable. One Hamilton biographer wrote that Hamilton was "indifferent" to the abstract theory of neutral rights and generally sympathetic to the British interpretation of neutral rights. In truth, Hamilton simply recognized that Great Britain was not going to dismantle its maritime system, regardless of American action. Such a demand could lead only to destructive war or humiliating diplomatic retreat. "Every body knows that the safety of Great Britain depends on her Marine," Hamilton wrote in "Defence" no. 6. "This was never more emphatically the case, than in the war in which she is now engaged. Her very existence as an independent power seems to rest on maritime superiority."[49]

As much as Hamilton might have hoped for an agreement barring the impressment of American seamen, this would have to wait for a future treaty. Hamilton defended the creation of a commission to adjudicate shipping claims as "an adequate atonement." He considered seizures under the orders of June 8 and November 6, 1793, as "injuries" rather than "insults." Hamilton also conceded that the British government might find support in international law for their claims under the Orders-in-Council.[50]

A combination of necessity, law, and common usage forced Jay to accept the British definition of what goods constituted contraband of war. "It is well understood that War abridges the Liberty of Trade of neutral nations," Hamilton observed, "and that it is not lawful for them to supply either of two belligerent parties with any article deemed contraband of war nor may they supply any article whatever to a place besieged blockaded or invested." Writers on the law of nations such as Vattel and Thomas Rutherforth considered goods not exclusively used for war, including timber and horses, as contraband. Under article 18 of the Jay Treaty, the United States was no worse off than before the treaty.[51]

Hamilton's last collaboration with Washington was the Farewell Address, which one historian has called the "apex" of the Hamilton-Washington partnership. On May 15, 1796, Washington sent for Hamilton's review and updated version of Madison's 1792 draft. "My wish is that the whole may appear in plain stile; and be handed to the public in an honest; unaffected; simple garb," the president instructed Hamilton. Furthermore, "the address should avoid personalities, allusions to particular measures, which may appear partial; and to expressions which could not fail to draw upon me attacks which I should wish to avoid, and might not find agreeable to repel." In the key foreign policy passages, Washington urged the United States to "avoid connecting ourselves with the Politics of any Nation," and he reiterated that his own political philosophy may be found in the Proclamation of Neutrality.[52]

Hamilton had spent most of his adult life as Washington's confidant, and he had no trouble turning a few hints into an extended essay. Certainly he did not force ideas on Washington that the president did not already share. Rather, Hamilton was acting out the final scene of the role he had played since 1793, that of the chief defender of neutrality. Washington knew the conclusion he wanted to reach. He relied on Hamilton for the explanation.

Naturally, Hamilton's philosophy of foreign policy matched Washington's, and much of the material from Hamilton's July 30, 1796, draft went into the Farewell Address with little or no change. From Hamilton's perspective, one of the main problems of the Washington years was the Republicans' hatred for Great Britain and their love for France. He therefore warned that any "nation, which indulges toward another a habitual hatred or a habitual fondness is in some degree a slave."[53]

Hamilton next moved on to restate the principles of the Proclamation of Neutrality. "The great rule of conduct for us in regard to foreign Nations ought to be to have as little *political* connection with them as possible—so far as we have already formed engagements let them be fulfilled—with circumspection indeed but with perfect good faith." Since 1793 Hamilton had advocated correct but unenthusiastic relations with France as the only way to prevent the 1778 treaty from leading to destruction. The "detached and distant situation" of the United States provided a natural barrier against "national injury" and "extended annoyance." To protect the freedom of action made possible by nature, the United States had to shun permanent alliances. Hamilton considered the French alliance a burden. He dismissed the idea that the United States could "expect or calculate upon real favours" from other nations.[54]

The Washington administration marked the triumph of the whig over the yeoman vision of diplomacy. Yet the whig version was not as unified as its yeoman counterpart. Hamilton accepted the outer framework of eighteenth-century whig diplomacy—separation from European politics, the unlikelihood of liberty in other nations, the lack of a natural community of interest with other nations, and the inability of the United States to force drastic changes in world politics. His republican realpolitik leaned more on realpolitik than on ideological republicanism. He did not accept the fear of power at the inner core of whig belief. The tools of foreign policy held no terrors for him. "In my opinion the real danger in our system is that the General Government organised as at present will prove too weak rather than too powerful," Hamilton wrote in a passage Washington left out of the Farewell Address.[55] When Hamilton was the theorist in chief, the split in the whig vision could not be seen. With Adams in power, it led to the breakup of the Federalist party.

CHAPTER SIX

The Bolingbrokean Moment

On July 20, 1799, Secretary of War James McHenry wrote to President John Adams explaining that he planned to delay the recruitment of twelve regiments of infantry in order to "husband our means." Adams agreed with McHenry's plan, but the letter triggered a deeper reaction from the president. "I can never think of our means, without Shuddering," Adams replied; "All the declamations as well as demonstrations of Trenchard & Gordon, Bolingbroke, Bernard & Walpole, Hume Burgh & Burke rush in upon my memory & frighten me out of my witts. The system of debts & taxes is levelling all governments in Europe."[1] In his reply to a routine letter, Adams laid out the intellectual basis for whig diplomacy. Of the thinkers listed, Adams's thought can be connected most closely to Bolingbroke. Like Bolingbroke, Adams fully agreed that the executive should "espouse no party" and should "govern like common father of his people." Adams's debt to Bolingbroke on the desirability of a president above party is generally acknowledged.[2] However, Adams expanded Bolingbroke's teachings and reinforced them with his practical experience in foreign policy to encompass a Bolingbrokean sense of foreign policy. Adams's conduct of the Quasi-War was a successful attempt to apply the whig vision to diplomatic practice, in essence a Bolingbrokean moment. During the Quasi-War with France, Adams pursued a policy of strict neutrality combined with vigorous defense of American commerce, both enforced by the navy and executed by a president who stood above party. Such a policy, Adams believed, was the only way to preserve the republic.[3]

In practice, Adams pursued a neutrality policy similar to the one Hamilton outlined to Washington. Adams later wrote to Thomas Truxton that "my system has been, for nine and twenty years at least, to do justice and maintain friendship with all nations as long as we possibly could, and have alliances with none if we could avoid it."[4] Unlike Hamilton, Adams accepted both the outer framework and the inner core of the eighteenth-century Opposition thought. The story of the Quasi-War is often presented as a personality clash between Adams and Hamilton. It is in reality the story of the breakdown of the whig consensus on foreign policy.

In recording the events of his inauguration day, Adams noted the coming difficulties as well as Washington's happiness to be rid of them. "He seemed to me to enjoy a Tryumph over me," Adams wrote his wife. "Methought I heard him think Ay! I am fairly out and you are fairly in! See which of Us will be happiest." One source of difficulty was the French reaction to the Jay Treaty. Adams supported the treaty and agreed with Hamilton that war would be fatal to the republic. Yet they differed on the reason why. Adams feared "Another War would add two or three Millions to our Debt, raise up a many-headed and many bellied Monster of an Army to tyrannize over Us, totally disadjust our present government and accelerate the Advent of Monarchy and Aristocracy by at least fifty years."[5]

A settlement with Great Britain, however temporary, naturally brought conflict with France. French foreign minister Charles Delacroix advised Pierre Adet, the French minister to the United States, to stir up anti-British feeling and bring the United States into war on the French side. Delacroix informed James Monroe, the American minister to France, that France considered the alliance ended the moment the Senate ratified the Jay Treaty. Threats turned into action on July 2, 1796, when the Directory decreed that France would treat American ships the same way Great Britain did, subjecting American commerce with Great Britain to French capture.[6]

A second source of difficulty was the cabinet that Adams inherited from Washington—Timothy Pickering as secretary of state, James McHenry as secretary of war, Oliver Wolcott as secretary of the treasury, and Charles Lee as attorney general. Adams retained all of these men, partly because there was no precedent for the cabinet to resign upon a change of administration and partly because of the difficulty in finding men willing to serve. To varying degrees, Pickering, Wolcott, and McHenry were politically closer to Hamilton than to Adams, and they consulted with the former secretary of the treasury on public affairs. Pickering was too stubborn and independent to be anyone's subordinate, and he looked to Hamilton as a kindred spirit rather than as a superior. Wolcott had served as Hamilton's deputy in the treasury department, and he was his closest ally. McHenry, completely out of his depth as secretary of war, relied on Hamilton for answers to presidential queries.[7]

Hamilton shared Adams's disgust for French actions toward the United States and a desire to make peace if possible. In "The Warning," which ran in the *Gazette of the United States* from January 27 to March 27, 1797, Hamilton made a stronger frontal assault against the principles of the French Revolution than in any of his previous newspaper essays. In the first article he wrote, "The conduct of France from the commencement of her successes, has by gradual development betrayed a spirit of universal domination." In a later article he continued, "'Tis our true policy to remain at peace, if we can, to negotiate our subjects of complaint as long as they shall be negotiable." This is what Hamilton believed, and he expected the president to follow such a course. If negotiation failed, armed resistance was the only honorable alternative. In either case, the United States had to defend itself on the high seas. "Whether our determination should be to lock up our Trade by embargoes, or to permit our commerce to float an unprotected prey to French Cruisers, our degradation and ruin will be equally complete."[8]

Hamilton supported the idea of sending a special bipartisan and sectionally balanced commission to France. "I would appoint a commission extraordinary to consist of M. Jefferson, or Mr. Madison, together with Mr. Cabot & Mr. Pinckney," Hamilton wrote to Pickering and other Federalists.[9] Hamilton no longer had direct access to the president, but he commanded the attention of the other leading Federalists. McHenry was an empty vessel into which Hamilton poured his opinions, and the secretary of war transmitted Hamilton's ideas verbatim to the president. In an answer to questions Adams posed to the cabinet, Hamilton argued that the "U States have the strongest motives to avoid war." France had not yet "gone to the *ne plus ultra*." Furthermore, "a considerable party" in the United States leaned toward France and might present a problem in the event of war.[10]

Adams described Hamilton as "a proud, conceited, aspiring mortal, always pretending to morality."[11] However, Adams had reached the same conclusion as Hamilton regarding a peace commission. He met with Jefferson on March 3, 1797, and asked the vice president elect if he would consider joining Pinckney, whom the French had rejected as Monroe's replacement, on a peace commission. Jefferson refused, arguing that it was inappropriate for the vice president to serve as a minister, and Adams agreed. Adams then suggested a commission of Pinckney and Madison or Elbridge Gerry. Jefferson agreed to ask Madison but did not expect him to accept, and when Adams suggested Madison to the cabinet the members unanimously opposed the appointment. On March 6, Jefferson told Adams that Madison would not serve. Adams then suggested Gerry as an independent member of the commission. The cabinet preferred Massachusetts Federalist Francis Dana. Adams relented, at least temporarily, and in May named Pinckney, Dana, and General John Marshall of Virginia as the peace commission. Adams knew that Dana hated ocean travel, and Adams "was always apprehensive he would decline." In June when Dana declined the appointment, Adams replaced him with Gerry.[12]

On March 25, 1797, Adams called for a special session of Congress to meet on May 15 to discuss defense measures. In the intervening period Adams received word of the French decree of March 2, declaring enemy goods on American ships to be lawful prizes and condemning American ships not carrying a *rôle d'équipage,* the proper crew manifest. France intended to inflict as much damage as possible on American shipping without a formal war. Adams approached the crisis from a whig perspective. As the French threat came from the sea, Adams advocated building a navy, combining his reading of Opposition Whig thought with his own experience. "The trident of Neptune is the scepter of the world," he wrote to Thomas Truxton. In an unused fragment of his speech to the special session, Adams argued, "it is a maxim among maritime people that with *wood, iron, and hemp and ships to employ them any nation may do itself justice.*" The United States was a natural seapower, and its commerce demanded protection.[13] By "commerce," Adams always meant the carrying trade as well as agricultural exports. "Commerce has made this Country what it is," Adams wrote in a draft of his first annual message. Aside from being politically dangerous, an army was of no use, as the French could not mount a land invasion. "Where is it possible to send thirty thousand Men here & we are double the number we were in 1775," Adams explained to Gerry. "We have four times the military skill and eight times the munitions of war. What would 30,000 men do here?"[14]

Adams addressed the special session on May 16, 1797. He blamed the French for the poor relations between the United States and France, citing the French rejection of Pinckney as minister and French attempts to influence the presidential election. Adams announced the new mission but also advised defensive preparations. "A naval power, next to the militia, is the most natural defence of the United States," Adams argued, echoing Bolingbroke. In June, William L. Smith of South Carolina submitted a program along Adams's lines, increasing the navy and providing for the arming of eighty thousand militia, which Congress approved. In July Congress voted to build twelve new frigates and improve coastal fortifications but defeated a motion to create a fifteen-thousand-man army. Hamilton fully approved the president's conduct.[15]

Before the envoys sailed at the end of July 1797, the Directory in France replaced the anti-American Delacroix with Charles Maurice de Talleyrand-Perigord, the chief architect of the Directory's American policy.[16] Despite the changes, Adams expected nothing from the mission, however. "It will be spun out into an immeasurable length, unless quickened by an embargo," he complained to Oliver Wolcott. "Talleyrand, I should suppose, could not be for war with this country," he wrote Pickering; "A continued appearance of umbrage, and continued depredations on a weak defenceless commerce, will be much more convenient for their views." The coup of 18 Fructidor (September 4, 1797) threatened to make relations worse, as the anti-American Jean François Reubell took control of foreign policy. "The internal commotions of France produce no external weakness, no diminution of exertion against her enemies," Marshall informed Pickering.[17]

Marshall, Pinckney, and Gerry met with each other in Paris on October 6, 1797, and called on Talleyrand two days later. Talleyrand asked the Americans to wait for official reception until he finished his report to the Directory. Official reception never came. Talleyrand sent four of his agents—Nicholas Hubbard, Jean Hottinguer, Pierre Bellamy, and Lucien Hauteval, labeled W, X, Y, and Z in the American dispatches—to negotiate. On October 18, Hottinguer presented Talleyrand's price for negotiation: an apology for Adams's speech of May 16, American assumption of American shipping claims against France, help in floating a loan in the Dutch money market, and a £50,000 bribe for Talleyrand. The only other option, Hottinguer later argued, was war, which would end in American defeat. Napoleon Bonaparte's victories in Italy buoyed the French spirit. In the Treaty of Campo Formio, France gave Venice to Austria as part of a peace settlement, and Bellamy suggested that the United States might also be carved up in a peace settlement if it allied with Great Britain against France.[18]

Over the next five months, negotiations stalled. "From our first arrival there has been a continuing effort to operate on our fears," Marshall wrote in his journal; "We have been threatened with a variety of ills, and among others with being ordered immediately to quit France." French tactics began to work on Gerry, who was willing to discuss making a loan at the end of the war. Talleyrand, seeing his opportunity, asked for one "impartial" envoy, namely Gerry, to remain in Paris, and for the other two to leave. Marshall was more than happy to comply, and he and Pinckney left Paris in April 1798. Gerry remained behind, believing that he alone stood between war and peace.[19]

The first group of dispatches, including documents dated as recently as January 8, 1798, arrived at Philadelphia in March 1798. Adams was willing to accept the formal etiquette of European diplomacy, but not outright extortion. The president was surprised and upset that the envoys had even talked to Talleyrand's agents. "Pinckney's answer to X, should have been We will not Say one Word in Answer to Propositions till We are recd. and meet a Minister on equal ground," Adams wrote in his personal notes. Convinced that the mission had failed, Adams asked Congress on March 19 for increased defensive preparations, but not a declaration of war. Despite French insolence and vague talk of invasion, the main French threat came from the sea, and this was where Adams intended to meet it. Adams asked Congress to increase the navy, improve coastal fortifications, and allow merchant ships to arm. "In all your proceedings, it will be important to manifest a zeal, vigor, and concert, in defence of the national rights proportional to the danger with which they are threatened," Adams told Congress. Republicans in Congress suspected that the crisis was a Federalist invention and on March 30 demanded to see the XYZ papers. The Federalists joined in and approved the demand on April 2. Adams immediately released the papers, embarrassing the Republicans and creating a backlash against both the French and the Republicans.[20]

President Adams himself contributed to the backlash, spending most of the spring and summer denouncing French action in his public addresses. "There is nothing in the conduct of our enemies more remarkable than their total contempt for the people," Adams wrote to the inhabitants of

Burlington County, New Jersey, "and of all real republican governments, while they screen themselves under some of their names and forms." To the Cincinnati of South Carolina, he wrote, "As to the French, I know of no government ancient or modern that ever betrayed so universal and decided a contempt of the people of all nations, as the present rulers of France." Despite his rhetoric, however, Adams refused to rule out a peaceful settlement. "I will never send another mission to France without assurances that they will be received, respected and honored as the representatives of a great, free, powerful and independent nation," Adams told Congress on June 21, 1798.[21]

Hamilton shared Adams's outrage at the XYZ Affair, and he also trod the increasingly fine line between peace and war. In "The Stand," which ran in the *New York Commercial Advertiser* from March 30 to April 21, 1798, Hamilton denounced the "studied contempt and systematic insult" shown to the American envoys. "Acting upon the pretension to universal empire, they [the French] have at length, in fact tho not in name, decreed war against all not in league with themselves; and towards this country in particular, they add to a long train of unprovoked aggressions and affronts the insupportable outrage of refusing to receive the extraordinary ambassadors whom we sent to endeavour to appease and conciliate." Having changed his manner since 1793, Hamilton let fly against the principles of the French Revolution itself rather than just the conduct of the French government. The revolution was a "frightful volcano of atheism, depravity, and absurdity," and an "engine of despotism and slavery." If successful, the French Revolution threatened to destroy civilization itself.[22]

In "The Stand" no. 6, Hamilton wrote, "Our true policy is, in the attitude of calm defiance, to meet the aggressions upon us by proportionate resistance, and to prepare for further resistance." To that end, he advocated a "respectable naval force" to protect American shipping and a "respectable army" to ward off invasion. The militia could not stand against battle-hardened French troops. Like Adams, Hamilton believed the United States was in a far better position to defend itself than during the American Revolution. It had an increased population in addition to the natural advantages of an ocean barrier and the materials to build a navy. Hamilton moved closer to believing that war was inevitable. Certainly it was better than a submissive peace. "Peace is doubtless precious, but it is a bauble compared with national independence, which includes national liberty."[23]

Adams was prepared to sail into a limited war but not to march into a full war. The president was a lifelong advocate of a navy, believing it to be "the most powerful, the safest and the cheapest National defence for this Country." Like Bolingbroke, Adams believed that a navy paid for itself by protecting commerce and could not endanger domestic liberties. "To arms then, my young friends,—to arms, especially by sea," Adams wrote in response to an address from the young men of Boston. On April 27, 1798, Congress authorized the president to obtain twelve twenty-four-gun ships. On April 30, Adams signed the bill creating the Department of the Navy.

The Senate confirmed Maryland merchant Benjamin Stoddert as secretary of the navy, Adams's second choice, on May 21. The navy's first task was to sweep the Atlantic coast of French privateers. The twenty-four-gun ship *Ganges* and the thirty-six-gun frigate *Constellation* largely completed this task by November 1798. Through most of 1798, however, for defense the navy relied on ten- to sixteen-gun revenue cutters.[24]

Adams recalled in retirement, "My hobby-horse was a navy; Alexander Hamilton's an army. I had no idea that France, involved as she was in Europe, could send any formidable invasion to America." Like Bolingbroke, Adams preferred to fight a limited naval war, over maritime issues, and to avoid foreign entanglements. Here Hamilton began to part with Adams. Hamilton agreed that the navy should be increased, but he also advocated creating a twenty-thousand-man standing army and a thirty-thousand-man provisional army, which Adams did not approve. Hamilton saw no reason for a formal declaration of war, as "a mitigated hostility still leaves a door open to negotiation." He also believed a British alliance was unnecessary. Interest would unite the two nations.[25]

Congress took up defensive measures in the summer of 1798 and favored Hamilton's program, although also approving the president's naval program. Federalists in the House of Representatives came close to a declaration of war, when Peleg Sprague of New Hampshire proposed attacking all French commerce. This motion failed on June 30, and a similar motion failed on July 2. The House modified this act to permit the seizure of armed French vessels anywhere in the world, which Congress and the president approved. On July 16, Congress authorized the president to recruit a fifty-thousand-man provisional army, which he had not asked for and did not want.[26]

Nor did Adams ever intend to ask for a declaration of war. He believed that the naval campaign was a sufficient response until French policy changed one way or the other. "Congress has already in my Judgement as well as in the opinion of the judges at Phyladelphia declared War, within the meaning of the Constitution, against that Republic, under certain restrictions and Limitations," Adams later explained to John Marshall, referring to the naval actions authorized in July 1798. Adams intended to conduct the limited war authorized by Congress at sea, and for that a large army was useless.[27]

The Federalist program had a domestic component as well. Both Federalists and Republicans tended to see political opposition as near treason. Fearful of Republican sympathy for the French Revolution, the Federalists moved to quiet opposition. The Alien and Sedition Acts included the Naturalization Act, designed to limit the political influence of immigrants, who tended to swell Republican ranks, by extending the waiting period for citizenship from five to fourteen years. The Alien Enemies Act allowed the president to expel aliens from hostile nations as he saw fit, and the Alien Friends Act allowed him to expel aliens from friendly nations he deemed dangerous. Finally, the Sedition Act punished "false, scandalous and malicious" statements against the president, Congress, or officers of the government in general. Adams attempted to shift the blame for the enactments to Hamilton. "Nor did I adopt his idea of an alien and sedition law," Adams wrote in 1809; "I recommended no such thing in my speech." However, even if Adams did not specifically ask for such legislation, he did not veto it.[28]

Congressional support for a large army showed that Adams did not have control of his party. The issue of who would command that army proved to Adams that his cabinet was disloyal. George Washington was the obvious choice, and Adams nominated the former president on July 4. Washington accepted, but on condition that he be allowed to choose his major generals and that he not be called to active duty unless Congress declared war. Until that time, the inspector general would command the army. Washington leaned toward either Henry Knox or Charles Cotesworth Pinckney as his deputy. Pickering, Wolcott, and McHenry lobbied heavily for Hamilton, however.[29]

Washington chose Hamilton as his deputy. Adams did not trust Hamilton with the command of an army and insisted that Knox was legally entitled to the inspector generalship. What followed was a comedy of errors. Washington did not know or care why Adams opposed Hamilton's appointment, and Adams never explained himself to Washington. "General Knox is legally entitled to rank next to General Washington and no other arrangement will give satisfaction," Adams informed McHenry. Adams openly resented the cabinet's interference, complaining to McHenry that "there has been too much intrigue in this business with General Washington and me." Washington grew tired of the conflict, and on September 25 he threatened to resign if the president did not comply with their agreement. When Adams received this letter, he knew he had lost. He could not afford an open rift with the hero of the revolution. On October 9, 1798, Adams wrote to Washington, telling him that he would date the commissions of Knox, Pinckney, and Hamilton on the same day, and Washington could settle the matter as he saw fit.[30]

Hamilton assumed that a conflict with France would bring a conflict with Spain and would provide an opportunity for the United States to conquer Louisiana. Throughout 1798 he was in steady contact with the Venezuelan revolutionary Francisco de Miranda, who had met with Prime Minister Pitt and who hoped for Anglo-American cooperation against Spain. American minister to Great Britain Rufus King hoped to be the midwife to the plan. Hamilton wanted the United States to take the lead in an assault on Spanish America, joining a British fleet to an American army. Hamilton anticipated that he would command the land force. "The Independency of the separated territory under a *moderate* government, with the joint guarantee of the cooperating powers, stipulating equal privileges in commerce, would be the sum of the results accomplished," Hamilton wrote to King on August 22, 1798.[31]

Adams greeted Miranda's plans with silence and later wrote to James Lloyd that Hamilton's designs on Spanish territory, requiring a large army and an alliance with Great Britain, were "in direct opposition to my system, and wholly subversive of it." Adams blamed French tyranny in part on French military aggression. "Could Mr. Pitt and Mr. Miranda believe me so fascinated, charmed, enchanted with what had happened in France," Adams asked Lloyd, "as to be desirous of engaging myself and my country in most hazardous and expensive and bloody experiments to excite similar horrors in South America?" Adams believed Hamilton wanted to launch a crusade to bring democracy to Spanish America, a prospect Adams considered "as absurd as similar plans would be to establish democracies among the birds, beasts and fishes."[32]

Hamilton did not intend to embark on a Harringtonian crusade for liberty but, rather, a military strike in defense of American national interest. In 1790 he had hoped to use the Nootka Sound crisis to take control of both sides of the Mississippi. Hamilton believed that at one stroke the United States could chase Spain from the Western Hemisphere, prevent a French invasion from the West, and advance the day that the American Hercules left its cradle. Naturally, the campaign would give Hamilton the everlasting fame he had craved since he was a young boy working in a countinghouse. Hamilton's tour on Washington's staff had been politically advantageous but, apart from an assault on a redoubt at Yorktown, short on glorious exploits. Forrest McDonald's description of Hamilton as a romantic is apt here, and doubtless the Miranda scheme appealed to that side of his character. Hamilton's biographers have placed the timing of Hamilton's commitment to war sometime between June and October 1798. August 22 may be a more precise answer. He clearly anticipated that the liberated colonies would not have free governments unless under Anglo-American tutelage. Like Montesquieu, Hamilton did not believe all nations were suited for liberty. St. Domingo, for example, could be administered only by a military or feudal government.[33]

Not coincidentally, Hamilton's impatience for decisive action grew after his appointment as inspector general. On January 26, 1799, he wrote to Harrison Gray Otis, a Federalist leader in the House of Representatives. Hamilton wanted a law authorizing the president to go to war with France if negotiations had not begun by August 1, 1799. Once at war, the United States should seize Louisiana and the Floridas. They were "the key of the Western Country," and Hamilton considered "the acquisition of those countries as essential to the permanency of the Union." Hamilton never gave up on the project. Even after Adams sent the second mission, Hamilton wanted to take Louisiana and the Floridas and "to squint at South America."[34]

Hamilton did not believe France could materially hurt the United States as much as Great Britain could. The danger of a war with France was internal subversion. Hamilton had come to see the Republicans as French servants, and some Republicans contributed to this perception. Virginia lawyer St. George Tucker asserted that, if the French landed, ten thousand Americans, including himself, would march with them. By early 1799 Hamilton believed that war would force French sympathizers to show their true loyalties. After the Virginia and Kentucky Resolutions passed, he proposed to send a force to "put Virginia to the test of resistance."[35]

Hamilton cannot be tied to any one thinker the way Adams can be linked to Bolingbroke. Hamilton came closest to resembling Algernon Sidney, who came at the end of a long line of republicanism with a strong martial component. Like Sidney, Hamilton saw no danger in military power wielded by a properly constructed government and no need to justify such action as a crusade for universal liberty. National interest would suffice. What Richard Kohn called "Federalist militarism" was a revival of the martial side of classical virtue, which both Hamilton and Adams had embraced during the American Revolution.[36] When war was inevitable, the martial ethic, which saw war as a positive rather than a destructive act, revived. Hamilton believed this time had come; Adams did not. Hamilton had constructed a plan to secure American interests, internally and externally, based on the martial ethic. All he needed was a declaration of war, which never came.

At the same time Hamilton was planning what to do with his new command, Adams began to receive information indicating that the army was, as he believed all along, unnecessary. There were three sources of diplomatic information that Adams trusted most. The first was his son, John Quincy Adams, currently the American minister to Prussia. The second was Elbridge Gerry, Adams's personal friend and one of the few "1775 men" still active in public affairs. The third was William Vans Murray, the American minister to the Netherlands. Murray, a Maryland Federalist, was a strong supporter of John Adams and a close friend of John Quincy Adams. Dispatches from these men along with the president's own analysis of the military situation brought about the shift from a war footing to the appointment of a second peace mission.[37]

John Quincy Adams spent much of his time observing French actions and reported in early 1798 that France was approaching the limits of its military capacity. "The preparations for the french expedition to England continue," Adams wrote his father in May, but those preparations took so long, "an opinion has lately been spreading, that it would eventually be abandoned." In letters to William Vans Murray, Minister Adams expressed his belief that, if the United States resisted French action, "the terrible Republic can hurt us little by sea." He applauded the American reaction to the XYZ Affair, noting that the French "are alarmed at the spirit which the publication raised in our country."[38]

Gerry did not similarly approve of American actions. He had remained in Paris after Marshall and Pinckney left, for fear that his departure would bring war, and he continued to meet with Talleyrand, who told Gerry that peace could still be achieved but also warned him not to leave. Pickering fi-nally ordered Gerry home in July. Gerry arrived in Boston on October 1, 1798, and went almost immediately to Quincy to meet with the president. Gerry had convinced himself he had prevented war, and he hoped to con-vince the president of the same thing. In later years, Adams credited Gerry for providing the evidence that France was willing to meet the conditions the president set in his speech of June 21.[39]

Adams may have exaggerated Gerry's immediate influence. In an effort to buy time, Talleyrand may have told Gerry exactly what the envoy wanted to hear, knowing Gerry would report immediately to the president. Adams had more official information from William Vans Murray. In July 1798, Talleyrand ordered Louis Pichon, the French minister to the Nether-lands, to begin informal negotiations with Murray. On July 17, Murray wrote Adams that France was afraid of full-scale war with the United States. Adams received Murray's letters on October 9. Adams responded that the letters "made a great impression on me." On October 20, Adams wrote to Pickering, asking his opinion on whether the president should re-quest a declaration of war or appoint a new minister to France. In any case, Murray's letters convinced Adams that there would be no invasion and offered a vindication of Adams's version of republican diplomacy. "If this nation sees a great army to maintain, without an enemy to fight, there may arise an enthusiasm that seems little forseen," Adams warned McHenry; "At present there is no more prospect of seeing a French army here, than there is in Heaven."[40]

The military situation tracked with Adams's analysis. By the fall of 1798, the navy was fully deployed, with between ten and fifteen ships on station. American action along with independent British action in the West In-dies reduced American losses to the French. British victories also worked in favor of the United States. On August 1, 1798, Admiral Horatio Nel-son destroyed the French fleet at the Battle of the Nile, stranding Napoleon Bonaparte's army in Egypt and curtailing French naval action in the Atlantic. Adams celebrated the "magnificent victory of Nelson," writing Francis Dana that the victory was "without a precedent or paral-lel." Adams later wrote his wife, "The English have exhibited an amaz-ing Example of Skill and Intrepidity, Performance and Firmness at Sea. We are a Chip off that Block."[41]

By December 1798, Adams clearly believed that the French would not and could not escalate the war. Whether they would make peace was a different matter. Despite various hints that France wanted to reach a set-tlement, there was still no official word, at least not one that would satisfy the conditions set forth in Adams's message of June 21. Adams therefore announced no policy changes in his annual message to Congress on De-cember 8. He observed that the French laws subjecting neutral ships carry-ing enemy goods to capture were still in operation and that such legisla-tion was "an unequivocal act of war on the commerce of the nations it attacks." "Hitherto, therefore," he continued, "nothing is discoverable in the conduct of France which ought to change or relax our measures of defence." Adams reminded Congress that "an efficient preparation for war can alone insure peace. . . . It is peace that we have uniformly and perseveringly cultivated; and harmony between us and France may be restored at her option." However, he would not send another minister, "without more determinate assurances."[42]

Murray's letters brought such assurances. Murray continued to meet with Pichon, who delivered messages from Talleyrand. Talleyrand wrote to Pichon on August 28, arguing that American prosperity "is more at the expense of Great Britain than us." Pichon passed this letter on to Murray on September 6. On October 7, Murray received a copy of a letter Talleyrand had written on September 28, in which Talleyrand promised that any minister Adams sent would be properly received. Murray thought Talleyrand's method unorthodox but believed that the letter satisfied Adams's conditions, and he sent it to the president. Adams received Murray's letters in January and February 1799. Probably on the basis of these letters, Adams ordered Pickering to draft a treaty to be proposed to France. Adams had sufficient information from "regular diplomatic sources" to make his decision. On February 1, 1799, Washington forwarded a letter to him from the poet Joel Barlow, who argued that France wanted peace with the United States. Washington added that he would support any honorable peace that Adams made. Adams gave no weight to Barlow's letter, but Washington's letter seemed to offer political cover for a new mission. On February 18, 1799, Adams nominated Murray as minister to France.[43]

In 1815 Adams wrote, "I desire no other inscription over my gravestone than: 'Here lies John Adams, who took upon himself the responsibility of the peace with France in the year 1800.'"[44] Adams had seen that the military fervor of 1798 was dead by 1799 and that his administration's actions had brought France back to the bargaining table. Adams believed that his diplomacy allowed him to remove the army as a domestic threat to republican government.

Although Adams did not nominate Murray solely for political gain it is clear that Adams believed, in Albert Hall Bowman's words, that "good policy was good politics." In execution Adams's policy married his Bolingbrokean conception of the presidency, as a leader acting alone for the general good, to the Bolingbrokean conception of the proper goals and methods of foreign policy. The Murray nomination also reflected Adams's long experience in diplomacy and his acceptance that American diplomats in Europe must act according to European rules. He accepted Talleyrand's use of Murray and Pichon as standard diplomatic practice. It is unlikely that the John Adams of 1778 would have approved of such a roundabout approach.[45]

The mission was the ruin of Hamilton's plans. On February 21, 1799, he wrote to Senator Theodore Sedgwick, urging to him to intervene. Sedgwick and four other Federalists—James Ross and William Bingham of Pennsylvania,

Jacob Reed of South Carolina, and Richard Stockton of New Jersey—met with Adams on February 23, hoping to talk him out of the peace mission. When Adams refused, the senators asked for a commission rather than a single envoy, to which Adams reluctantly agreed. Two days after the meeting, Adams named Chief Justice Oliver Ellsworth and Patrick Henry, both Federalists, as Murray's colleagues.[46]

The cabinet met at the president's house on March 10, 1799, to draft instructions. The president and cabinet unanimously agreed on three requirements for a treaty. First, France should indemnify American citizens for spoliation claims. Second, France should compensate shipowners for ships seized for lack of a *rôle d'équipage*. Third, the United States would offer no guarantee for French territory. As the cabinet drafted instructions, Patrick Henry declined his appointment, and Adams named Governor William R. Davie of North Carolina as his replacement.[47]

Congress adjourned in mid-March 1799, and Adams left for Quincy soon after without having ordered the new envoys to sail. The delay was not an accident but was tied directly to American sea power, as Opposition thought and Adams's own diplomatic experience dictated it should be. In March twenty American ships were on station in the Caribbean, but most of them were due to rotate out for repairs. By June only five ships remained, none with more than twenty-four guns. Adams pursued a twin policy of preparation and negotiation and would not launch a new mission without sufficient sea power to defend American shipping in the event of failure. In the meantime, Adams could read dispatches and issue orders as easily from Quincy as from Philadelphia.[48]

On June 18, 1799 (30 Prarial on the French calendar), most of the Directory fell from power. Several weeks later, Talleyrand resigned and was replaced by his ally, Karl Reinhard. Pickering believed the coup to be sufficient reason to suspend the mission, "the men lately in power, who gave the assurances you required, relative to the mission, being ousted in a manner indicative of a revolution in the public mind." Adams advised Pickering to maintain defensive preparations but to make no changes in policy. Adams did not intend to provoke a war. "If the spirit of exterminating vengeance ever arises," Adams wrote Pickering, "it shall be conjured up by them, not me."[49]

Adams did not wish to send the mission prematurely. "I have no reason or motive to precipitate the mission," he wrote Stoddert on September 4, 1799. On September 16, he wrote Pickering that it would be better to wait until after hurricane season to send the envoys. By September American naval strength was restored in the Caribbean. In October Adams arrived at Trenton, where the government had moved after a yellow fever epidemic in Philadelphia. On October 16, Adams ordered Ellsworth and Davie to sail, and the envoys left for Europe on November 3. "All my calculations lead me to regret the measure," Hamilton wrote to Washington, citing political instability in France and the danger of war with France's enemies.[50]

Ellsworth and Davie arrived in Paris on March 2, 1800, meeting a new government. Napoleon Bonaparte had overthrown the Directory on 18 Brumaire (November 9, 1799), establishing himself as First Consul. He wanted better relations with the neutral powers of northern Europe, and a settlement with the United States would improve his image. To establish the groundwork, Bonaparte repealed the law of January 18, 1798, which subjected American vessels to capture. On February 9, 1800, he declared two weeks of mourning in honor of George Washington, who had died on December 14, 1799. Bonaparte appointed Talleyrand as his foreign minister, but he turned negotiations over to a three-man commission made up of his older brother, Joseph Bonaparte, and two Counsellors of State who supported the coup, Pierre Louis Roederer and Charles Pierre Claret Fleurieu.[51]

Negotiations made no progress until September 11, 1800, when Roederer observed that the most important goal to the Americans was to end the 1778 alliance and the guarantee of French territory. The French were willing to grant this concession but only at the price of giving up the indemnities. On September 13, the American envoys agreed to postpone discussion of the indemnities, suspend the 1778 treaties, and simply restore normal relations. The two sides completed a draft on September 27 and signed the Provisional Treaty of Amity and Commerce on October 1. Bonaparte asked that the agreement be downgraded to a convention. The Convention of Mortefontaine, negotiated at Joseph Bonaparte's estate of the same name, was signed on October 3, 1800. The treaty did not exactly conform to instructions, but as Murray explained to the secretary of state, "it was our duty & for the honor & interest of the government & people of the United States, that we should agree to that treaty, rather than make none."[52]

The treaty was concluded too late to affect the presidential election of 1800. On May 1, the Republicans secured all of New York's twelve electoral votes. Adams learned of the results on May 3 and acted to distance himself from the Hamilton program. Adams cut off Hamilton's influence over military policy by demanding and receiving McHenry's resignation, replacing him with moderate Massachusetts Federalist Samuel Dexter. On May 10, Adams asked Pickering to resign. Pickering refused, and on May 12, 1800, Adams fired him. Adams appointed John Marshall as Pickering's replacement. This may have been Adams's attempt to distance himself from the domestic program, which fell under the secretary of state's jurisdiction. Marshall opposed the Alien and Sedition Acts, writing that they would do more harm than good. By 1800 Marshall was exactly the type of Federalist Adams wanted in his cabinet.[53]

The cabinet purge angered Hamilton to the point where he almost preferred to elect Jefferson than reelect Adams. "If we must have an enemy at the head of the Government, let it be one whom we can oppose," Hamilton wrote Sedgwick. Hamilton's true object was to swing the election to Adams's running mate, Charles Cotesworth Pinckney. Throughout the summer,

Hamilton distributed a private letter to Federalist leaders, cataloguing Adams's supposed faults. Hamilton condemned Adams's nomination of Murray as bad policy and bad form, as Adams had not consulted the cabinet. "When unhappily, an ordinary man dreams himself to be a FREDERICK and through vanity refrains from counselling with his constitutional advisers, he is apt to fall into the hands of miserable intriguers, with whom his self-love is more of ease, and who without difficulty slide into his confidence, and by flattering, govern him." Republican resurgence and a Federalist split denied Adams a second term. On December 3, 1800, South Carolina gave its eight votes to Thomas Jefferson and Aaron Burr, putting the two Republicans in a first place tie.[54]

On December 11, 1800, Davie arrived in the United States with a copy of the convention. Adams sent it to the Senate five days later. The convention stalled in the Federalist-controlled Senate and was rejected 16–14 on January 23, 1801. Political pressure from merchants led the Senate to reconsider. The Senate expunged article 2, which stated that the 1778 treaties were suspended, and finally approved the convention 22–9 on February 3, 1801, bringing the Quasi-War to a formal end a month before Adams left office. Hamilton believed the treaty was deeply flawed, but he supported ratification as the only way to save the Federalist party.[55]

To a keen student of British political history such as Adams, the end of the administration looked familiar. "We federalists are much in the situation of the party of Bolingbroke and Harley, after the treaty of Utrecht, completely and totally routed and defeated," Adams wrote to Benjamin Stoddert a few weeks after leaving office. Adams advised his youngest son to read *The Idea of a Patriot King* to see another instance where one party sought a war with France, "for the pretext to raise a regular army . . . for the purpose of Patronage and Influence." As the Bolingbrokean moment ended, Adams could himself take some solace in a passage from *The Idea of a Patriot King*. "It is true that a prince, who gives just reasons to expect that his reign will be that of a Patriot King, may not always meet, and from all persons, such returns as such expectations deserve," Bolingbroke wrote, "but they must not hinder either the prince from continuing to give them, or the people from continuing to acknowledge them."[56]

John Adams believed he had acted the part of a patriot president; the people, however, had not acknowledged it. "I shall leave the State with its coffers full, and the fair prospect of a peace with all the world smiling in its face," Adams remarked in his final months in office. He concluded that peace and neutrality depended on naval preparation. "We cannot, without committing a dangerous imprudence, abandon those measures of self-protection, which are adapted to our situation," he told Congress in his last annual message. As he left public office, he abandoned any hope that foreign policy based on the more idealistic elements of republican ideology could reform the world; for example, the small-navy principle that free ships make free goods had become part of republican ideology. If all nations adopted this principle, theoretically all naval wars would come to an end. "However desirable this may be to Humanity, how much soever Phylosophy may approve of it, and Christianity desire it," Adams wrote to Marshall, "I am clearly convinced that it will never take place." The United States could not rely on the goodwill of other nations, nor on the justice of its policies or the nature of its government, but only on the strength of its navy.[57] As president, Adams replaced the classical virtue embodied in the Model Treaty with the whig republican realpolitik described by Bolingbroke and confirmed by Adams's own diplomatic experience.

CHAPTER SEVEN

Yeoman Virtue and the Wilderness

If one were to pinpoint the moment Jefferson joined the opposition, it might be July 7, 1793. He had just read the second and third "Pacificus" essays, and he begged Madison to reply. "For god's sake my dear Sir, take up your pen, select the most striking heresies, and cut him to pieces in the face of the public." Jefferson's use of religious terminology describing his opponents and their ideas is instructive; the yeoman vision of republicanism he helped create and defend had risen to the level of religious faith, threatened by the "reign of witches" that was Federalist rule.[1]

The yeoman faith rested on three broad tenets. The first was that, despite all evidence to the contrary, the French Revolution represented the cause of liberty. "Genet is a madman but do not let us quarrel with his nation," Kentucky congressman George Nicholas wrote to James Madison. Long after the fact, Jefferson wrote of the "horrors of the French revolution" (which the Federalists used for their own purposes) and of "the atrocities of Robespierre." French excesses were merely bumps on the road to liberty. Furthermore, French military success was not dangerous to the United States. Republicanism trumped the balance of power. "We have every motive in America to pray for her success, not only from a general attachment to the liberties of mankind, but from a particular regard to our own," Madison wrote in 1793. A few months after leaving office, Jefferson argued that the United States should "make common cause" with France to guarantee her West Indian islands. Jefferson openly hoped for a French conquest of Great Britain. He had "little doubt of dining with Pichegru in London next autumn," and the chance to "hail the dawn of liberty and republicanism in that island" could convince Jefferson to cross the Atlantic.[2]

The second tenet was that the United States could use its economic power to coerce other nations, particularly Great Britain, without recourse to war. "War is not the best engine for us to resort to. Nature has given us one in our *commerce* which, if properly managed, will be better instrument for obliging the interested nations of Europe to treat us with justice," Jefferson wrote Pinckney at the beginning of the French crisis. In commercial terms, yeoman republicanism held that the United States was the stronger party. "We send necessaries to her," Madison argued during the British crisis. "She sends superfluities to us."[3]

The third tenet derived from the second. Commercial coercion had to be a substitute for war, because war was dangerous, if not fatal, to republics. "Perhaps it is a universal truth that the loss of liberty at home is to be charged agst. danger real or pretended from abroad," Madison wrote Jefferson. In 1799 Jefferson restated to Elbridge Gerry his opinion of the proper means of defense. He favored a militia and "such a naval force only as may protect our coasts and harbours." He opposed a standing army and a navy on the scale built by Adams. A standing army "may overawe the public sentiment," and a navy would drag the United States into war, which would "grind us with public burthens & sink us under them."[4]

Fear of executive power made Madison a strong opponent of Washington's policy toward France, on both constitutional and policy grounds. He denied that the president had the authority to declare neutrality without congressional approval. The president could not go further than a statement that the United States was at war or peace. "The right to decide the question [of peace or war] . . .," he wrote Jefferson in June 1793, "seems to me to be essentially & exclusively involved in the right of the Legislature, of declaring war in a time of peace, and in the P[resident]. & S[enate]. of making peace in time of war."[5]

Madison, writing as "Helvidius," responded to Hamilton in the *Gazette of the United States*. These essays constitute a definitive treatise on the yeoman constitutional theory of foreign relations. The Constitution left the question of control of foreign policy vague. Madison, who in the convention and in the *Federalist* essays clearly favored a prominent role for the legislature, resolved that question in favor of the legislature. As Madison pointed out in Federalist no. 41, the United States was physically removed from European politics. Therefore, the president's power to repel sudden attacks would not figure into the power to conduct foreign policy. Madison sought to reverse the British formula of diplomatic initiative. In Great Britain, war power belonged to the king. Yeoman theory feared the growth of executive power and sought to put the war power in as many hands as possible. Madison placed the power to decide on war with Congress and then expanded the war power to include all matters that could affect the decision between war and peace, that is, every aspect of foreign policy. Madison's formulation placed Congress at the beginning of the policy process, reducing the president's role to administration rather than formation of policy. Madison also linked legislative control to a reliance on international law. Madison had not expected the rise of the executive. "I see, and *politically feel* that will be the weak branch of the Government," Madison wrote to Edmund Randolph in 1789. Events had since proven otherwise.[6]

In his first "Helvidius" essay, Madison argued that a declaration of war was law and as such was the province of the legislature. "It is one of the most deliberative acts that can be performed, and when performed, has the effect of *repealling* all the *laws* operating in a state of peace, so far as they are inconsistent with a state of war." According to the Constitution, Madison continued, this power rested with Congress. He discounted the presidential power over the military as having no bearing on the questions of foreign policy. "Those who are to *conduct a war* cannot in the nature of things, be proper or safe judges, whether *a war ought* to be *commenced, continued, or concluded.*" In his second essay, Madison followed this theme to its logical conclusion. Congress had the right not only to declare war but also "to judge the causes of war," which implied that Congress, and not the president, should lead in making foreign policy. "The executive has no other discretion than to convene and give information to the legislature on occasions that may demand it," Madison wrote, "and whilst this discretion is duly exercised the trust of the executive is satisfied, and that department is not responsible for the consequences."[7]

Madison in his third essay directly attacked Hamilton's views regarding the French treaties. Citing such authorities as Vattel and Burlamaqui in his defense, Madison argued that the 1778 treaties remained in force despite the change in the French government. Like Jefferson, Madison saw the issue of the validity of the 1778 treaties through the lens of his approval of the French Revolution. Madison returned to the issues of legislative and executive power in his final two essays. "In no part of the constitution is more wisdom to be found than in the clause which confides the question of war or peace to the legislature, and not to the executive department," Madison wrote in "Helvidius" no. 4 and went on to repeat the argument "that the executive has no right, in any case to decide the question, to decide whether there is or is not cause for declaring war." Madison also repeated a central tenet of yeoman republicanism when he wrote that "the executive is the department of power most distinguished by its propensity to war." Madison attacked the Proclamation of Neutrality in his final essay, no. 5. "In exercising the Constitutional power of deciding a question of war, the Legislature ought to be as free to decide, according to its own sense of the public good, on one side or the other side." Washington's proclamation, he continued, was improper in this light.[8]

As the Republican leader in the House of Representatives, Madison took the lead on forming policy toward Great Britain. On January 3, 1794, he introduced resolutions recommending commercial discrimination against Great Britain, using the same arguments he had used five years before. "We stand with respect to the nation exporting those luxuries in the relation of an opulent individual to the labor in producing the superfluities, for his accommodation," he told the House of Representatives; "the former can do without those luxuries, the consumption of which gives bread to the latter." On January 23, Madison discounted the possibility of war, arguing that "every consideration of interest must prevent it." On March 25, the House of Representatives moved to stronger measures, taking up a sequestration of British debts and a non-importation act. The Committee of the Whole approved non-importation on April 15. Madison complained to Jefferson that the appointment of Jay as envoy extraordinary "has had the effect of impeding all legislative measures for extorting redress from G.B." Jefferson agreed. "A more degrading measure could not have been proposed," he wrote to Monroe. Jefferson shared Madison's belief that a non-importation act would more likely bring a settlement than war. "My opinion of the British government," he wrote Washington, "is that nothing will force them to do justice but the loud voice of their people, and this can never be excited but by destroying their commerce."[9]

Madison and Jefferson opposed the Jay Treaty from the beginning, but there was little either could do, as member of the House of Representatives and private citizen, beyond public and private criticism. By signing the treaty the United States "relapsed into some dependence" on Great Britain, Madison argued in his pamphlet *Political Observations*. He continued to oppose the treaty after its ratification. He summed up Republican anger in a draft petition, writing that the treaty "is in its present form unworthy the voluntary acceptance of an Independent people, and is not dictated to them by the circumstances in which providence has kindly placed them." The treaty turned Jefferson against diplomacy itself. Jefferson had not decided if the United States needed no treaties, but certainly "we should be better without any such as this." Jefferson told Senator Henry Tazewell that "acquiescence under insult is not the way to escape war."[10]

As in 1793, Madison took the lead in presenting the Jeffersonian view to the public. He attacked the treaty both as bad policy and as a violation of the Constitution. He drafted a petition to the Virginia General Assembly in which he argued that the treaty interfered with the power of Congress to regulate commerce. When the House of Representatives convened in December 1795, Madison observed to Monroe that there was, "a clear *majority who disapprove the treaty* but it *will dwindle* under the *influence of causes well known* to you." Hoping to soften opposition, Washington submitted Pinckney's Treaty with Spain (which secured the right of deposit at New Orleans) to the Senate at the same time the House took up the appropriations needed to carry out the Jay Treaty. In the House, the Federalists played on the fear of war if the United States did not approve the appropriations.[11]

Jefferson had complete confidence that the House of Representatives would scuttle a treaty he considered "nothing more than a treaty of alliance between England and the Anglomen of this country against the legislature and people of the United states." In March 1796, Madison led the attack on the treaty's constitutionality. The congressional power over appropriations placed the treaty before the House of Representatives, but Madison continued to base his arguments on the congressional war power. He joined in the demand that Washington deliver all of the papers connected with the treaty, and when the president refused, Madison complained that Washington had interfered with Congress's right to ask for such information.[12] Madison believed that the Jay Treaty made the treaty-making power of the Senate and president superior to the war powers of Congress. The Constitution, he asserted, made the treaty power subordinate to the war power. He argued that the Jay Treaty was essentially an alliance with a power at war, and the treaty could drag the United States into the war without congressional approval. The United States could send troops around the world, or keep a standing army at home in peacetime, all as a result of the abuse of the treaty-making power. "Under this aspect," Madison argued, "the Treaty power would be tremendous indeed." The Federalists would make the "Treaty power in a manner omnipotent," he charged, and this interpretation of the treaty power was "inadmissible, in a Constitution marked throughout with limitations & checks."[13] Madison attacked the provisions of the treaty in April. The treaty endangered American interests in the Northwest by allowing the British to take part in the Indian trade, and it completely reversed American policy by acceding to the British interpretation of neutral rights and by rejecting "free ships, free goods." In the end Madison urged the House of Representatives to reject the appropriations needed to implement the treaty. The Committee of the Whole voted 50–49 in favor of implementation on April 29, 1796. The next day the House passed the appropriations 51–48.[14]

Jefferson and Madison anticipated that settlement with Great Britain would bring conflict with France. They differed over whether Adams could resolve it successfully. Madison wrote Jefferson that "an awful scene appears to be opening upon us." He expected that war would be "the fruit of the British Treaty." Jefferson was willing to give his old partner in independence the benefit of the doubt. Jefferson believed that Adams was "detached from Hamilton." Adams did not want war with France, nor would he "truckle to England as servilely as has been done."[15]

Jefferson's hopes for Adams soon vanished. After Jefferson told the president that Madison would not accept an appointment to France and the president told Jefferson the cabinet had already rejected Madison, the two did not speak again. The president, Jefferson recorded, "returned to his former party views." Jefferson considered Adams's speech of May 16, 1797, an attempt to talk the country into war. Gerry's presence on the peace commission was Jefferson's only reason for hope, and he implored Gerry to make peace with France. Madison fully expected that Adams would "go indirectly to war, by using the frigates as convoys and arming private vessels of which the owners & mariners will often be British subjects under American colours." Madison compared Adams unfavorably to Washington, with Adams "taking as great pains to get into war, as [Washington] took to keep out of it."[16]

If France represented the cause of liberty and the Federalists the leading edge of monarchism, France was blameless. Jefferson considered Adams's speech of March 19, 1798, "almost insane" and believed it "the only obstacle to negociation." Jefferson also blamed the merchants engaged in the carrying trade, who needed "the lottery of war to get themselves to rights." Madison considered Adams's speech a product of the president's well-known "violent passions" and further proof of the whig doctrine that "the Ex. is the branch of power most interested in war & most prone to it." With the president and the Senate in complete control of foreign policy, "it is evident that the people are cheated out of the best ingredients in their Govt. the safeguards of peace which is the greatest of their blessings."[17]

The particulars of the XYZ Affair had no influence on the yeoman theory. To Jefferson the XYZ Affair was a "delusion," or a "dish cooked up by Marshall, where the swindlers are made to appear as the French government." Even when Jefferson admitted to Archibald Stuart that France had given cause for war, he added that the British treated the United States no better. Madison did not consider Talleyrand's actions cause for war, but he fully expected the Federalists to use them as such.[18]

In the fall of 1798, Madison and Jefferson helped the Virginia and Kentucky legislatures draft responses to the Alien and Sedition Acts. Jefferson's draft of the Kentucky Resolutions declared the acts unconstitutional, as Congress could punish only certain acts and the president had no constitutional authority to evict aliens, who were under the jurisdiction of the states in which they resided. Jefferson concluded that "nullification of the act is the rightful remedy." The Kentucky legislature dropped the word "nullification." Madison's Virginia Resolutions did not go quite as far. Madison did declare that the acts were unconstitutional, but he advocated no action beyond sending the resolutions to other states.[19]

Madison expanded on the Virginia Resolutions in his Report of 1800, which he wrote as a member of the Virginia House of Delegates. By 1800 Madison had moved closer to Jefferson's view of the powers of the union. "The constitution of the United States was formed by a sanction of the states, given by each in its sovereign capacity," he asserted, using an argument he had rejected thirteen years before. The states therefore had a right to determine whether the Constitution had been violated and to decide which issues "may be of sufficient magnitude as to require their interposition." Madison went on, "Consolidation of the states into one sovereignty, would be to transform the republican system of the United States into a monarchy," and he opposed the Alien and Sedition Acts on those grounds. The acts concentrated power in the hands of the president. The states had not only a right to declare acts unconstitutional but also a right to coordinate efforts among the several states. By 1800 Madison was willing to give the states a greater role in national affairs than he had favored in 1787, a shift dictated by the need to preserve republican government. The doctrine of state interposition may be seen as the reverse side of the negative on state laws.[20]

In 1799 Madison wrote an anonymous essay, "Political Reflections," that summed up the yeoman fear of Federalist diplomacy. He argued that *"the fetters imposed on liberty at home have ever been forged out of the weapons provided for the defence against real, pretended, or imaginary dangers from abroad."* Jefferson noted the damage done to agrarianism, writing that the United States had gone "navigation mad, and commerce mad, and navy mad, which is worst of all." When in power Jefferson and Madison planned on a diplomacy that favored agriculture over shipping, and commercial coercion over armies and navies. Jefferson and Madison never abandoned the reformative aspects of republican diplomacy. It had not failed for them in the 1790s; it merely had not been tried. The Federalists were the main block on yeoman diplomacy. In 1799 Jefferson wrote to Edmund Pendleton that if Massachusetts could "emerge from the deceptions under which they are kept by their clergy, lawyers & English presses, our salvation would be sure & easy."[21]

Madison and Jefferson fully expected American agricultural produce to act as the republican sword and shield against monarchy at home and abroad. However, yeoman diplomacy depended for success on the other nations of Europe acting in ways that allowed the United States the luxury of ideological purity. Whig diplomacy put no such expectations on the world. Eight years in the wilderness shaped the mature form of yeoman diplomacy. The next sixteen years in power demonstrated how yeoman diplomacy would collapse when Great Britain, Spain, and France did not act out the roles that Jefferson and Madison planned for them.

PRESIDENT JEFFERSON AND SENATOR WILLIAM PLUMER of New Hampshire identified the weakness in the yeoman vision during a conversation they had in 1806. Plumer wrote in his memoranda, "[I] observed that our form of government appeared to me better calculated for the regulation of our own internal concerns than to regulate our relations with other nations." Jefferson agreed, believing that "our constitution is a peace establishment — It is not calculated for war. War would endanger its existence." The yeoman virtue at the heart of Jefferson and Madison's republicanism and diplomacy promised a way out of war. Jefferson and Madison believed the farmer at his plow was the model republican citizen, and the safest tool of diplomacy. Agricultural production would achieve diplomatic goals without recourse to weapons more dangerous to republican government.[22]

The diplomacy of yeoman virtue saw the American advantage in a combination of the reliance on personal virtue in classical republicanism and the whig reliance on institutions and geography. Each would prevent war with a European power. In his first inaugural address, Jefferson called the American people "too high-minded to endure the degradations of the others." More important, the United States was "separated by nature and a wide ocean from the exterminating havoc of one quarter of the globe," with "room enough for our descendants to the thousandth generation." The United States wanted "peace, commerce and honest friendship with all nations, entangling alliances with none."[23]

Yeoman diplomacy ruled out what whig diplomacy considered normal military preparations. Albert Gallatin argued that "pretended tax-preparations and army-preparations against contingent wars tend only to encourage wars." Jefferson agreed. "Were armies to be raised whenever a speck of war is visible in our horizon, we never should have been without them," he told Congress in 1806. In his first annual message, Jefferson recommended a militia for defense. He considered diplomacy itself an excuse to raise taxes and multiply offices. He cheered the reduction of the diplomatic corps in 1801 and looked forward to letting "every treaty drop off without renewal."[24]

The yeoman vision saw the possibility of universal liberty, with the United States in the lead. "It is impossible not to be sensible that we are acting for all mankind," Jefferson wrote in 1802. After Napoleon's coup in 1799, the brotherhood of republics disappeared, and Jefferson and Madison came to believe that liberty could be achieved more easily in territories influenced or controlled by the United States. In January 1803, Jefferson announced a policy of "preparing [the Indians] ultimately to participate in the benefits of our Government." The French inhabitants of Louisiana would also have to be trained for liberty, and Madison "expected that every blessing of liberty will be extended to them as fast as they shall be prepared and disposed to receive it." Jefferson considered "our new citizens" to be "as incapable of self government as children."[25]

The productive power of the yeoman farmer and Europe's need for that production would permit the United States to achieve its ends without using unrepublican methods. The United States would avoid war "even in support of principles which we mean to pursue," Jefferson wrote Thomas Paine; "We believe we can enforce those principles as to ourselves by peaceful means, now that we are likely to have our public councils free of foreign views." The peaceful method was, of course, to use trade as a reward and punishment. With trade, the United States would avoid both war and the normal course of diplomacy. In his third annual message, Jefferson argued that "with productions and wants which render our commerce and friendship useful to them and theirs to us, it cannot be the interest of any to assail us, nor ours to disturb them." Madison saw a more aggressive use of trade. "Indeed, if a commercial weapon can be properly shaped for the Executive hand," he wrote in 1805, "it is more and more apparent to me that it can force all the nations having colonies in this quarter of the globe, to respect our rights."[26]

Jefferson and Madison unwittingly staked the survival of republican government on events they could not control. Both assumed that national interests, like human nature, were fixed—and fixed in a way that benefited the United States. Spain would recognize its own military and political weakness and would submit to American demands. Great Britain would recognize its economic weakness, depending on the United States to buy British manufactures and feed British colonies, and would follow the Spanish lead. France would act as the friend of the United States to prevent American friendship with Great Britain. For his part, Madison expected greater reason from nations than he did from the American people. He had no direct experience (as John Adams had) to make him believe otherwise; there was no foreign-policy equivalent of his electoral defeat of 1777. Jefferson's own experience in diplomacy might have shown the weakness of yeoman diplomacy, but he interpreted this experience to mean that the yeoman theory had never been given a fair test, especially in the Federalist years. The republican realpolitik of yeoman diplomacy rested more on republicanism than on realpolitik. Jefferson and Madison succeeded when the world acted, or appeared to act, as they expected. They failed when the vagaries of diplomacy did not conform to the yeoman theoretical model.

The two diplomatic issues that shaped the yeoman vision—control of the Mississippi River and trade with Europe and its colonies—best reveal the connection between republican ideology and diplomacy. Had the French Revolution not intervened, Jefferson would likely have spent most of his term as secretary of state dealing with Spain and the Mississippi valley. His report of March 18, 1792, foreshadowed his policy as president. Jefferson claimed a right under the law of nations to navigate the entire length of the Mississippi, even where it flowed between Spanish banks. Jefferson considered free navigation "essential to the interests of both parties." Pinckney's Treaty had temporarily settled the Mississippi question in 1795, and it promised to do so as long as Spain owned Louisiana. As Rufus King put it, the Spanish were "quiet neighbours" and posed little threat to American interests. Then Napoleon Bonaparte decided to use Louisiana in combination with the reconquest of St. Domingo as the basis for a new French empire in North America. French and Spanish negotiators concluded the Treaty of St. Ildefonso on October 1, 1800, in which Spain ceded Louisiana and six warships to France in exchange for an Italian kingdom for the Duke of Parma. France was not to take possession of Louisiana until it had delivered the Italian territory. The retrocession of Louisiana combined with the signing of the Peace of Amiens between France and Great Britain on March 27, 1802, promised to give France a free hand in North America.[27]

Soon after the secret Treaty of St. Ildefonso was signed, rumors of its conclusion circulated among European diplomats. In late March 1801, Rufus King wrote from London that Spain had ceded Louisiana and the Floridas to France. Two months later, Madison wrote that "intelligence has come thro' several channels, which makes it probable that Louisiana has been ceded to France." Jefferson feared the worst. Previously he had considered France the nation least likely to cause trouble for the United States, as France held no territory in North America. He called New Orleans the "one single spot, the possessor of which is our natural and habitual enemy." If France had New Orleans, Jefferson wrote to Robert R. Livingston, minister to France, that would be the day the United States would ally with Great Britain. To avoid this event, Jefferson asked his friend Pierre S. DuPont de Nemours to lobby the French government to cede New Orleans and the Floridas to the United States. The Floridas were as important as the port of New Orleans itself. "Whatever power, other than ourselves, holds the country east of the Mississippi becomes our natural enemy," the president warned DuPont de Nemours. Madison wrote Livingston in October 1802 that if he could acquire New Orleans and the Floridas "the happiest of issues will be given to one of the most perplexing occurrences."[28]

Spain suspended the American right of deposit at New Orleans on October 18, 1802, which led the Jefferson administration to conclude that neither France nor Spain was a safe neighbor. If the United States did not own New Orleans, then Europe's wars would engulf North America. "We shall get entangled in European politics, and more, be much less happy and prosperous," Jefferson warned Monroe; "This can only be prevented by a successful issue to your present mission." For France or Spain, the price of peace was the cession of New Orleans. Otherwise, within two years the owner would face two hundred thousand American militia who would not hesitate to defend their rights.[29]

Madison and Jefferson agreed that anything threatening American access to the Mississippi threatened the survival of republican government in two ways. First, permanent closure of New Orleans would force United States prematurely into manufactures in the East and would detach the West from the union. Second, the United States might have to force the port open through war, which would bring armies, debts, and foreign entanglements. To the westerners, the Mississippi was "the Hudson, the Delaware, the Potomac and all the navigable rivers of the atlantic States formed into one stream," Madison wrote to Pinckney.[30] Officially, Madison argued that the West was fully attached to the union and would not throw in with France to protect its interests. Madison also believed that all sections agreed on the importance of the Mississippi, with the only dispute being over "the degree of patience which ought to be exercised during the appeal to friendly modes of redress."[31] The union had come too close to collapse over the same issue in the 1780s for Madison to be completely confident. "We are fully aware of the tendency of the reported Cession of Louisiana, to plant in our neighbourhood troubles of different kinds, and to prepare the way for very serious events," Madison wrote to Rufus King in London. "A mere neighbourhood could not be friendly to the harmony which both countries [France and the United States] have so much an interest in cherishing," he wrote to Livingston on May 1, 1802, "but if a possession of the mouth of the Mississippi is to be added to the other causes of discord, the worst events are to be apprehended." Madison instructed Livingston to "spare no effort" to determine the extent of the retrocession and to convince France to cede New Orleans and the Floridas to the United States. Madison issued similar instructions to Charles Pinckney, minister to Spain, in case Spain still owned the Floridas. Madison proposed to make the Mississippi "a common boundary, with a common use of its navigation, for [the United States] and Spain."[32]

For the Republicans, some sort of purchase was a policy better suited to republican government than the military solution advocated by some

Federalists, including Hamilton. On February 16, 1803, Senator James Ross, a Pennsylvania Federalist, sponsored a resolution authorizing the president to call up the militia and appropriate $5 million for an expedition against New Orleans whenever the president deemed it necessary. Madison believed that the resolution "drove at war thro' a delegation of unconstitutional power to the Executive." Madison was as unwilling in 1803 as he was in 1793 to use the president's role as commander in chief to formulate foreign policy. Jefferson believed the Federalists were more interested in finding an excuse to create an army than in acquiring New Orleans.[33]

As long as France was at peace with Great Britain, Bonaparte was intent on building his American empire. In September 1802, Livingston reported to Madison that his attempts to discuss New Orleans were "premature" and that France planned to take possession of Louisiana. The defeat of the French army in St. Domingo and the ice-choked French ports that prevented resupply made Bonaparte more willing to sell. The prospect of renewed war with Great Britain further motivated the French consul. Livingston sought to take advantage of the situation in January 1803, when he again offered to buy New Orleans and the Floridas. He added a buffer zone north of the Arkansas River, becoming the first negotiator to suggest a cession of land west of the Mississippi.[34]

While trying to purchase New Orleans, Jefferson planned to win the race to the Mississippi valley. Soon after Spain closed New Orleans, Jefferson planned a reconnaissance mission to the west bank of the Mississippi (which would become the Lewis and Clark expedition) and for the purchase of land from the Indians on the east bank. The president unveiled this policy in a confidential message to Congress on January 18, 1803. He hoped to induce the Indians to settle on farms and sell excess land to the United States. Furthermore, he planned to license traders who would undercut private merchants and ensure peaceful relations. It was a project similar to the military colonies proposed in Jefferson's instructions to George Rogers Clark in 1780. As Jefferson explained to William Henry Harrison of the Indiana Territory, he wanted to purchase excess land and to plant settlements on the Mississippi as a hedge against the French occupation of Louisiana. In the spring of 1803, Jefferson sent troops and arms to strategic points along the Mississippi and to Fort Adams, near New Orleans.[35]

In January 1803, Jefferson appointed James Monroe as special envoy to assist in negotiations. Madison issued instructions on March 2, directing Monroe and Livingston to purchase New Orleans and the Floridas, with no mention of acquiring land to the west of the Mississippi. As a fallback position, if France would not sell New Orleans, Madison advised the envoys to secure free navigation of the rivers of West Florida. By mid-April Bonaparte was prepared to sell all of Louisiana, which he believed to be worthless without New Orleans, in order to prevent an Anglo-American alliance. On April 30, 1803, French and American negotiators concluded an agreement in which the United States was to pay $15 million for all of French Louisiana. The envoys signed formal agreements on May 2 and 9. Borders were not defined precisely, nor were the Floridas specifically mentioned, although Monroe later recalled that the Americans understood the cession to include territory west of the Perdido River. In any case, the French project for an American empire was at an end.[36]

To the Republicans, the only problem with the Louisiana Purchase was the lack of any explicit constitutional sanction to purchase territory. Most of the constitutional handwringing, curiously, came after the purchase was complete. In January 1803, Attorney General Levi Lincoln proposed to add New Orleans and the Floridas to the Mississippi Territory and Georgia. As a resident of Massachusetts, Lincoln saw a political difficulty in adding new slave states, but none in making existing slave states bigger. Albert Gallatin disagreed. He did not think the Constitution conferred a power to enlarge existing states any more than it did to enlarge the entire union. Without enthusiasm Gallatin recommended an interpretation of the treaty power that included the purchase of territory.[37]

The news that Livingston and Monroe had purchased all of Louisiana revived the constitutional issue. Jefferson appears to have considered everything east of the Mississippi as within the bounds of the United States, but territory west of the Mississippi required a special arrangement. In July 1803, Jefferson drafted an amendment that made Louisiana part of the union, prohibited the admission of states north of the Arkansas River without another amendment, and provided for the eventual admission of Florida. "Let us not make it [the Constitution] a blank page by construction," Jefferson warned Wilson Cary Nicholas. Madison's draft stated that Louisiana would become a part of the United States and that Congress could incorporate "other adjacent territories which shall be justly acquired." Madison also provided for the severance of any part of the territory with the consent of the voting inhabitants. The United States had a deadline of October 30 to ratify the treaty, otherwise Napoleon would likely withdraw it. There was no time to amend the Constitution. Republicans in the Senate embraced the idea of implied powers and ratified the treaty.[38]

Jefferson, in his third annual message, attributed the Louisiana Purchase to French wisdom and his own policies. "The enlightened government of France" properly recognized what would serve the interests of both nations. He dismissed the notion that luck or random chance played the greatest role in the purchase, directing his critics to look into the War Department's files from April 1801 to April 1802 to see the preparations made on the east bank of the Mississippi to ensure that the United States would be ready in the event of a renewed European war. "We did not by our intrigues produce the war," Jefferson wrote to Horatio Gates, "but we availed ourselves of it when it happened." One of Jefferson's most sympathetic biographers agreed with Jefferson's assessment, arguing that the president "played the game [of strategic procrastination] to perfection."[39]

Republican policy demonstrated the preeminence of ideological republicanism in the republican realpolitik. A republican political economy depended on American control of New Orleans. Jefferson and Madison formed a policy to purchase the city when the policy had no chance of success and kept it in place until conditions were right for it to work. Jefferson and Madison based their policy on Spanish weakness and French friendship, which would operate in favor of the United States. This strategy worked in Louisiana, but it would not work in West Florida.

"The annexation of Louisiana was an event so portentous as to defy measurement; it gave a new force to politics, and ranked in historical importance next to the Declaration of Independence and the adoption of the Constitution,—events of which it was the logical outcome," wrote Henry Adams, himself no admirer of Jefferson or Madison.[40] More recent commentators have also seen the Louisiana Purchase as the end result of Madison's political philosophy. Ralph Ketcham wrote that, by doubling the size of the nation, Madison provided more land for yeoman farmers. The Louisiana Purchase was, therefore, "perfectly suited [to] Republican political and social theory." Such an analysis, however, reads history backward, by assuming that Federalist no. 10 was a call for expansion and that Madison intended to acquire all of Louisiana. Certainly Madison approved the purchase, but for him the main problem was securing the navigation of the Mississippi River. Like Madison, Jefferson saw no limits to the size of the republic. "But who can limit the extent to which the federative principle may operate effectively?" Jefferson asked Congress in 1805. "The larger our association the less it will be shaken by local passions." Yet the union of the whole continent was unnecessary. "Whether we remain in one confederacy," Jefferson wrote to Priestly, "or form into Atlantic and Mississippi confederacies, I believe not very important to the happiness of either part."[41]

Reading history backward distorts not only the study of the Louisiana Purchase but also its epilogue, the pursuit of West Florida. To some, West Florida was a grand psychic crisis; the white whale that haunted Jefferson and Madison. Henry Adams called West Florida Jefferson's "overmastering passion." Tucker and Hendrickson saw Jefferson's frustration at not acquiring West Florida in the first place as the mainspring of Republican policy and that this frustration outweighed the actual value of the territory. In terms of size, West Florida was insignificant compared to a purchase that doubled the size of the United States. Yet its location made it vital. Jefferson and Madison believed that republican government depended on American access to the Mississippi. West Florida bordered not only the Mississippi but New Orleans itself. Possession of West Florida meant absolute control of the Mississippi; without this the vast tracts of land beyond the Mississippi meant nothing. For this reason, Jefferson flatly refused to give up any territory that would allow Spain access to the Mississippi.[42]

Madison shared Jefferson's desire to secure the Floridas, as well as his reluctance to give up lands west of the Mississippi River. Spanish possession of West Florida, bordering New Orleans, prevented American control of the mouth of the Mississippi and threatened to drag the United States into a European war. Both Monroe and Livingston considered West Florida a part of the Louisiana Purchase. Madison's instructions to Monroe of July 29, 1803, fifteen days after receipt of the purchase treaty, listed the Floridas as the main objective. Madison wrote that Monroe should not trade western territory, as it was potentially too valuable to the United States, and West Florida was worthless to France or Spain without New Orleans. In 1804 Madison warned Monroe and Pinckney not to make any agreement that allowed Spain back onto the banks of the Mississippi.[43]

The Jefferson administration was convinced that the United States already owned West Florida according to the terms of both the retrocession to France and the American purchase. In 1762 France had ceded its territory east of the Mississippi River, excluding the island of New Orleans, to Great Britain. At the same time, France ceded New Orleans and the land west of the Mississippi River to Spain. The British had divided Florida into two provinces at the Perdido River. The British cession of the Floridas to Spain in 1783 reunited the old French province of Louisiana. Under the treaty of St. Ildefonso, Spain ceded Louisiana as it existed in 1762, which the Americans understood to include territory extending to the Perdido River. Jefferson studied the relevant treaties himself to reach this conclusion. The French government did not explicitly say whether the Louisiana Purchase included West Florida. Jefferson denied any hostility against Spain. "We want nothing of *hers* & we want no nation to possess what is hers," he wrote to the American minister to Spain.[44]

Through Madison's first term as president, the Floridas were the main focus of the Republicans' Spanish diplomacy. Madison revived the arguments he had used against Spain in the 1780s, that the rise of American power could not be stopped. Madison was unable to understand why Spain did not see that its best interests were to give up the Floridas. "*The Spanish Government must understand in fact that the United States can never consider the amiable relations between Spain and them as definitively and permanently secured, without an* arrangement on this subject," Madison wrote to Monroe on July 29, 1803. Madison's instructions to Charles Pinckney, written the same day, are similar in tone, arguing that the United States would eventually possess the Floridas, and Spain would be wise to bow to the inevitable. The Floridas revived Madison's twenty-year quarrel with what he saw as Spanish stubbornness. "What is it that Spain dreads?" Madison wrote to Pinckney, using the same language and arguments as in his 1785 letter to Lafayette:

> She dreads, it is presumed, the growing power of this country, and the direction of it against her possessions within its [the United States'] reach. Can she annihilate this power? No. Can she sensibly retard its growth? No. Does not common prudence then advise her, to conciliate by every proof of friendship and confidence the good will of a nation whose power is formidable to her; instead of yielding to the impulses of jealousy, and adopting obnoxious precautions, which can have no other effect than to bring on prematurely the whole weight of the Calamity which she fears.

Alexander Hamilton would have seized West Florida outright. John Adams would have prepared to seize the territory while giving Spain a chance to surrender it. Republican fear of executive power left Jefferson and Madison with few alternatives beyond waiting for France and Spain to see reason, which they defined as acceding to American wishes. In November 1803, Congress passed the Mobile Act, which extended American revenue laws to the territory acquired from France and gave the president the power to create a customs district for Mobile, even though that port fell within the disputed area with Spain.[45]

When France took Spain's side on its West Florida claim, Madison could not understand why France would pursue a policy that "might end in placing the United States on the side of Great Britain." French hostility forced Jefferson to play a dangerous card, a potential alliance with Great Britain. Jefferson suggested it to Madison in a letter of August 7, 1805. Madison responded on August 20, agreeing in theory. In practice, however, he saw no chance of a treaty that would not commit the United States to Great Britain's wars. Jefferson believed that "hostile and treacherous intentions against us on the part of France" left no other choice.[46]

On August 27, 1805, the president expanded on his plan to offer an alliance to Great Britain. The alliance would be conditional on the United States going to war with France or Spain during the present war in Europe. Fear of such an alliance would lead France and Spain to make the necessary concessions to avoid it. There would be no war and therefore no activation of the alliance. Great Britain would accept the potential alliance out of a supposed desire to see the English-speaking world united against France. Jefferson's proposal demonstrates how the diplomacy of classical and yeoman virtue matched each other. In 1776 John Adams believed the promise of American friendship and the fear of American enmity would be sufficient diplomatic tools. As classical virtue turned to whig virtue, Adams gave up on this idea, but Jefferson never did. If the yeoman thesis was not true, the United States would be forced to resort to a military structure that yeoman theory considered fatal to liberty. Madison shared the assumptions of yeoman virtue, but even he did not believe Great Britain would sign an alliance with little or nothing in return. Madison believed that an arrangement with Great Britain might be necessary to secure West Florida, but the price—either a mutual guarantee of territory or concessions on neutral trade—would be much too high.[47]

Even without a cost-free British alliance, Jefferson hoped that the expanding war in Europe would bring a settlement. "This gives us our great desideratum, time," the president wrote to Madison. Jefferson fell back on the theory that war would force the great powers to bid for American neutrality. He proposed to work through France, assuming that Spain would do what France told it to and that France would see its interest in acting as a friend of the United States. The cession of the Floridas would guarantee peace with the United States. On November 12, 1805, the cabinet agreed to ask for the Floridas and to set the western boundary of Louisiana at the Colorado River of Texas, ceding the claim of Texas to the Rio Grande. The United States would offer $5 million up front, $4 million of which would come back in spoliation claims.[48]

Two days later Madison received a letter from John Armstrong, the minister to France, detailing a September meeting with an unidentified French agent, who had presented a proposal in Talleyrand's handwriting in which the United States would pay $10 million and receive the Floridas, and threatening war if Spain disagreed. Spain and the United States should agree to the Colorado River of Texas as the boundary and a thirty-league neutral zone on either side. Armstrong balked at the price, which the agent lowered to $7 million. Jefferson and the cabinet leapt at the agreement.[49] Presumably, Jefferson should have known better than to accept at face value the promises of anonymous French agents, or of Talleyrand himself. Yet France now played the role Jefferson and Madison had assigned it, the constant friend of the United States, and could threaten force when the United States could not. The French offer had to be genuine if the United States was to avoid war.

In February 1806 Congress passed the Two Million Dollar Act, which officially provided $2 million for unspecified diplomatic expenses. In reality, the money was intended to buy the Floridas from Spain. The act passed by a wide margin, but it created a rift in the Republican party. John Randolph of Roanoke, hitherto one of Jefferson's staunchest supporters, henceforth became one of his sharpest critics, charging that the act was little more than a bribe and beneath the dignity of a republic.[50]

Spanish intransigence led Jefferson to consider war. Spain would not give up the Floridas, and France would not back up the United States. By the end of 1806, Jefferson believed that "with Spain we shall have blows; but they will hasten, instead of preventing a peaceable settlement." In 1807 Jefferson still counted on "the friendship of the emperor [Napoleon]," who would force Spain to give up the Floridas "or abandon her to us." If Spain stood alone, its defeat was certain. "We ask but one month to be in possession of the city of Mexico," Jefferson boasted. Jefferson's new eagerness to use force came not only from his frustration with Spain but also from his belief that any war with Spain would be short and completely victorious. A war would not be long enough to create a permanent army, nor would it add significantly to the debt, and it would not endanger republican government.[51]

By 1807 the maritime crisis with Great Britain overshadowed Florida, which remained an unanswered question well into Madison's presidency. External events promised to work in Madison's favor. The Spanish Empire collapsed in 1810. Most of Spain's American provinces moved toward independence, and West Florida was among them. American settlers dominated the West Florida legislature and on September 26, 1810, proclaimed the Republic of West Florida. This solved the constitutional problems of annexing new territory and incorporating new citizens into the union. On October 10, the new republic asked to be annexed by the United States. Madison had closely watched the developments of the summer of 1810. On July 17 the president advised Secretary of State Robert Smith that Governor David Holmes of Mississippi Territory should monitor events. "It would be well for him also to be attentive to the means of having his Militia in a state for any service that may be called for," Madison wrote, believing that European interference was the greatest danger. When the West Florida government asked for annexation, it gave Madison the chance to act without appearing to overstep the bounds of executive authority. Madison wrote on October 19 that he expected the West Floridians to call for help from either Great Britain or the United States. After receiving communications from Baton Rouge, Madison issued a secret proclamation on October 27, 1810, informing Congress of his intention to occupy West Florida from the Mississippi to the Perdido.[52]

Madison hoped that the same circumstances that delivered West Florida into American hands would work in East Florida as well. On January 3, 1811, Madison asked Congress for the power to annex East Florida if the residents of that province asked him to do so. Congress, complying with Madison's request, authorized George Mathews and John McKee to occupy East Florida under certain circumstances: specifically if an insurgent movement overthrew the Spanish government and asked for American intervention or in response to British interference. In March 1812, Mathews responded to an uprising on Amelia Island by invading the island. Madison believed that Mathews had acted prematurely, and he disapproved of Mathews's attempts to stir up a revolt, writing that "Mathews has been playing a strange comedy, in the face of common sense, as well as of his instructions." Madison disavowed Mathews's conduct, and he had Secretary of State Monroe send official notification.[53]

The Florida episode revealed two elements of Madison's diplomacy: first, that in dealing with European power his version of republican diplomacy limited executive action and tended to be overtaken by events, and second, that his conception of how nations should act had not moved beyond the belief that nations would act purely in their own interests. Madison defined those interests in terms of acceding to American wishes, which led him to overestimate the diplomatic value of American friendship to France and Spain. Fortune had turned in favor of the United States with the Louisiana Purchase, but it was of little help in acquiring the Floridas.

Nothing in the history of the Louisiana Purchase and the subsequent annexation of West Florida told Jefferson or Madison that the yeoman theory was mistaken. If it was, a republican diplomacy was impossible. They believed France had acted as the friend of the United States in 1803 by ceding New Orleans. After a fashion, Spanish weakness permitted the annexation of West Florida. Preparation for these events could be likened to standing by with a bucket to be ready when the apples fell off the tree. Yet the desire to conquer without war, and to score diplomatic victories with a minimum of diplomacy, left much to chance. The maritime crisis with Great Britain, which ran concurrently with the Louisiana and West Florida episodes, demonstrated what happened when the yeoman machine completely broke down.

CHAPTER EIGHT

Yeoman Virtue at Sea

The yeoman ambivalence about commerce, and particularly the idea of an American carrying trade, was never far from the surface. The third president betrayed no state secrets when he told British diplomat Augustus John Foster "that he wished the United States had never possessed a single ship." Jefferson preferred that other nations carry American goods. "He would," Foster recorded in his journal, "have laid the American ports open to all the world, let foreigners dispute, if they liked it, which should supply at the cheapest rate the richest agricultural market in the universe." In his first inaugural address in March 1801, Jefferson called for the "encouragement of agriculture, and of commerce as its handmaid." Clearly, agriculture was to be the dominant interest. "Agriculture, manufactures, commerce and navigation, the four pillars of our prosperity, are the most thriving when left most free to individual enterprise," Jefferson told Congress in December 1801. Of course, both Jefferson and Madison believed that free trade would favor agriculture over the other branches of the economy.[1]

In the 1780s Jefferson speculated that, in the event of war between Great Britain and France, the United States would assume most of the neutral trade. Both Jefferson and Madison expected that such a situation would be temporary. Eventually other nations would reclaim neutral trade, and the American share would never grow so great as to divert the United States from agriculture. "On the restoration of peace in Europe, that portion of the general carrying trade which had fallen to our share during the war, was abridged by the returning competition of the belligerent powers," Jefferson told Congress in 1802; "This was to be expected, and was just." With the revival of war, non-American neutral shipping vanished from the Atlantic and the United States assumed more of the world's carrying trade. American freight values jumped from $6 million in 1790 to over $40 million on the eve of the Embargo. The value of the reexport trade, the trade at the heart of the British crisis, increased between four and ten times. Yeoman diplomacy supported an American shipping industry only large enough to carry American goods to market; most of the new carrying trade was, in John Randolph's words, a "fungus of war," which put the agricultural mass of the country at the mercy of the port cities of the East Coast. The carrying trade presented a dreadful paradox for yeoman diplomacy. If the United States gave up neutral trade, it would submit to Great Britain as mistress of the high seas and sacrifice American independence. If the United States defended its absolute right to the neutral trade, it risked war with Great Britain, which would bring taxes, debts, navies, armies, and eventually monarchy.[2]

Yeoman republicanism resolved this ideological quandary by asserting the American right to the West Indian trade and by conducting a policy that assumed the American carrying trade was more valuable to Europe than to the United States. Madison returned to the argument at the center of his diplomatic thought, that the West Indies depended on the United States "for the supplies essential to their existence." Jefferson saw American commerce as "the means of peaceable coercion." Republican policy would make the United States "honestly neutral, and truly useful to both belligerents."[3]

Henry Adams wrote that Jefferson and Madison took control of a republic they considered "an enlarged Virginia." Madison's attitude fit that description more than Jefferson's. Jefferson had once been willing to put his commercial misgivings aside for national purposes. In the end, Madison triumphed. "As to the merits of our measures against England, Mr. Madison is justly entitled to his full share of the measures of my administration," Jefferson wrote upon leaving office. "Our principles were the same, and we never differed sensibly in the application of them."[4]

The maritime crisis that tested yeoman principles began in earnest in 1805. In the spring of that year, the Lords Commissioners of Appeals handed down the *Essex* decision upholding the Rule of 1756, that trade considered illegal in peacetime could not be made legal in wartime, and barring neutrals from plying the French and Spanish colonial trades. The *Essex* decision revised the *Polly* decision handed down by the Admiralty Court in 1800, which permitted a "broken voyage," allowing neutral participation in the colonial trades if broken by a stop at a neutral port. The *Essex* decision closed that loophole and upheld the doctrine of continuous voyage. Lord Nelson's victory over the combined Spanish and French fleets at Trafalgar on October 21, 1805, assured British naval supremacy for the rest of the war.[5]

The same day as Trafalgar, James Stephen, a pro-ministry writer, published *War in Disguise; or the Frauds of the Neutral Flags,* a quasi-official defense of the British crackdown on neutral trade in the West Indies. *War in Disguise* was similar to Sheffield's *Observations on the Commerce of the American States,* in that both works reflected popular and official British anger toward the United States, and both portrayed control of the West Indian trade as vital to the preservation of British naval supremacy. Stephen argued that the so-called neutral trade with the West Indies was in fact French and Spanish trade carried on under American flags. Neutrals had always carried at least some of the French and Spanish trade, but by 1805 the United States carried almost all of it. Stephen had a simple solution: Great Britain should seize all ships involved in the French and Spanish colonial trade, and after Trafalgar, Great Britain seemed able to make good on that threat.[6]

Madison wrote Jefferson on September 14, 1805, that the Rule of 1756 "threatens more loss and vexation to neutrals than all the belligerent claims put together." Three weeks later, Madison noted that he was working on his refutation of the Rule of 1756. The fruit of Madison's labors, *An Examination of the British Doctrine, which subjects to Capture a Neutral Trade, not open in a Time of Peace,* appeared in January 1806. The *Examination* served to confirm the link between republican government and the law of nations, which had always been present in Madison's thought.[7]

Madison denied that trade between a colonial port and a foreign port was in principle different from direct trade with the mother country. Madison wrote that "a trade between a colony and a foreign port is, in a like manner, precisely the same with the trade between a foreign port and the parent country." The counter to the Rule of 1756 was the principle that "free ships make free goods," which Madison based on the law of nations. Madison cited Hugo Grotius as the father of the law of nations and argued that nothing in Grotius's work could justify the Rule of 1756 and most of Grotius's work supported neutral rights. Vattel concurred "in establishing the general freedom of commerce, with the exception of things relating to the war."[8]

British practice as well as the law of nations invalidated the Rule of 1756. Great Britain "cannot surely demure to the example of her own proceedings," Madison wrote. "And it is here, perhaps, more than anywhere else, that the claim ought to shrink from examination." No precedent for the Rule of 1756 existed before the Seven Years' War, and the Rule of 1756 was not even a fixed feature of British practice. Great Britain opened its West Indian trade to the United States under article 12 of the Jay Treaty (the article rejected by the Senate) and in the Orders-in-Council of June 27, 1805. The practice of other nations was no support for current British policy. Madison cited Edward Long's *History of Jamaica,* noting that Spain opened its colonial trade to the Dutch to alleviate a shortage of Spanish ships and sailors.[9]

Madison concluded that Great Britain aimed at nothing less than complete domination of the West Indian trade, and the United States was the only remaining obstacle. The British government invented the Rule of 1756 as legal cover for a seaborne monopoly. "And thus we arrive at the *true foundation* of the principle which has so often varied its attitudes of defense, and when driven from one stand, has been so ready to occupy another," Madison wrote. "Finding no asylum elsewhere, it at length asserts, as its *true foundation, a mere superiority of force.*" Madison argued nothing "was more disrespectful to neutral nations, or more fatal to the liberty and interests of neutral commerce," than the Rule of 1756; "if she will not answer for herself all the world will answer for her," he wrote, "that she would not [accept the capture of British ships under laws similar to the Rule of 1756], and what is more, she ought not."[10]

Henry Adams called the rights Madison defended, "worthless unless supported by the stronger force."[11] The *Examination* revealed that Madison had failed to make the leap from republican theory to diplomatic practice. The *Examination* seems to rest on the assumption of the diplomacy of the American Revolution, that the United States had justice on its side and that all the United States needed to do was make its claims known to the world. Madison wrote an effective answer to the theory set forth by Stephen in *War in Disguise*. Economic coercion was an insufficient answer to the reality of Trafalgar.

Great Britain bolstered its control of the high seas by declaring French-controlled Europe under a state of blockade on May 16, 1806. To maintain naval supremacy, Great Britain needed seamen, which exacerbated the second sore point with the United States, that of impressment and the right of search. Better pay and milder discipline on American ships led many British sailors to desert. The British did not recognize American naturalization and included American citizens in its hunt for deserters. "Every attempt of Great Britain to enforce her principle of 'once a subject and always a subject' beyond the case of *her own subjects* ought to be repelled," Jefferson told Gallatin in 1803. Madison believed there could be no justification for impressment.[12]

Impressment, like neutral trade, seemed to allow no settlement. On April 3, 1807, the cabinet agreed to bar British subjects from American ships if the British renounced impressment. Gallatin conducted a study of the American merchant marine and concluded that half the eighteen thousand sailors in the foreign trade were British subjects, according to American rules of naturalization. Madison sought to salvage the proposal by suggesting the United States further bar foreign sailors who joined during the current war. Jefferson disagreed, and he dropped the issue. Neither Jefferson nor Madison wanted such a large merchant marine, but they could not abandon it without crippling American trade.[13]

In March 1806, the Jefferson administration agreed they would approve a settlement on neutral trade based on the *Polly* decision, which would permit an indirect trade between European colonies in America and Europe. The same month, Congressman Andrew Gregg, a Pennsylvania Republican, proposed a non-importation bill that would halt all imports from Great Britain. Ideally, non-importation would force concessions. In April Congress passed a limited bill that would take effect on November 15. The administration publicly denied and privately affirmed that the bill, and non-importation generally, was to be used as a weapon. Madison instructed Monroe and William Pinkney, joint negotiators in London, to tell the

British government that the act was no cause for war. Madison wanted to maintain the fiction that such acts were designed to promote domestic manufactures. Jefferson acknowledged to one congressional sympathizer that the act was "necessary even to alarm the British merchants" and force the ministry to change policy.[14]

To the real threat of non-importation Jefferson added the empty threats of alliances and military action. "All we can do," he wrote Thomas Paine, "is to encourage others to declare & guarantee neutral rights, by excluding all intercourse with any other that infringes them & so leave a niche in their compact for us, if our treaty making power shall chuse to occupy it." Jefferson extolled to Monroe the natural friendship of the United States and Great Britain, and he hoped the Fox ministry would agree. "The only rivalry that can arise is on the ocean." Yet if the negotiation failed, the United States would actively join with other neutrals "to take part in the great counterpoise to her navy." Furthermore, the United States had the materials to build its own navy.[15]

Madison and Jefferson gave Monroe and Pinkney responsibility for turning the rights asserted in the *Examination* into policy. Madison continued to assume that interest would force Great Britain to open its West Indian trade, which was a "permanent object of the United States," with geographical proximity and economic necessity in the West Indies working in favor of the United States. Monroe and Pinkney began negotiations on August 27, 1806, and soon realized that the British government would not concede on the vital issues. On November 11, the envoys informed Madison there was no chance of a settlement of the impressment issue. The two sides signed a treaty on December 31 that reestablished trade relations and ignored impressment. "We are sorry to add that this treaty contains no provision against the impressment of our seamen," the envoys wrote to Madison on January 3, 1807. They hoped an informal agreement would curtail the practice, even if Great Britain did not renounce the right of search. To Monroe and Pinkney, the treaty seemed the only protection for American commerce in a world torn by Anglo-French war. Napoleon's Berlin Decree of November 21, 1806, declaring Great Britain in a state of blockade, removed any safe haven for American commerce.[16]

The Jefferson administration took a hard line on impressment. The cabinet met on February 2, 1807, and in response to Monroe and Pinkney's letter of November 11 unanimously agreed to reject any treaty that remained silent on impressment. Madison wrote Monroe and Pinkney the next day with a new set of instructions, putting repeal of impressment at the top of the list, followed by the rights of colonial trade and a further definition of a legal blockade.[17] When the administration received the Monroe-Pinkney Treaty, it was naturally a disappointment. Madison wrote to Monroe and Pinkney on May 20, explaining why Jefferson rejected the treaty. Impressment was the leading issue. The president "laments more especially, that the British Government has not yielded to the just and cogent considerations which forbid the practice of its Cruizers in visiting and impressing the Crews of our vessels, covered by an independent flag, and guarded by the laws of the high seas, which ought to be sacred to all nations," Madison wrote. The Monroe-Pinkney Treaty might have performed the same function for the Republicans as the Jay Treaty did for the Federalists, to buy time, build up forces, and prepare for a more vigorous defense of American rights. Whig diplomacy did not consider the United States in a position to give orders to Great Britain. Yeoman diplomacy held that British economic weakness gave the United States the advantage. Madison again argued that economically Great Britain needed the United States too much to risk war.[18]

Contrary to American hopes, Great Britain was undeterred in its quest for command of the seas. Both Great Britain and France combined to decree neutral shipping out of legal existence. The British Order-in-Council of January 7, 1807, made all trade with French or French-allied ports subject to capture. An Order of November 11, 1807, required that all neutrals obtain British licenses. Napoleon responded with the Milan Decree of December 17, 1807, which subjected to capture any neutral ship with a British license.[19]

The *Chesapeake* affair of June 22, 1807, in which the British frigate *Leopard* attacked and seized four sailors from the unprepared American ship, was the strongest example of British high-handedness on impressment. Jefferson's first reaction was to pull back from the sea. "Reason & the usage of civilized nation require that we should give them an opportunity of disavowal & reparation," he wrote to a son-in-law, Congressmen John W. Eppes. "Our own interest, too, the very means of making war, requires that we should give time to our merchants to gather in their vessels & property & our seamen now afloat." Jefferson also refused to take any action committing the country to war, as only Congress had that power. Jefferson gave up on a change in policy on neutral trade, believing that the British navy depended on the "lawful plunder" of the Rule of 1756.[20] By the end of October, Jefferson still hoped that Great Britain would disavow the attack on the *Chesapeake*. This would solve the dilemma of policy. Congress was unlikely to declare war, and Jefferson feared that a non-importation "will end in war & give her [Great Britain] the choice of the moment of declaring it." On December 18, 1807, Jefferson recommended an embargo, and on December 22 he signed the Embargo Act, which prohibited American ships from clearing out of American ports. Combined with reimposition of the non-importation act of 1806, the Embargo closed American trade to the world.[21]

The yeoman vision of diplomacy posited that the Embargo was the republic's ultimate weapon. It rejected the martial aspect of classical virtue in favor of the yeoman virtue of economic independence, which would prevent creating a military organization and consequently an internal threat to civil liberty. It also risked little except a branch of trade that Jefferson and Madison believed to be incompatible with a yeoman political economy. Implicitly, the Embargo would have the domestic effect of reorienting American political economy back toward agriculture by effectively killing the domestic carrying trade, or at least making it subordinate to agriculture, and forcing France and Great Britain to bid for the right to buy American agricultural produce.

The Embargo was, however, another example of the gap between theory and practice. In Federalist no. 10, Madison had listed numerous reasons that caused factions. In explaining the actions of nations, particularly Great Britain, Madison narrowed these reasons down to rational economic interest. He did not appreciate the role of British pride, political anti-Americanism, or other factors in Anglo-American diplomacy. Jefferson, despite his long career in diplomacy, had the same blind spot. Indeed, a belief in yeoman diplomacy demanded these blind spots. If Great Britain was not vulnerable to economic pressure, there was no hope for what Jefferson and Madison considered a republican diplomacy. However, by 1807 Great Britain believed that it was in a death struggle with Napoleon and that American actions aided France. No amount of economic data could change this perception. Jefferson and Madison were certainly aware of non-economic factors, and Madison noted that only the "pride of the Cabinet" made Great Britain resist economic pressure. Nevertheless, such observations did not influence yeoman diplomacy.[22]

Madison instructed Pinkney to tell the British government that the Embargo was not a hostile act or an excuse for war. Yet from the beginning he saw the Embargo as an offensive rather than a defensive measure, although he was careful not to portray it as a war measure. Madison wrote in the *National Intelligencer* on December 23, 1807, that "war cannot be the result" and that the "embargo violates the rights of none." The Embargo was designed to protect Americans from misfortunes on the ocean, "where no harvest is to be reaped but that of danger, of spoliation and of disgrace." The Embargo was also a weapon that would punish Spain by cutting off its food supply, France by removing American ships from the French colonial trade, and Great Britain by cutting off supplies to its colonies and by not buying its manufactures. Writing to Pinkney on October 21, Madison completely discounted the possibility of Canada and the maritime provinces acting as alternate suppliers for the British West Indies.[23]

In his second *National Intelligencer* essay, Madison described the Embargo as a sword that "may be drawn at a moment's warning" and discussed its domestic effects. He believed that the only American group vulnerable to the Embargo would be those merchants involved in the Atlantic carrying trade or those who would dare risk violating the act. "We are certain that the farmer, the planter and the mechanic will approve it from the security it offers to the public interest," he wrote, "and if the merchants be honest and enlightened, as we trust they are, they will perceive the indissoluble connection between their solid and permanent prosperity and the general welfare." In other words, merchants who dealt primarily in delivering American goods to market would be protected. Those who gambled on John Randolph's "fungus of war" were on their own.[24]

Jefferson was less clear about the coercive power of the Embargo. Two weeks after he signed the act, he considered it a play for time. He wrote John Taylor that "time may produce peace in Europe," which "removes all causes of difference, till another European war." Jefferson did not expect a war with Great Britain but nonetheless saw the Embargo as a potentially permanent policy. Within a few months, Jefferson moved toward a coercive position. He observed that "our embargo, added to the exclusions from the continent will be most easily felt in England and Ireland," which would lead Liverpool merchants to mobilize against the Orders-in-Council.[25]

The Embargo ultimately failed as a coercive policy. It had no effect on France and did little economic damage in Great Britain, serving only to convince the British government that the United States would not fight. The Embargo did far more damage to the American economy and nearly drove New England into revolt. Madison attributed the "artificial excitements" stirred up in New England to disaffection. Few opponents went to the extreme of one anonymous Bostonian, who planned to pay four friends four hundred dollars to shoot the president if he did not remove the Embargo by October 10, 1808.[26]

Both Jefferson and Madison put a good face on bad policy by celebrating the growth of domestic manufactures. "Homespun has become the spirit of the time," Jefferson wrote in November 1808; "I think it an useful one, & therefore that it is a duty to encourage it by example." Six weeks before leaving office, he claimed, "I have lately inculcated the encouragement of manufactures to the extent of our own consumption at least." Madison informed Pinkney that the Embargo "created a zeal for homespun," and he speculated that the United States might encourage a large-scale manufacture of cotton goods.[27]

Neither Jefferson nor Madison had acquired any newfound love for domestic manufactures. Madison expected that Pinkney, as minister to Great Britain, would pass along the twenty-year-old threat of American manufactures to the British government. The yeoman vision presumed that economic coercion had a fail-safe mechanism—that Great Britain would change policy to preserve its markets and prevent the growth of another manufacturing power. Whig republicanism welcomed manufactures; yeoman republicanism saw them as a bluff that might destroy the republic if called.

Jefferson in his last annual message acknowledged only the political failure of the "candid and liberal experiment." He believed the Embargo demonstrated "the moderation and firmness which govern our councils" and "the necessity of unity in support of the laws." In private, Jefferson concluded that the carrying trade was the root of the republic's problems and brought about the crisis he had feared since 1785. He placed commerce on a lower moral plane, denouncing "the exercise of commerce, merely for profit," when that commerce brought the risk of war or of undermining the Embargo. In a letter to Thomas Leiper he denied, in a defensive tone, that he supported a "Chinese policy" of complete isolation but, rather, stated that he sought to restore the proper balance of agriculture, manufacturing, and commerce. Commerce (that is, the carrying trade) was the whole problem, as he had outlined in 1785. Jefferson denounced the idea of "converting this great agricultural country into a city of Amsterdam,—a mere headquarters for carrying on the commerce of all nations with one another."[28]

When Madison succeeded Jefferson as president in 1809, he still believed in the Embargo but had to find a politically acceptable replacement. On March 1, 1809, Congress approved the Non-Intercourse Act, which barred French and British ships from American ports after May 20 and allowed the president to revoke the ban if either power changed its policies toward the United States. Madison attributed the act to "aversion to war, the inconveniences by or charged on the embargo, the hope of favorable changes in Europe, the dread of civil convulsions in the East, and the policy of permitting the discontented to be reclaimed to their duty by losses at sea." Madison had little faith in the act and believed "it seems to be as little satisfactory out of doors, as it was within."[29]

As each of his three predecessors in office had done, Madison pledged to defend American neutrality. "Indulging no passions which trespass on the rights or the repose of other nations, it has been the glory of the United States to cultivate peace by observing justice, and to entitle themselves to the respect of the nations at war, by fulfilling their neutral obligations with the most scrupulous impartiality," Madison said in his first inaugural address. Privately, Madison considered Great Britain the worse threat to the United States and believed that most of the country, especially the South and West, shared his view. Even "the calculating & commercial spirit of N. England" should recognize "the disadvantage of renouncing the trade with all the world beside G.B. for the portion which her single market would afford."[30]

David Erskine, the new British minister, offered a republican solution to the Anglo-American crisis. Foreign Minister George Canning instructed Erskine to promise a repeal of the Orders-in-Council if the United States enforced commercial restrictions against France and formally accepted the Rule of 1756. Erskine knew that the United States would never accept Canning's terms. Madison detected fear in the British envoy and proof that the Embargo had worked. "Private letters from individuals in England, leave no doubt that a great dread prevailed of our perseverence in the Embargo," Madison wrote Jefferson. Madison and secretary of state Robert Smith agreed with Erskine to reopen trade and offered to relinquish the direct trade between France and its colonies in exchange for a treaty legalizing indirect colonial trade. Erskine agreed to drop the demand for British enforcement of American commercial laws. Erskine and Smith signed a note on April 18 that would act as a conditional agreement pending the arrival of a special envoy to negotiate a formal treaty. On April 19, Madison issued a proclamation announcing that Great Britain had agreed to repeal its Orders on June 10 and that trade with Great Britain could resume at that time.[31]

Throughout his presidency, Madison leapt to accept whatever diplomatic offers confirmed the yeoman vision, and he ignored any difficulties. "You will see that it [the agreement] puts an end to the two immediate difficulties with G.B. and has the air of a policy in her to come to a thorough adjustment," Madison wrote to his brother-in-law John G. Jackson. For Madison, the note with Erskine provided a full if belated vindication of yeoman diplomacy's greatest weapon, the Embargo. "It remains now to be seen what course will be taken by France," Madison wrote to Pinkney, "whether it will be prescribed by her interest & duty, or by her pride & her anger." Madison was fully attuned to the role of pride and anger in domestic politics, but strangely deaf to it in diplomacy. As he explained to Jefferson, Madison had little doubt that France, if not "bereft of common sense," would pursue the logical course of repealing its decrees. "Besides the general motive to follow the example of G.B. she cannot be insensible to the dangerous tendency of prolonging the commercial suffering of her Allies, particularly Russia, all of them already weary of such a state of things, after the pretext for enforcing it shall have ceased."[32]

Madison's commitment to the yeoman vision prevented him from seeing that Great Britain could well act out of political hatred and against its own interests. The British government rejected the Erskine agreement on May 21, 1809, even though the United States already considered it operational. Canning replaced Erskine with Francis Jackson, who loathed the United States. Madison was not willing, without a fight, to let go of a republican solution to the Anglo-American conflict. Madison drafted Robert Smith's October 19, 1809, letter to Jackson, arguing that the British government had not shown sufficient reason for disavowing the treaty. Madison also restated the American case against the Orders-in-Council. Madison wrote to Pinkney in October complaining of Jackson's conduct, especially his "mean & insolent attempt to defraud the U.S. of the exculpatory explanation dictated by the respect due them, and particularly . . . the insinuation in Jackson's answer that this Govt. colluded with Mr. E[rskine] in violating his instructions." Madison remarked to Jefferson, "Jackson is proving himself a worthy instrument of his Patron Canning." By early November, Madison had concluded that the United States could no longer negotiate with Jackson. In his annual message, Madison described the collapse of negotiations and recommended organizing the militia. Nor was France the constant friend Madison expected. On March 23, 1810, Napoleon issued the Rambouillet Decree, which subjected all American ships in French ports to capture.[33]

The Erskine fiasco left Madison in the same position he had been in a year before, but with the added embarrassment of the failed agreement. Some in Congress had grown tired of commercial diplomacy, and they had settled on war as the only honorable option left. "But I prefer the troubled ocean of war, demanded by the honor and independence of the country, with all its calamities, and desolations," Henry Clay told the House of Representatives on February 22, 1810, "to the putrescent pool of ignominious peace." Madison had not decided on war and believed that most of the country had not either. Madison also ruled out the other extreme of submission to Great Britain. Political considerations ruled out a direct revival of the Embargo, the president's preferred solution. The legislation known as Macon's Bill no. 2 seemed to offer an alternative. The bill barred French and British ships from American ports, like the expired Non-Intercourse Act. Macon's Bill allowed American ships to trade with any nation, but if one belligerent repealed its decrees against neutral shipping, the president could reimpose non-intercourse on the other power. Madison still mourned the loss of the Embargo and was skeptical of lesser measures. "G. Britain may indeed conceive that she now has a compleat interest in perpetuating the actual state of things, which gives her the full enjoyment of our trade, and enables her to cut it off with every other part of the World; at the same time that it increases the chance of such resentments in France at the inequality, as may lead to hostilities with the United States," Madison complained to Pinkney in May 1810. Madison conceded that the scheme could work if it led France to "turn the tables on G. Britain, by compelling her either to revoke her orders, or to lose the commerce of this country."[34]

France took the chance to turn the United States against Great Britain in August 1810. Word of Macon's Bill reached Paris by July. Unfounded rumors of war with the United States and hopes of promoting Anglo-American conflict led Napoleon to take the opening provided by the bill and hint that he might revoke French decrees. On August 5, the Duc de Cadore informed Minister John Armstrong that France would revoke the Berlin and Milan Decrees as of November 1 if Great Britain repealed its Orders-in-Council, or if the United States reimposed non-intercourse on Great Britain, as required by Macon's Bill. Napoleon had little to risk and much to gain in offering a reversal of policy. Madison, on the other hand, risked much in accepting the Cadore letter as a statement of French policy.[35]

Madison's defenders have generally absolved him of the charge of naiveté in accepting the Cadore letter without proof that France would repeal its decrees. Irving Brant wrote that "Madison took a logical position, but with no other evidence to support it," and Clifford Egan argued that Madison did not act out of "ignorance, fear, timidity or wishful thinking." Madison did act out of a certain desperation to preserve the yeoman form of diplomacy. He accepted the Cadore letter because his political system required that the letter be an accurate representation of French policy. "It promises us, at least an extraction from the dilemma, of a mortifying peace, or a war with both the great belligerents," Madison wrote to Caesar A. Rodney. French action would at least force the British hand regarding the Rule of 1756 and the "Mock-Blockades." "I do not believe that Congs. will be disposed, or permitted by the Nation to a tame submission," Madison wrote Jefferson, "the less so as it would be not only perfidious to the other belligerent, but irreconcilable with an honorable neutrality." Madison's target was always the entire British maritime policy regarding trade, blockades, and impressment, which demanded atonement.[36]

Acceptance of the Cadore letter promised a return to the full use of the one weapon the United States did have—its trade. Madison did not think in terms of war and would not for another year. For Madison, the Cadore letter and anticipated British intransigence gave political cover for a return to the Embargo, at least against Great Britain, a policy that Madison had always considered the proper weapon of a republic and the only answer to British naval tyranny. If the letter was not true, the entire structure of yeoman diplomacy would collapse.

On November 2, 1810, Madison announced that he would reimpose non-intercourse on Great Britain under the terms of Macon's Bill no. 2. The wait for official French word of repeal became longer and increasingly embarrassing. In his second annual message, Madison told Congress that the government had received no word on the repeal of the Berlin and Milan Decrees, and therefore Great Britain would not repeal its Orders-in-Council. "On the whole our prospects are far from being very flattering," Madison wrote to Jefferson, "yet a better chance seems to exist than, with the exception of the adjustment with Erskine, has presented itself, for closing the scene of rivalship in plundering & insulting us, & turning into a competition for our commerce & friendship." For Madison's diplomacy to work, he had to believe that the Berlin and Milan Decrees had been repealed; the success of republican diplomacy depended on Napoleon's being a man of his word. The French government continued to seize American ships under municipal regulations, and Madison himself realized it was "extremely difficult to keep the public mind awake to the distinction between the decrees relating to the trade of the U.S. with England, & those relating to the trade with F. herself."[37]

The British themselves did not share Madison's faith in the goodwill of the French government. The foreign minister warned Augustus John Foster, Jackson's replacement, to make no concessions that would undermine British naval supremacy. Madison's futile meetings with Foster combined with a deteriorating domestic political situation produced a belligerent annual message for 1811. On November 5, 1811, Madison admitted to Congress and to himself that France had not revoked the Berlin and Milan Decrees, and therefore that Great Britain would not repeal its Orders-in-Council. Madison moved on to suggest the option he had been dreading and that he had hoped commercial diplomacy would replace. The president recommended raising a regular army and a short-term additional army, purchasing cannon and other ordnance, and increasing the navy.[38]

The next seven months were a countdown to war at three different speeds. Henry Adams wrote that Madison "stood midway between the masses of his followers," that is, the Republicans with Henry Clay, John C. Calhoun, and Felix Grundy pushing the president to bolder action, and

John Randolph of Roanoke trying to block any war measure. Madison held out no hope for a change in British policy. Madison wrote Jefferson on February 7, 1812, "all that we see from G.B. indicated an adherence to her mad policy towards the U.S." Two months later Madison wrote Jefferson that Great Britain seemed to "prefer war with us, to a repeal of their orders in Council!" and he concluded, "We have nothing left therefore, but to make ready for it."[39]

On June 1, 1812, Madison delivered the war message that had been seven months—if not seven years—in the making. Madison declared that the diplomacy of a republic must match its domestic institutions. The acceptance of British tyranny on the high seas was incompatible with independence or republicanism. Madison began with impressment, a "crying enormity" that no nation could tolerate. He moved on to the "pretended blockades, without the presence of an adequate force and sometimes without the probability of applying one," which the British used as an excuse to seize American commerce. The ultimate question was "Whether the United States should continue passive under these progressive usurpations and these accumulated wrongs, opposing force to force in defence of their national rights." Madison made no specific recommendations but clearly favored a declaration of war. In the end, he concluded that war, even with all its dangers, was safer for republican government than submission. "When the U.S. assumed and established their rank among the Nations of the Earth," the president wrote to an unidentified correspondent, "they assumed & established a common Sovereignty on the high seas, as well as an exclusive sovereignty within their territorial limits."[40]

Most commentators correctly state that Madison went to war because the dignity of republican government demanded it. Madison differed from the younger Republicans in Congress in that the so-called War Hawks warmly embraced the martial aspect of the classical tradition. In December 1811, John C. Calhoun invoked "the last redress of a nation's wrongs." At the same time, Felix Grundy agreed that "the only justifiable course left was to put the nation in arms." Madison followed the eighteenth-century Opposition fear of war.[41]

Madison's yeoman diplomacy led him into a disastrous contradiction. He made the dismantling of the British maritime program his sine qua non and, in doing so, touched on the one sacrosanct issue in British politics. He would not accept lesser agreements, such as the Monroe-Pinkney Treaty. War was almost inevitable. At the same time, Madison's republicanism prevented him from building the military, especially the navy, and denied the United States any real weapon against Great Britain. "In a state of military and psychological unpreparedness," Bradford Perkins wrote, "the United States embarked upon a war to recover the self-respect destroyed by Republican leaders."[42]

As the Senate debated a declaration of war, Great Britain removed the ostensible cause by repealing the Orders-in-Council on June 16, 1812. Repeal was not, however, a disavowal, and Great Britain still claimed the rights it momentarily chose not to exercise. Furthermore, the repeal said nothing about permanently ending impressment, a stipulation Madison always demanded in any settlement. "Although a repeal of the orders susceptible of explanations meeting the views of this Government had taken place before this pacific advance was made to Great Britain, the advance was declined from an avowed repugnance of impressment during the armistice, and without any intimation that the arrangement proposed with respect to seamen would be accepted," Madison told Congress in his fourth annual message. "On the issue of the war are staked our national sovereignty on the high seas and the security of an important class of our citizens, whose occupation give proper value to those of every other class," Madison said in the second inaugural message, marking a shift, at least in public, since 1792 in his opinion of sailors. In January Madison endorsed the Seamen's Bill, which revived his 1807 attempt to reduce the danger on the high seas by reducing the number of American sailors. The bill offered to exclude foreigners from the American merchant marine if Great Britain gave up the right of search.[43]

Madison hoped to conduct the war in a republican manner. His model was the first years of the American Revolution, which supposed that an armed and patriotic citizenry could defeat Great Britain with a few quick thrusts, particularly against Canada. He was soon disappointed on both counts. By September 1812, Madison concluded that only "high bounties & short enlistments, however objectionable, will fill the ranks." Hopes for a successful campaign against Canada, which Madison saw as the weak link of empire and the most convenient target, were dashed by a number of factors: the timidity of General William Hull in the Northwest; squabbling among generals Stephen Van Renssalaer, Daniel Tompkins, and Alexander Smyth at Niagara; and the refusal of the militia to cross the border with General Henry Dearborn at Plattsburgh. These and other factors kept Canada in British hands.[44]

Madison was not opposed to an early and honorable end to the war, and Russia promised to provide such an ending. On March 8, 1813, Russian minister to the United States Andrei de Daschkov offered his government's services as mediator. "We shall endeavor to turn the good will of Russia to the proper account," Madison wrote to Jefferson two days later. The Russian offer promised the chance to end a war that had already lasted longer than planned, and it presented an opportunity to force Great Britain to negotiate over maritime rights. In Madison's framework, Russia replaced France as the American friend who could pressure Great Britain. "We are encouraged in this policy by the known friendship of the Emperor Alexander to this country; and the probability that the greater affinity between the Baltic and American ideas of maritime law, than between the former and G.B. will render this interposition as favorable as will be consistent with the character assumed by him," Madison explained to John Nicholas. Madison informed Congress on May 25, 1813, that he accepted the mediation, and he nominated Albert Gallatin, John Quincy Adams, and James A. Bayard as commissioners. British foreign minister Lord Castlereagh suspected that Russia would favor a neutral rights agenda, and he rejected the mediation, offering instead to negotiate directly with the United States.[45]

By the time the Madison administration received word of Castlereagh's offer in January 1814, the military balance had tilted in Great Britain's favor, in both Europe and America. The American cause was implicitly linked with Napoleon's success. Napoleon's defeat at Leipzig in October 1813, combined with British victories in Spain, spelled the beginning of the end for the French emperor. Allied troops entered Paris on March 31, 1814, making thousands of British battle-hardened troops available for potential use against the United States. The British army burned Washington on August 27 and occupied eastern Maine on September 1, 1814.[46]

Yeoman diplomacy had previously been impervious to battlefield results. As the Royal Navy took control of the Chesapeake, Madison began to moderate his diplomatic demands. The cabinet met on June 23 and 24, 1814, to discuss impressment. The whole cabinet, with Attorney General Richard Rush dissenting, agreed not to insist on a solution as a peace ultimatum. The cabinet (except for Secretary of War John Armstrong and Secretary of the Navy William Jones) also determined not to accept a treaty that said nothing about impressment. The cabinet (except for Rush, who wanted to wait on dispatches from Europe) would agree to a treaty that referred impressment to a separate treaty. After dispatches arrived from Gallatin and Bayard, the cabinet met on June 27 and agreed to accept a treaty silent on impressment, as long as American diplomats did not surrender American claims on the matter or admit British claims. Initial dispatches from Ghent, indicating a British hard line, led Madison to the unorthodox step of making negotiations in progress a matter of congressional debate and public record.[47]

On February 18, 1815, Madison transmitted the Treaty of Ghent to Congress. By most accounts, this treaty signaled the end of the first party system. Madison himself signed a bill chartering the second Bank of the United States. He advocated a system of internal improvements but, on his last day in office, vetoed a bill establishing a fund for that purpose. For Madison, the War of 1812 was a vindication of republican government. "The war has proved moreover that our free Government, like other free governments, though slow in its early movements, acquires in its progress a force proportional to its freedom, and that the union of these states, the guardian of the freedom and safety of all and each is strengthened by every occasion that puts it to the test," Madison wrote in his fifth annual message, voicing a sentiment more in tune with the classical virtue of 1776. "It was a struggle due to the Independence of the present and to the security of future generations," Madison wrote after the war.[48]

Madison also considered the war a vindication of yeoman diplomacy. Yeoman republicanism still intended to reform the world, even if whig diplomacy did not. "If a purification of the Maritime Code ever takes place, the task seems to be reserved for the United States," Madison wrote to Charles J. Ingersoll in 1814. "Under such auspices, truth, justice, humanity, and universal good, will be inculcated with an advantage which must gradually and peaceably enlist the civilized world, against a Code which violates all these obligations," Madison concluded. John Adams had abandoned that hope by the time he left office. Madison wrote in 1827 that the United States would become the world's dominant sea power and would act with more justice than Great Britain.[49]

The history of yeoman and whig diplomacy ran on parallel tracks with the architects of each finding their careers ending in a war crisis over neutral rights. Adams's whig diplomacy allowed him to uphold American rights on the ocean without entering a formal war that might have torn the nation apart. Madison's yeoman diplomacy, built on the assumption that the United States could use trade to order other nations about, led the country into a war that it nearly lost and that nearly divided the union. It is perhaps the highest irony that Adams, who had the most right to condemn Madison as a failure, concluded that, despite "a thousand Faults and blunders, his Administration has acquired more glory, and established more Union, than all his three Predecessors, Washington Adams and Jefferson, put together."[50]

Conclusion

Debate over American foreign policy inevitably involves the search for the soul of America. Such a debate is perhaps more philosophical than practical in current events, but to the founding generation it was a question of the utmost urgency. The United States, as a republic, had self-imposed limits on its already limited power. The new nation lived among countries with far greater power and far fewer self-imposed limits. The proper balance between ideological purity and practical diplomacy, between republicanism and realpolitik, was a matter of life and death. The connection between republican ideology and diplomacy is a vital question, but one that has received relatively little scholarly attention from either diplomatic or intellectual historians. This study is meant to fill that gap.

This study establishes that republican ideology exercised a control over the making of foreign policy as it did over domestic policy. James Hutson argues that Americans would have found and relied on the idea of a balance of power without ever reading the English Opposition works.[1] Ideology explains how the early republic used that idea of balance. As republicans, the figures in this study believed that republics rested on virtue, be it of the sword, the law, or the plow. This sense of virtue was naturally reflected in diplomacy. Therefore, Adams, Jefferson, Madison, and Hamilton conceived of this balance in a manner different from Metternich or Catherine the Great.

Diplomatic historians, especially those who pay less attention to the ideological side, generally divide thinkers into "idealists" and "realists." Felix Gilbert saw the diplomacy of the American Revolution as idealistic, especially as it intended to reform international practice. James Hutson, reviewing the career of John Adams, comes down on the side of realism, denying that revolutionary diplomacy was revolutionary in conception or execution; the Model Treaty was not meant to remake the world, nor did Adams intend to rewrite the rules of diplomatic conduct. Gerald Stourzh marked Hamilton as a realist. Paul Varg puts the dichotomy of realists and idealists among the founders in its classic form: Hamilton was a realist who accepted the international system as it was; Jefferson and Madison were idealists driven by natural rights political theory to remake the world.[2]

The realist/idealist division is a false one. To paraphrase Jefferson, they were all realists, and at least until the 1780s they were all idealists. Jefferson and Madison calculated power against goals, just as Adams and Hamilton did. The fact that Jefferson and Madison calculated wrongly is a separate issue. One might also ask where the idealism was in the threat to starve the West Indies, or where the realism was in the plot to liberate South America. The realism of Adams and Hamilton was the product of the recalculation of power, the shift from classical to whig virtue. Hutson is incorrect in arguing that Adams's thoughts on diplomacy did not change during the course of the American Revolution.[3] Adams's own statements contradict this argument. However, the idea that the United States could remake the world died in Paris and was buried in London. The yeoman system never underwent such a recalculation.

The debate over the primacy of foreign policy is related to that of idealism and realism. Stourzh argues that Hamilton placed foreign policy above domestic policy. Tucker and Hendrickson portray Jefferson as a statesman whose main goal was to find a way to subordinate foreign policy to domestic policy.[4] This debate also represents a false division. Republicanism did not make a sharp distinction between foreign and domestic policy. More properly, the debate over primacy is about how the whig and yeoman schools viewed the tools of diplomacy. Hamilton, with a seventeenth-century conception of power, did not fear an army or a navy. Adams, influenced by Bolingbroke, favored a navy but feared a permanent army. Yeoman diplomacy feared both. Whig diplomacy held that the United States could neither reform nor escape the world of diplomacy. Yeoman diplomacy wanted to escape the international system by reforming it.

The three strains of republicanism often came to the same destination from different paths. For example, all believed that a nation's interests and diplomacy reflected the nature of its government and society. Americans sought limited and balanced government and the freedom to trade as widely as possible. All four figures in this study concluded that Americans were not on any permanent basis a Spartan people, although they praised and demanded such martial virtue in times of crisis. Adams and Hamilton had arrived at this conclusion by the end of the revolution; Jefferson and Madison never considered martial virtue the foundation of the republic. Whig and yeoman strains of republicanism disagreed on whether the United States should pursue manufactures and shipping as well as agriculture. This disagreement went to the heart of what they believed was entailed in republican diplomacy.

The first rule adopted by all three versions of American republicans was that political and physical separation from the hazards of continental European politics was essential to liberty. Bolingbroke and "Cato," as contemporary critics of Walpole's foreign policy, warned against Walpole's engagements on the European continent (dictated in part by the Hanoverian connection) where Great Britain had no essential interests. Classical virtue saw European entanglements as a source of moral corruption. Whig virtue saw that a relatively weak United States would be overwhelmed by Europe's wars. Yeoman virtue saw involvement in European wars as a precursor to standing armies at home. The principle that separation preserved republican government can be seen most obviously in the Declaration of Independence, and it was the central assumption of early American diplomacy.

A rule related to physical separation was that separation should be enforced by methods not dangerous to domestic liberty. Hamilton had the least fear of the tools of diplomacy, but only if it was a free government using those tools. Here he was more similar to Harrington than to Bolingbroke. Adams followed the Opposition Whigs in believing that the navy was the constitutionally safest form of defense. It could not overthrow the government, as could a standing army. A navy also paid for itself by protecting overseas commerce, a valuable source of economic power and a training ground for sailors. This difference was the fundamental split in whig republicanism.

Yeoman republicanism considered both navy and army as interests separate from the common good, drains on the treasury, and sources of executive patronage and corruption. Jefferson and Madison therefore believed that economic power could play the strategic role of a navy. Opposition Whigs in Britain did not address economic coercion as a means of foreign policy but suggested the idea by emphasizing the role played by the American colonies in ensuring British wealth. The careers of John Adams and James Madison, both of which concluded with maritime crises, are instructive on this point. In 1776 Adams believed that the economic power of America, both as a market for manufactures and a supplier of staple goods, could substitute, at least temporarily, for a substantial navy. By the 1780s Adams gave up on economic coercion as effective policy. During the Quasi-War, he waged a naval war in defense of commerce, particularly the American carrying trade, in a manner he considered consistent with republican ideology and the lessons he had learned as a diplomat.

Yeoman republicanism, on the other hand, went beyond Opposition thought to lump a navy with a standing army as a threat to liberty. Jefferson and Madison believed that a large domestic carrying trade was inconsistent with a primarily agrarian republic. They saw American economic power as its own defense and framed the commercial discrimination bills of the 1790s and the Embargo of 1807 to achieve American goals without recourse to military force. Yeoman diplomacy forced them to believe that American commerce was more powerful than it was in reality, and that nations would always act out of rationally defined interests. Yeoman republicanism was more bound to a particular theory and was more innovative than the other two strains, but it was also the greatest failure. Yet, in the opinion of Jefferson and Madison, failure came from outside sources, such as Federalist Anglophilia or New England's treason, rather than from the theory itself.

A third rule, tied to the proper weapons of foreign policy, was that the power of the executive, while necessary for administration and for balance within a government, was to be tightly controlled. Hamilton's version of whig diplomacy differed somewhat from this consensus. He followed Harrington in believing that a popular government could use power without a danger to liberty. Adams believed in a strong executive more than Madison did, but Adams was also careful to conduct himself as a republicanized version of Bolingbroke's Patriot King. Adams, in defense of his own administration, pointed out that he had preserved the republic by refusing to follow measures pressed on him by Hamilton. Jefferson and Madison feared executive power more than Adams did, and Madison's political essays and Jefferson's correspondence throughout the 1790s provide a variation on the Opposition Whig thesis that executive tyranny could result from an unrestrained power to conduct foreign relations. In power, Jefferson and Madison may have come close to violating their own rules while attempting to acquire Louisiana and the Floridas, but their circumspection may be evidence that they were no more comfortable with their own use of executive power than they were with that of the Federalists.

It is a tricky game to take a current event in American diplomacy and ask, What would Jefferson (or Madison, or Hamilton, or Adams) do? Statesmen and commentators are less interested in the founders in the context of their own times than in what lessons might be extracted. The founders, of course, used classical and English history the same way, as a source of ancient wisdom to be mined for use in their own time.

Future generations saw the founding generation itself as the source of ancient authority. In his 1931 article "The Permanent Bases of American Foreign Policy," former presidential candidate John W. Davis wrote that "the first [base] in point of time, if not in point of importance, is to abstain as far as possible from any participation in foreign questions in general and European questions in particular." In support of his argument, Davis cited John Adams and the Farewell Address without reference to the earlier republican ideology that had produced those statements of policy.[5]

John Adams, Thomas Jefferson, Alexander Hamilton, and James Madison came to serve the function in later American thought that Grotius, Vattel, Harrington, Bolingbroke, and "Cato" served for the founding generation. Even if American statesmen no longer cited the Opposition Whigs in debates over foreign policy, it cannot be said that their ideas and concerns faded from the American consciousness. "Free ships make free goods" reappeared in the Civil War, at the Hague Peace Conferences, and upon American entry into World War I.

The idea of separation from foreign politics, put forth by the Opposition and transmitted most prominently through the Farewell Address, has been at the center of every subsequent debate over American action throughout the world, most obviously in the American entry into World War I, World War II, and the cold war. Madison might have called it the most durable lesson of the founding generation. Historian and Washington biographer Curtis P. Nettels testified against the North Atlantic Treaty on the grounds that the agreement violated the tradition, laid down in the Farewell Address, against permanent alliances. In 1951 Senator Robert A. Taft echoed John Adams's version of whig republicanism when he advocated a defense policy based on a large navy and air force but opposed the provision in NATO that committed American ground troops to Europe.[6] Adams's whig republicanism was something of a lost tradition in the cold war. Statesmen of that era took the Hamiltonian/Harringtonian belief that an elected government could wield great power, and they combined this with the yeoman (and classical) belief in the possibility of universal liberty. The yeoman fear of executive power (without the agrarian base) resurfaced in the Bricker Amendment and the War Powers Act, to name but two examples. The end of the cold war divorced whig from yeoman virtue: the whig strain focused on maintaining American power and did not share the yeoman hope of spreading democracy.

The consequences of September 11, 2001, demonstrate how events can force a statesman from one category of virtue to another. As presidential candidate, George W. Bush opposed the new foreign involvements of the Clinton years. He spoke of acting abroad with "modesty" and "humility" and expressed doubt about promoting the spread of democracy, apart from acting as an example. In other words, Governor Bush embraced something of the whig view. The attacks of September 11 and the subsequent wars in Afghanistan and Iraq caused President Bush to reverse course. In a speech on April 28, 2003, he argued that "freedom is God's gift to every person in every nation," restating the natural rights argument. He put the responsibility for spreading liberty on the shoulders of the United States. "Yet, the security of our nation and the hope of millions depend on us," he told the United Nations on September 12, 2002, "and Americans do not turn away from duties because they are hard."[7] In peace, President Bush was a Bolingbrokean; in war, a Harringtonian.

The question of what constitutes a republican foreign policy has not been and cannot be answered for all time. John Adams, Thomas Jefferson, James Madison, and Alexander Hamilton were among the first to grapple with it. Their search for a republican realpolitik formed the guide subscribed to by each succeeding generation charged with keeping the republic.

Notes

ABBREVIATIONS

AFC	*Adams Family Correspondence,* ed. L. H. Butterfield, Marc Friedlaender, and Richard Allen Ryerson
AP	Adams Papers
ASP:FR	*American State Papers: Foreign Relations*
DAJA	John Adams, *Diary and Autobiography of John Adams*
LOWJM	James Madison, *Letters and Other Writings of James Madison*
PAH	Alexander Hamilton, *The Papers of Alexander Hamilton*
PJA	John Adams, *Papers of John Adams*
PJM	James Madison, *The Papers of James Madison*
PJM:PS	James Madison, *The Papers of James Madison: Presidential Series*
PJM:SS	James Madison, *The Papers of James Madison: Secretary of State Series*
PTJ	Thomas Jefferson, *The Papers of Thomas Jefferson*
TJPapers	Thomas Jefferson Papers
WJA	John Adams, *The Works of John Adams*
WJM	James Madison, *The Writings of James Madison*
WoTJ	Thomas Jefferson, *The Works of Thomas Jefferson*
WrTJ	Thomas Jefferson, *The Writings of Thomas Jefferson*

1: THE REPUBLICAN WORLD

1. Benjamin Franklin cited from James McHenry, anecdote, 18—, in Max Farrand, ed., *The Records of the Federal Convention of 1787,* 4 vols. (New Haven: Yale University Press, 1911–1937), 4:85; John Quincy Adams, *The Jubilee of the Constitution: A Discourse Delivered at the Request of the New York Historical Society* (New York: S. Coleman, 1839), 73.

2. Diary entries of Jan. 16, July 19, August 7, 1756, and June 26–27, 1760, in John Adams, *Diary and Autobiography of John Adams,* 4 vols., ed. L. H. Butterfield (Cambridge, Mass.: Harvard University Press, 1961; hereafter cited as *DAJA*), 1:2, 35, 40, 142, also 3:264, 358.

3. Jefferson to Robert Skipwith, August 3, 1771, in Thomas Jefferson, *The Papers of Thomas Jefferson,* 30 vols. to date, ed. Julian Boyd et al. (Princeton, N.J.: Princeton University Press, 1950– ; hereafter cited as *PTJ*), 1:79.

4. Jefferson to John Nowell, June 14, 1807, in Thomas Jefferson, *The Works of Thomas Jefferson,* 12 vols., ed. Paul Leicester Ford (New York: G. P. Putnam's Sons, 1904–1905; hereafter cited as *WoTJ*), 10:416.

5. Report of Jan. 23, 1783, in James Madison, *The Papers of James Madison,* 17 vols. to date, ed. William T. Hutchinson et al. (Chicago and Charlottesville: University of Chicago Press and University Press of Virginia, 1959– ; hereafter cited as *PJM*), 6:84–92.

6. Hamilton, "The Farmer Refuted," [Feb. 23,] 1775, in Alexander Hamilton, *The Papers of Alexander Hamilton,* 27 vols., ed. Harold C. Syrett et al. (New York: Columbia University Press, 1961–1987; hereafter cited as *PAH*), 1:86.

7. Forrest McDonald, *Novus Ordo Seclorum: The Intellectual Origins of the Constitution* (Lawrence: University Press of Kansas, 1985), 8.

8. Thomas Paine, *Common Sense,* ed. Isaac Kramnick (1776; New York: Penguin, 1976), 87.

9. Charles Secondat, Baron de Montesquieu, *The Spirit of the Laws,* 2 vols., ed. and trans. Thomas Nugent (1749; New York: Hafner, 1949), 1:127–28; Paine, *Common Sense,* 81.

10. Hamilton to Edward Stevens, Nov. 11, 1769, *PAH* 1:4; Adams to Abigail Adams, May 29, 1775, in L. H. Butterfield, Marc Friedlaender, and Richard Allen Ryerson, eds., *Adams Family Correspondence,* 6 vols. to date (Cambridge, Mass.: Harvard University Press, 1963– ; hereafter cited as *AFC*), 1:207; John Adams, Fragmentary draft of *A Dissertation on the Canon and Feudal Law,* Feb. 1765, *DAJA* 1:257.

11. John Adams, "Discourses on Davila," in John Adams, *The Works of John Adams,* 10 vols., ed. Charles Francis Adams (Boston: Little, Brown, 1850–1856; hereafter cited as *WJA*), 6:399; Hamilton, "Tully No. III," August 28, 1794, *PAH* 17:159; Adams to Richard Rush, May 14, 1821, *WJA* 10:397; Montesquieu, *Spirit of the Laws,* 1:6; Hamilton to the Marquis de Lafayette, Jan. 6, 1799, *PAH* 22:404.

12. Jefferson to Samuel Kercheval, July 12, 1816, *WoTJ* 12:7; Thomas Jefferson, *Notes on the State of Virginia,* ed. William Peden (1787; Chapel Hill: University of North Carolina Press, 1954), 165; Jefferson to Tench Coxe, June 1, 1795, *PTJ* 28:373.

13. Felix Gilbert, *To the Farewell Address: Ideas of Early American Foreign Policy* (Princeton, N.J.: Princeton University Press, 1961), 44–75, 115–36. The survey of the "republican synthesis" in this study derives from Bernard Bailyn, *The Ideological Origins of the American Revolution* (Cambridge, Mass.: Harvard University Press, 1967); Gordon S. Wood, *The Creation of the American Republic, 1776–1787* (Chapel Hill: University of North Carolina Press, 1969); Lance Banning, *The Jeffersonian Persuasion: Evolution of a Party Ideology* (Ithaca, N.Y.: Cornell University Press, 1978); and Drew R. McCoy, *The Elusive Republic: Political Economy in Jeffersonian America* (Chapel Hill: University of North Carolina Press, 1980). Robert E. Shalhope's two articles—"Toward a Republican Synthesis: The Emergence of an Understanding of Republicanism in American Historiography," *William and Mary Quarterly,* 3rd ser., 29, no. 1 (Jan. 1972): 49–80, and "Republicanism and Early American Historiography," *William and Mary Quarterly,* 3rd ser., 39, no. 2 (April 1982): 334–55—provide an overview of the literature of republicanism. For the English and European background, see Caroline Robbins, *The Eighteenth-Century Commonwealthman: Studies in the Transmission, Development, and Circumstance of English Liberal Thought from the Restoration of Charles II*

until the War with the Thirteen Colonies (Cambridge, Mass.: Harvard University Press, 1959); Isaac Kramnick, *Bolingbroke and His Circle: The Politics of Nostalgia in the Age of Walpole* (Cambridge, Mass.: Harvard University Press, 1968); and J. G. A. Pocock, *The Machiavellian Moment: Florentine Political Thought and the Atlantic Republican Tradition* (Princeton, N.J.: Princeton University Press, 1975).

14. Michael H. Hunt, *Ideology and U.S. Foreign Policy* (New Haven: Yale University Press, 1987), 19–124; Hans J. Morgenthau, *In Defense of the National Interest: A Critical Examination of American Foreign Policy* (New York: Alfred A. Knopf, 1951), 7, 13; George Kennan, *American Diplomacy, 1900–1950* (New York: Mentor Books, 1952), 82–83.

15. Wood, *Creation*, 21–22; Bailyn, *Ideological Origins*, 55–59.

16. McDonald, *Novus Ordo Seclorum*, 70–82; Bailyn, *Ideological Origins*, 22–54; Kramnick, *Bolingbroke*, 33–34, 167–68; Robbins, *Commonwealthman*, 9–21.

17. Paul A. Rahe, *Republics Ancient and Modern: Classical Republicanism and the American Founding* (Chapel Hill: University of North Carolina Press, 1992), 57–59, 72–76, 324, 333–34; Carl J. Richard, *The Founders and the Classics: Greece, Rome, and the American Enlightenment* (Cambridge, Mass.: Harvard University Press, 1994), 12–25, 55, 90–91, 126–27; Z. S. Fink, *The Classical Republicans: An Essay in the Recovery of a Pattern of Thought in Seventeenth-Century England* (Evanston, Ill.: Northwestern University Press, 1945), 3–4; Polybius, *The Histories of Polybius*, 2 vols., trans. Evelyn S. Shuckburgh (Bloomington: Indiana University Press, 1962), 1:167.

18. Montesquieu, *Spirit of the Laws*, 1:120; Samuel Adams to John Scollay, Dec. 30, 1780, in Paul H. Smith, ed., *Letters of Delegates to Congress, 1774–1789*, 26 vols. (Washington, D.C.: Library of Congress, 1976–1998), 16:515; Adams to Richard Rush, July 14, 1813, in Adams Papers, Massachusetts Historical Society (hereafter cited as AP), reel 95.

19. Harrington, "Oceana," in James Harrington, *The Political Works of James Harrington*, ed. J. G. A Pocock (New York: Cambridge University Press, 1977), 161, 304, 167, 205.

20. Ibid., 332; Pocock, *Machiavellian Moment*, 389; Harrington, "Oceana," 157 ("middle people"); Lois G. Schwoerer, *"No Standing Armies!" The Antiarmy Ideology in Seventeenth-Century England* (Baltimore: Johns Hopkins University Press, 1974), 50; Harrington, "Oceana," 164–65, 332 ("commonwealth"). See also Michael Walzer, *The Revolution of the Saints: A Study in the Origins of Radical Politics* (Cambridge, Mass.: Harvard University Press, 1965), 290; Blair Worden, "James Harrington and 'The Commonwealth of Oceana,' 1656," in David Wootton, ed., *Republicanism, Liberty, and Commercial Society, 1649–1776* (Stanford, Calif.: Stanford University Press, 1994), 103, 106.

21. Harrington, "Oceana," 320–21 ("increase"); Fink, *Classical Republicans*, 81–82; Harrington, "Oceana," 160 ("sea").

22. Harrington, "Oceana," 323.

23. Hamilton, "The Farmer Refuted," [Feb. 23,] 1775, *PAH* 1:122; Jefferson, "Original Rough draught" of the Declaration of Independence, *PTJ* 1:423. See also Garrett Ward Sheldon, *The Political Philosophy of Thomas Jefferson* (Baltimore: Johns Hopkins University Press, 1991), 41–45; Michael Zuckert, *The Natural Rights Republic: Studies in the Foundation of the American Political Tradition* (Notre Dame, Ind.: University of Notre Dame Press, 1996), 28.

24. Algernon Sidney, *Discourses Concerning Government*, ed. Thomas G. West (1698; Indianapolis: Liberty Fund, 1990), 6 ("better, wiser"), 166, 212 ("good men").

25. Ibid., 198, 157–58, 205 (quotations); Allan Craig Houston, *Algernon Sidney and the Republican Heritage in England and America* (Princeton, N.J.: Princeton University Press, 1991), 159–61.

26. For William's wars, see Angus McInnis, "When Was the English Revolution," *History* 67, no. 221 (Oct. 1982): 389–92; for William's standing army, Schwoerer, *"No Standing Armies"*, 162, 184–85. Daniel Defoe, *Some Reflections on a Pamphlet lately Publish'd, Entitled, An Argument Shewing that a Standing Army is inconsistent with a Free Government, and Absolutely Destructive to the Constitution of the English Monarchy*, 2nd ed. (London: E. Whitlock, 1697), 13, 19; John Trenchard, *An Argument Shewing, that a Standing Army is inconsistent with a Free Government, and absolutely destructive to the Constitution of the English Monarchy* (London, 1698), 7–8, 10–11, 24, 26.

27. Rodger D. Parker, "The Gospel of Opposition: A Study in Eighteenth-Century Anglo-American Ideology" (unpublished Ph.D. dissertation, Wayne State University, 1975), 169; Charles Davenant, "An Essay Upon Ways and Means," and "An Essay on the Probable Methods of Making a People Gainers in the Balance of Trade," in Charles Davenant, *The Political and Commercial Works of that Celebrated Writer Charles D'Avenant, LL.D.*, 5 vols., ed. Sir Charles Whitworth (London: R. Horsman, 1771), 1:15–16 ("strength"); 2:192–93 ("extent"); Joyce Appleby, *Economic Thought and Ideology in Seventeenth-Century England* (Princeton, N.J.: Princeton University Press, 1978), 78–79; Davenant, "Balance of Trade" and "An Essay upon Universal Monarchy," in Davenant, *Works*, 2:275, 309, 4:3–4 ("Commonwealths").

28. Jeremy Black, *British Foreign Policy in the Age of Walpole* (Edinburgh, Scotland: John Donald, 1985), 112; J. R. Jones, *Britain and the World, 1649–1815* (Atlantic Highlands, N.J.: Humanities Press, 1980), 189–97; Paul Langford, *The Eighteenth Century, 1688–1815* (New York: St. Martin's Press, 1976), 18–19, 32–33, 89–103; Arthur McCandless Wilson, *French Foreign Policy during the Administration of Cardinal Fleury, 1726–1743: A Study in Diplomacy and Commercial Development* (Cambridge, Mass.: Harvard University Press, 1936), 291–94.

29. Jonathan Swift, *The Conduct of the Allies,* in *Political Tracts, 1711–1713,* ed. Herbert Davis (Princeton, N.J.: Princeton University Press, 1951), 19, 38.

30. Bernard Capp, *Cromwell's Navy: The Fleet in the English Revolution, 1648–1660* (New York: Oxford University Press, 1989), 87, 96–97; Christine Gerrard, *The Patriot Opposition to Walpole: Politics, Poetry, and National Myth, 1725–1742* (New York: Oxford University Press, 1994), 9–10.

31. Kramnick, *Bolingbroke,* 8–13.

32. Adams to Thomas Jefferson, Dec. 25, 1813, in Lester J. Cappon, ed., *The Adams-Jefferson Letters* (Chapel Hill: University of North Carolina Press, 1988), 410; Henry St. John, Viscount Bolingbroke, *A Dissertation on Parties,* in *The Works of Lord Bolingbroke,* 4 vols. (London: Henry G. Bohn, 1844), 2:27 ("Magna Carta"), 75, 86–87, 93 ("key-stone"), 163; Kramnick, *Bolingbroke,* 26–28.

33. Kramnick, *Bolingbroke,* 184–85; Parker, "Gospel of Opposition," 270; Bolingbroke, *Dissertation on Parties* and "A Letter to William Windham," in *Works,* 2:98, 1:115; Richard Pares, "American versus Continental Warfare, 1739–1763," *English Historical Review* 51, no. 204 (July 1936): 436–40; Bolingbroke, *Dissertation on Parties* and *Letters on the Study and Use of History,* in *Works,* 2:28, 330–31; Henry St. John, Viscount Bolingbroke, *Contributions to the "Craftsman,"* ed. Simon Varey (London: Oxford University Press, 1982), no. 511, April 17, 1736, 206–7 ("Opportunities"); Bolingbroke, "Remarks on the History of England," in *Works,* 1:379 (Queen Elizabeth).

34. Bolingbroke, Craftsman no. 114, Sept. 7, 1728, in *Contributions*, 54, 64–65; Jones, *Britain and the World*, 174–76; Charles Jenkinson, Earl of Liverpool, *A Collection of all the Treaties of Peace, Alliance and Commerce between Great Britain and Other Powers*, 3 vols. (1785; New York: August M. Kelley, 1969), 2:5–144 (whole treaty), 2:40–65 (Anglo-French articles); Bolingbroke, *The Idea of a Patriot King*, in *Works*, 2:414 (quotation).

35. Parker, "Gospel of Opposition," 269–70; Bolingbroke, *Patriot King*, in *Works*, 2:374, 412 (quotations).

36. Bolingbroke, *Patriot King*, in *Works*, 2:375 ("salvation"), 396–97 ("corruption"), 406 ("espouse"), 416 ("multiply"). See also Kramnick, *Bolingbroke*, 167–68.

37. John Taylor to Wilson Cary Nicholas, Sept. 5, 1801, in Thomas Jefferson, *The Jefferson Papers*, Collections of the Massachusetts Historical Society, 7th ser. (Boston: Massachusetts Historical Society, 1900), 1:102; Bolingbroke, *Patriot King*, in *Works*, 2:393, 416–18; see also Kramnick, *Bolingbroke*, 33–34.

38. John Trenchard, *A Short History of Standing Armies in England* (London, 1698), 3–4; "Cato," Letter 70, March 17, 1721/22, in John Trenchard and Thomas Gordon, *Cato's Letters: Or Essays on Liberty, Civil and Religious, and other Important Subjects*, 2 vols., ed. Ronald Hamowy, 6th ed. (1755; Indianapolis: Liberty Fund, 1995), 2:505–6; Parker, "Gospel of Opposition," 55–56; Kramnick, *Bolingbroke*, 118.

39. "Cato," Letters 93, 95, Sept. 8, 22, 1722, in Trenchard and Gordon, *Cato's Letters*, 2:665, 682.

40. "Cato," Letter 64, Feb. 3, 1721/22, ibid., 1:447, 446; Letter 106, Dec. 8, 1722, ibid., 2:749.

41. "Cato," Letter 93, Sept. 8, 1722, ibid., 2:667; Paine, *Common Sense*, 100.

42. Peter Douglas Brown, *William Pitt, Earl of Chatham: The Great Commoner* (London: George Allen and Unwin, 1978), 33, 46–47, 61, 79–80; Fred Anderson, *Crucible of War: The Seven Years' War and the Fate of Empire in British North America, 1754–1766* (New York: Alfred A. Knopf, 2000), 212–13.

43. Robbins, *Commonwealthman*, 364–65; Adams to James Burgh, Dec. 28, 1774, in *Papers of John Adams*, 10 vols. to date, ed. Robert J. Taylor et al. (Cambridge, Mass.: Harvard University Press, 1977– ; hereafter cited as *PJA*), 2:205; James Burgh, *Political Disquisitions: An Enquiry into Public Errors, Defects, and Abuses*, 3 vols. (1774–1775; New York: Da Capo Press, 1971), 1:403 ("first works"), 408, 2:388, 349 ("No nation"), 379 ("man of courage"), 389 ("Militia"), 281–90 (colonial contribution).

44. Edward Vose Gulick, *Europe's Classical Balance of Power* (Ithaca, N.Y.: Cornell University Press, 1955), 24–25, 45; Daniel G. Lang, *Foreign Policy in the Early Republic: The Law of Nations and the Balance of Power* (Baton Rouge: Louisiana State University Press, 1985), 2–10, 35–36; Peggy K. Liss, *Atlantic Empires: The Network of Trade and Revolution, 1713–1826* (Baltimore: Johns Hopkins University Press, 1983), 1.

45. For Grotius, see James Madison, "An Examination of the British Doctrine, which Subjects to capture a Neutral Trade not Open in Time of Peace," in *The Writings of James Madison*, 9 vols., ed. Gaillard Hunt (New York: G. P. Putnam's Sons, 1900–1910; hereafter cited as *WJM*), 7:210. For von Pufendorf, see J. H. Burns, ed., *The Cambridge History of Political Thought, 1450–1700* (New York: Cambridge University Press, 1991), 690. For Vattel, see Lang, *Foreign Policy*, 15–16; John Adams, "Defence of the Constitutions of Government of the United States of America," vol. 1, in *WJA* 4:377; Francis Stephen Ruddy, *International Law in the Enlightenment: The Background of Emmerich de Vattel's "Les Droits des Gens"* (Dobbs Ferry, N.Y.: Oceana, 1975), 280–85.

46. Emmerich de Vattel, *The Law of Nations,* ed. Joseph Autty (1758; Philadelphia: L. & J. W. Johnson, 1876), Preliminaries, lxiii, par. 21; Jean-Jacques Burlamaqui, *The Principles of Natural and Politic Law,* 2 vols., 4th ed., trans. Thomas Nugent (Boston: Joseph Bumstead, 1792), 2:208. See also Hedley Bull, *The Anarchical Society: A Study of Order in World Politics* (New York: Columbia University Press, 1977), 48; Lang, *Foreign Policy,* 16–20; Peter S. Onuf and Nicholas Onuf, *Federal Union, Modern World: The Law of Nations in an Age of Revolution, 1776–1814* (Madison, Wis.: Madison House, 1993), 10–22.

47. Thomas Hobbes, *Leviathan: or the Matter Forme and Power of a Commonwealth Ecclesiastical and Civil,* ed. Michael Oakeshott (1651; New York: Collier Books, 1962), 99–100; Burlamaqui, *Principles,* 1:121; Samuel Freiherr von Pufendorf, *The Law of Nature and Nations,* 5th ed., trans. Basil Kennett (London: J. & J. Bonwicke, 1749), 108; Vattel, *Law of Nations,* bk. 3, ch. 3, par. 47, 311; John Locke, *Two Treatises of Government,* ed. Peter Laslett (1690; New York: Cambridge University Press, 1963), par. 134, 401; also Bull, *Anarchical Society,* 24–27; Lang, *Foreign Policy,* 35.

48. Burlamaqui, *Principles,* 1:120; Hugo Grotius, *The Rights of War and Peace,* trans. A. C. Campbell (1625; New York: M. Walter Dunne, 1901), 389–90; Vattel, *Law of Nations,* bk. 1, ch. 22, par. 282, 125–26 ("nation"), and bk. 3, ch. 7, par. 112, 336.

49. Elizabeth Fox-Genovese, *The Origins of Physiocracy: Economic Revolution and Social Order in Eighteenth-Century France* (Ithaca, N.Y.: Cornell University Press, 1976), 9–11, 306; McCoy, *Elusive Republic,* 67–68; Adam Smith, *An Inquiry into the Nature and the Causes of the Wealth of Nations,* 2 vols., ed. Edwin Cannan (Chicago: University of Chicago Press, 1976), 2:95.

50. Charles M. Andrews, *The Colonial Period of American History,* 4 vols. (New Haven: Yale University Press, 1934–1938), 4:13–20, 323; Michael Kammen, *Empire and Interest: The American Colonies and the Politics of Mercantilism* (Philadelphia: J. B. Lippencott, 1970), 5–6, 48–49; Adam Smith, *Wealth of Nations,* 1:457, 495, 2:180.

51. David Hume, "Of Commerce," in *Essays: Moral, Political, and Literary,* ed. Eugene F. Miller (1777; Indianapolis: Liberty Fund, 1985), 256–57; also McCoy, *Elusive Republic,* 19–30; Adam Ferguson, *An Essay on the History of Civil Society* (1767; New York: Garland, 1971), 36.

52. Montesquieu, *Spirit of the Laws,* 1:96; McCoy, *Elusive Republic,* 46–49, 56–60, 66–69, 107–10; Jefferson, *Notes on Virginia,* 164–65.

53. Bailyn, *Ideological Origins,* 22 ("switchboard"), 99–102; Richard H. Kohn, *Eagle and Sword: The Federalists and the Creation of the Military Establishment in America, 1783–1802* (New York: Free Press, 1975), 2–6; John W. Shy, *Toward Lexington: The Role of the British Army in the Coming of the American Revolution* (Princeton, N.J.: Princeton University Press, 1965), 140–43, 376, 380–81.

54. Robert W. Tucker and David C. Hendrickson, *The Fall of the First British Empire: Origins of the War of American Independence* (Baltimore: Johns Hopkins University Press, 1982), 56–57; John E. Crowley, *This Sheba, SELF: The Conceptualization of Economic Life in Eighteenth-Century America* (Baltimore: Johns Hopkins University Press, 1974), 127–31; John W. Tyler, *Smugglers and Patriots: Boston Merchants and the Advent of the American Revolution* (Boston: Northeastern University Press, 1986), 22–23, 172; Pauline Maier, *From Resistance to Revolution: Colonial Radicals and the Development of American Opposition to Britain, 1765–1776* (New York: Alfred A. Knopf, 1972), 137–38; McCoy, *Elusive Republic,* 94–95.

55. Tucker and Hendrickson, *First British Empire,* 50–56; Kammen, *Empire and Interest,* 129; Robert Middlekauff, *The Glorious Cause: The American Revolution, 1763–1789*

(New York: Oxford University Press, 1982), 153–54; P. D. G. Thomas, *British Politics and the Stamp Act Crisis: The First Phase of the American Revolution, 1763–1767* (London: Oxford University Press, 1975), 31–32; Jack M. Sosin, *Agents and Merchants: British Colonial Policy and the Origins of the American Revolution, 1763–1775* (Lincoln: University of Nebraska Press, 1965), 89; Paine, *Common Sense,* 83.

2: THE ARC OF VIRTUE

1. Adams to Benjamin Rush, Feb. 25, 1808, in Alexander Biddle, ed., *Old Family Letters: Copied from the Originals for Alexander Biddle* (Philadelphia: J. B. Lippencott, 1892), 178.

2. James H. Hutson, *John Adams and the Diplomacy of the American Revolution* (Lexington: University Press of Kentucky, 1980), 1–8 (poem quoted p. 5); Adams to Benjamin Rush, May 23, 1807, in Biddle, *Old Family Letters,* 143 ("legend"); Adams to Nathan Webb, Oct. 12, 1755, *PJA* 1:5 (quotations).

3. Adams, Diary entry, March 31, 1774, *DAJA* 2:95 ("Cession"); Adams to Hendrik Calkoen, Oct. 4, 1780, *PJA* 10:200.

4. Wood, *Creation,* 21–22; Bailyn, *Ideological Origins,* 55–59; John Adams, *A Dissertation on the Canon and Feudal Law,* Feb. 1765, *DAJA* 1:255–56.

5. Adams to Mercy Otis Warren, Jan. 8, April 16, 1776, *PJA* 3:398, 4:125.

6. Gerard Clarfield, "John Adams: The Marketplace and American Foreign Policy," *New England Quarterly* 52, no. 3 (Sept. 1979): 348–50; Jack N. Rakove, *The Beginnings of National Politics: An Interpretive History of the Continental Congress* (New York: Alfred A. Knopf, 1979), 49; Adams to James Warren, April 6, 1777 ("shackles"), July 17, 1774 (non-exportation), Oct. 20 ("Inhabitants"), Oct. 28, 1775 ("Shield"), *PJA* 5:145, 2:110, 3:216, 254–55.

7. Adams, "Autobiography," *DAJA* 3:314, 327; H. James Henderson, *Party Politics in the Continental Congress* (New York: McGraw Hill, 1974), 40–41; List of Grievances, Oct. 14, 1774, *PJA* 2:162; Adams, Notes of Debates, Oct. 17 [?], 1774, *DAJA* 2:154; Don Higginbotham, *The War of American Independence: Military Attitudes, Policies, and Practice, 1763–1789* (New York: Macmillan, 1971), 109–14.

8. Adams, "Autobiography," *DAJA* 3:327.

9. Adams, "Thoughts on Government," *PJA* 4:88 ("single assembly"), 91 ("Frugality"), 92 ("people"); John R. Howe Jr., *The Changing Political Thought of John Adams* (Princeton, N.J.: Princeton University Press, 1966), 16–18; Douglass Adair, "Fame and the Founding Fathers," in Douglass Adair, *Fame and the Founding Fathers,* ed. Trevor Colbourn (New York: W. W. Norton, 1974), 8; Adams to Unknown, April 27, 1777, *PJA* 5:163 ("ambition").

10. Samuel Flagg Bemis, *The Diplomacy of the American Revolution,* rev. ed. (Bloomington: University of Indiana Press, 1957), 32; Rakove, *National Politics,* 81, 96.

11. John Dickinson's speech notes of July 1, 1776, in *Letters of Delegates,* 4:354; Patrick Henry to Adams, May 20, 1776, *PJA* 4:201; also John E. Selby, *The Revolution in Virginia, 1775–1783* (Williamsburg, Va.: Colonial Williamsburg, dist. University Press of Virginia, 1988), 95–98.

12. Adams to Abigail Adams, April 12, 1776, *AFC* 1:377 (independence); Adams, *DAJA* 3:327 ("Foreign powers"); Adams to John Winthrop, June 23, 1776, *PJA* 4:331–32 ("Commerce"); Adams, Diary entry, March 1, 1776, *DAJA* 2:236; Committee of Secret Correspondence to Silas Deane, March 2, 1776, in Smith, *Letters of Delegates,* 4:321.

13. Adams to C. F. W. Dumas, Jan. 31, 1781, in John Adams, *Correspondence of the Late President Adams, Originally Published in the Boston Patriot* (Boston: Everett and Munroe, 1809), 366; Adams to Edmund Jennings, written before July 14, 1780, published Jan. 17, 1782, *PJA* 9:542; Hutson, *Diplomacy,* 28–31; Adams to Benjamin Rush, April 18, 1813, in Biddle, *Old Family Letters,* 450–51.

14. Model Treaty, editorial note, *PJA* 4:263; Max Savelle, *The Origins of American Diplomacy: The International History of Anglo-America, 1492–1763* (New York: Macmillan, 1967), 150–51; Model Treaty, *PJA* 4:265–77, 290–300.

15. Gilbert, *Farewell Address,* 43, 46–48; Adams, "Autobiography," *DAJA* 3:329; Charles Royster, *A Revolutionary People at War: The Continental Army and American Character, 1775–1783* (Chapel Hill: University of North Carolina Press, 1979), 12–23; Adams to Abigail Adams, Sept. 2, 1777, *AFC* 2:336.

16. Committee of Secret Correspondence to the Commissioners, Dec. 30, 1776, in Benjamin Franklin, *The Papers of Benjamin Franklin,* 36 vols. to date, ed. Leonard W. Labaree, William B. Wilcox, Claude A. Lopez, et al. (New Haven: Yale University Press, 1959–), 23:97; Rakove, *National Politics,* 115; Gerald Stourzh, *Benjamin Franklin and American Foreign Policy* (Chicago: University Press, 1954), 136–40.

17. Hutson, *Diplomacy,* 33–34, 37; Stourzh, *Benjamin Franklin,* 154–55; Adams to James Warren, July 26, August 4, 1778, *PJA* 6:321, 347.

18. Charles Francis Adams, *The Life of John Adams,* 2 vols. (Philadelphia: J. B. Lippencott, 1871), 1:395; Rakove, *National Politics,* 249–55; Hutson, *Diplomacy,* 42–43; Louis W. Potts, *Arthur Lee: A Virtuous Revolutionary* (Baton Rouge: Louisiana State University Press, 1981), 154–59, 185–86; Adams, Diary entry, Feb. 8, 1779, *DAJA* 2:345.

19. Adams to Abigail Adams, April 12, 1778, *AFC* 3:9 ("Republican"); Adams, *DAJA* 4:118 ("Scene"); Hutson, *Diplomacy,* 11; Stourzh, *Benjamin Franklin,* 164–65; Claude-Anne Lopez, *Mon Cher Papa: Franklin and the Ladies of Paris* (New Haven: Yale University Press, 1966), 10 ("very French"); Peter Shaw, *The Character of John Adams* (Chapel Hill: University of North Carolina Press, 1976), 137–38; Franklin to Samuel Huntington, August 9, 1780, in Franklin, *Papers,* 33:162 ("too free"); Adams to the Comte de Vergennes, July 18, 1781, *WJA* 7:445.

20. Hutson, *Diplomacy,* 41, 49–51; Rakove, *National Politics,* 255–56; Worthington C. Ford, ed., *Journals of the Continental Congress, 1774–1789,* 34 vols. (Washington, D.C.: GPO, 1904–1937), 14:456–60; Richard B. Morris, *The Peacemakers: The Great Powers and American Independence* (New York: Harper and Row, 1965), 15–18; William C. Stinchcombe, *The American Revolution and the French Alliance* (Syracuse, N.Y.: Syracuse University Press, 1969), 65–66, 73–76.

21. Adams to the President of Congress, no. 49, April 19, 1781, *PJA* 9:166, 164 ("Spirit of Commerce"), 166, 168, 177 ("Infant Hercules"), 180–81 ("free Port"). The editors of the Adams Papers consider Pownall's pamphlet the single greatest influence on Adams's diplomacy. Ibid., 9:158.

22. Adams to the President of Congress, Oct. 14, 1780, ibid., 10:270; Stinchcombe, *French Alliance,* 151; R. Arthur Bowler, *Logistics and the Failure of the British Army in America, 1775–1783* (Princeton, N.J.: Princeton University Press, 1975), 93, 123–24.

23. Jonathan R. Dull, *The French Navy and American Independence: A Study of Arms and Diplomacy, 1774–1787* (Princeton, N.J.: Princeton University Press, 1975), 154–57; Adams to Benjamin Rush, Sept. 19, 1779, *PJA* 8:153; Dull, *French Navy,* 178–79; Adams to Samuel Huntington, March 10, 1780, AP reel 98 ("trifle"); Adams to Vergennes, July 13, 1780, *PJA* 9:524; Hutson, *Diplomacy,* 68–70.

24. Hutson, *Diplomacy*, 71–73, 78–79; Bemis, *American Revolution*, 150–56.

25. Adams to the President of Congress, Feb. 1, 1781, in Francis Wharton, ed., *The Revolutionary Diplomatic Correspondence of the United States*, 6 vols. (Washington, D.C.: GPO, 1889), 2:244–47; Adams to the President of Congress, April 10, 1780, *PJA* 9:121–24; David M. Griffiths, "American Commercial Diplomacy in Russia, 1780 to 1783," *William and Mary Quarterly*, 3rd ser., 27, no. 3 (July 1970): 382–83.

26. Hutson, *Diplomacy*, 79–82, 93.

27. Adams to Franklin, June 13, 1782, in Wharton, *Diplomatic Correspondence*, 5:491; Adams, Memorial of April 19, 1781, *WJA* 7:399–401; Jonathan R. Dull, *A Diplomatic History of the American Revolution* (New Haven: Yale University Press, 1985), 124–25; Hutson, *Diplomacy*, 110–14.

28. Adams to Franklin, May 23, 1781, *WJA* 7:422; Franklin to Arthur Lee, March 21, 1777, in Franklin, *Papers*, 23:511; also Stourzh, *Benjamin Franklin*, 160–61; Adams to the President of Congress, August 4, 1779, *PJA* 8:109.

29. Stinchcombe, *French Alliance*, 153–54, 157–59, 162, 174.

30. Hutson, *Diplomacy*, 97–98; Howe, *Political Thought*, 120; Royster, *Revolutionary People*, 190; Adams to Franklin, August 25, 1781, *WJA* 7:459; Adams to Abigail Adams, Dec. 2, 1781, *AFC* 4:382; Adams to Robert R. Livingston, Feb. 19, 1782, *WJA* 7:513; Hutson, *Diplomacy*, 116.

31. Morris, *Peacemakers*, 307–10; Dull, *Diplomatic History*, 145–47.

32. Morris, *Peacemakers*, 346–50; Hutson, *Diplomacy*, 117–19; Adams, Diary entry, Nov. 5, 1782, *DAJA* 3:46–47.

33. Adams, *DAJA* 4:5 ("Naval Power"); Adams, Diary entry, Nov. 25, 1782, ibid., 3:72–74; Morris, *Peacemakers*, 376.

34. Adams, Diary entry, Nov. 29, 1782, *DAJA* 3:79–81; Morris, *Peacemakers*, 377–81.

35. Adams to James Warren, Dec. 12, 1782, in *Warren-Adams Letters*, 2 vols. (Boston: Massachusetts Historical Society, Collections, 1917–1925), 2:186; Robert R. Livingston to the Peace Commissioners, March 25, 1783, in Wharton, *Diplomatic Correspondence*, 6:338–40; Jay, Adams, and Franklin to Livingston, July 18, 1783, in John Jay, *The Correspondence and Public Papers of John Jay*, 4 vols., ed. Henry P. Johnston (New York: G. P. Putnam's Sons, 1890–1894), 2:556; Adams, Diary entry, Feb. 18, 1783, *DAJA* 3:108.

36. Adams, Diary entry, Nov. 11, 1782, *DAJA* 3:52. Adams wrote a similar letter to Livingston on the same day, see Wharton, *Diplomatic Correspondence*, 5:877–78. Adams to Thomas Mifflin, Sept. 5, 1783, *WJA* 8:146; Hutson, *Diplomacy*, 142–43; Adams to Warren, March 20, 1783, in *Warren-Adams Letters*, 2:142; Adams, Diary entry, April 30, 1783, *DAJA* 3:115–16.

37. Adams to Abigail Adams, Feb. 27, 1783, *AFC* 5:103.

38. Adams to Livingston, June 23, 1783, in Wharton, *Diplomatic Correspondence*, 6:500 ("commerce"); Frederick W. Marks III, *Independence on Trial: Foreign Affairs and the Making of the Constitution* (Baton Rouge: Louisiana State University Press, 1973), 54–56; Charles R. Ritcheson, *Aftermath of Revolution: British Policy toward the United States, 1783–1795* (Dallas: Southern Methodist University Press, 1969), 6–9; Adams to Abigail Adams, Sept. 4, 1783, *AFC* 5:233 ("Repetition").

39. S. Basedo and H. Robertson, "The Nova Scotia–British West Indies Commercial Experiment in the Aftermath of the American Revolution, 1783–1802," *Dalhousie Review* 61, no. 1 (Spring 1981): 53–54; Herbert C. Bell, "British Commercial Policy in the West Indies, 1783–1793," *English Historical Review* 31, no. 123 (July 1916): 440; Adams to Livingston, July 9, 14, 18, 1783, *WJA* 8:86, 97, 107.

40. John Holroyd, Earl of Sheffield, *Observations on the Commerce of the American States* (1784; New York: August M. Kelley, 1970), 2 ("light"), 86, 59–60, 152 ("carrying trade"), 174–75 ("navigation"), 188, 198.

41. Adams to John Jay, July 19, 1785, *WJA* 8:282 (quotations); Ritcheson, *Aftermath of Revolution*, 42; Adams to Jay, June 17, 1785, *WJA* 8:269–71.

42. Adams to Jay, June 26, August 6, Nov. 4, 1785, *WJA* 8:274, 289–90, 337; Ritcheson, *Aftermath of Revolution*, 17; Adams to Jay, Dec. 3, 1785, *WJA* 8:350–56.

43. Adams to Jay, August 25, Oct. 21, 1785, *WJA* 8:303, 326–27.

44. Lord Carmaerthen to Adams, Feb. 28, 1786, Jay to Adams, Nov. 1, 1786, in Mary A. Giunta et al., eds. *The Emerging Nation: A Documentary History of the Foreign Relations of the United States under the Articles of Confederation, 1780–1789*, 3 vols. (Washington, D.C.: NHPRC, 1996), 3:110–11, 362.

45. Adams to Jay, May 25, 1786, *WJA* 8:394–96; Adams to Cotton Tufts, May 20, 1786, AP reel 368 (quotation); Ritcheson, *Aftermath of Revolution*, 63–67, 77–78.

46. Adams to Jay, Dec. 6, 1785, *WJA* 8:356.

47. Jeremy Black, *British Foreign Policy in an Age of Revolutions, 1783–1793* (New York: Cambridge University Press, 1994), 111; W. O. Henderson, "The Anglo-French Commercial Treaty of 1786," *Economic History Review*, 2nd ser., 10, no. 1 (August 1957): 105–6; Adams to Jay, Oct. 27, 1786, Nov. 30, 1787, Feb. 14, 1788, *WJA* 8:416, 463–64, 476.

48. Clarfield, "John Adams," 345–47; Gilbert, *Farewell Address*, 65–66; Adams to Jay, August 10, 1785, Feb. 26, 1786, *WJA* 8:299, 380–81.

49. Adams to John Quincy Adams, Sept. 9, 1785, *AFC* 6:355; Adams to the Marquis de Lafayette, Jan. 21, 1786, AP reel 113; Adams to Rufus King, Feb. 14, 1786, in Rufus King, *The Life and Correspondence of Rufus King*, 6 vols., ed. Charles R. King (New York: G. P. Putnam's Sons, 1894–1900), 1:161; Adams to Samuel Adams, Jan. 26, 1786, AP reel 113.

50. Adams to Jay, May 16, 1786, *WJA* 8:391; Adams to Cotton Tufts (family friend), July 4, 1786, AP reel 386; Howe, *Political Thought*, 106–7, 125–26, 130–31, 152–53.

51. McCoy, *Elusive Republic*, 71–72; Wood, *Creation*, 104; Adams to Warren, July 4, 1786, in *Warren-Adams Letters*, 2:277.

52. Adams to Hendrik Calkoen, Oct. 27, 1780, *PJA* 10:249 (see also his letters to Vergennes, July 26, and John Luzac, Sept. 15, 1780, ibid., 46, 152); John J. McCusker and Russell R. Menard, *The Economy of British North America, 1607–1789* (Chapel Hill: University of North Carolina Press, 1985), 92; Adams to Rufus King, June 14, 1786, AP reel 113.

53. McCoy, *Elusive Republic*, 97–100; Wood, *Creation*, 569–74; Adams to Jay, Dec. 6, 1785, *WJA* 8:357.

54. Anne Robert Turgot to Richard Price, March 22, 1778, *WJA* 4:278–81; Pocock, *Machiavellian Moment*, 526. C. Bradley Thompson makes the opposite argument, that classical virtue played little or no role in Adams's thought, but he underestimates the classical element in Adams's earlier thought. See C. Bradley Thompson, *John Adams and the Spirit of Liberty* (Lawrence: University Press of Kansas, 1998), 192–201.

55. John Adams, *Defence of the Constitutions*, in *WJA* 4:283 ("inventions"), 5:289 ("poverty"), 6:209 ("frugality"), 6:95–96 ("country").

56. Ibid., 6:209, 4:391–92, 6:488.

57. Ibid., 4:296; Adams to John Taylor of Caroline, Letter 13, 1814, *WJA* 6:173;

Montesquieu, *Spirit of the Laws*, 1:156; Adams, *WJA* 4:358, 381–82, 359. Wood argues that "Adams could not understand that in America by 1787 the magistracy and senators had become somehow as representative of the people as the houses of representatives." Wood, *Creation*, 586; Adams, *WJA* 4:380 ("America").

58. Howe, *Political Thought*, 147.

59. Adams, *WJA* 6:219.

3: TILLERS OF THE EARTH

1. Jefferson to Madison, [March 24, 1793], *PTJ* 25:442.

2. Charles S. Sydnor, *Gentlemen Freeholders: Political Practices in Washington's Virginia* (Chapel Hill: University of North Carolina Press, 1952), 19–26, 51–58; Douglass Adair, ed., "James Madison's Autobiography," *William and Mary Quarterly*, 3rd ser., 2, no. 2 (April 1945): 199–200 (quotation).

3. Thomas Jefferson, *A Summary View of the Rights of British America*, in *PTJ* 1:123–24; Jefferson, Query 13, "Constitution," Query 19, "Manufactures," Query 22, "Public Revenue and Expenses," in *Notes on Virginia*, 127 ("free trade"), 164–65, 174 ("our interest").

4. Jefferson, *Notes on Virginia*, 175–76.

5. Adrienne Koch, *Jefferson and Madison: The Great Collaboration* (New York: Alfred A. Knopf, 1950), 3–6; Dumas Malone, *Jefferson and His Time*, 6 vols. (Boston: Little, Brown, 1948–1981), 1:406 (quotation).

6. Jefferson to Richard Henry Lee, August 30, 1778, *PTJ* 2:210.

7. Madison to Edmund Randolph, May 20, 1783, to Edmund Pendleton, Jan. 9, 1787, *PJM* 7:59–60, 9:244–45.

8. Jefferson to Bernardo de Galvez, Nov. 8, 1779, to George Rogers Clark, Jan. 30, Dec. 25, 1780, *PTJ* 3:168, 273–77, 4:237 ("Empire"). See also Merrill D. Peterson, *Thomas Jefferson and the New Nation* (New York: Oxford University Press, 1970), 182–83.

9. Irving Brant, *James Madison*, 6 vols. (Indianapolis: Bobbs-Merrill, 1941–1961), 1:82; Ralph Ketcham, *James Madison: A Biography* (New York: Macmillan, 1971), 96–98; Madison to Jay, Oct. 17, 1780, *PJM* 2:130–32; Virginia Delegates to Jefferson, Dec. 13, 1780, *PJM* 2:242.

10. Lance Banning, *The Sacred Fire of Liberty: James Madison and the Founding of the Federal Republic* (Ithaca, N.Y.: Cornell University Press, 1995), 42; also McDonald, *Novus Ordo Seclorum*, 204–5; Madison to Joseph Jones, Nov. 25, 1780 ("Obsticles"), to Edmund Randolph, Feb. 25, 1783, *PJM* 2:203, 6:287.

11. Stinchcombe, *French Alliance*, 174; Ketcham, *James Madison*, 93–94; Brant, *James Madison*, 2:137–44; Motion on John Adams's Commission and Instructions, July 12, 1781, *PJM* 3:188; Virginia Delegates to Thomas Nelson, Oct. 9, 1781, *PJM* 3:281; Madison, Comments on Instructions to Peace Commissioners, July 24, August 8, 1782, *PJM* 4:437, 5:33–34.

12. Vernon G. Setser, *The Commercial Reciprocity Policy of the United States, 1774–1829* (Philadelphia: University of Pennsylvania Press, 1937), 65–67; Madison to Jefferson, May 13, to Randolph, May 20, Randolph to Madison, May 24, 1783, Madison to Monroe, June 21, 1785, *PJM* 7:39, 61, 73, 8:307.

13. T. H. Breen, *Tobacco Culture: The Mentality of the Great Planters on the Eve of the Revolution* (Princeton, N.J.: Princeton University Press, 1985), 38–39, 89–95; Selby, *Revolution in Virginia*, 27–30; Emory G. Evans, "Private Indebtedness and the Revolution in

Virginia, 1776 to 1796," *William and Mary Quarterly*, 3rd ser., 28, no. 3 (July 1971): 349; Jacob M. Price, *Capital and Credit in British Overseas Trade: The View from the Chesapeake, 1700–1776* (Cambridge, Mass.: Harvard University Press, 1980), 135–37; Bruce A. Ragsdale, *A Planters' Republic: The Search for Economic Independence in Revolutionary Virginia* (Madison, Wis.: Madison House, 1996), 23–26.

14. Gilbert, *Farewell Address*, 72–73; Thomas Jefferson, Elbridge Gerry, and Hugh Williamson, Report on a Letter from the American Ministers in Europe, [Dec. 20, 1783,] *PTJ* 6:393–96; Jefferson to Monroe, Nov. 11, 1784, *PTJ* 7:511–12.

15. Jefferson to Madison, Nov. 11, 1784 ("hostility"), March 18, 1785, *PTJ* 7:506, 8:40.

16. Jefferson to Jay, August 23, 1785, ibid., 8:426 (quotations); see also Jefferson to Monroe, Feb. 6, to G. K. van Hogendorp, Oct. 13, 1785, ibid., 7:638–39, 8:623.

17. Jefferson to Jay, August 23, 1785, ibid., 8:426–27.

18. Jefferson to John Langdon, Sept. 11, 1785, ibid., 512; Merrill D. Peterson, "Thomas Jefferson and Commercial Policy, 1783–1793," *William and Mary Quarterly*, 3rd ser., 22, no. 4 (Oct. 1965): 589–90.

19. "Bill Restricting Foreign Vessels to Certain Virginia Ports," June 8, 1784, *PJM* 8:64–65; Drew R. McCoy, "The Virginia Port Bill of 1784," *Virginia Magazine of History and Biography* 83, no. 3 (July 1975): 291–92; Madison to Jefferson, July 3, 1784, *PJM* 8:93; Jefferson to Madison, Nov. 11, 1784, *PTJ* 7:503.

20. Richard S. Chew III, "A New Hope for the Republic" (unpublished M.A. thesis, College of William and Mary, 1992), 16–17; Madison to Jefferson, August 20, 1784, to Monroe, August 7, 1785, to Jefferson, April 16, 1781, to Edmund Randolph, Feb. 25, 1783, to James Monroe, August 7, 1785, *PJM* 8:102–3 ("trade of G.B."), 333–35, 3:72, 6:287, 8:335 ("carriers"). For the Port Bill, see McCoy, "Port Bill," 299–303. McCoy has called the Port Bill "a classic mercantilist measure in that it specifically encouraged the development of native (i.e. Virginian) seamen." McCoy, "Port Bill," 293. Richard Chew is closer to the mark in arguing that encouragement of seamen was a minor part of the bill. Chew, "New Hope," 51–52.

21. Peterson, *New Nation*, 315–16; Lawrence S. Kaplan, *Jefferson and France: An Essay on Politics and Political Ideas* (New Haven: Yale University Press, 1967), 20–21; Jefferson to John Langdon, Sept. 11, 1785, *PTJ* 8:512.

22. Jacob M. Price, *France and the Chesapeake: A History of the French Tobacco Monopoly, 1674–1791, and of Its Relationship to the British and American Tobacco Trades*, 2 vols. (Ann Arbor: University of Michigan Press, 1973), 2:738; Jefferson to Vergennes, August 15, 1785, *PTJ* 8:385–86, 388–89.

23. Malone, *Jefferson and His Time*, 2:40; Price, *France and the Chesapeake*, 2:758.

24. Price, *France and the Chesapeake*, 2:750–56, 760–68.

25. Jefferson to Thomas Pleasants, August 8, to Jay, May 27, Oct. 23, 1786, to Montmorin, July 23, 1787, *PTJ* 9:472, 583–84, 10:485, 11:616.

26. Price, *France and the Chesapeake*, 2:769, 773–74; Doron S. Ben-Atar, *The Origins of Jeffersonian Commercial Policy and Diplomacy* (New York: St. Martin's Press, 1993), 81.

27. Jefferson to Jay, Oct. 23, 1786, to Madison, Jan. 30, 1787 (partially in code), July 31, 1788 (partially in code), *PTJ* 10:484, 11:95–96, 13:440.

28. Black, *Age of Revolution*, 139–55; Jefferson to Alexander Donald, Sept. 17, to Burrill Carnes, Sept. 22, 1787, *PTJ* 12:132–33 (quotation), 164.

29. Marks, *Independence on Trial*, 25–32.

30. Norman K. Risjord, *Chesapeake Politics, 1781–1800* (New York: Columbia University Press, 1978), 235–38; Patricia Watlington, *The Partisan Spirit: Kentucky Politics, 1779–1792* (Chapel Hill: University of North Carolina Press, 1972), 89–93; Samuel Flagg Bemis, *Pinckney's Treaty: America's Advantage from Europe's Distress, 1783–1800,* rev. ed. (New Haven: Yale University Press, 1960), 118–24.

31. Madison to Jefferson, August 20, 1784, *PJM* 8:107 (yeoman vision); Monroe to Madison, May 31, Madison to Monroe, June 21 (partially in code), Monroe to Madison, August 14, 1786, ibid., 9:68–69, 82, 104; Madison, Resolution Reaffirming American Rights to Navigate the Mississippi, Nov. 29, 1786, and Resolution to Transfer Negotiations with Spain to Madrid, April 18, 1787, ibid., 9:182–83, 388.

32. Jay to Jefferson, Jan. 19, Jefferson to Jay, May 23, 1786, *PTJ* 9:185, 569.

33. Jefferson to Archibald Stuart, Jan. 25, 1786, ibid., 9:218.

34. Jefferson to Madison, Jan. 30, 1787, ibid., 11:93.

35. Madison to the Marquis de Lafayette, March 20, 1785, *PJM* 8:251–53.

36. Madison to Jefferson, March 18, 1786, ibid., 8:502; Jefferson to Edmund Randolph, Feb. 15, 1783, to John Page, August 20, to Madison, Sept. 1, 1785, *PTJ* 6:248 ("pride"), 8:419, 460–61.

37. "Notes on Ancient and Modern Confederacies," April–June 1786, *PJM* 9:8 ("Romans"), 8–11 (Helvetic Confederacy), 16–17 ("Grotius").

38. Ketcham, *James Madison,* 185; Madison to George Washington, Nov. 8, 1786, to Edmund Pendleton, Feb. 24, 1787, *PJM* 9:166, 294–95 ("present System").

39. Madison to Jefferson, March 19, 1787, in *PJM* 9:318–19. Charles F. Hobson argues that the negative on state laws was central to Madison's solution to the republican crisis. Hobson, "The Negative on State Laws: James Madison, the Constitution and the Crisis of Republican Government," *William and Mary Quarterly,* 3rd ser., 36, no. 2 (April 1979): 218, 221–23.

40. Madison, "Vices of the Political System of the United States," April–June 1787, *PJM* 9:349, 353–57 (quotations 355–57).

41. Ketcham, *James Madison,* 186–87; David Hume, "Idea of a Perfect Commonwealth," in Hume, *Essays,* 522–26. Douglass Adair was the first to point out the connection between Hume and Federalist no. 10. See "'That Politics May Be Reduced to a Science': David Hume, James Madison, and the Tenth Federalist," in Adair, *Founding Fathers,* 93–106.

4: Extending the Sphere

1. Forrest McDonald, *Alexander Hamilton: A Biography* (New York: W. W. Norton, 1979), 217.

2. Hamilton, "A Full Vindication of the Measures of Congress," [Dec. 15], 1774, *PAH* 1:47 (American rights), 58 (G.B.), 55 ("trade"), 58, 61, 46–47 (vice).

3. Hamilton, "The Farmer Refuted," [Feb. 23,] 1775, ibid., 1:88, 94, 129, 152.

4. Hamilton to Jay, Nov. 26, 1775, ibid., 1:177; Broadus Mitchell, *Alexander Hamilton,* 2 vols. (New York: Macmillan, 1957–1962), 1:76; Hamilton to George Clinton, Feb. 13, 1778, *PAH* 1:425; McDonald, *Hamilton,* 18–19.

5. Hamilton to George Clinton, Feb. 13, 1778, to John Laurens, June 30, 1780, *PAH* 1:427, 2:347.

6. McDonald, *Hamilton,* 4–5.

7. Hamilton to James Duane, Sept. 3, 1780, to Robert Morris, April 30, 1781, *PAH* 2:401, 408, 617–18.

8. Hamilton, Continentalist no. 6, July 4, 1782, ibid., 3:103 ("preach"); Gerald Stourzh, *Alexander Hamilton and the Idea of Republican Government* (Stanford, Calif.: Stanford University Press, 1970), 70–73; Hamilton, Continentalist no. 5, April 18, 1782, *PAH* 3:76 ("paradoxes"), 77, and Continentalist, no. 6, July 4, 1782, *PAH* 3:102 ("interwoven").

9. Stourzh, *Alexander Hamilton,* 180–84; Karl-Friedrich Walling, *Republican Empire: Alexander Hamilton on War and Free Government* (Lawrence: University Press of Kansas, 1999), 9–10; McDonald, *Hamilton,* 112; Hamilton, Continentalist, no. 1, July 12, 1781, *PAH* 2:651 ("History"), and Continentalist no. 4, August 30, 1781, *PAH* 2:670.

10. Ketcham, *James Madison,* 190–92; Madison, "Virginia Plan," *PJM* 10:15–17; Madison's notes for May 29, 1787, in Farrand, *Records,* 1:18–23.

11. Madison's notes, June 1, 1787, in Farrand, *Records,* 1:64–65 (Pinckney and Sherman); Rufus King's notes, June 1, ibid., 1:70; Convention Journal, June 4–5, ibid., 1:93–94, 116.

12. Madison's notes, June 18, ibid., 1:283, 289 ("principles"), 290 ("Republican Govt."); Robert Yates's notes, June 22, ibid., 1:381.

13. Madison's notes, June 29, August 17, ibid., 1:465 (quotations), 2:318–19.

14. Madison's notes, June 25, 29, ibid., 1:401–2 (Pinckney), 467 (Hamilton); Stourzh, *Alexander Hamilton,* 126–28.

15. Madison's notes, August 21, 29, in Farrand, *Records,* 2:361 (quotation), 361–64, 449–52.

16. McCoy, *Elusive Republic,* 121–24, 131–34. McDonald correctly points out that Madison's nationalism was always tempered by his concern for Virginia's interests in *Novus Ordo Seclorum,* 204–5. Wood, *Creation,* 475.

17. Clinton Rossiter called Hamilton's "Publius" the "real Hamilton." However, both Hamilton and Madison shaded their arguments to secure ratification. Clinton Rossiter, *Alexander Hamilton and the Constitution* (New York: Harcourt, Brace, and World, 1964), 59.

18. Hamilton, Federalist no. 1, Oct. 27, Federalist no. 8, Nov. 20, 1787, in Alexander Hamilton, John Jay, and James Madison, *The Federalist,* ed. Jacob E. Cooke (Middletown, Conn.: Wesleyan University Press, 1961), 5, 46.

19. Federalist no. 23, Dec. 18, 1787, Federalist no. 31, Jan. 1, 1788, Federalist no. 70, March 15, 1788, ibid., 150, 195, 471.

20. Federalist no. 7, Nov. 17, 1787, ibid., 43 ("labyrinths"); Federalist no. 6, Nov. 14, 1787, ibid., 28, 31, 28–29 ("causes"), 32 ("objects"), 33 ("contests"); Federalist no. 7, Nov. 17, 1787, ibid., 36–39.

21. Federalist no. 11, Nov. 24, 1787, ibid., 66–67 ("Suppose"), 69–70, 72–73 ("honor").

22. Federalist no. 8, Nov. 20, 1787, ibid., 44 ("aspect"), 47–49.

23. Federalist nos. 25, 26, 28, 29, Dec. 21, 23, 26, 1787, Jan. 9, 1788, ibid., 161–62 ("Militia"), 166, 167 ("power"), 178 ("essential"), 185 ("common sense").

24. William Appleman Williams, "The Age of Mercantilism: An Interpretation of the American Political Economy, 1763–1828," *William and Mary Quarterly,* 3rd ser., 15, no. 4 (Oct. 1958): 424–26.

25. Madison, Federalist no. 10, Nov. 22, 1787, *The Federalist,* 57 ("faction"), 58–59 ("source"); Douglass Adair, "'That Politics May Be Reduced to a Science':

David Hume, James Madison, and the Tenth Federalist," in Adair, *Founding Fathers,* 95–97; Gordon S. Wood, "Interests and Disinterestedness in the Making of the Constitution," in Richard Beeman, Stephen Botein, and Edward C. Carter II, eds., *Beyond Confederation: Origins of the Constitution and American National Identity* (Chapel Hill: University of North Carolina Press, 1987), 71–74.

26. Madison, Federalist no. 10, Nov. 22, 1787, *The Federalist,* 62 (re. Montesquieu, *Spirit of the Laws,* 1:120), 63–64 ("sphere").

27. Madison, Federalist nos. 14, 51, Nov. 30, 1787, Feb. 6, 1788, ibid., 85–86, 351–52. Rahe advances a similar argument in *Republics Ancient and Modern,* 586–91.

28. Madison, Federalist no. 41, Jan. 18, 1788, *The Federalist,* 271–72, 274–75.

29. Ibid., 275.

30. Madison, Federalist no. 53, February 9, 1788, ibid., 364.

31. Ketcham, *James Madison,* 280–82; Stanley Elkins and Eric McKitrick, *The Age of Federalism: The Early American Republic, 1788–1800* (New York: Oxford University Press, 1993), 9–74; Madison, Speech of April 8, 1789, *PJM* 12:65–66.

32. Madison, Speeches of April 9, 21, 1789, *PJM* 12:71–72, 100.

33. Madison, Speech of April 9, 1789, ibid., 12:71; Rahe, *Republics Ancient and Modern,* 733; Madison, Speech of April 25, 1789, *PJM* 12:112; Madison to Jefferson, June 30, 1789, *PJM* 12:269–70; Jerald A. Combs, *The Jay Treaty: Political Battleground of the Founding Fathers* (Berkeley: University of California Press, 1970), 78–79; Madison, Speech of May 4, 1790, *PJM* 13:218.

34. McCoy argues that Madison, in addition to breaking the British hold on American trade, did indeed hope to develop a domestic shipping. However, McCoy has ignored Madison's view of sailors in "Republican Distribution of Citizens." McCoy, *Elusive Republic,* 137–45.

35. Paul A. Varg, *New England and Foreign Relations, 1789–1850* (Hanover, N.H.: University Press of New England, 1983), 11–17; Madison, Speeches of April 21, May 4, 1789, June 25, 1790, *PJM* 12:101–2, 126, 13:256.

36. Madison, "Fashion," March 20, 1792, *PJM* 14:258.

37. Madison, "Republican Distribution of Citizens," March 3, 1792, ibid., 14:245; McCoy, *Elusive Republic,* 156–58. McCoy does not mention Madison's passage on sailors in his discussion of the *National Gazette* essays.

38. Jefferson, Opinion of the Secretary of State, August 28, 1790, *PTJ* 17:130; Ben-Atar, *Jeffersonian Commercial Policy,* 94–95.

39. Hamilton, Conversation with George Beckwith [Oct. 1789], *PAH* 5:483; Elkins and McKitrick, *Age of Federalism,* 123–31; John R. Nelson Jr., *Liberty and Property: Political Economy and Policymaking in the New Nation, 1789–1812* (Baltimore: Johns Hopkins University Press, 1987), 52–53; Hamilton to Jefferson, [Jan. 13, 1791], *PAH* 7:426.

40. Hamilton, Report on Public Credit, Jan. 9, 1790, *PAH* 6:69–76; McDonald, *Hamilton,* 168–71.

41. Hamilton, First Report on the Further Provision for Public Credit, Dec. 13, 1790, *PAH* 7:233; Hamilton, Second Report on the Further Provisions Necessary for Establishing Public Credit, Dec. 14, 1790, ibid., 7:306 ("fact"), 306–9, 322; Hamilton, Opinion on the Constitutionality of an Act to Establish a Bank, Feb. 23, 1791, ibid., 8:102 ("necessary and proper"); McDonald, *Hamilton,* 202–3.

42. Hamilton, Report on Manufactures, Dec. 5, 1791, *PAH* 10:230 ("expediency"), 236 ("industry"), 246 ("no natural difference"), 247, 293.

43. Nelson, *Liberty and Property,* 56; Hamilton, Report on Manufactures, *PAH* 10:257, 275–76 (quotation), 288–89, 291.

44. McCoy, *Elusive Republic*, 152–55; Ketcham, *James Madison*, 312–15; Elkins and McKitrick, *Age of Federalism*, 146–50; Richard R. Beeman, *The Old Dominion and the New Nation, 1788–1801* (Lexington: University Press of Kentucky, 1972), 67–71; Madison, Speech of April 22, 1790, *PJM* 13:167.

45. Speech of Feb. 8, 1791, *PJM* 13:386; Madison to Pendleton, Jan. 21, 1792, ibid., 14:195; Madison, "Consolidation," Dec. 3, 1791, "Fashion," March 20, 1792, "The Union: Who Are Its Real Friends?" March 31, 1792, ibid., 14:139, 259, 275.

46. Jefferson, Opinion on the Constitutionality of the Bank, Feb. 15, 1791, and Notes on the Constitutionality of Bounties to Encourage Manufactures, [Feb. 1792], *PTJ* 19:276, 23:173; Jefferson to Lafayette, June 16, 1792, ibid., 24:85 ("stock jobbers"); Jefferson, Notes of a Conversation with George Washington, July 10, 1792, ibid., 24:211.

47. Thomas Jefferson, *The Complete Anas of Thomas Jefferson*, ed. Franklin B. Sawvel (New York: Roundtable, 1903), 30, 36 (quotation); Hamilton to Edward Carrington, May 26, 1792, *PAH* 11:437.

5: THE CAUSE OF LIBERTY

1. Robert R. Palmer, *The Age of the Democratic Revolution*, 2 vols. (Princeton, N.J.: Princeton University Press, 1959–1964), 1:479–87.

2. Banning, *Jeffersonian Persuasion*, 158–59; Peterson, *New Nation*, 377–80; Jefferson to Count de Trondin-Diodati, August 3, to Madison, August 28, 1789, *PTJ* 15:326, 366.

3. Edward Handler, *America and Europe in the Political Thought of John Adams* (Cambridge, Mass.: Harvard University Press, 1964), 4–5; Adams to Benjamin Rush, Sept. 30, 1805, in Biddle, *Old Family Letters*, 82; William Maclay, diary entry, April 27, 1790, in Kenneth R. Bowling and Helen E. Viet, eds., *The Diary of William Maclay and Other Notes on Senate Debates* (Baltimore: Johns Hopkins University Press, 1988), 254.

4. Adams, "Discourses on Davila," *WJA* 6:324, 250, 257.

5. Ibid., 6:270, 273, 276, 399.

6. Jefferson to Jonathan B. Smith, April 26, 1791, *PTJ* 20:290 (quotation); Jefferson, *Anas*, 36–37; Jefferson to George Mason, Feb. 4, 1791, *PTJ* 19:241.

7. Jefferson to Madison, June 29, William Short to Jefferson, Oct. 12, 1792, Jefferson to Short, Jan. 3, Jefferson to Joseph Fay, March 18, 1793, *PTJ* 24:134, 75, 25:14, 402.

8. Palmer, *Democratic Revolution*, 2:36–44; Harry Ammon, *The Genet Mission* (New York: W. W. Norton, 1973), 2–7, 12–31, 44–46; Albert Hall Bowman, *The Struggle for Neutrality: Franco-American Diplomacy during the Federalist Era* (Knoxville: University of Tennessee Press, 1974), 41–44; Elkins and McKitrick, *Age of Federalism*, 331–34.

9. Adams to Abigail Adams, Dec. 20, 1793, AP reel 376; Adams to Tench Coxe, April 25, 1793, AP reel 116. See also Samuel Flagg Bemis, *Jay's Treaty: A Study in Commerce and Diplomacy*, rev. ed. (New Haven: Yale University Press, 1962), 185.

10. McDonald, *Hamilton*, 265–66; Bowman, *Struggle for Neutrality*, 52–54; Combs, *Jay Treaty*, 109–13; Alexander DeConde, *Entangling Alliance: Politics and Diplomacy under George Washington* (Durham, N.C.: Duke University Press, 1958), 151–53, 205–6; James D. Richardson, ed., *A Compilation of the Messages and Papers of the Presidents, 1789–1902*, 10 vols. (Washington, D.C.: Bureau of National Literature and Art, 1905–1906), 1:156 ("duty"); Jefferson to Madison, April 28, June 23, 1793, *PTJ* 25:619 ("scrap in Vattel"), 26:346.

11. Thomas Jefferson, Opinion on the Treaties with France, April 28, 1793, *PTJ* 25:608–9.

12. Ibid., 25:610–11, 613 ("just cause"), 617 ("government").

13. Malone, *Jefferson and His Time*, 3:66; Jefferson to Madison, April 28, to Monroe, May 5, to Harry Innes, May 23, 1793, *PTJ* 25:619, 661, 26:100.

14. Jefferson to Madison, May 19, 1793, *PTJ* 26:62.

15. DeConde, *Entangling Alliance*, 205–6; Bowman, *Struggle for Neutrality*, 41–44.

16. Ammon, *Genet Mission*, 65–71.

17. Ibid., 72–73; Jefferson to Monroe, June 28, 1793, *PTJ* 26:393; Ammon, *Genet Mission*, 80, 86.

18. Jefferson to Madison, July 7, 1793, *PJM* 26:444; Jefferson, Dissenting Opinion on the *Little Sarah*, July 8, 1793, ibid., 26:450–51; Ammon, *Genet Mission*, 90–94.

19. Jefferson to Madison, August 3, 1793, *PTJ* 26:606; Ammon, *Genet Mission*, 108–10; Notes of a Cabinet Meeting on Edmond Charles Genet, August 20, 1793, *PTJ* 26:730–32; Jefferson to Madison, Sept. 1, 1793, *PTJ* 27:6.

20. Ammon, *Genet Mission*, 112, 155–59, 171–72.

21. Jefferson, *Report on Commerce*, Dec. 16, 1793, *PTJ* 27:574.

22. Ibid., 574–75.

23. [Hamilton,] "No Jacobin," no. 8, August 26, 1793, *PAH* 15:283 ("every nation"); "Pacificus," no. 6, July 17, 1793, ibid., 106 (GRECIAN HORSE); Hamilton to Washington, April 14, 1794, ibid., 16:272 ("Hercules").

24. Hamilton to Jay, April 9, 1793, ibid., 14:298.

25. Hamilton and Henry Knox to Washington, May 2, 1793, ibid., 369, 377, 386.

26. Hamilton to George Washington, May 2, 1793, ibid., 398–99, 403, 406–8. See also Gilbert L. Lycan, *Alexander Hamilton and American Foreign Policy* (Norman: University of Oklahoma Press, 1970), 141–42.

27. Hamilton to George Washington, May 15, 1793, *PAH* 14:454–56; Hamilton to Richard Harrison, [June 13–15, 1793], ibid., 539; Cabinet meeting, July 8, 1793, ibid., 15:71.

28. Hamilton to Unknown, May 18, to Henry Lee, June 22, 1793, ibid., 14:475–76 (all quotations except last one), 15:14–15 ("jealousy").

29. Hamilton, Defence of the President's Neutrality Proclamation, [May 1793,] ibid., 14:503, 507.

30. "Pacificus" no. 1, June 29, no. 7, July 27, 1793, ibid., 15:37 (quotations), 40, 43, 130.

31. "Pacificus" no. 2, July 3, 1793, ibid., 56–60.

32. "Pacificus" no. 3, July 6, 1793, ibid., 65 ("naval force"), 67 ("contest"), 68.

33. "Pacificus" no. 4, July 10, 1793, ibid., 84, 86.

34. "Pacificus" no. 5, July 13–17, no. 6, July 17, 1793, ibid., 91, 95, 102.

35. "Pacificus" no. 5, July 13–17, no. 6, July 17, 1793, ibid., 92, 106.

36. "No Jacobin" no. 2, August 5, no. 6, August 23, 1793, ibid., 186 ("violation"), 268–69.

37. "Americanus" no. 1, Jan. 31, 1794, ibid., 669–71.

38. Hamilton, "Views of the French Revolution," [1794], ibid., 26:739 ("Theories"); Hamilton, "The Cause of France," [1794], ibid., 17:585 ("Liberty"); Hamilton, "Relations with France," [1795–1796], ibid., 19:522.

39. "Americanus" no. 1, Jan. 31, no. 2, Feb. 7, 1794, ibid., 15:673, 16:13, 14–15 (quotations).

40. Ritcheson, *Aftermath of Revolution*, 298–302.

41. Hamilton to Washington, April 14, 1794, *PAH* 16:266–67.

42. Ibid., 272 ("estimate"), 273–75, 276 ("error"), 278–79; Combs, *Jay Treaty*, 108.

43. Elkins and McKitrick, *Age of Federalism*, 399–401; Lycan, *Foreign Policy*, 226–28; Bemis, *Jay's Treaty*, 291–96.

44. Bemis, *Jay's Treaty*, 296, 304–6; Hamilton to Randolph, July 8, 1794, conversation with George Hammond, [July 1–10], 1794, *PAH* 16:578, 548; Ritcheson, *Aftermath of Revolution*, 353.

45. Elkins and McKitrick, *Age of Federalism*, 406–14; Combs, *Jay Treaty*, 158–60; Bemis, *Jay's Treaty*, 348–73; Ritcheson, *Aftermath of Revolution*, 353.

46. See Bemis, *Jay's Treaty*, 467–69, for the text of article 12. McDonald, *Hamilton*, 316; Hamilton to Rufus King, June 11, to William Bradford, June 13, 1795, *PAH* 18:371, 374; Hamilton [to Washington], "Remarks on the Treaty of Amity Commerce and Navigation lately made between the United States and Great Britain," [July 9–11, 1795], *PAH* 18:451; Combs, *Jay Treaty*, 160–61.

47. Hamilton, "The Defence" no. 5, August 7, no. 2, July 25, 1795, *PAH* 19:94 ("War, or disgrace"), 18:495 ("Few nations"), 498–99 ("dangerous mistakes").

48. Hamilton, "The Defence" no. 8, August 15, no. 10, August 26, no. 22, Nov. 5–11, 1795, ibid., 19:116–17, 175 ("general spirit"), 395.

49. John C. Miller, *Alexander Hamilton: Portrait in Paradox* (New York: Harper and Brothers, 1959), 386, 429; Hamilton, "The Defence" no. 6, August 8, 1795, *PAH* 19:106.

50. Hamilton, "The Defence" no. 6, August 8, no. 15, Sept. 12–14, 1795, *PAH* 19:105, 264–65 ("adequate atonement").

51. Hamilton, "The Defence" no. 33, Dec. 19, 1795, ibid., 501 (quotation), 505–8.

52. Lycan, *Foreign Policy*, 286 ("apex"); Washington to Hamilton, May 15, 1796, *PAH* 20:175; Draft of May 15, 1796, in Victor Hugo Paltsits, *Washington's Farewell Address* (New York: New York Public Library, 1935), 169, 171. See also Matthew Spalding and Patrick J. Garrity, *A Sacred Union of Citizens: George Washington's Farewell Address and the American Character* (Lanham. Md.: Rowman & Littlefield, 1996), 50; Gilbert, *Farewell Address*, 123–34; Paltsits, *Farewell Address*, 31–54.

53. Draft of Washington's Farewell Address, July 30, 1796, *PAH* 20:282. For the final version, see Washington's Farewell Address, Sept. 19, 1796, in Richardson, *Messages and Papers*, 1:221.

54. Draft of July 30, 1796, *PAH* 20:284, 286; Farewell Address, in Richardson, *Messages and Papers*, 1:222–23.

55. Draft of July 30, 1796, *PAH* 20:277.

6: THE BOLINGBROKEAN MOMENT

1. James McHenry to Adams, July 20, 1799, AP reel 395; Adams to McHenry, July 27, 1799, AP reel 120.

2. Bolingbroke, *Works*, 2:401; Shaw, *Character*, 247–48; Ralph Ketcham, *Presidents above Party: The First American Presidency, 1789–1829* (Chapel Hill: University of North Carolina Press, 1984), 94–97; Elkins and McKitrick, *Age of Federalism*, 536–37; Alexander DeConde, *The Quasi-War: The Politics and Diplomacy of the Undeclared War*

with France, 1797–1801 (New York: Charles Scribner's Sons, 1966), 4–6; Bruce Minoff, "John Adams and the Presidency," in Thomas E. Cronin, ed., *Inventing the American Presidency* (Lawrence: University Press of Kansas, 1989), 304.

3. Adams to James Lloyd, March 29, 1815, *WJA* 10:147.

4. Ralph Adams Brown, *The Presidency of John Adams* (Lawrence: University Press of Kansas, 1975), 38–41; Adams to Thomas Truxton, Dec. 13, 1803, AP reel 118.

5. Adams to Abigail Adams, March 5, 1797, AP reel 383; Adams to Jefferson, May 11, 1794, in Cappon, *Adams-Jefferson Letters*, 255.

6. Combs, *Jay Treaty*, 186–88; Bowman, *Struggle for Neutrality*, 237–44.

7. C. F. Adams, *Life of John Adams*, 2:214–16; Stephen G. Kurtz, *The Presidency of John Adams: The Collapse of Federalism* (Philadelphia: University of Pennsylvania Press, 1957), 238, 269–80; Leonard D. White, *The Federalists: A Study in Administrative History* (New York: Macmillan, 1948), 238–41. Pickering, McHenry, and Lee were each last on Washington's list of candidates for their respective posts. Kurtz, *Presidency*, 414–15; Gerard Clarfield, *Timothy Pickering and American Diplomacy, 1795–1800* (Columbia: University of Missouri Press, 1969), 90–92.

8. Hamilton, "The Warning" no. 1, Jan. 27, no. 2, Feb. 7, no. 3, Feb. 27, 1797, *PAH* 20:494, 510–11, 519.

9. William Stinchcombe, *The XYZ Affair* (Westport, Conn.: Greenwood, 1980), 23; Hamilton to Timothy Pickering, March 22, 1797, *PAH* 20:545–46. See also Hamilton to Washington, Jan. 25–31, to Theodore Sedgwick, Feb. 26, to McHenry, March, to William L. Smith, April 5, 1797, *PAH* 20:480, 522, 571, 575; Lycan, *Foreign Policy*, 308–9.

10. Hamilton to McHenry, April 29, 1797, *PAH* 21:63–64. McDonald argues that the possibility of internal discord made Hamilton willing to go further to make peace with France. McDonald, *Hamilton*, 333.

11. Adams to Abigail Adams, Jan. 9, 1797, AP reel 383.

12. This account is based on a variety of sources, including Kurtz, *Presidency*, 228–29, and DeConde, *Quasi-War*, 13–28. Adams described his meeting with Jefferson in Adams to Elbridge Gerry, April 6, 1797, and Letter 13 to the *Boston Patriot*, 1809, *WJA* 8:538, 9:286–87. Jefferson's version is in "Notes on Conversations with George Washington and John Adams, after Oct. 13, 1797," *PTJ* 29:551–52. McHenry later recalled that he was the only member to criticize Gerry. McHenry to Pickering, Feb. 23, 1811, in Henry Cabot Lodge, *Life and Letters of George Cabot* (Boston: Little, Brown, 1877), 204–5. Adams discussed Dana in Adams to Gerry, June 20, 1797, *WJA* 8:546. John Marshall appears second to Madison on a list of proposed envoys in John Adams's hand, AP reel 386.

13. For the French decree, see R. A. Brown, *Presidency*, 39–40, and Bowman, *Struggle for Neutrality*, 276–77. Adams to Thomas Truxton, Nov. 30, 1802, in Dudley W. Knox, ed., *Naval Documents Related to the Quasi-War between the United States and France*, 7 vols. (Washington, D.C.: GPO, 1935–1938), 5:174–75; Draft of speech of May 16, 1797, AP reel 387; Frederic H. Haynes, "John Adams and American Sea Power," *American Neptune* 25, no. 1 (Jan. 1965): 38–43.

14. Speech fragment, Nov. 22, 1797, AP reel 387; Adams to Gerry, May 3, 1797, AP reel 117.

15. Adams, Speech of May 16, 1797, *WJA* 9:113–15; Kurtz, *Presidency*, 234–35; DeConde, *Quasi-War*, 26–31; R. A. Brown, *Presidency*, 42–45; Hamilton to Oliver Wolcott, June 6, 1797, *PAH* 21:99.

16. DeConde, *Quasi-War*, 35; Stinchcombe, *XYZ Affair*, 32–35.

17. Adams to Oliver Wolcott, Oct. 27, to Pickering, Oct. 31, 1797, *WJA* 8:558–59; Bowman, *Struggle for Neutrality,* 310–14; Marshall to Pickering, Sept. 9, 1797, in John Marshall, *The Papers of John Marshall,* 10 vols. to date, ed. Herbert A. Johnson et al. (Chapel Hill: University of North Carolina Press, 1974–), 3:134.

18. Stinchcombe, *XYZ Affair,* 54–59; Marshall's journal entry and American Envoys to Timothy Pickering, Oct. 22, 1797, in Marshall, *Papers,* 3:173, 255–67. The October 30 meeting with Talleyrand is described in American Envoys to Timothy Pickering, Nov. 8, 1797, in Marshall, *Papers,* 3:284.

19. Marshall's journal, Feb. 4, 1797, in Marshall, *Papers,* 3:195–96; Stinchcombe, *XYZ Affair,* 109–13; Marshall's journal, March 14, 1798, in Marshall, *Papers,* 3:229–31; George Athan Billias, *Elbridge Gerry: Founding Father and Republican Statesman* (New York: McGraw-Hill, 1976), 274–75.

20. R. A. Brown, *Presidency,* 48–49; Stinchcombe, *XYZ Affair,* 71; Paper in John Adams's hand titled "Remarks/ No. 1 Oct. 22, 1797," AP reel 386 (the date refers to the date of the first dispatch describing the meeting with Hottinguer); Adams, Speech of March 19, 1798, *WJA* 9:156–57; R. A. Brown, *Presidency,* 50–52.

21. Adams to the Inhabitants of Burlington County, New Jersey, May 8, 1798, *WJA* 9:191; to the Cincinnati of South Carolina, Sept. 17, 1798, ibid., 232–33; Adams, Message of June 21, 1798, ibid., 159.

22. Hamilton, "The Stand" no. 1, March 30, no. 2, April 4, no. 3, April 7, 1798, *PAH* 21:382–83 ("contempt"), 391 ("volcano"), 402.

23. Hamilton, "The Stand" no. 6, April 19, no. 1, March 30, no. 7, April 21, 1798, ibid., 438 ("policy"), 386–87 ("respectable"), 385–86, 443 ("Peace").

24. Adams to Jefferson, Oct. 15, 1822, in Cappon, *Adams-Jefferson Letters,* 585; Adams to the Young Men of Boston, May 22, 1798, *WJA* 9:194; DeConde, *Quasi-War,* 90–91; Michael A. Palmer, *Stoddert's War: Naval Operations during the Quasi-War with France, 1798–1801* (Columbia: University of South Carolina Press, 1987), 7–10, 18–19, 52–53.

25. Adams to James Lloyd, Feb. 21, 1815, *WJA* 10:127; Hamilton to McHenry, [Jan. 27–Feb. 11], 1798, *PAH* 21:342–43, 345; also Hamilton to Sedgwick, March [1–15], to Pickering, March 25, 1798, *PAH* 21:361–63, 380; Kurtz, *Presidency,* 293–94; Manning J. Dauer, *The Adams Federalists* (Baltimore: Johns Hopkins University Press, 1953), 145–50.

26. R. A. Brown, *Presidency,* 58; DeConde, *Quasi-War,* 96–107; Kurtz, *Presidency,* 321–24.

27. Ferling, *John Adams: A Life* (Knoxville: University of Tennessee Press, 1992), 355–56; Adams to Marshall, Sept. 4, 1800, in Marshall, *Papers,* 4:255. In the case of *Bas v. Tingy,* the Supreme Court unanimously ruled that the naval legislation of July 1798 constituted a limited declaration of war against France. James Brown Scott, ed., *The Controversy over Neutral Rights between the United States and France, 1797–1800: A Collection of American State Papers and Judicial Decisions* (New York: Oxford University Press, 1917), 106–15; Reginald C. Stuart, *War and American Thought: From the Revolution to the Monroe Doctrine* (Kent, Ohio: Kent State University Press, 1982), 88. William J. Murphy Jr. notes that utility outweighed ideology in Adams's thinking on the army, in "John Adams: The Politics of the Additional Army," *New England Quarterly* 52, no. 2 (June 1979): 246.

28. Kohn, *Eagle and Sword,* 215–18; John R. Howe Jr., "Republican Thought and the Political Violence of the 1790s," *American Quarterly* 19 no. 2 (Summer 1967): 150; James Morton Smith, *Freedom's Fetters: The Alien and Sedition Laws and American*

Civil Liberties (Ithaca, N.Y.: Cornell University Press, 1956), 22–34, 47–48, 51–52, 94–95; Adams, Letter 13 to the *Boston Patriot*, 1809, *WJA* 9:291; Ferling, *A Life*, 366; Elkins and McKitrick, *Age of Federalism*, 588.

29. DeConde, *Quasi-War*, 96–97; Kohn, *Eagle and Sword*, 234–37; Douglas Southall Freeman, *George Washington*, 7 vols. (New York: Charles Scribner's Sons, 1948–1957), 7:518–23.

30. DeConde, *Quasi-War*, 97–98; Adams to McHenry, August 14, 29, 1798, *WJA* 8:580, 587–88; Washington to Adams, Sept. 25, 1798, also to McHenry, Sept. 16, 1798, in George Washington, *The Writings of George Washington*, 39 vols., ed. John C. Fitzpatrick (Washington, D.C.: GPO, 1931–1944), 36:456, 447; Adams to Washington, Oct. 9, 1798, *WJA* 8:600–601.

31. DeConde, *Quasi-War*, 116–18; Dauer, *Adams Federalists*, 172–80; Hamilton to Rufus King, August 22, to Francisco de Miranda, August 22, 1798, *PAH* 21:154–56.

32. Adams to James Lloyd, March 29, 27, 1815, *WJA* 10:147, 149, 145.

33. Hamilton to Washington, Sept. 15, 1790, *PAH* 7:52–53; Miller, *Hamilton*, 467–69, 497–98; Lycan, *Foreign Policy*, 330, 375–78; Walling, *Republican Empire*, 242; Adair, *Founding Fathers*, 10–13; McDonald, *Hamilton*, 4–5. For biographers, see Miller, *Hamilton*, 470; Lycan, *Foreign Policy*, 360. Hamilton to Pickering, Feb. 21, 1799, *PAH* 22:492.

34. Hamilton to Harrison Gray Otis, Jan. 26, to McHenry, June 27, 1799, *PAH* 22:440–41, 23:227 ("squint").

35. Kohn, *Eagle and Sword*, 216; Hamilton to Sedgwick, Feb. 2, 1799, *PAH* 22:453.

36. Kohn, *Eagle and Sword*, 284.

37. Dauer, *Adams Federalists*, 89; Adams to Gerry, Feb. 13, 1797, *WJA* 8:525; Peter P. Hill, *William Vans Murray: Federalist Diplomat* (Syracuse, N.Y.: Syracuse University Press, 1971), 1–45.

38. John Quincy Adams to John Adams, May 8, 1798, AP reel 133; John Quincy Adams to William Vans Murray, March 6, June 19, 1798, in John Quincy Adams, *The Writings of John Quincy Adams*, 7 vols., ed. Worthington C. Ford (New York: Macmillan, 1913–1917), 2:266, 310.

39. For Gerry, see Billias, *Elbridge Gerry*, 285–86, 294–95; DeConde, *Quasi-War*, 146–47; Kurtz, *Presidency*, 340–44. Adams, Letter 3 to the *Boston Patriot*, 1809, *WJA* 9:246.

40. DeConde downplays Gerry's influence in *Quasi-War*, 161, see also 147–48, 162–63; Vans Murray to Adams, July 1, 17, 1798, *WJA* 8:677–82; Adams to Pickering, Oct. 29, 20, 1798, *WJA* 8:614–15 ("great impression"), 609; Adams to McHenry, Oct. 22, 1798, *WJA* 8:613.

41. Palmer, *Stoddert's War*, 72–81; DeConde, *Quasi-War*, 161; Adams to Francis Dana, Dec. 3, 1798, to Abigail Adams, Jan. 1, 1799, AP reels 117, 393.

42. Adams, Speech of Dec. 8, 1798, *WJA* 9:129–30.

43. DeConde, *Quasi-War*, 151–52, 159–60, 178–79; Vans Murray to John Adams, August 20, Oct. 7, 1798, and *WJA* 8:688–90; Talleyrand to Pichon, August 28, 1798, *WJA* 8:690–91; Adams, Letter 7 to the *Boston Patriot*, 1809, *WJA* 9:262; Adams to Pickering, Jan. 15, 1799, *WJA* 8:621; Adams, Letter 1 to the *Boston Patriot*, 1809, *WJA* 9:241–42 ("sources"); Washington to Adams, Feb. 1, 1799, in Washington, *Writings*, 37:119–20.

44. Adams to James Lloyd, Jan. 1815, *WJA* 10:113.

45. Bowman, *Struggle for Neutrality*, 368 (quotation); Kohn, *Eagle and Sword*,

258–59; Kurtz, *Presidency,* 308–9, 335–36; Ketcham, *Presidents above Party,* 99; Stephen G. Kurtz, "The French Mission of 1799–1800: Concluding Chapter in the Statecraft of John Adams," *Political Science Quarterly* 80, no. 4 (Dec. 1965): 598.

46. Hamilton to Sedgwick, Feb. 21, 1799, *PAH* 22:493; Adams, Letter 4 to the *Boston Patriot,* 1809, *WJA* 8:248–50; DeConde, *Quasi-War,* 185; Richard E. Welch Jr., *Theodore Sedgwick, Federalist: A Political Portrait* (Middleton, Conn.: Wesleyan University Press, 1965), 187–89.

47. Pickering, Account of March 10, 1799, meeting, in Timothy Pickering Papers, Massachusetts Historical Society, reel 10; DeConde, *Quasi-War,* 186–87.

48. R. A. Brown, *Presidency,* 102–7; Kurtz, "French Mission," 555; Palmer, *Stoddert's War,* 108–9.

49. Bowman, *Struggle for Neutrality,* 384–87; Pickering to Adams, Sept. 11, 1799, AP reel 396; Adams to Pickering, August 6, 1799, *WJA* 9:11.

50. Adams to Benjamin Stoddert, Sept. 4, to Pickering, Sept. 16, 1799, *WJA* 9:20, 30; DeConde, *Quasi-War,* 219–22; Palmer, *Stoddert's War,* 241; Hamilton to Washington, Oct. 21, 1799, *PAH* 23:545.

51. DeConde, *Quasi-War,* 223–31.

52. Ibid., 237–57; Vans Murray to Marshall, Oct. 1, 1800, in Marshall, *Papers,* 4:310.

53. Kurtz also makes this connection in *Presidency,* 358–59. DeConde, *Quasi-War,* 269–72; Ferling, *A Life,* 393–94; Kohn, *Eagle and Sword,* 264; White, *Federalists,* 252; Elkins and McKitrick, *Age of Federalism,* 729–30; Marshall to "A Freeholder," Sept. 20, 1798, in Marshall, *Papers,* 3:505.

54. Hamilton to Sedgwick, May 10, 1800, *PAH* 24:475; Hamilton, "Letter from Alexander Hamilton, Concerning the Public Conduct and Character of John Adams, Esq. President of the United States, October, 24, 1800," ibid., 25:214; DeConde, *Quasi-War,* 277–85.

55. DeConde, *Quasi-War,* 288–92; Richard C. Rohrs, "The Federalist Party and the Convention of 1800," *Diplomatic History* 12, no. 3 (Summer 1988): 250–51; Hamilton to Sedgwick, Dec. 22, 1800, *PAH* 25:270.

56. Adams to Stoddert, March 31, 1801, *WJA* 9:582; Adams to Thomas Boylston Adams, Jan. 15, 1801, Adams Family Collection, Library of Congress; Bolingbroke, *Works,* 2:387.

57. Adams to Francis A. Vanderkemp, Dec. 28, 1800, *WJA* 9:577; Adams, Speech of Nov. 22, 1800, ibid., 145; Adams to Marshall, Oct. 3, 1800, in Marshall, *Papers,* 4:313.

7: YEOMAN VIRTUE AND THE WILDERNESS

1. Jefferson to Madison, July 7, 1793, to John Tyler Sr., June 4, 1798, *PTJ* 26:444, 30:389 ("witches").

2. George Nicholas to Madison, Feb. 9, 1794, *PJM* 15:256; Jefferson, *Anas,* 38 ("horrors"); Jefferson to Tench Coxe, June 1, 1795, *PTJ* 28:183 ("atrocities"); Madison to Nicholas, March 15, 1793, *PJM* 14:472 ("motive"); Jefferson to Madison, April 3, 1794, to William Branch Giles, April 27, 1795, *PTJ* 28:49 ("common cause"), 337 ("Pichegru").

3. Jefferson to Pinckney, May 29, 1797, *PTJ* 29:405; Madison's speech, Jan. 14, 1794, *PJM* 15:187.

4. Madison to Jefferson, May 13, 1798, *PJM* 17:130; Jefferson to Gerry, Jan. 26, 1799, *PTJ* 30:646. See also Banning, *Jeffersonian Persuasion*, 259–63.

5. Madison to Jefferson, May 8, June 13, 1793, *PJM* 15:13, 29.

6. Lang, *Foreign Policy*, 133–35; Edward Keynes, *Undeclared War: Twilight Zone of Constitutional Power* (University Park: Pennsylvania State University Press, 1982), 33; Madison to Randolph, May 31, 1789, *PJM* 13:190.

7. "Helvidius" no. 1, August 24, 1793, *PJM* 15:69–71; "Helvidius" no. 2, August 31, 1793, ibid., 82, 86.

8. "Helvidius" no. 3, Sept. 7, no. 4, Sept. 14, no. 5, Sept. 18, 1793, ibid., 98–99, 108–9, 116.

9. Madison, Speeches of Jan. 3, 23, 1794, in ibid., 169, 206; Combs, *Jay Treaty*, 121–22; Madison to Jefferson, May 11, 1794, *PJM* 15:327; Jefferson to Monroe, April 24, to Washington, May 14, 1794, *PTJ* 28:55, 75.

10. Madison, *Political Observations*, April 20, 1795, *PJM* 15:516; Madison, Draft of a Petition, Sept. 1795, ibid., 16:75–76; Jefferson to Henry Tazewell, Sept. 13, 1795, *PTJ* 28:466.

11. Madison, Petition to the General Assembly, Oct. 12, 1795, *PJM* 16:102; Madison to Monroe, Dec. 20, 1795 (partly in code), ibid., 170; Combs, *Jay Treaty*, 180–83; DeConde, *Entangling Alliances*, 133; Bemis, *Pinckney's Treaty*, 267–81.

12. Jefferson to Edmund Rutledge, Nov. 30, 1795, *PTJ* 28:542; Madison, Speeches of March 7, April 6, 1796, *PJM* 16:254, 292–93.

13. Madison, Speech of March 10, 1796, *PJM* 16:258–59, 262.

14. Madison, Speech of April 15, 1796, ibid., 316–25; Combs, *Jay Treaty*, 186–88.

15. Madison to Jefferson, Jan. 22, to James Madison Sr., March 12, 1797, *PJM* 16:471, 500–501; Jefferson to Archibald Stuart, Jan. 4, 1797, *PTJ* 29:253; Jefferson to Madison, Jan. 22, 1797, *PJM* 16:471.

16. Jefferson, "Notes on Conversations with George Washington and John Adams, after Oct. 13, 1797," *PTJ* 29:552; Jefferson to Thomas Mann Randolph, May 19, 1797, ibid., 385 (re. Adams's speech of May 16); Jefferson to Gerry, May 13, 1797, ibid., 364; Madison to Jefferson, Feb. 12, 18, 1798, *PJM* 17:78, 82.

17. Jefferson to Monroe, March 21, to Peter Carr, April 12, to Monroe, March 21, 1798, *PTJ* 30:191, 267, 191; Madison to Jefferson, April 2, 1798, *PJM* 17:104.

18. Jefferson to John Taylor, Nov. 26, 1798, to Edmund Pendleton, Jan. 29, 1799, to Archibald Stuart, June 8, 1798, *PTJ* 30:588, 661, 397; Madison to Jefferson, April 22, 1798, *PJM* 17:118.

19. Thomas Jefferson, Draft of Kentucky Resolutions [Nov. 1798], *WoTJ* 8:462–68, 471; Malone, *Jefferson and His Time*, 3:406–7; Madison, Virginia Resolutions, Dec. 21, 1798, *PJM* 17:188–90.

20. Madison, Report of 1800, *PJM* 17:309 ("constitution"), 309–10 ("interposition"), 315 ("consolidation"), 315–16, 324–28, 348; Hobson, "Negative on State Laws," 234–35.

21. [Madison,] "Political Reflections," *Philadelphia Aurora and General Advertizer*, Feb. 23, 1799, *PJM* 17:242; Jefferson to Joseph Priestly, Jan. 18, 1800, to Pendleton, April 22, 1799, *WoTJ* 9:95, 65.

22. Conversation of April 2, 1806, between Jefferson and Plumer in William Plumer, *William Plumer's Memorandum of Proceedings in the United States Senate, 1803–1807*, ed. Everett Somerville Brown (New York: Macmillan, 1923), 470.

23. Thomas Jefferson, First Inaugural Address, March 4, 1801, in Richardson, *Messages and Papers*, 1:323.

24. Albert Gallatin to Jefferson, ca. Nov. 16, 1801, in Albert Gallatin, *The Writings of Albert Gallatin*, 3 vols., ed. Henry Adams (Philadelphia: J. B. Lippencott, 1879), 1:71; Jefferson, Sixth Annual Message, Dec. 2, 1806, First Annual Message, Dec. 8, 1801, *WoTJ* 10:319, 9:335; Jefferson to William Short, Oct. 3, 1801, *WoTJ* 9:309 (quotation).

25. Jefferson to Joseph Priestly, June 19, 1802, *WoTJ* 9:381; Jefferson, Special Message to Congress, Jan. 18, 1803, in Richardson, *Messages and Papers*, 1:352; Madison to Robert R. Livingston, Jan. 31, 1804, in *The Papers of James Madison: Secretary of State Series*, 6 vols. to date, ed. Robert A. Rutland et al. (Charlottesville: University Press of Virginia, 1986– ; hereafter cited as *PJM:SS*), 6:407; Jefferson to DeWitt Clinton, Dec. 2, 1803, *WoTJ* 10:55.

26. Jefferson to Thomas Paine, March 18, 1801, *WoTJ* 9:213; Jefferson, Third Annual Message, Oct. 17, 1803, ibid., 10:43; Madison to Jefferson, Sept. 14, 1805, in James Morton Smith, ed., *The Republic of Letters: The Correspondence between Thomas Jefferson and James Madison, 1776–1826*, 3 vols. (New York: W. W. Norton, 1995), 3:1185.

27. Thomas Jefferson, Report on Negotiations with Spain, March 18, 1792, *PTJ* 23:302–3; Rufus King to Madison, April 2, 1803, in King, *Correspondence*, 4:242; Alexander DeConde, *This Affair of Louisiana* (New York: Charles Scribner's Sons, 1976), 95–102.

28. Rufus King to Madison, March 29, 1801, *PJM:SS* 1:55; Madison to Monroe, June 1, 1801, ibid., 1:245; Jefferson to Robert R. Livingston, April 18, 1802, in Jefferson, *WoTJ* 9:364–65; Jefferson to Pierre S. Dupont de Nemours, April 25, 1802, in Gilbert Chinard, ed., *The Correspondence of Jefferson and Du Pont de Nemours* (Baltimore: Johns Hopkins University Press, 1931), 46–47; Jefferson to Dupont de Nemours, Feb. 1, 1803, *WoTJ* 9:439 ("whatever power"); Madison to Livingston, Oct. 15, 1802, *PJM:SS* 4:24–25.

29. DeConde, *Louisiana*, 119–21; Arthur P. Whitaker, *The Mississippi Question, 1795–1803: A Study in Trade, Politics, and Diplomacy* (New York: D. Appleton-Century, 1934), 189–92; Jefferson to Monroe, Jan. 13, to Livingston, Feb. 3, 1803, *WoTJ* 9:419–20 (quotation), 442; Madison to Livingston, Dec. 17, 1802, *PJM:SS* 4:198.

30. McCoy, *Elusive Republic*, 197–98; Madison to Charles Pinckney, Nov. 27, 1802, *PJM:SS* 4:147.

31. Madison to Monroe and Livingston, March 2, to Charles Pinckney, Jan. 10, 1803, *PJM:SS* 4:366–67, 370, 246 (quotation).

32. Madison to Rufus King, May 1, to Livingston, May 1, to Pinckney, May 11, 1802, ibid., 3:173, 175–76, 215–16.

33. McDonald, *Hamilton*, 357–58; DeConde, *Louisiana*, 140; Madison to Monroe, March 1, 1803, *PJM:SS* 4:361; Jefferson to Monroe, Jan. 10, 1803, *WoTJ* 9:416.

34. Livingston to Madison, Sept. 1, 1802, *PJM:SS* 3:536; DeConde, *Louisiana*, 130–31, 149–54.

35. Mary P. Adams, "Jefferson's Reaction to the Treaty of San Ildefonso," *Journal of Southern History* 21, no. 2 (May 1955), 182–86; Jefferson, Confidential Message, Jan. 18, 1803, in Richardson, *Messages and Papers*, 1:352–53; Jefferson to William Henry Harrison, Feb. 27, 1803, in Thomas Jefferson, *The Writings of Thomas Jefferson*, 20 vols., ed. Andrew A. Lipscomb and Albert Bergh (Washington, D.C.: Thomas Jefferson Memorial Association, 1904–1905; hereafter cited as *WrTJ*), 10:371; M. P. Adams, "Jefferson's Reaction," 177–81.

36. DeConde, *Louisiana*, 135–36; Madison to Monroe and Livingston, March 2, 1803, *PJM:SS* 4:370–72; DeConde, *Louisiana*, 165–72; James Monroe, *The Autobiography of James Monroe*, ed. Stuart Gerry Brown (Syracuse, N.Y.: Syracuse University Press, 1959), 164.

37. Everett Somerville Brown, *The Constitutional History of the Louisiana Purchase, 1803–1812* (Berkeley: University of California Press, 1920), 17–22.

38. Jefferson, Draft of an Amendment to the Constitution [July 1803], *WoTJ* 10:3–7; Jefferson to Wilson Cary Nicholas, Sept. 9, 1803, ibid., 418–19; Madison, Proposed Constitutional Amendment [ca. July 9, 1803], *PJM:SS* 5:156; Brown, *Constitutional History*, 62–65; DeConde, *Louisiana*, 184–92.

39. Jefferson, Third Annual Message, Oct. 17, 1803, *WoTJ* 10:36; Jefferson to Horatio Gates, July 11, 1803, ibid., 13; Peterson, *New Nation*, 761–62.

40. Henry Adams, *History of the United States during the Administrations of Thomas Jefferson and James Madison*, 9 vols. (New York: Charles Scribner's Sons, 1889–1891), 2:49.

41. Ketcham, *James Madison*, 420; Jefferson, Second Inaugural Address, March 4, 1805, in Richardson, *Messages and Papers*, 1:379; Jefferson to Joseph Priestly, Jan. 29, 1804, *WoTJ* 10:71.

42. H. Adams, *History*, 2:245; Robert W. Tucker and David C. Hendrickson, *Empire of Liberty: The Statecraft of Thomas Jefferson* (New York: Oxford University Press, 1990), 159, 163; Jefferson to John Dickinson, August 9, 1803, *WoTJ* 10:29.

43. Livingston to Jefferson, May 26, 1803, Thomas Jefferson Papers, Library of Congress (hereafter cited as TJPapers), reel 28; Monroe to Madison, May 28, Madison to Monroe, July 29, 1803, *PJM:SS* 5:72–77, 7:53–54, 57–58; Madison to Monroe, April 15, to Monroe and Pinckney, July 8, 1804, *WJM* 7:141–52, 153–55.

44. Isaac Joslin Cox, *The West Florida Controversy, 1798–1813: A Study in American Diplomacy* (Baltimore: Johns Hopkins University Press, 1918), 84–85; Thomas Jefferson, "The Limits and Bounds of Louisiana," Sept. 7, 1803, in *Documents Relating to the Purchase and Exploration of Louisiana* (Boston: Houghton Mifflin, 1904), 33–36; Jefferson to James Bowdoin, April 27, 1805, *WoTJ* 10:140.

45. Madison to Monroe, July 29, to Pinckney, July 29, Oct. 12, 1803, *PJM:SS* 5:240, 246, 512–13; DeConde, *Louisiana*, 214–16; Brant, *James Madison*, 4:192–93.

46. Madison to John Armstrong, June 6, 1805, *WJM* 7:184; Kaplan, *Jefferson and France*, 114–15; Jefferson to Madison, August 7, Madison to Jefferson, August 20, Jefferson to Madison, August 27, 1805, in Smith, *Republic of Letters*, 3:1376, 1380.

47. Jefferson to Madison, August 27, 1805, in Smith, *Republic of Letters*, 3:1382; Madison to Jefferson, Sept. 1, 1805, ibid., 1384.

48. Jefferson to Madison, Oct. 23, 1805, ibid., 1394–95; Jefferson, Entry for Nov. 12, 1805, in *Anas*, 232–33; Malone, *Jefferson and His Time*, 5:62–63.

49. C. Edward Skeen, *John Armstrong, Jr., 1758–1843: A Biography* (Syracuse, N.Y.: Syracuse University Press, 1981), 76–77; Clifford L. Egan, *Neither Peace nor War: Franco-American Relations, 1803–1812* (Baton Rouge: Louisiana State University Press, 1983), 55; Jefferson, Entry for Nov. 19, 1805, in *Anas*, 233–34.

50. Ketcham, *James Madison*, 233; Norman K. Risjord, *The Old Republicans: Southern Conservatism in the Age of Jefferson* (New York: Columbia University Press, 1965), 46–50.

51. Cox, *West Florida Controversy*, 243–50; Jefferson to John Langdon, Dec. 22, 1806, TJPapers, reel 37; Jefferson to James Bowdoin, April 2, 1807, *WoTJ* 10:381.

52. H. Adams, *History*, 5:306–8; Cox, *West Florida Controversy*, 416–17; Madison to Robert Smith, July 17, 1810, in James Madison, *The Papers of James Madison: Presidential Series*, 4 vols. to date, ed. Robert A. Rutland et al. (Charlottesville: University Press of Virginia, 1984– ; hereafter cited as *PJM:PS*), 2:419; Madison to Jefferson, Oct. 19, 1810, and Proclamation of October 27, 1810, *PJM:PS* 2:585, 595–96.

53. H. Adams, *History*, 6:237–40; Brant, *James Madison*, 5:442–44; Cox, *West Florida Controversy*, 522–24; Rembert W. Patrick, *Florida Fiasco: Rampant Rebels on the Georgia-Florida Border, 1810–1815* (Athens: University of Georgia Press, 1954), 49–50, 68, 120–22; J. C. A. Stagg, *Mr. Madison's War: Politics, Diplomacy, and Warfare in the Early American Republic, 1783–1830* (Princeton, N.J.: Princeton University Press, 1983), 98–100; Madison to Congress, Jan. 3, 1811, *PJM:PS* 3:93–94; Madison to Jefferson, April 24, 1812, in Smith, *Republic of Letters*, 3:1694; Monroe to George Mathews, April 4, 1812, in *American State Papers: Foreign Relations*, 6 vols. (Washington, D.C.: Gales and Seaton, 1833–1861; hereafter cited as *ASP:FR*), 3:572.

8: Yeoman Virtue at Sea

1. Sir Augustus John Foster, *Jeffersonian America: Notes on the United States of America Collected in the Years 1805–6–7 and 11–12* (San Marino, Calif.: Huntington Library, 1954), 81; Jefferson, First Inaugural Address, March 4, 1801, in Richardson, *Messages and Papers*, 1:323 (Jefferson used similar language in an address to the General Assembly of Rhode Island, May 26, 1801, *WrTJ* 10:263); Jefferson, First Annual Message, Dec. 8, 1801, *WoTJ* 9:339.

2. Jefferson, Second Annual Message, Dec. 15, 1802, *WoTJ* 9:408; Douglas C. North, *The Economic Growth of the United States, 1790–1860* (Englewood Cliffs, N.J.: Prentice-Hall, 1961), 28, 44; Bradford Perkins, *Prologue to War: England and the United States, 1805–1812* (Berkeley: University of California Press, 1961), 112.

3. Madison to Monroe, March 6, 1805, *WJM* 7:174–75; Jefferson to George Logan, March 21, 1801, *WoTJ* 9:220; Jefferson to James Bowdoin, July 10, 1806, *WrTJ* 11:119–20.

4. H. Adams, *History*, 1:210; Jefferson to Wilson Cary Nicholas, May 25, 1809, *WoTJ* 11:108.

5. Perkins, *Prologue to War*, 76–80.

6. Ibid., 77–78; James Stephen, *War in Disguise; or, the Frauds of the Neutral Flags*, 2nd American ed. (New York: I. Riley, 1806), 57, 103, 148.

7. Madison to Jefferson, Sept. 14, also Oct. 5, 1805, in Smith, *Republic of Letters*, 3:1386, 1390; Onuf and Onuf, *Federal Union*, 208–9.

8. Madison, *An Examination of the British Doctrine*, in *WJM* 7:206 ("trade"), 209–15 (Grotius), 230 (Vattel).

9. Ibid., 268 (quotations), 272–73, 235; Madison's extracts, James Madison Papers, Library of Congress, 2nd series, reel 25.

10. Madison, *Examination*, in *WJM* 7:299–300, 346 ("we arrive"), 374–75 ("disrespectful").

11. H. Adams, *History*, 2:327.

12. Perkins, *Prologue to War*, 104–6; Reginald Horsman, *The Causes of the War of 1812* (Philadelphia: University of Pennsylvania Press, 1962), 27–29; James Fulton Zimmerman, *Impressment of American Seamen* (New York: Columbia University Press, 1925), 18–21; Jefferson to Gallatin, July 12, 1803, *WoTJ* 10:15; Madison to Monroe, Jan. 5, 1804, *PJM:SS* 6:291.

13. Jefferson, Entry for April 3, 1807, in *Anas*, 254; Burton Spivak, *Jefferson's English Crisis: Commerce, Embargo, and the Republican Revolution* (Charlottesville: University Press of Virginia, 1979), 65; Madison to Jefferson, April 17, Jefferson to Madison, April 21, 1807, in Smith, *Republic of Letters*, 3:1467–69.

14. Jefferson, Entry for March 14, 1806, in *Anas*, 236; Spivak, *English Crisis*, 32–46; Perkins, *Prologue to War*, 108–12; Madison to Monroe and Pinkney, May 17, 1806, *WJM* 7:376; Jefferson to Jacob Crowninshield, May 13, 1806, *WoTJ* 10:267.

15. Jefferson to Paine, March 25, to Monroe, May 4, 1806, *WoTJ* 10:248, 263.

16. Madison to Monroe and Pinkney, May 17, 1806, *WJM* 7:391–92; H. Adams, *History*, 3:407–9; Horsman, *Causes of War*, 76–92; Spivak, *English Crisis*, 62–65; Monroe and Pinkney to Madison, Jan. 3, 1807, *ASP:FR* 3:137–40, 146.

17. Jefferson, *Anas*, 251–52; Madison to Monroe and Pinkney, Feb. 3, 1807, *WJM* 7:397–404.

18. Madison to Monroe and Pinkney, May 20, 1807, *WJM* 7:415–16 (quotations), 444–45.

19. H. Adams, *History*, 3:416, 103; Horsman, *Causes of War*, 121.

20. Jefferson to John W. Eppes, July 12, to William H. Cabell, June 29, 1807, *WoTJ* 10:457–58 (quotation), 433; also Jefferson to George Clinton, July 6, 1807, ibid., 449, and Jefferson to Thomas Mann Randolph, July 5, to John Page, July 9, to Cabell, July 16, 1807, TJPapers, reel 38; Jefferson to Paine, Sept. 6, 1807, *WoTJ* 10:493 ("plunder").

21. Jefferson to Randolph, Oct. 26, 1807, TJPapers, reel 39 (quotation); Jefferson, Special Message on Commercial Depredations, Dec. 18, 1807, *WoTJ* 10:530–31; Brant, *James Madison*, 4:397–402; Ketcham, *James Madison*, 457; Spivak, *English Crisis*, 68–71, 103–10.

22. Madison to Pinkney, May 1, 1808, William Pinkney Papers, Princeton University.

23. Madison to Pinkney, Dec. 23, 1807, *WJM* 7:468; Madison, *Daily National Intelligencer*, Dec. 23, 1807; Madison to Pinkney, Oct. 21, 1807, William Pinkney Papers, Princeton University.

24. Madison, *Daily National Intelligencer*, Dec. 25, 1807.

25. Jefferson to John Taylor, Jan. 6, to Randolph, Feb. 6, 1808, TJPapers, reel 40; Jefferson to Caesar Rodney, April 24, 1808, *WoTJ* 11:29.

26. Ketcham, *James Madison*, 462; North, *Economic Growth*, 55–58; Horsman, *Causes of War*, 142–43; Spivak, *English Crisis*, 200–201; Unknown (Bostonian) to Jefferson, Sept. 19, 1808, TJPapers, reel 42; Madison to Pinkney, Jan. 3, 1809, *WJM* 8:42 (quotation).

27. Jefferson to Abraham Bishop, Nov. 13, 1808, to Thomas Leiper, Jan. 21, 1809, *WoTJ* 11:72, 90; Madison to Pinkney, July 21 (quotation), 3, 1808, William Pinkney Papers, Princeton University.

28. Jefferson, Eighth Annual Message, Nov. 8, 1808, *WoTJ* 11:64; Jefferson to Gallatin, May 27, 1808, *WrTJ* 12:66; Jefferson to Thomas Leiper, Jan. 21, to Stoddert, Feb. 18, 1809, *WoTJ* 11:90–91, 98.

29. Brant, *James Madison*, 5:38–39; Madison to Pinkney, March 17, 1809, *PJM:PS* 1:56.

30. Madison, First Inaugural Address, March 4, 1809, *PJM:PS* 1:16; Madison to Gerry, March 14, 1809, ibid., 44.

31. H. Adams, *History*, 5:71–72; Madison to Jefferson, April 9, 1809, *PJM:PS* 1:107; Ketcham, *James Madison*, 492–93; Madison, Proclamation of April 19, 1809, *PJM:PS* 1:125–26.

32. Madison to John G. Jackson, April 21, to Pinkney, April 21, to Jefferson, April 24, 1809, *PJM:PS* 1:128, 128, 135.

33. Perkins, *Prologue to War*, 220–21; Smith to Francis James Jackson, Oct. 19,

1809, *ASP:FR* 3:311–14; Madison to Pinkney, Oct. 23, to Jefferson, Nov. 6, 1809, *PJM:PS* 2:27–28, 55; Madison, draft of Smith to Pinkney, ca. Nov. 9, and First Annual Message, Nov. 29, 1809, *PJM:PS* 2:65–67, 91–93; Perkins, *Prologue to War*, 244–45.

34. Henry Clay, Speech of Feb. 22, 1810, in Henry Clay, *The Papers of Henry Clay*, 11 vols., ed. James F. Hopkins, Mary M. W. Hargreaves, et al. (Lexington: University Press of Kentucky, 1959–1993), 1:449; Perkins, *Prologue to War*, 239–42; Madison to Pinkney, Jan. 23, May 23, 1810, *PJM:PS* 2:195, 348 (quotations).

35. Egan, *Neither Peace nor War*, 121–24.

36. Brant, *James Madison*, 5:214; Egan, *Neither Peace nor War*, 122–23; Madison to Caesar A. Rodney, Sept. 30, to Jefferson, Oct. 19, to Pinkney, Oct. 30, 1810, *PJM:PS* 2:565, 585, 604.

37. Madison, Presidential Proclamation, Nov. 2, 1810, *PJM:PS* 2:612–13; Madison, Second Annual Message, Dec. 5, 1810, ibid., 3:50–51; Madison to Jefferson, March 18, 1811, ibid., 3:225; Egan, *Neither Peace nor War*, 141; Madison to Richard Cutts, May 23, 1811, *PJM:PS* 3:315.

38. Marquis Wellesley to Augustus John Foster, April 10, 1811, in Bernard Mayo, ed., "Instructions to the British Ministers to the United States, 1791–1812," *Annual Report of the American Historical Association for the Year 1936*, vol. 3 (Washington, D.C.: GPO, 1941), 317–18; Brant, *James Madison*, 5:374; Stagg, *Mr. Madison's War*, 78–81; Roger H. Brown, *The Republic in Peril: 1812* (New York: Columbia University Press, 1964), 33–35; Julius W. Pratt, *The Expansionists of 1812* (New York: Macmillan, 1925), 50; Madison, Third Annual Message, Nov. 5, 1811, *PJM:PS* 4:2–4.

39. H. Adams, *History*, 6:175; Madison to Jefferson, Feb. 7, April 3, 1812, *PJM:PS* 4:168, 287.

40. Madison, Special Message to Congress, June 1, 1812, *PJM:PS* 4:433–37; Madison to Unknown, July 25, 1812, *WJM* 8:204–5.

41. For the dignity of republican government, see especially Brown, *Republic in Peril*, 14–15; Ketcham, *James Madison*, 530–33; Steven Watts, *The Republic Reborn: War and the Making of Liberal America, 1790–1820* (Baltimore: Johns Hopkins University Press, 1987), 160; Brown, *Republic in Peril*, 50 (Calhoun), 52 (Grundy). Watts argues that the War Hawks overcame a *classical* fear of war. *Republic Reborn*, 240–46.

42. Perkins, *Prologue to War*, 437.

43. Stagg, *Mr. Madison's War*, 115–19; Madison, Fourth Annual Message, Nov. 4, 1812, *WJM* 8:226; Madison, Second Inaugural Message, March 4, 1813, *WJM* 8:236; Stagg, *Mr. Madison's War*, 295–96.

44. Madison to Monroe, Sept. 21, 1812, James Monroe Papers, Library of Congress, Series 1, reel 5; Stagg, *Mr. Madison's War*, 4–7, 201–5; Harry L. Coles, *The War of 1812* (Chicago: University of Chicago Press, 1965), 38–39; Donald R. Hickey, *The War of 1812: A Forgotten Conflict* (Urbana: University of Illinois Press, 1989), 72–75, 81–84, 86–88.

45. Andrei de Daschkov to Monroe, March 8, 1813, *ASP:FR* 3:624; Madison to Jefferson, March 10, 1813, in Smith, *Republic of Letters*, 3:1718; Brant, *James Madison*, 6:155–63; Madison to John Nicholas, April 2, 1813, *WJM* 8:243–44; Madison, Message to the Special Session of Congress, May 25, 1813, *WJM* 8:244–47; H. Adams, *History*, 7:343; Stagg, *Mr. Madison's War*, 299–302.

46. Hickey, *War of 1812*, 158, 182–83, 190–203; Stagg, *Mr. Madison's War*, 369–72, 382–86.

47. Cabinet Memorandum, June 23–24, 1814, in Madison, *Letters and Other Writings of James Madison*, ed. William C. Rives. 4 vols. (Philadelphia: J. B. Lippencott, 1865; hereafter cited as *LOWJM*), 3:408; Madison, *ASP:FR* 3:695.

48. Banning, *Jeffersonian Persuasion,* 301; Brant, *James Madison,* 6:403; Ketcham, *James Madison,* 604–5; Watts, *Republic Reborn,* 300–301; Madison, Seventh Annual Message, Dec. 5, 1815, Veto Message, March 3, 1817, Fifth Annual Message, Dec. 7, 1813, *WJM* 8:342, 386–88, 274; Madison to Thomas Charlton, June 29, 1815, *LOWJM* 2:607.

49. Madison to Charles J. Ingersoll, July 28, 1814, *WJM* 8:285; Madison to C. C. Cambreleng, March 8, 1827, *LOWJM* 3:567.

50. Adams to Jefferson, Feb. 2, 1817, in Cappon, *Adams-Jefferson Letters,* 508.

CONCLUSION

1. Hutson, *Diplomacy,* 2.

2. Gilbert, *Farewell Address,* 60–75; Hutson, *Diplomacy,* 1, 147, 150–54; Stourzh, *Alexander Hamilton,* 126–28; Paul A. Varg, *Foreign Policies of the Founding Fathers* (East Lansing: Michigan State University Press, 1963), 146.

3. Hutson, *Diplomacy,* 142.

4. Stourzh, *Alexander Hamilton,* 148–49; Tucker and Hendrickson, *Empire of Liberty,* 232–33.

5. John W. Davis, "The Permanent Bases of American Foreign Policy," *Foreign Affairs* 10, no. 1 (Oct. 1931): 1–3.

6. Lawrence Kaplan, *The United States and NATO: The Formative Years* (Lexington: University Press of Kentucky, 1984), 14; Robert A. Taft, *A Foreign Policy for Americans* (Garden City, N.Y.: Doubleday, 1951), 19–20.

7. Bush quoted in Andrew J. Bacevich, *American Empire: The Realities and Consequences of U.S. Diplomacy* (Cambridge, Mass.: Harvard University Press, 2002), 202; Bush, Speeches of April 28, 2003, and Sept. 12, 2002, posted on www.whitehouse.gov.

Bibliography

PRIMARY SOURCES

Manuscripts

Adams Family Collection, Library of Congress

Adams Papers, Massachusetts Historical Society (cited in notes as AP)

Cutts-Madison Collection, Library of Congress

Albert Gallatin Papers, New York University

General Records of the Department of State, National Archives

Elbridge Gerry Papers, Massachusetts Historical Society

Thomas Jefferson Papers, Library of Congress (cited in notes as TJPapers)

James Madison Papers, Library of Congress

James Madison Papers, New York Public Library

James Monroe Papers, Library of Congress

James Monroe Papers, New York Public Library

Timothy Pickering Papers, Massachusetts Historical Society

William Pinkney Papers, Princeton University

Newspaper

Daily National Intelligencer [Washington, D.C.]

Published Works

Adair, Douglass, ed. "James Madison's Autobiography." *William and Mary Quarterly,* 3rd ser., 2, no. 2 (April 1945): 191–209.
Adams, John. *Correspondence of the Late President Adams, Originally Published in the Boston Patriot.* Boston: Everett and Munroe, 1809.
———. *Diary and Autobiography of John Adams.* Edited by L. H. Butterfield. 4 vols. Cambridge, Mass.: Harvard University Press, 1961. Cited in notes as *DAJA.*
———. *The Earliest Diary of John Adams.* Edited by L. H. Butterfield. Cambridge, Mass.: Harvard University Press, 1966.
———. *Papers of John Adams.* Edited by Robert J. Taylor et al. 10 vols to date. Cambridge, Mass.: Harvard University Press, 1977– . Cited in notes as *PJA.*

———. *The Works of John Adams*. Edited by Charles Francis Adams. 10 vols. Boston: Little, Brown, 1850–1856. Cited in notes as *WJA*.

Adams, John Quincy. *The Jubilee of the Constitution: A Discourse Delivered at the Request of the New York Historical Society*. New York: S. Coleman, 1839.

———. *The Writings of John Quincy Adams*. Edited by Worthington C. Ford. 7 vols. New York: Macmillan, 1913–1917.

American State Papers: Foreign Relations. 6 vols. Washington, D.C.: Gales and Seaton, 1833–1861. Cited in notes as *ASP:FR*.

Annals of the Congress of the United States. 42 vols. Washington, D.C.: Gales and Seaton, 1834–1856.

Biddle, Alexander, ed. *Old Family Letters: Copied from the Originals for Alexander Biddle*. Philadelphia: J. B. Lippencott, 1892.

Bolingbroke, Henry St. John, Viscount. *Contributions to the "Craftsman."* Edited by Simon Varey. London: Oxford University Press, 1982.

———. *Historical Writings*. Edited by Isaac Kramnick. Chicago: University of Chicago Press, 1972.

———. *The Works of Lord Bolingbroke*. 4 vols. London: Henry G. Bohn, 1844.

Bowling, Kenneth R., and Helen E. Viet, eds. *The Diary of William Maclay and Other Notes on Senate Debates*. Baltimore: Johns Hopkins University Press, 1988.

Burgh, James. *Political Disquisitions: An Inquiry into Public Errors, Defects, and Abuses*. [1774–1775.] 3 vols. New York: Da Capo Press, 1971.

Burke, Edmund. *Reflections on the Revolution in France*. 1790. Edited by Thomas H. D. Mahoney. Indianapolis: Bobbs-Merrill, 1955.

Burlamaqui, Jean Jacques. *The Principles of Natural and Politic Law*. 4th ed. Translated by Thomas Nugent. 2 vols. Boston: Joseph Bumstead, 1792.

Butterfield, L. H., Marc Friedlaender, and Richard Allen Ryerson, eds. *Adams Family Correspondence*. 6 vols. to date. Cambridge, Mass.: Harvard University Press, 1963– . Cited in notes as *AFC*.

Cappon, Lester J., ed. *The Adams-Jefferson Letters*. Chapel Hill: University of North Carolina Press, 1988.

Chinard, Gilbert, ed. *The Correspondence of Jefferson and Du Pont de Nemours*. Baltimore: Johns Hopkins University Press, 1931.

Clay, Henry. *The Papers of Henry Clay*. Edited by James F. Hopkins, Mary M. W. Hargreaves, et al. 11 vols. Lexington: University Press of Kentucky, 1959–1993.

Cunningham, William. *Correspondence Between the Hon. John Adams, late President of the United States, and the Late William Cunningham, Esq., Beginning in 1803, and Ending in 1812*. Boston: E. S. Cunningham, 1823.

Davenant, Charles, *The Political and Commercial Works of that Celebrated Writer Charles D'Avenant, LL.D*. Edited by Sir Charles Whitworth. 5 vols. London: R. Horsman, 1771.

Defoe, Daniel. *Some Reflections on a Pamphlet lately Publish'd, Entitled, An Argument Shewing that a Standing Army is inconsistent with a Free Government, and Absolutely Destructive to the Constitution of the English Monarchy*. 2nd ed. London: E. Whitlock, 1697.

Documents Relating to the Purchase and Exploration of Louisiana. Houghton Mifflin, 1904.

Farrand, Max, ed. *The Records of the Federal Convention of 1787*. 4 vols. New Haven: Yale University Press, 1911–1937.

Ferguson, Adam. *An Essay on the History of Civil Society*. [1767.] New York: Garland, 1971.

Fleet, Elizabeth, ed. "Madison's 'Detached Memoranda.'" *William and Mary Quarterly,* 3rd ser., 3, no. 4 (October 1946): 534–68.

Ford, Worthington C., ed. *Journals of the Continental Congress, 1774–1789.* 34 vols. Washington, D.C.: GPO, 1904–1937.

———. "Letters of William Vans Murray to John Quincy Adams, 1797–1803." *Annual Report of the American Historical Association for the Year 1912.* Washington, D.C.: GPO, 1914.

———. *Statesman and Friend: Correspondence of John Adams with Benjamin Waterhouse 1784–1822.* Boston: Little, Brown, 1927.

Foster, Sir Augustus John. *Jeffersonian America: Notes on the United States of America Collected in the Years 1805–6–7 and 11–12.* San Marino, Calif.: Huntington Library, 1954.

Franklin, Benjamin. *The Papers of Benjamin Franklin.* Edited by Leonard W. Labaree, William B. Wilcox, Claude A. Lopez, et al. 36 vols. to date. New Haven: Yale University Press, 1959– .

———. *The Writings of Benjamin Franklin.* Edited by Albert Henry Smyth. 10 vols. New York: Macmillan, 1907.

Gallatin, Albert. *The Writings of Albert Gallatin.* Edited by Henry Adams. 3 vols. Philadelphia: J. B. Lippencott, 1879.

Gibbs, George, ed. *Memoirs of the Administrations of George Washington and John Adams.* 2 vols. New York, 1846.

Giunta, Mary A., et al., eds. *The Emerging Nation: A Documentary History of the Foreign Relations of the United States under the Articles of Confederation, 1780–1789.* 3 vols. Washington, D.C.: NHPRC, 1996.

Grotius, Hugo. *The Rights of War and Peace.* [1625.] Translated by A. C. Campbell. New York: M. Walter Dunne, 1901.

Hamilton, Alexander. *The Papers of Alexander Hamilton.* Edited by Harold C. Syrett et al. 27 vols. New York: Columbia University Press, 1961–1987. Cited in notes as *PAH.*

Hamilton, Alexander, John Jay, and James Madison. *The Federalist.* Edited by Jacob E. Cooke. Middletown, Conn.: Wesleyan University Press, 1961.

Haraszti, Zoltan, ed. "The 32nd Discourse on Davila." *William and Mary Quarterly,* 3rd ser., 11, no. 1 (January 1954): 89–92.

Harrington, James. *The Political Works of James Harrington,* ed. J. G. A. Pocock. New York: Cambridge University Press, 1977.

Hobbes, Thomas. *Leviathan: or the Matter Forme and Power of a Commonwealth Ecclesiastical and Civil.* [1651.] Edited by Michael Oakeshott. New York: Collier Books, 1962.

Hume, David. *Essays: Moral, Political, and Literary.* [1777.] Edited by Eugene F. Miller. Indianapolis: Liberty Fund, 1985.

Jay, John. *The Correspondence and Public Papers of John Jay.* Edited by Henry P. Johnston. 4 vols. New York: G. P. Putnam's Sons, 1890–1894.

———. *John Jay: Unpublished Papers.* Edited by Richard B. Morris. 2 vols. New York: Harper and Row, 1975–1980.

Jefferson, Thomas. *The Complete Anas of Thomas Jefferson.* Edited by Franklin B. Sawvel. New York: Roundtable, 1903.

———. *The Jefferson Papers.* Collections of the Massachusetts Historical Society, 7th ser., vol. 1. Boston: Massachusetts Historical Society, 1900.

———. *Notes on the State of Virginia.* 1787. Edited by William Peden. Chapel Hill: University of North Carolina Press, 1954.

————. *The Papers of Thomas Jefferson.* Edited by Julian Boyd et al. 30 vols. to date. Princeton, N.J.: Princeton University Press, 1950– . Cited in notes as *PTJ.*

————. *The Works of Thomas Jefferson.* Edited by Paul Leicester Ford. 12 vols. New York: G. P. Putnam's Sons, 1904–1905. Cited in notes as *WoTJ.*

————. *The Writings of Thomas Jefferson.* Edited by Andrew A. Lipscomb and Albert Bergh. 20 vols. Washington, D.C.: Thomas Jefferson Memorial Association, 1904–1905. Cited in the notes as *WrTJ.*

King, Rufus. *The Life and Correspondence of Rufus King.* Edited by Charles R. King. 6 vols. New York: G. P. Putnam's Sons, 1894–1900.

Knox, Dudley W., ed. *Naval Documents Related to the Quasi-War between the United States and France.* 7 vols. Washington, D.C.: GPO, 1935–1938.

"Letters of John Adams and John Quincy Adams, 1776–1838." *Bulletin of the New York Public Library* 10, no. 4 (April 1906): 227–50.

Liverpool, Charles Jenkinson, Earl of. *A Collection of all the Treaties of Peace, Alliance and Commerce between Great Britain and Other Powers.* 1785. 3 vols. New York: August M. Kelley, 1969.

Locke, John. *Two Treatises of Government.* 1690. Edited by Peter Laslett. New York: Cambridge University Press, 1963.

Madison, James. *Letters and Other Writings of James Madison.* Edited by William C. Rives. 4 vols. Philadelphia: J. B. Lippencott, 1865. Cited in notes as *LOWJM.*

————. *The Papers of James Madison.* Edited by William T. Hutchinson, William M. E. Rachal, et al. 17 vols. to date. Chicago and Charlottesville: University of Chicago Press and University Press of Virginia, 1959– . Cited in notes as *PJM.*

————. *The Papers of James Madison: Presidential Series.* Edited by Robert A. Rutland, J. C. A. Stagg, et al. 4 vols. to date. Charlottesville: University Press of Virginia, 1984– . Cited in notes as *PJM:PS.*

————. *The Papers of James Madison: Secretary of State Series.* Edited by Robert A. Rutland et al. 6 vols. to date. Charlottesville: University Press of Virginia, 1986– . Cited in the notes as *PJM:SS.*

————. *The Writings of James Madison.* Edited by Gaillard Hunt. 9 vols. New York: G. P. Putnam's Sons, 1900–1910. Cited in notes as *WJM.*

Marshall, John. *The Papers of John Marshall.* Edited by Herbert A. Johnson et al. 10 vols. to date. Chapel Hill: University of North Carolina Press, 1974– .

Mayo, Bernard, ed. "Instructions to the British Ministers to the United States, 1791–1812." In *Annual Report of the American Historical Association for the Year 1936,* vol. 3. Washington, D.C.: Government Printing Office, 1941.

Monroe, James. *The Autobiography of James Monroe.* Edited by Stuart Gerry Brown. Syracuse, N.Y.: Syracuse University Press, 1959.

————. *The Writings of James Monroe.* Edited by Stanislaus Murray Hamilton. 7 vols. New York: G. P. Putnam's Sons, 1898–1903.

Montesquieu, Charles Secondat, Baron de. *The Spirit of the Laws.* [1749.] Edited and translated by Thomas Nugent. 2 vols. New York: Hafner, 1949.

Paine, Thomas. *Common Sense.* [1776.] Edited by Isaac Kramnick. New York: Penguin, 1976.

Plumer, William. *William Plumer's Memorandum of Proceedings in the United States Senate 1803–1807.* Edited by Everett Somerville Brown. New York: Macmillan, 1923.

Polybius. *The Histories of Polybius.* Translated by Evelyn S. Shuckburgh. 2 vols. Bloomington: Indiana University Press, 1962.

Powell, J. H., ed. "Some Unpublished Correspondence of John Adams and Richard Rush, 1811–1822." 3 parts. *Pennsylvania Magazine of History and Biography* 60, no. 4, and 61, nos. 1 and 2 (October 1936, January, April 1937): 419–54, 26–53, 137–64.

Pufendorf, Samuel Freiherr von. *The Law of Nature and Nations.* 5th ed. Translated by Basil Kennett. London: J. & J. Bonwicke, 1749.

Richardson, James D., ed. *A Compilation of the Messages and Papers of the Presidents, 1789–1902.* 10 vols. Washington, D.C.: Bureau of National Literature and Art, 1905–1906.

Robbins, Caroline, ed. *Two English Republican Tracts.* New York: Cambridge University Press, 1969.

Scott, James Brown, ed. *The Controversy over Neutral Rights between the United States and France, 1797–1800: A Collection of American State Papers and Judicial Decisions.* New York: Oxford University Press, 1917.

Sheffield, John Holroyd, Earl of. *Observations on the Commerce of the American States.* [1784.] New York: August M. Kelley, 1970.

Sidney, Algernon. *Discourses Concerning Government.* [1698.] Edited by Thomas G. West. Indianapolis: Liberty Fund, 1990.

Smith, Adam. *An Inquiry into the Nature and the Causes of the Wealth of Nations.* [1776.] Edited by Edwin Cannan. 2 vols. Chicago: University of Chicago Press, 1976.

Smith, James Morton, ed. *The Republic of Letters: The Correspondence between Thomas Jefferson and James Madison 1776–1826.* 3 vols. New York: W. W. Norton, 1995.

Smith, Paul H., ed. *Letters of Delegates to Congress, 1774–1789.* 26 vols. Washington, D.C.: Library of Congress, 1976–1998.

Stephen, James. *War in Disguise; or, the Frauds of the Neutral Flags.* 2nd American ed. New York: I. Riley, 1806.

Swift, Jonathan. *Political Tracts, 1711–1713.* Edited by Herbert Davis. Princeton, N.J.: Princeton University Press, 1951.

Trenchard, John. *An Argument Shewing, that a Standing Army is inconsistent with a Free Government, and absolutely destructive to the Constitution of the English Monarchy.* London, 1698.

———. *A Short History of Standing Armies in England.* London, 1698.

Trenchard, John, and Thomas Gordon. *Cato's Letters: Or Essays on Liberty, Civil and Religious, and other Important Subjects.* [1755.] 6th ed. Edited by Ronald Hamowy. 2 vols. Indianapolis: Liberty Fund, 1995.

Turner, Frederick Jackson, ed. "Correspondence of the French Ministers to the United States, 1791–1797." In *Annual Report of the American Historical Association for 1903,* vol. 2. Washington, D.C.: GPO, 1904.

Vattel, Emmerich de. *The Law of Nations.* [1758.] Edited by Joseph Autty. Philadelphia: L. & J. W. Johnson, 1876.

Warren-Adams Letters. 2 vols. Boston: Massachusetts Historical Society, Collections, 1917–1925.

Washington, George. *The Writings of George Washington.* Edited by John C. Fitzpatrick. 39 vols. Washington, D.C.: GPO, 1931–1944.

Wharton, Francis, ed. *The Revolutionary Diplomatic Correspondence of the United States.* 6 vols. Washington, D.C.: GPO, 1889.

Wolff, Christian. *The Law of Nations Treated according to a Scientific Method.* 1764. Translated by Joseph H. Drake. London: Oxford University Press, 1934.

Secondary Sources

Adair, Douglass. *Fame and the Founding Fathers.* Edited by Trevor Colbourn. New York: W. W. Norton, 1974.

Adams, Charles Francis. *The Life of John Adams.* 2 vols. Philadelphia: J. B. Lippencott, 1871.

Adams, Henry. *History of the United States during the Administrations of Thomas Jefferson and James Madison.* 9 vols. New York: Charles Scribner's Sons, 1889–1891.

Adams, Mary P. "Jefferson's Reaction to the Treaty of San Ildefonso." *Journal of Southern History* 21, no. 2 (May 1955): 173–88.

Ammon, Harry. *The Genet Mission.* New York: W. W. Norton, 1973.

———. *James Monroe: The Quest for National Identity.* New York: McGraw-Hill, 1971.

Anderson, Fred. *Crucible of War: The Seven Years' War and the Fate of Empire in British North America, 1754–1766.* New York: Alfred A. Knopf, 2000.

Anderson, William G. "John Adams, the Navy, and the Quasi-War with France." *American Neptune* 30, no. 2 (April 1970): 117–32.

Andrews, Charles M. *The Colonial Period of American History.* 4 vols. New Haven: Yale University Press, 1934–1938.

Appleby, Joyce. *Capitalism and a New Social Order: The Republican Vision of the 1790s.* New York: New York University Press, 1984.

———. *Economic Thought and Ideology in Seventeenth-Century England.* Princeton, N.J.: Princeton University Press, 1978.

———. *Liberalism and Republicanism in the Historical Imagination.* Cambridge, Mass.: Harvard University Press, 1992.

Bacevich, Andrew J. *American Empire: The Realities and Consequences of U.S. Diplomacy.* Cambridge, Mass.: Harvard University Press, 2002.

Bailyn, Bernard. *The Ideological Origins of the American Revolution.* Cambridge, Mass.: Harvard University Press, 1967.

———. *The Origins of American Politics.* New York: Alfred A. Knopf, 1968.

Banner, James M., Jr. *To the Hartford Convention: The Federalists and the Origins of Party Politics in Massachusetts 1789–1815.* New York: Alfred A. Knopf, 1970.

Banning, Lance. "The Hamiltonian Madison: A Reconsideration." *Virginia Magazine of History and Biography* 92, no. 1 (January 1984): 3–28.

———. "James Madison and the Nationalists." *William and Mary Quarterly,* 3rd ser., 40, no. 20 (April 1983): 227–55.

———. "Jeffersonian Ideology Revisited: Liberal and Classical Ideas in the New American Republic." *William and Mary Quarterly,* 3rd ser., 43, no. 1 (January 1986): 3–19.

———. *The Jeffersonian Persuasion: Evolution of a Party Ideology.* Ithaca, N.Y.: Cornell University Press, 1978.

———. *The Sacred Fire of Liberty: James Madison and the Founding of the Federal Republic.* Ithaca, N.Y.: Cornell University Press, 1995.

Basedo, S., and H. Robertson. "The Nova Scotia–British West Indies Commercial Experiment in the Aftermath of the American Revolution, 1783–1802." *Dalhousie Review* 61, no. 1 (Spring 1981): 53–69.

Beard, Charles A. *An Economic Interpretation of the Constitution of the United States.* New York: Macmillan, 1913.

Beeman, Richard, Stephen Botein, and Edward C. Carter II, eds. *Beyond Confederation: Origins of the Constitution and American National Identity.* Chapel Hill: University of North Carolina Press, 1987.

Bell, Herbert C. "British Commercial Policy in the West Indies, 1783–1793." *English Historical Review* 31, no. 123 (July 1916): 429–41.

Bemis, Samuel Flagg. *The Diplomacy of the American Revolution.* Bloomington: Indiana University Press, 1957.

———. *Jay's Treaty: A Study in Commerce and Diplomacy.* Rev. ed. New Haven: Yale University Press, 1962.

———. *Pinkney's Treaty: America's Advantage from Europe's Distress, 1783–1800.* Rev. ed. New Haven: Yale University Press, 1960.

Bemis, Samuel Flagg, ed. *American Secretaries of State and Their Diplomacy.* 10 vols. New York: Alfred A. Knopf, 1927–1928.

Ben-Atar, Doron S. *The Origins of Jeffersonian Commercial Policy and Diplomacy.* New York: St. Martin's Press, 1993.

Billias, George Athan. *Elbridge Gerry: Founding Father and Republican Statesman.* New York: McGraw-Hill, 1976.

Black, Jeremy. *British Foreign Policy in an Age of Revolutions, 1783–1793.* New York: Cambridge University Press, 1994.

———. *British Foreign Policy in the Age of Walpole.* Edinburgh, Scotland: John Donald, 1985.

Bowler, R. Arthur. *Logistics and the Failure of the British Army in America, 1775–1783.* Princeton, N.J.: Princeton University Press, 1975.

Bowman, Albert Hall. *The Struggle for Neutrality: Franco-American Diplomacy during the Federalist Era.* Knoxville: University of Tennessee Press, 1974.

Boyd, Julian P. *Number 7: Alexander Hamilton's Secret Attempts to Control American Foreign Policy.* Princeton, N.J.: Princeton University Press, 1964.

Brant, Irving. *James Madison.* 6 vols. Indianapolis: Bobbs-Merrill, 1941–1961.

Breen, T. H. *Tobacco Culture: The Mentality of the Great Planters on the Eve of Revolution.* Princeton, N.J.: Princeton University Press, 1985.

Briggs, Herbert Whittaker. *The Doctrine of Continuous Voyage.* Baltimore: Johns Hopkins University Press, 1926.

Brown, Everett Somerville. *The Constitutional History of the Louisiana Purchase, 1803–1812.* Berkeley: University of California Press, 1920.

Brown, Peter Douglas. *William Pitt, Earl of Chatham: The Great Commoner.* London: George Allen and Unwin, 1978.

Brown, Ralph Adams. *The Presidency of John Adams.* Lawrence: University Press of Kansas, 1975.

Brown, Richard D. *Modernization: The Transformation of American Life 1600–1865.* New York: Hill and Wang, 1976.

Brown, Robert E. *Charles Beard and the Constitution: A Critical Analysis of "An Economic Interpretation of the Constitution."* Princeton, N.J.: Princeton University Press, 1956.

Brown, Roger H. *The Republic in Peril: 1812.* New York: Columbia University Press, 1964.

Buel, Richard, Jr. *Securing the Revolution: Ideology in American Politics, 1789–1815.* Ithaca, N.Y.: Cornell University Press, 1972.

Bull, Hedley. *The Anarchical Society: A Study of Order in World Politics.* New York: Columbia University Press, 1977.

Burns, J. H., ed. *The Cambridge History of Political Thought, 1450–1700.* New York: Cambridge University Press, 1991.

Capp, Bernard. *Cromwell's Navy: The Fleet in the English Revolution, 1648–1660.* New York: Oxford University Press, 1989.

Chew, Richard S., III. "A New Hope for the Republic." Unpublished M.A. thesis, College of William and Mary, 1992.

Chinard, Gilbert. *Honest John Adams*. Boston: Little, Brown, 1933.

Clarfield, Gerard. "John Adams: The Marketplace and American Foreign Policy." *New England Quarterly* 52, no. 3 (September 1979): 345–57.

———. *Timothy Pickering and American Diplomacy, 1795–1800*. Columbia: University of Missouri Press, 1969.

Clauder, Anna Cornelia. *American Commerce as Affected by the Wars of the French Revolution and Napoleon, 1793–1812*. Philadelphia: University of Pennsylvania Press, 1932.

Colbourn, H. Trevor. *The Lamp of Experience: Whig History and the Intellectual Origins of the American Revolution*. Chapel Hill: University of North Carolina Press, 1965.

Coles, Harry L. *The War of 1812*. Chicago: University of Chicago Press, 1965.

Combs, Jerald A. *The Jay Treaty: Political Battleground of the Founding Fathers*. Berkeley: University of California Press, 1970.

Cooke, Jacob E. "Country above Party: John Adams and the 1799 Mission to France." In *Fame and the Founding Fathers*, ed. Edmund P. Willis. Bethlehem, Pa.: Moravian College, 1967.

Cox, Isaac Joslin. "The Border Missions of General George Mathews." *Mississippi Valley Historical Review* 12, no. 3 (December 1925): 309–33.

———. *The West Florida Controversy, 1798–1813: A Study in American Diplomacy*. Baltimore: Johns Hopkins University Press, 1918.

Cronin, Thomas E., ed. *Inventing the American Presidency*. Lawrence: University Press of Kansas, 1989.

Crosby, Alfred W., Jr. *America, Russia, Hemp, and Napoleon: American Trade with Russia and the Baltic, 1783–1812*. Columbus: Ohio State University Press, 1965.

Crowley, John E. *The Privileges of Independence: Neomercantilism and the American Revolution*. Baltimore: Johns Hopkins University Press, 1993.

———. *This Sheba, SELF: The Conceptualization of Economic Life in Eighteenth-Century America*. Baltimore: Johns Hopkins University Press, 1974.

Dauer, Manning J. *The Adams Federalists*. Baltimore: Johns Hopkins University Press, 1953.

Davis, John W. "The Permanent Bases of American Foreign Policy." *Foreign Affairs* 10, no. 1 (October 1931): 1–12.

DeConde, Alexander. *This Affair of Louisiana*. New York: Charles Scribner's Sons, 1976.

———. *Entangling Alliance: Politics and Diplomacy under George Washington*. Durham, N.C.: Duke University Press, 1958.

———. *The Quasi-War: The Politics and Diplomacy of the Undeclared War with France, 1797–1801*. New York: Charles Scribner's Sons, 1966.

Dull, Jonathan R. *A Diplomatic History of the American Revolution*. New Haven: Yale University Press, 1985.

———. *The French Navy and American Independence: A Study of Arms and Diplomacy, 1774–1787*. Princeton, N.J.: Princeton University Press, 1975.

Egan, Clifford L. *Neither Peace nor War: Franco-American Relations, 1803–1812*. Baton Rouge: Louisiana State University Press, 1983.

Elkins, Stanley, and Eric McKitrick. *The Age of Federalism: The Early American Republic, 1788–1800*. New York: Oxford University Press, 1993.

Ellis, Joseph J. *American Sphinx: The Character of Thomas Jefferson*. New York: Alfred A. Knopf, 1997.

———. *Passionate Sage: The Character and Legacy of John Adams*. New York: W. W. Norton, 1993.

Epstein, David F. *The Political Theory of "The Federalist."* Chicago: University of Chicago Press, 1984.

Evans, Emory G. "Private Indebtedness and the Revolution in Virginia, 1776 to 1796." *William and Mary Quarterly*, 3rd ser., 28, no. 3 (July 1971): 349–74.

Farrand, Max. *The Framing of the Constitution of the United States*. New Haven: Yale University Press, 1913.

Ferguson, E. James. *The Power of the Purse: A History of American Public Finance, 1776–1790*. Chapel Hill: University of North Carolina Press, 1961.

Ferling, John. "John Adams, Diplomat." *William and Mary Quarterly*, 3rd ser., 51, no. 2 (April 1994): 227–52.

———. *John Adams: A Life*. Knoxville: University of Tennessee Press, 1992.

———. "'Oh That I Was A Soldier': John Adams and the Anguish of War." *American Quarterly* 36, no. 2 (Summer 1984): 258–75.

Field, James A., Jr. *America and the Mediterranean World 1776–1882*. Princeton, N.J.: Princeton University Press, 1969.

Fink, Z. S. *The Classical Republicans: An Essay in the Recovery of a Pattern of Thought in Seventeenth-Century England*. Evanston, Ill.: Northwestern University Press, 1945.

Fischer, David Hackett. *The Revolution in American Conservatism: The Federalist Party in the Era of Jeffersonian Democracy*. New York: Harper and Row, 1965.

Flaumenhaft, Harvey. *The Effective Republic: Administration and Constitution in the Thought of Alexander Hamilton*. Durham, N.C.: Duke University Press, 1992.

Fox-Genovese, Elizabeth. *The Origins of Physiocracy: Economic Revolution and Social Order in Eighteenth-Century France*. Ithaca, N.Y.: Cornell University Press, 1976.

Freeman, Douglas Southall. *George Washington*. 7 vols. New York: Charles Scribner's Sons, 1948–1957.

Fuller, Hubert Bruce. *The Purchase of Florida: Its History and Diplomacy*. Cleveland: Burrows Brothers, 1906.

Galpin, W. Freeman. *The Grain Supply of England during the Napoleonic Period*. Ann Arbor: University of Michigan Press, 1925.

Gerrard, Christine. *The Patriot Opposition to Walpole: Politics, Poetry, and National Myth, 1725–1742*. New York: Oxford University Press, 1994.

Gilbert, Felix. *To the Farewell Address: Ideas of Early American Foreign Policy*. Princeton, N.J.: Princeton University Press, 1961.

Graebner, Norman A. *Foundations of American Foreign Policy: A Realist Appraisal from Franklin to McKinley*. Wilmington, Del.: Scholarly Resources, 1985.

Griffiths, David M. "American Commercial Diplomacy in Russia, 1780 to 1783." *William and Mary Quarterly*, 3rd ser., 27, no. 3 (July 1970): 379–410.

Gulick, Edward Vose. *Europe's Classical Balance of Power*. Ithaca, N.Y.: Cornell University Press, 1955.

Gummere, Richard M. *The American Colonial Mind and the Classical Tradition: Essays in Comparative Culture*. Cambridge, Mass.: Harvard University Press, 1963.

Hagan, Kenneth J. *This People's Navy: The Making of American Sea Power*. New York: Free Press, 1991.

Handler, Edward. *America and Europe in the Political Thought of John Adams*. Cambridge, Mass.: Harvard University Press, 1964.

Haraszti, Zoltan. *John Adams and the Prophets of Progress*. Cambridge, Mass.: Harvard University Press, 1952.

Harvey, Ray Forrest. *Jean Jacques Burlamaqui: A Liberal Tradition in American Constitutionalism*. Chapel Hill: University of North Carolina Press, 1937.

Hayes, Frederic H. "John Adams and American Sea Power." *American Neptune* 25, no. 1 (January 1965): 35–45.

Heaton, Herbert. "Non-Importation, 1806–1812." *Journal of Economic History* 1, no. 2 (November 1941): 178–98.

Henderson, W. O. "The Anglo-French Commercial Treaty of 1786." *Economic History Review*, 2nd ser., 10, no. 1 (August 1957): 104–12.

Hickey, Donald R. "The Monroe-Pinkney Treaty of 1806: A Reappraisal." *William and Mary Quarterly*, 3rd ser., 44, no. 1 (January 1987): 65–88.

———. *The War of 1812: A Forgotten Conflict*. Urbana: University of Illinois Press, 1989.

Higginbotham, Don. *The War of American Independence: Military Attitudes, Policies, and Practice, 1763–1789*. New York: Macmillan, 1971.

Hill, Peter P. *William Vans Murray: Federalist Diplomat*. Syracuse, N.Y.: Syracuse University Press, 1971.

Hobson, Charles F. "The Negative on State Laws: James Madison, the Constitution and the Crisis of Republican Government." *William and Mary Quarterly*, 3rd ser., 36, no. 2 (April 1979): 215–35.

Hoffman, Ronald, and Peter J. Albert, eds. *Diplomacy and Revolution: The Franco-American Alliance of 1778*. Charlottesville: University Press of Virginia, 1981.

———. *Peace and the Peacemakers: The Treaty of 1783*. Charlottesville: University Press of Virginia, 1986.

Hofstadter, Richard. *The Idea of a Party System: The Rise of Legitimate Opposition in the United States, 1780–1840*. Berkeley: University of California Press, 1969.

Holder, Jean S. "The John Adams Presidency: War Crisis Leadership in the Early Republic." Unpublished Ph.D. dissertation, American University, 1983.

Horn, David Bayne. *Great Britain and Europe in the Eighteenth Century*. London: Oxford University Press, 1967.

Horsman, Reginald. *The Causes of the War of 1812*. Philadelphia: University of Pennsylvania Press, 1962.

Houston, Allan Craig. *Algernon Sidney and the Republican Heritage in England and America*. Princeton, N.J.: Princeton University Press, 1991.

Howe, John R., Jr. *The Changing Political Thought of John Adams*. Princeton, N.J.: Princeton University Press, 1966.

———. "Republican Thought and the Political Violence of the 1790s." *American Quarterly* 19, no. 2 (Summer 1967): 147–65.

Hunt, Michael H. *Ideology and U.S. Foreign Policy*. New Haven: Yale University Press, 1987.

Hutson, James H. *John Adams and the Diplomacy of the American Revolution*. Lexington: University Press of Kentucky, 1980.

Jensen, Merrill. *The New Nation: A History of the United States during the Confederation 1781–1789*. New York: Alfred A. Knopf, 1950.

Johnstone, Robert M., Jr. *Jefferson and the Presidency: Leadership in the Young Republic*. Ithaca, N.Y.: Columbia University Press, 1978.

Jones, J. R. *Britain and the World, 1649–1815*. Atlantic Highlands, N.J.: Humanities Press, 1980.

Kammen, Michael. *Empire and Interest: The American Colonies and the Politics of Mercantilism.* Philadelphia: J. B. Lippencott, 1970.

Kaplan, Lawrence S. *Colonies into Nation: American Diplomacy, 1763–1801.* New York: Macmillan, 1972.

———. *Entangling Alliances with None: American Foreign Policy in the Age of Jefferson.* Kent, Ohio: Kent State University Press, 1987.

———. *Jefferson and France: An Essay on Politics and Political Ideas.* New Haven: Yale University Press, 1967.

———. *The United States and NATO: The Formative Years.* Lexington: University Press of Kentucky, 1984.

Kaplan, Lawrence S., ed. *The American Revolution and "A Candid World."* Kent, Ohio: Kent State University Press, 1977.

Kennan, George. *American Diplomacy, 1900–1950.* New York: Mentor Books, 1952.

Ketcham, Ralph. *James Madison: A Biography.* New York: Macmillan, 1971.

———. "James Madison and the Nature of Man." *Journal of the History of Ideas* 19, no. 1 (January 1958): 62–76.

———. *Presidents above Party: The First American Presidency, 1789–1829.* Chapel Hill: University of North Carolina Press, 1984.

Keynes, Edward. *Undeclared War: Twilight Zone of Constitutional Power.* University Park: Pennsylvania State University Press, 1982.

Koch, Adrienne. *Jefferson and Madison: The Great Collaboration.* New York: Alfred A. Knopf, 1950.

Koch, Adrienne, and Harry Ammon. "The Virginia and Kentucky Resolutions: An Episode in Jefferson's and Madison's Defense of Civil Liberties." *William and Mary Quarterly,* 3rd ser., 5, no. 2 (April 1948): 145–76.

Kohn, Richard H. *Eagle and Sword: The Federalists and the Creation of the Military Establishment in America, 1783–1802.* New York: Free Press, 1975.

Kramnick, Isaac. *Bolingbroke and His Circle: The Politics of Nostalgia in the Age of Walpole.* Cambridge, Mass.: Harvard University Press, 1968.

———. "Republican Revisionism Revisited." *American Historical Review* 87, no. 3 (June 1982): 629–64.

Kurtz, Stephen G. "The French Mission of 1799–1800: Concluding Chapter in the Statecraft of John Adams." *Political Science Quarterly* 80, no. 4 (December 1965): 543–57.

———. "The Political Science of John Adams, a Guide to His Statecraft." *William and Mary Quarterly,* 3rd ser., 25, no. 4 (Oct. 1968): 605–13.

———. *The Presidency of John Adams: The Collapse of Federalism.* Philadelphia: University of Pennsylvania Press, 1957.

Kurtz, Stephen G., and James H. Hutson, eds. *Essays on the American Revolution.* Chapel Hill: University of North Carolina Press, 1973.

LaFeber, Walter. "Foreign Policies of a New Nation: Franklin, Madison, and the 'Dream of a New Land to Fulfill with People in Self-Control,' 1750–1804." In *From Colony to Empire: Essays in the History of American Foreign Relations,* ed. William Appleman Williams. New York: John Wiley and Sons, 1972.

Lang, Daniel G. *Foreign Policy in the Early Republic: The Law of Nations and the Balance of Power.* Baton Rouge: Louisiana State University Press, 1985.

Langford, Paul. *The Eighteenth Century, 1688–1815.* New York: St. Martin's Press, 1976.

Lint, Gregg L. "John Adams on the Drafting of the Treaty Plan of 1776." *Diplomatic History* 2, no. 3 (Summer 1978): 313–20.

Liss, Peggy K. *Atlantic Empires: The Network of Trade and Revolution, 1713–1826*. Baltimore: Johns Hopkins University Press, 1983.

Lodge, Henry Cabot. *Life and Letters of George Cabot*. Boston: Little, Brown, 1877.

Logan, John A., Jr. *No Transfer: An American Security Principle*. New Haven: Yale University Press, 1961.

Lopez, Claude-Anne. *Mon Cher Papa: Franklin and the Ladies of Paris*. New Haven: Yale University Press, 1966.

Lycan, Gilbert L. *Alexander Hamilton and American Foreign Policy*. Norman: University of Oklahoma Press, 1970.

Lyon, Wilson E. "The Directory and the United States." *American Historical Review* 43, no. 3 (April 1938): 514–32.

———. "The Franco-American Convention of 1800." *Journal of Modern History* 12, no. 3 (September 1940): 305–33.

———. *Louisiana in French Diplomacy, 1759–1804*. Norman: University of Oklahoma Press, 1934.

Macpherson, C. B. *The Political Theory of Possessive Individualism: Hobbes to Locke*. New York: Oxford University Press, 1962.

Maier, Pauline. *From Resistance to Revolution: Colonial Radicals and the Development of American Opposition to Britain, 1765–1776*. New York: Alfred A. Knopf, 1972.

Malone, Dumas. *Jefferson and His Time*. 6 vols. Boston: Little, Brown, 1948–1981.

Marks, Frederick W., III. *Independence on Trial: Foreign Affairs and the Making of the Constitution*. Baton Rouge: Louisiana State University Press, 1973.

Matson, Cathy D., and Peter S. Onuf. *A Union of Interests: Political and Economic Thought in Revolutionary America*. Lawrence: University Press of Kansas, 1990.

Matthews, Richard K. *If Men Were Angels: James Madison & the Heartless Empire of Reason*. Lawrence: University Press of Kansas, 1995.

May, Henry F. *The Enlightenment in America*. New York: Oxford University Press, 1976.

Mayer, David N. *The Constitutional Thought of Thomas Jefferson*. Charlottesville: University Press of Virginia, 1994.

McCoy, Drew R. *The Elusive Republic: Political Economy in Jeffersonian America*. Chapel Hill: University of North Carolina Press, 1980.

———. *The Last of the Fathers: James Madison and the Republican Legacy*. New York: Cambridge University Press, 1989.

———. "Republicanism and American Foreign Policy: James Madison and the Political Economy of Commercial Discrimination, 1789 to 1794." *William and Mary Quarterly*, 3rd ser., 31, no. 4 (October 1974): 633–46.

———. "The Virginia Port Bill of 1784." *Virginia Magazine of History and Biography* 83, no. 3 (July 1975): 288–303.

McCusker, John J., and Russell R. Menard. *The Economy of British North America, 1607–1789*. Chapel Hill: University of North Carolina Press, 1985.

McDonald, Forrest. *Alexander Hamilton: A Biography*. New York: W. W. Norton, 1979.

———. *E Pluribus Unum: The Formation of the American Republic 1776–1790*. Boston: Houghton Mifflin, 1965.

———. *Novus Ordo Seclorum: The Intellectual Origins of the Constitution*. Lawrence: University Press of Kansas, 1985.

———. *The Presidency of George Washington*. Lawrence: University Press of Kansas, 1974.

———. *The Presidency of Thomas Jefferson*. Lawrence: University Press of Kansas, 1976.

McInnis, Angus. "When Was the English Revolution." *History* 67, no. 221 (October 1982): 377–92.

Melvin, Frank E. *Napoleon's Navigation System: A Study of Trade Control during the Continental Blockade.* New York: D. Appleton, 1919.

Middlekauff, Robert. *The Glorious Cause: The American Revolution, 1763–1789.* New York: Oxford University Press, 1982.

Miller, John C. *Alexander Hamilton: Portrait in Paradox.* New York: Harper and Brothers, 1959.

Mitchell, Broadus. *Alexander Hamilton.* 2 vols. New York: Macmillan, 1957–1962.

Morgan, Edmund S. "The Puritan Ethic and the American Revolution." *William and Mary Quarterly,* 3rd ser., 24, no. 1 (January 1967): 3–43.

Morgenthau, Hans J. *In Defense of the National Interest: A Critical Examination of American Foreign Policy.* New York: Alfred A. Knopf, 1951.

Morris, Richard B. *The Peacemakers: The Great Powers and American Independence.* New York: Harper and Row, 1965.

Murphy, Orville T. *Charles Gravier, Comte de Vergennes: French Diplomacy in the Age of Revolution, 1719–1787.* Albany: State University of New York Press, 1982.

Murphy, William J., Jr. "John Adams: The Politics of the Additional Army." *New England Quarterly* 52, no. 2 (June 1979): 234–49.

Nelson, John R., Jr. *Liberty and Property: Political Economy and Policymaking in the New Nation, 1789–1812.* Baltimore: Johns Hopkins University Press, 1987.

North, Douglas C. *The Economic Growth of the United States, 1790–1860.* Englewood Cliffs, N.J.: Prentice-Hall, 1961.

O'Brien, Conor Cruise. *The Long Affair: Thomas Jefferson and the French Revolution, 1785–1800.* Chicago: University of Chicago Press, 1996.

Onuf, Peter S., and Nicholas Onuf. *Federal Union, Modern World: The Law of Nations in an Age of Revolution, 1776–1814.* Madison, Wis.: Madison House, 1993.

Owsley, Frank Lawrence, Jr., and Gene A. Smith. *Filibusters and Expansionists: Jeffersonian Manifest Destiny, 1800–1821.* Tuscaloosa: University of Alabama Press, 1997.

Palmer, Michael A. *Stoddert's War: Naval Operations during the Quasi-War with France, 1798–1801.* Columbia: University of South Carolina Press, 1987.

Palmer, Robert R. *The Age of the Democratic Revolution.* 2 vols. Princeton, N.J.: Princeton University Press, 1959–1964.

Paltsits, Victor Hugo. *Washington's Farewell Address.* New York: New York Public Library, 1935.

Pangle, Thomas L. *The Spirit of Modern Republicanism: The Moral Vision of the American Founders and the Philosophy of Locke.* Chicago: University of Chicago Press, 1988.

Parker, Rodger D. "The Gospel of Opposition: A Study in Eighteenth-Century Anglo-American Ideology." Unpublished Ph.D. dissertation, Wayne State University, 1975.

Patrick, Rembert W. *Florida Fiasco: Rampant Rebels on the Georgia-Florida Border, 1810–1815.* Athens: University of Georgia Press, 1954.

Perkins, Bradford. *Castlereagh and Adams: England and the United States 1812–1823.* Berkeley: University of California Press, 1964.

———. *The First Rapprochement: England and the United States, 1795–1805.* Berkeley: University of California Press, 1955.

———. *Prologue to War: England and the United States, 1805–1812.* Berkeley: University of California Press, 1961.

Peterson, Merrill D. "Thomas Jefferson and Commercial Policy, 1783–1793." *William and Mary Quarterly*, 3rd ser., 22, no. 4 (October 1965). p. 584–610.

————. *Thomas Jefferson and the New Nation*. New York: Oxford University Press, 1970.

Pocock, J. G. A. *The Machiavellian Moment: Florentine Political Thought and the Atlantic Republican Tradition*. Princeton, N.J.: Princeton University Press, 1975.

Potts, Louis W. *Arthur Lee: A Virtuous Revolutionary*. Baton Rouge: Louisiana State University Press, 1981.

Pratt, Julius W. *The Expansionists of 1812*. New York: Macmillan, 1925.

Price, Jacob M. *Capital and Credit in British Overseas Trade: The View from the Chesapeake, 1700–1776*. Cambridge, Mass.: Harvard University Press, 1980.

————. *France and the Chesapeake: A History of the French Tobacco Monopoly, 1674–1791, and of Its Relationship to the British and American Tobacco Trades*. 2 vols. Ann Arbor: University of Michigan Press, 1973.

Rahe, Paul A. *Republics Ancient and Modern: Classical Republicanism and the American Founding*. Chapel Hill: University of North Carolina Press, 1992.

Ragsdale, Bruce A. *A Planters' Republic: The Search for Economic Independence in Revolutionary Virginia*. Madison, Wis.: Madison House, 1996.

Rakove, Jack N. *The Beginnings of National Politics: An Interpretive History of the Continental Congress*. New York: Alfred A. Knopf, 1979.

————. *James Madison and the Creation of the American Republic*. Glenview, Ill.: Scott, Forsman, 1990.

Richard, Carl J. *The Founders and the Classics: Greece, Rome, and the American Enlightenment*. Cambridge, Mass.: Harvard University Press, 1994.

Risjord, Norman K. *Chesapeake Politics, 1781–1800*. New York: Columbia University Press, 1978.

————. *The Old Republicans: Southern Conservatism in the Age of Jefferson*. New York: Columbia University Press, 1965.

Ritcheson, Charles R. *Aftermath of Revolution: British Policy toward the United States, 1783–1795*. Dallas: Southern Methodist University Press, 1969.

Robbins, Caroline. *The Eighteenth-Century Commonwealthman: Studies in the Transmission, Development and Circumstance of English Liberal Thought from the Restoration of Charles II until the War with the Thirteen Colonies*. Cambridge, Mass.: Harvard University Press, 1959.

Rogers, Daniel T. "Republicanism: The Career of a Concept." *Journal of American History* 79, no. 1 (June 1992): 11–38.

Rohrs, Richard C. "The Federalist Party and the Convention of 1800." *Diplomatic History* 12, no. 3 (Summer 1988): 237–60.

Rossiter, Clinton. *Alexander Hamilton and the Constitution*. New York: Harcourt, Brace, and World, 1964.

————. *Conservatism in America*. 2nd rev. ed. Cambridge, Mass.: Harvard University Press, 1982.

Royster, Charles. *A Revolutionary People at War: The Continental Army and American Character, 1775–1783*. Chapel Hill: University of North Carolina Press, 1979.

Ruddy, Francis Stephen. *International Law in the Enlightenment: The Background of Emmerich de Vattel's "Les Droits des Gens."* Dobbs Ferry, N.Y.: Oceana, 1975.

Rutland, Robert A. *The Presidency of James Madison*. Lawrence: University Press of Kansas, 1990.

Saul, Norman E. *Distant Friends: The United States and Russia, 1763–1867*. Lawrence: University Press of Kansas, 1991.

Savelle, Max. *The Origins of American Diplomacy: The International History of Anglo-America, 1492–1763*. New York: Macmillan, 1967.

Scanlon, James E. "A Sudden Conceit: Jefferson and the Louisiana Government Bill of 1804." *Louisiana History* 9, no. 2 (Spring 1968): 139–62.

Schwoerer, Lois G. *"No Standing Armies!" The Antiarmy Ideology in Seventeenth-Century England*. Baltimore: Johns Hopkins University Press, 1974.

Scott, H. M. *British Foreign Policy in the Age of the American Revolution*. New York: Oxford University Press, 1990.

Selby, John E. *The Revolution in Virginia, 1775–1783*. Williamsburg, Va.: Colonial Williamsburg, dist. University Press of Virginia, 1988.

Setser, Vernon G. *The Commercial Reciprocity Policy of the United States, 1774–1829*. Philadelphia: University of Pennsylvania Press, 1937.

Shalhope, Robert E. "Republicanism and Early American Historiography." *William and Mary Quarterly*, 3rd ser., 39, no. 2 (April 1982): 334–55.

———. "Toward a Republican Synthesis: The Emergence of an Understanding of Republicanism in American Historiography." *William and Mary Quarterly*, 3rd ser., 29, no. 1 (January 1972): 49–80.

Sharp, James Roger. *American Politics in the Early Republic: The New Nation in Crisis*. New Haven: Yale University Press, 1993.

Shaw, Peter. *The Character of John Adams*. Chapel Hill: University of North Carolina Press, 1976.

Sheldon, Garrett Ward. *The Political Philosophy of Thomas Jefferson*. Baltimore: Johns Hopkins University Press, 1991.

Shy, John. *Toward Lexington: The Role of the British Army in the Coming of the American Revolution*. Princeton, N.J.: Princeton University Press, 1965.

Sloan, Herbert E. *Principle and Interest: Thomas Jefferson and the Problem of Debt*. New York: Oxford University Press, 1995.

Smith, Gene A. *"For the Purposes of Defense:" The Politics of the Jeffersonian Gunboat Program*. Newark: University of Delaware Press, 1995.

Smith, James Morton. *Freedom's Fetters: The Alien and Sedition Laws and American Civil Liberties*. Ithaca, N.Y.: Cornell University Press, 1956.

Smith, Page. *John Adams*. 2 vols. Garden City, N.Y.: Doubleday, 1962.

Sosin, Jack M. *Agents and Merchants: British Colonial Policy and the Origins of the American Revolution, 1763–1775*. Lincoln: University of Nebraska Press, 1965.

Spalding, Matthew, and Patrick J. Garrity. *A Sacred Union of Citizens: George Washington's Farewell Address and the American Character*. Lanham, Md.: Rowman and Littlefield, 1996.

Spivak, Burton. *Jefferson's English Crisis: Commerce, Embargo, and the Republican Revolution*. Charlottesville: University Press of Virginia, 1979.

Stagg, J. C. A. *Mr. Madison's War: Politics, Diplomacy, and Warfare in the Early American Republic, 1783–1830*. Princeton, N.J.: Princeton University Press, 1983.

Steel, Anthony. "Impressment in the Monroe-Pinkney Negotiation, 1806–1807." *American Historical Review* 57, no. 2 (January 1952): 352–69.

Stinchcombe, William C. *The American Revolution and the French Alliance*. Syracuse, N.Y.: Syracuse University Press, 1969.

———. *The XYZ Affair*. Westport, Conn.: Greenwood, 1980.

Stourzh, Gerald. *Alexander Hamilton and the Idea of Republican Government*. Stanford, Calif.: Stanford University Press, 1970.

———. *Benjamin Franklin and American Foreign Policy*. Chicago: University of Chicago Press, 1954.

Stuart, Reginald C. "James Madison and the Militants: Republican Disunity and Replacing the Embargo." *Diplomatic History* 6, no. 2 (Spring 1982): 145–67.

———. *War and American Thought: From the Revolution to the Monroe Doctrine.* Kent, Ohio: Kent State University Press, 1982.

Sydnor, Charles S. *Gentlemen Freeholders: Political Practices in Washington's Virginia.* Chapel Hill: University of North Carolina Press, 1952.

Taft, Robert A. *A Foreign Policy for Americans.* Garden City, N.Y.: Doubleday, 1951.

Thomas, P. D. G. *British Politics and the Stamp Act Crisis: The First Phase of the American Revolution, 1763–1767.* London: Oxford University Press, 1975.

Tucker, Robert W., and David C. Hendrickson. *Empire of Liberty: The Statecraft of Thomas Jefferson.* New York: Oxford University Press, 1990.

———. *The Fall of the First British Empire: Origins of the War of American Independence.* Baltimore: Johns Hopkins University Press, 1982.

Tyler, John W. *Smugglers and Patriots: Boston Merchants and the Advent of the American Revolution.* Boston: Northeastern University Press, 1986.

Varg, Paul A. *Foreign Policies of the Founding Fathers.* East Lansing: Michigan State University Press, 1963.

———. *New England and Foreign Relations, 1789–1850.* Hanover, N.H.: University Press of New England, 1983.

Walling, Karl-Friedrich. *Republican Empire: Alexander Hamilton on War and Free Government.* Lawrence: University Press of Kansas, 1999.

Walsh, Correa Moylan. *The Political Science of John Adams: A Study in the Theory of Mixed Government and the Bicameral System.* New York: G. P. Putnam's Sons, 1915.

Walters, Raymond, Jr. *Albert Gallatin: Jeffersonian Financier and Diplomat.* New York: Macmillan, 1957.

Walzer, Michael. *The Revolution of the Saints: A Study in the Origins of Radical Politics.* Cambridge, Mass.: Harvard University Press, 1965.

Watlington, Patricia. *The Partisan Spirit: Kentucky Politics, 1779–1792.* Chapel Hill: University of North Carolina Press, 1972.

Watts, Steven. *The Republic Reborn: War and the Making of Liberal America, 1790–1820.* Baltimore: Johns Hopkins University Press, 1987.

Whitaker, Arthur P. *The Mississippi Question, 1795–1803: A Study in Trade, Politics, and Diplomacy.* New York: D. Appleton-Century, 1934.

White, Leonard D. *The Federalists: A Study in Administrative History.* New York: Macmillan, 1948.

———. *The Jeffersonians: A Study in Administrative History.* New York: Macmillan, 1951.

Williams, William Appleman. "The Age of Mercantilism: An Interpretation of the American Political Economy, 1763–1828." *William and Mary Quarterly,* 3rd ser., 15, no. 4 (October 1958): 419–37.

Wilson, Arthur McCandless. *French Foreign Policy during the Administration of Cardinal Fleury, 1726–1743: A Study in Diplomacy and Commercial Development.* Cambridge, Mass.: Harvard University Press, 1936.

Wood, Gordon S. *The Creation of the American Republic, 1776–1787.* Chapel Hill: University of North Carolina Press, 1969.

Wootton, David, ed. *Republicanism, Liberty, and Commercial Society, 1649–1776.* Stanford, Calif.: Stanford University Press, 1994.

Worden, Blair. "The Commonwealth Kidney of Algernon Sidney." *Journal of British Studies* 24, no. 1 (January 1985): 1–40.

Yarbrough, Jean M. *American Virtues: Thomas Jefferson on the Character of a Free People.* Lawrence: University Press of Kansas, 1998.

Zimmerman, James Fulton. *Impressment of American Seamen.* New York: Columbia University Press, 1925.

Zuckert, Michael P. *Natural Rights and the New Republicanism.* Princeton, N.J.: Princeton University Press, 1994.

———. *The Natural Rights Republic: Studies in the Foundation of the American Political Tradition.* Notre Dame, Ind.: University of Notre Dame Press, 1996.

Index